ZOMBIES
ON THE ROCK
EXTINCTION

ZOMBIES
ON THE ROCK
PAUL CARBERRY

ENGEN
BOOKS

Published in Canada by Engen Books, St. John's, NL.

A CIP catalogue record for this book is available from Library and Archives Canada.

Copyright © 2021 Paul Carberry

ISBN: 978-1-77478-009-1

Distributed by:
Engen Books
www.engenbooks.com
submissions@engenbooks.com

First mass market paperback printing: October 2021

Cover Design: Matthew LeDrew

For Jason Baker

For all those late night chats about surviving
the zombie apocalypse in Newfoundland.

CHAPTER 1
AND I WISHED FOR SO LONG

Frigid winds cut through the dead trees, throwing off drifts of snow from the pale grey trunks. Snow clung to the withered branches overhead, giving the woods a skeletal appearance. With each gust, cold seeped into Eric's bones. White powder snuck into his boots and melted around his ankles, magnifying the coldness numbing his feet. Stars danced at the edge of his vision every time he closed his eyes. Desperately wanting to rest, he couldn't allow himself the luxury, pursued by the dead relentlessly, their gnashing teeth snapping at his heels. No matter how hard he pushed himself, he struggled to distance himself from their grasps. His heavy breathing produced a mist rising in front of his face; his ribs ached. High above, the clouds were threatening to burst. Each time the wind picked up, it displayed mother nature's capability to shift this gentle snowfall into a blizzard.

Orange hues outlined the woods, the waning embers of a dying sun refusing to go softly. Eric used his forearms to shield his eyes from the protruding branches. Obscured by swirling snow, stray branches poked at the tender flesh of his face, the rigid twigs finding various ways to cut into his cheeks. Several trickles of blood warmed his numb flesh, serving as a grim reminder that he was still alive. Just six months ago he would have taken it for granted, would have cursed every time the branches slapped him in the face. Things were different now. Undead abominations wandered the earth, craving flesh without remorse. Relentless, they chased after him through the snow-covered forest. Eric kept his eyes down, not willing to turn around no matter how distressing the cacophony became. Hungry growls, hollow moans, anguished cries, and snapping jaws joined in a sinister symphony. Thousands of footsteps caused the earth to tremble in their wake.

"Just follow the hoofprints," Eric said between laboured breaths, "not that much further."

Spooked, his horse tossed him into the snow, demolishing Eric's plans. Destiny is elegant, maddeningly so. Now, everything he had struggled for was in jeopardy. The thick layers of white crust tugged at his ankles, putting a strain on his knees. Lactic acid accumulated in his calves and thigh muscles, approaching near critical levels, threatening to go on strike. With each stride, the muscle fibres twitched and cramped, every second a grueling struggle.

Slap

A tree branch whipped across his face, providing a jolt of energy. Another wave of adrenaline elevated the burning sensation in his quadriceps. He embraced those stinging jabs with open arms, keeping him alert. Light snow, falling for hours now, had left a delicate powder over everything. Eric knew if this kept up, it would bury the prints he had been following. He looked up at the solemn grey clouds that had swept overhead, casting gnarled shadows that stretched out for him.

He tripped on a concealed root. Pain ripped up from his foot and raced all the way up his exhausted legs. With an unbraced crash, Eric's mouth filled with snow. Until then, he'd been ignoring how dry his mouth had become. Dehydrated and cracked lips stung with fierce pain as water dribbled over his lips. Tremors from the ground raced into his heart, urging it to beat faster. With an anguished groan, Eric pulled himself to his feet, using an old birch close by to haul himself up. Instinct took over. His hand found its way back to the grip of his revolver resting in the holster dangling from his hip. He craned his neck to peer over his shoulder, surprised to find that the herd was still lagging, having gained some ground on the shuffling corpses. His hand traced the wooden butt, never resting long enough in one place to gain a grip on the weapon. Fear escaped his lungs in a deep, drawn-out sigh. With enough distance between them, Eric allowed himself a moment to catch his breath. Zombies staggered through the snow, their clumsy feet finding fallen branches and twisted roots. The unfortunate ones fell hard into the snow, the pressing herd behind them had no remorse.

A sickening *crunch* popped in the crisp air as the dead trampled their fallen comrades. Before long, the sound shifted to a wet slapping. It reminded Eric of walking through deep muck, the thick substance tugging at your boots. He laughed with glee at the disturbing noises. He took another glimpse at the depth of the herd. Unable to find an end to the enormous swarm of shuffling cadavers, it cut his laughter abruptly short. He turned back to his trail. On the first step, his legs felt like cinder blocks. It took several strides before he discovered his rhythm again.

Smack

A tree branch dug into his forehead, tearing open a deep cut just above his eyebrow. Crimson tears dripped over his eye, falling onto his jacket and jeans. The surge of adrenaline gave him the false hope that he could sprint all the way back to Grand Falls. He didn't know if he would make it there in time to start the assault. They would just have to wait. The Republic of Newfoundland was counting on him.

Hours passed with excruciating slowness. There was a lingering thought in the back of Eric's mind that rose with the setting sun. He was at risk of getting lost. The clouds obscured the stars from him. Not that it mattered to him. If Jason were here, he could have navigated by them. Eric wished that he had never let Jason go search for Tracy—or maybe he should have gone with them. Things could have been different. A squall of wind picked up a wall of snow and pelted him in the face. Mockery from mother nature. After an open stretch of field, Eric had ducked back into another stretch of forest. His pace slowed. Branches and bushes grouped closely together made it harder for him to maintain his distance from the herd.

Stumbling through the darkening evening, Eric searched for any source of light. The sky above was a rich shade of black. No stars pierced the blackened canvas, the clouds spitting snow. He heard the trees snapping and groaning against the undead as they advanced into the forest. Dead bodies pressing against each other, cramming each other through any crack or crevice between the trees. The staggering corpses stuffed into the thick woodland like midday traffic on a lively street. They pressed so hard against each other they toppled over some weaker seedlings. Loud, snapping cracks echoed into the night air as the tree trunks split. Thunderous booms echoed nearby. Every booming thud sent shivers down Eric's spine. The relentless noise and foul smell nipping at his heels never once allowed him a chance to gain his breath.

A narrow opening revealed itself just beyond the branches ahead, and an interminable stretch of barren white stretched out ahead. He dragged himself towards the gap, his fists gripping the branches to aid him through. The moment he reached the clearing, the snow underneath his feet deepened. No longer sheltered from the harsh blizzard that was brewing, Eric was forced to push forward with his head slanted down into his chest. He trudged through the knee-deep snow with feverish determination.

The wind let up, allowing Eric to survey the surrounding landscape. He needed to get his bearings before he lost his direction completely. A green sign jutted out of the snow, the writing on the enormous billboard obscured by a cloak of white. He shuffled over to the sign, trudging through the snow, pounding his fist against the wooden poll. Dollops of snow fell off the distance marker, revealing reflective white letters on the board.

Grand Falls-Windsor 12 KM

"Almost there," he announced. "Better late than never."

Eric spotted a set of snowmobile tracks and followed it towards Grand Falls. It didn't alleviate the difficulty of navigating through the deep snow, but it kept him on course. Purple hues gave way to a soft, silvery glow from the town's light pollution. Darkness loomed over the township like a predator waiting for its opportunity to strike. Behind him, the blackness of the herd spilled onto the highway from the forest. The pavement trembled beneath their death march. Eric wasn't sure if they were following him anymore, or if they were drawn to the lights like moths to the flame. It didn't matter. The plan was going ahead, albeit behind schedule, just as the Republic had envisioned. Another hour and Eric would send up the flare. He wondered if they had waited for him, or if they'd lost hope and retreated.

He swung around, gazing back at the shuffling herd. The black mass appeared to flow as one giant, hideous creature. The swarm of shadows flowed like mercury over the snow, swallowing up the white surface in its wake. Far in front of him, the road twisted up the hill and faded out of view. Once he reached the crest of that hill, the town would be close enough to fire the flare. It had to be. Or he would be too late. His legs burned; every strand of muscle fibre sizzled like a string on fire beneath his skin. He cursed himself for letting the horse get spooked. That flare should have gone up a long time ago. At any moment he expected to hear the eruption of gunfire, signalling the beginning of the war between the Republic of Newfoundland and The Highway Hangmen. Outnumbered and under armed, the Republic wouldn't stand a chance in a fair fight. Backed up by the Silver Skull Cartel, the Hangmen held the clear advantage on paper.

BRRRAAAAAPPPPPP

A deafening clap cut through the frosty midnight air. The unmistakable grumble of a snowmobile engine tore across the tundra.

"Damn it," Eric muttered in frustration.

Realization set in. This wasn't some arbitrary route. It was a patrol path. Eric was caught in a stretch of wide-open space. The only place to hide lay behind him now, inhabited by the undead. Two pairs of headlights appeared at the bend in the road, the rumble growing louder. Light flooded across the drifts of snow at the edge of the road. Thousands of tiny sparkles of light caught in the freshly fallen snow. Eric's hand shot down to the handle of his revolver. This time he didn't hesitate to draw it.

BRRRAAAAAAAPPPPPPP

The engines growled and grumbled angrily, drawing attention to the two riders as they drifted into view. Eric found himself trapped between a rock and a dead place. The purr of the snowmobiles caught the attention of the undead herd, driving them mad. Their groans strengthened, deeper and more determined. Two snow machines sped into view, the bright LEDs casting the drivers in a stark silhouette. Eric knew there was no where hide. A raised hand brought the two snowmobiles to an abrupt halt. Behind the brilliant headlights, the vague outline of the two figures neared each other. They had seen him and were deliberating what they would do next. Moonlight caught on the steel barrel of a rifle. Even from this distance, that threatening image could not be ignored. It stood out starkly against the darkness behind them. Drawn to the ready position, the gleaming light faded into a faint flicker as they pointed the barrel toward Eric.

Eric dove into the snow, trying to burry himself beneath the fallen powder. Even though he was a sitting duck out here, he wasn't about to make the shot easy. His heart thudded, waiting for the thundering reverberation of gunfire to explode. Moments dragged past slowly, drawing out the ordeal as the pressure in his heart built up to the point of bursting. The low grumble of the snow machines roared to life again. With a quick glance Eric noticed that the two riders had separated, approaching him from the left and the right.

The repugnant scent of the dead was slithering up behind him. It washed over him in waves like the rising tide, the wind pushing it back momentarily before the next wave pushed further over him. Eric closed his dominant eye now, trying to protect it from the bright light. He turned around and noticed that the herd was no longer a shifting black mass. The faint rays of light now crashed over them. Their forms beginning to materialize, growing out of the shadows, coming into focus. Countless shuffling limbs took shape, the disfigured faces still silhouetted by their own shadows. The whirr of the engines focused in on his position. Eric had to shield his face with his left arm against the bright lights. He tucked his revolver into his waistband, the cold metal sending a shiver down his spine as it pressed against the flesh of his back. Hopefully they hadn't seen the gun—it would have been a last resort. Firing off the revolver out here would be detected in Grand Falls. He needed to get the herd closer to town. If the warning came too early, the Republic's plan wouldn't work out the way they needed it too. Everything needed to fall into place for this to work.

"Hands in the air," a demanding voice boomed. They cut the engines, the low grumble immediately giving way to the hungry moans. "You think you could escape from town without the boss knowing?" His speech was soaked with too much alcohol, slurring his words. The hairs of his overgrown moustache dipped into his mouth with globules of frozen saliva.

"Hey, do you hear that?" a female voice questioned from the right, the harmony of the undead drawing her attention. Her gaze wandered past Eric, towards the shuffling corpses as they poured out of the shadows. Her strawberry blond hair poured out from underneath her orange toque, the wind tossing the split ends.

The man cut the engine to his snowmobile, ignoring his partner's question. The springs sighed with a mechanical grunt as he stepped off the running boards. "Now you count your lucky stars the boss needs workers, or I'd shoot you here on da'spot."

"Hey, Harry!" She tried to catch his attention with a wave of her hands. "Look over there!" Her voice shivered with fear.

"What is it, Helen?" Harry shot back, his voice full of venom. "You're interrupting my fun."

"I've never seen so many of them in one place." Helen's voice heavy with awe, the words falling out of her mouth. "We have to warn the others. We don't have time to deal with this fucker."

Eric couldn't let them escape. If they warned the others of what was coming, before he could signal the others, their assault would fail before it began. He raised his hands over his head and got down on his knees. "You can't leave me here. They will eat me." He tried his best to sound fragile and afraid.

"Harry, come on, lets go," Helen urged her partner. She pulled the throttle and thrusted the snow machine around in a tight circle, ready to flee the surging hoard.

"Now wait a second, Helen." He let the gun fall to his waist, the strap bearing the weight. "This will only take a second. Now put yer hands behind your back. Nice and easy, mister." Harry took out a length of rope underneath his leather vest. A sliver of silver light reflected off the Highway Hangman skull embroidered on his vest, the wind forcing the flaps of the open vest to ruffle. Frankie shifted his shotgun behind his back, freeing his hands to tie the rope.

Eric studied Helen, waiting for his opportunity to strike. An expression of fear distorted her face, her bright red lips pressed tight against her teeth in a thin frown. She bobbed up and down on the seat, eager to ride away. The sour stench of death poured over them, the hungry snapping teeth chattering together. "Harry, we have to go." Her voice had raised another octave. "They are heading straight for town."

"Now, mister," Harry burped, the sickly-sweet aroma of whisky gushing out of his belly, "just take your medicine." He nodded his head down towards the rope, allowing the length of rope in the middle to droop down.

"Goddamn, Harry, please," Helen pleaded.

Hysteria was settling in, acting like a vale, distracting Helen's attention. Harry was leaning in, his breath hot on Eric's neck. Her whimpering cry invited his impatient glare. "For fuck's sake, Helen." He turned his head to bark at her. Eric let his hand fall down to the handle of his revolver and moved quickly. The deafening clap of the gun cut off Harry's sentence, the bullet cutting off his final thought abruptly.

CHAPTER 2
ALL THE PRECIOUS MOMENTS

Clarence was as pale as a ghost. Janet stood behind her husband in the doorway, her eyes wide with panic. "I said my water broke."

"What do I do?" Clarence asked, his tone laden with terror and doubt. Overwhelmed by the dire situation he was facing, he looked like a child afraid to ride their bike for the first time.

"First thing we need to do is get her comfortable," Dana replied without having to think. "Where is your bedroom?" Surprised by her own sudden outburst, Dana took control of this situation without retaining control over her own emotions. She wasn't certain of what she was doing and had no formal training; she just let the words tumble out of her mouth. Maternal instinct. It was necessary for her to experience this firsthand. There was a life growing inside of her. If she didn't know how to deliver a baby, how would she face the problem herself? It would fester and nibble away at her confidence until it conquered her. This was an important test. A scientific experiment—identifying what worked and what failed so she would have a fighting chance when the moment arrived. She felt guilty for a moment, but that faded. It didn't matter what her motives were; she was trying to do the right thing, and that was all that mattered.

Hank eased over to Janet, nudging his shoulder under her own. "Lead the way, Clarence." He appeared lost, his eyes immense and distant. "Clarence?" Hank snapped his fingers, drawing him back from whatever universe he had wandered off into.

"Just up these stairs. It's the door at the end of the hallway." Clarence pointed towards the wooden staircase. Old pine panels, lacquered to a gloss and well looked after, glistened with the faint flicker of the old propane lamps. The antique brass lamps adorned with intricate designs gave the log cabin a Victorian charm.

Dana glanced over towards Clarence. His broad shoulders sagged, and his chin was bent down to his collar. "We need extra blankets and pillows." Dana reached out and shook him. "Do you have those?" She wanted to reach up and slap him. He drifted back and forth from reality. For a moment he'd appear focused, then his eyes would slide down a slippery slope, and he'd vanish again. "Clarence!" Dana screamed. "Wake up. Janet needs you to be with her."

His heavy eyes peered down at her. An icy shudder traveled up Dana's spine. A gapping frown accompanied his vacant stare. "Sheets are in the linen closet." Clarence paused for a moment. "In the bathroom."

"Clarence, can you help Janet get comfortable?" Dana wished they didn't need him. Concerned that he was just going to get in the way, or something much worse, she avoided making eye contact with him, afraid that his condition was catching.

Clarence lumbered up the stairs, his heavy footsteps rattling the floorboards of the cabin. Dana waited for him to disappear from view before allowing the reality of the situation to unnerve her. A trembling sigh escaped her throat. She took a moment to control her breathing, trying her best to regain her composure. Dana drew a deep breath and held it in her lungs before exhaling—repeating this until she found herself back in control. The floorboards above her head creaked with commotion. Janet's soft voice consoled Clarence. For the second time tonight, Dana let out a hearty chuckle from deep inside her belly. She could scarcely contain herself, muffling the noises with her hand as best she could, not wanting anyone upstairs to overhear her. The fireplace was pushing out a lot of heat, and the radiant waves of energy washed over her. She sat on the arm of a chesterfield, not daring to sit down into the cushion. Daydreams came to life, bleeding into reality, causing a feverish dream to spring to life.

Eric sat across from her in the rocking chair, an infant child nestled into his shoulders. A white blanket covered them both. His eyes were closed, and his head was tilted to one side to monitor the baby. Dana could see herself knitting a hat and matching mittens, her chair facing the warmth of the fireplace. A cup of tea rested on the side table beside her, the steam rising in swirls around her rosy cheeks. The gentle click clack of the rocking chair lulled her to sleep. A gentle breeze blew outside, tossing snow harmlessly against the window.

A blood curdling shriek from upstairs shattered Dana's momentary paradise.

Sprinting upstairs, skipping every second step, Dana rushed towards the door at the end of the hallway. It was slightly ajar, obstructing the view of what was awaiting her on the other side. Screams and sobs echoed off the wooden walls. "What's going on in here?" Dana called out, forcing the door open.

Janet lay in the bed, her knees curled into her chest, her hand crushing Clarence's. Sweat dripping down her face, eyes squeezing shut, and the corners of her mouth scrunching into her cheeks, Janet was misery personified. Hank stood at the foot of the bed with a bundle of bed sheets tucked underneath his armpit. "Contractions?" He shifted to stare at Dana. After everything they had been through together, this was the first time she noticed a concerned expression plastered on his face. Before, even when things appeared bleak, Hank had remained tranquil and collected.

"It's okay, sweetheart," Clarence cooed, "it will pass." His voice sounded convinced, but his pale complexion betrayed his tone.

"Jesus Christ," Janet cursed, "that hurts!" She sobbed into her knees. "I can't do this."

"You can do it, honey," Clarence reassured his wife. "You can do this."

"Do you have anything for the pain?" Hank spoke up. "Anything at all?"

"We have codeine tablets," Clarence admitted.

"Is that safe for the baby?" Hank asked Dana.

Dana didn't have the answer. "I don't think so?" Her

eyes engaged Janet's, passing along her condolences to the suffering woman. "I wouldn't want to risk it."

"It's not your risk to take." Janet glared back at Dana. Feral hate fumed from her eyes. "Clarence, I need something for the pain, or I won't make it," she ordered.

"I don't feel comfortable with that." Clarence looked distressed. "They may be right," he declared.

Janet reached out and snatched a fistful of his sweater. "I may pass out with the pain," she growled. "Now go get me those fucking pills." A fearful scream escaped her throat, full of self-pity. Clarence turned to face Dana, searching for an answer, searching for guidance. Once he realized that she didn't have any, he sauntered past her and lumbered into the bathroom. Cabinet doors opened and banged closed; scrapping and rattling sounds filtered out of the bathroom as he rummaged for the pill vial.

Dana didn't understand what Janet was going through. She wasn't about to make a choice for her. Hell, she may have a made a valid point about fainting. Nobody there was capable of making that decision for her; she was the only person who understood how much pain she was experiencing. Not Hank or Clarence. Fear tightened its grip on Dana's heart. Realizing that she would soon suffer the same fate as Janet crippled her. Janet's eyes were wet with pain. Drenched with sweat, her skin tone took on a translucent glow. Purple veins ran like raging rivers underneath the skin. Her chest rose and fell in heavy, heaving sighs. Expecting the next contraction was just as exhausting as the actual pain she was bracing herself against.

"Here you are." Clarence rattled the tablets in his hand, the tablets battering off the plastic vial. He tossed the bottle to his wife. "I'm going down to the kitchen for a moment. I'll be right back."

"What the fuck are you going down there for?" Janet's neck tensed as another contraction took hold.

"There's a bottle of George Street Rum above the fridge." Clarence walked away.

Dana reached out and grasped him by the wrist. Her hand didn't even come close to wrapping around his thick forearm. "I am sure she shouldn't be drinking."

"It's not for her," Clarence said with contempt. "I need something to calm my nerves." He lumbered down the hall. The entire top floor seemed to sigh with relief when he headed down the stairs.

"FFFHHHHUUUUUAAAA!!!"

Janet screamed bloody murder, turning her face shades of red and purple. Spittle escaped from the corners of her mouth. She doubled over in pain, burying her face back into her knees. Hands turned into fists and pounded her legs as she attempted to deal with the pain.

Dana grabbed a pillow and slipped it between Janet's wailing fists and her legs. The pillow absorbed the brunt of her punishment, the jolts silenced by the down feathers. "Try to breathe." Dana tried to coach Janet, placing her hand on Janet's back, rubbing it in circular motions. Sharp, boney segments of her spine pushed outwards at the curve of her backside. The bottle of pills rested in a fold in the bedsheet at Janet's feet.

"FFFFUUUCCCCCCCKKK!"

Tears welled up in her eyes, and her eyelashes stuck together. Veins rippled across her forehead as her face turned a reddish shade of royal purple. Dreadful, guttural sounds caught in Janet's throat as she tried to stifle her pained screams, which carried throughout the entire cabin and deep into the woods. To ease the pain, she tried to control her breathing, but quick breaths did little to ease the pain, and deep breaths were hard to hold on to.

Dana recognized the expression on Hank's face in the window's reflection. "What is it Hank?"

"I don't know?" Hank leaned in, cupping his hands on the window. "It looks like a giant shadow creeping towards us through the blackness."

Clarence appeared in the doorway, a bottle half full with amber fluid dangling from his hand. "Janet, you will be all right."

"I think we need to leave." Hank's skin went pale, his eyes wide with terror.

"What's going on out there?" Dana questioned.

"I think we are about to have some unliving guests joining us soon."

CHAPTER 3
IT'S NOT LIKE WINGS HAVE FALLEN

Gilbert Byrne shivered against the frigid winter winds, kicking up a swirling white cloak around him. Cold seeped up from the ground beneath him, forcing him to suffer through it. He didn't know how much longer he should remain up on the top of this hilltop. There was nothing to shelter him from the elements. With nothing to break the wind and snow, he found it challenging to see anything through the high-powered rifle scope. Doucette, long vanished into the blizzard, had stepped into the thick of the trees below twenty minutes ago now. Worried, Byrne continued to scan the patrol on the other side. He was afraid that if he got up, he would get disoriented and lose sight of the clearing. He held the perfect angle. The perfect angle, everything below was on display from this vantage point—when the weather cooperated, that was.

Byrne traced out the patrolman's entire route. At the center was the gas station. Heading to the east was a church with a green roof and a center spire topped off by a giant white cross that vanished when the snow picked up. After that, the path lead down a paved street with a sparse scattering of households, some of them lit up with an electrical radiance. At the end of the path was a red, two-story Cape Cod house with a blazing fire on the front lawn in an oil drum. The patrol would meet up with another guard at this house. Huddling over the warmth of the fire, they'd have a short conversation and then head back on their separate routes. The path to the right curved down a road between the houses, leading to a small park with a giant brick building in the center. Often, the patrol man would take a drink from his flask at his last post, sharing it with the person tending the fire or the next patrolman.

"What have you got yourself into, Byrne?" he muttered to himself. Anticipation built up and boiled over. His trigger finger itched. He waited for a pause in the weather. Byrne could pick out the patrolman down below, the halogen flashlight bobbing up and down as he walked the boundary of an old gas station. At the edge of his route, he met up with another patrolman. Byrne watched them have a smoke and a joke. Jealousy grew every time he saw that tiny red circle flare to life. He wanted a smoke so bad it was causing his skin to crawl all over from withdrawal. "If you had stayed with the boys, you could have as many smokes as you wanted." If he had been in one of the foxholes, he could've sneaked in a few fags, depending on whose trench he found himself in. Smith would have shared one or two with him.

A howl of wind picked up a blanket of snow, tossing it across his vision like a sheet being spread over a bed. When it died off, he scoured the horizon again. Right to left, just as he was instructed. Something caught his attention. A figure moved in the shadows at the edge of the treeline. The figure was wearing army fatigues. He realized it was Doucette. He searched for the patrolman and found that he was talking to the guard on the far left. Byrne determined that this would be the perfect time to make a move towards the gas station. The guard on the right would be farthest away at this moment, leaving the building deserted.

Doucette moved out of the darkness and sprinted across the field towards the gas station. He must have been watching the patrol and figured out their timings. Byrne didn't know what he was up to. He pushed himself up from the snow. His back cracked and his knees ached from being in the prone position for so long. He took a moment to look through the scope and found Doucette kneeling in front of the gas station door, trying to pick the lock. Byrne turned his attention back towards the patrolman, who had already made his way back. If Doucette didn't find a place to hide, the guard would spot him in under two minutes—less if the weather calmed. The light from the gas station sign lit up the entrance to the store, placing Doucette in plain sight. Once the guard made the turn around the old church, he'd discover Doucette trying to break into the building.

Byrne took off his glove, unable to operate the radio with them on. The green power light gave off a luminous glow. He turned the dial, making sure it was on the correct channel. "Doucette, come in." Static crackled. An ensuing lengthy pause was finally interrupted by Doucette's rough voice.

"What is it Byrne?"

"The patrol is headed your way. You got a minute tops before he spots you."

"Thanks for the heads up."

"Do you want me to take him out?"

Laughter erupted from the other end. Byrne took up aim with the scope and found that Doucette was making his way back around the building. *"When the patrol heads back to the left and gets behind that church, give me a heads up. I'll try to get in that building again."*

"You got it," Byrne responded. He kept his eye on the patrol man, waiting for him to complete another rotation of his route. Byrne found that his trigger finger itched even more now.

"Okay, you can make your move now. He just rounded the corner." Byrne watched as the patrol rounded the edge of the church.

"If he comes back and I'm still out here, you can shoot him."

Byrne's heart skipped a beat. "No problem." Waves of joy and excitement crashed over him, the surge of adrenaline wrecking havoc on his deprived system. It had been hours since he last ate. The endorphins made his head swim.

"Don't get trigger-happy up there."

"Roger that." Byrne let go of the call button. "I got this, don't you worry about a thing." His finger itched more than ever now, anticipation doing little to relieve the sensation. Through his scope, he watched Doucette run back to the door. Once he discovered him fiddling with the lock, Byrne took another glance around. Scanning from right to left, he didn't expect to find much. When the wind picked up a puff of snow, he didn't wait for it to die down. He just kept scanning the area back and forth. Every time he crossed the gas station, Doucette was still knelt there, making no progress with the door. On his fourth pass, a blur of colour passed through the periphery of his scope.

"What the hell was that?" Byrne took a break from the scope, looking over the top of the sniper rifle. Below, shadows shrouded the silvery landscape. Panic settled in, establishing a home deep in his chest, causing a chain re-action. Until now, his eyes hadn't felt dry, and his hands weren't trembling. The rifle rattled in his grip, the tripod legs shifting back and forth. He looked through the scope, finding it difficult to focus. His field of view danced be-fore his eyes.

"How are things looking up there?"

Byrne tried his best to concentrate, unable to look through the scope, it was giving him a headache. "Damn it, tunnel vision." Tears of frustration welled up, the frigid air freezing them on his cheek. With no other choice, he had to squint over the top of the scope, giving his eye a respite from the high-powered lens.

"Hey, how much time do I have?"

Must have been a figment of his imagination, the blur of colour just a ghost. There was nobody on the path near the front of the church. "You still got time." He respond-ed.

"Good, I'm just about in. There, I got it."

Byrne watched him with his bare eye, slipping into the gas station. "What do you see?"

"Oh shit."

A loud, high-pitched wail of static forced Byrne to drop the radio. He heard muffled voices and heavy breathing over the incessant hum of static. Byrne got to one knee—his position vulnerable. If anyone down below looked up, he would be in plain sight. Something deep inside told him it didn't matter anymore.

"Fuck he got me."

Surprised, Byrne took a moment to process what Doucette had said. "Who got you?" He didn't understand what was happening.

"There was a guy taking inventory in the back room when I roamed in."

Bile and acid ran up Byrne's throat as the realization settled in over him. He retched the noxious fluids over his knee, long ropes of clear, thick vomit dangled from his lips.

"He got one marvellous shot in before I put him down." Doucette choked on his own words. His voice sounded wet, like he was speaking under water.

"Do you need me to come get you?" Byrne wiped his face with the back of his sleeve.

"No, it's too late for me. Would you do me a favor?"

"Anything you want, brother." Another wave of nausea rose over Byrne. The fear of being out here alone wasn't something he had expected.

"Don't miss the shot."

"What shot? You told me not to open fire until the flare went up." Doubt had already settled in about Eric. Byrne wasn't about to start the war.

"Jones didn't make it." Doucette coughed, the fluids in his throat dampening the noise. *"There's no turning back.*

Take out the patrol's silen….." Silence fell over the radio.

Byrne looked up at the dreary night sky. Black clouds over head opened up, spilling out a heavy, cascading load of snow. With the wind pelting snow in his face, he took another peek through his scope. There was nothing except a wall of white flurries shielding everything from his vision. Even if the sight in his eyes settled down, there was no way he could make the shot from here in this weather. At least now he could move underneath the cover of the terrible weather. He bolted to his feet, his joints cracking and his lower back stiffening. His legs argued at first, but thanked him after they got to stretch out a little. Slowly, his body shook out the kinks, and he ran down the hill towards the tree line. He didn't want to get caught out in the open. Byrne caught a flash of light piercing through the snow ahead. A mysterious figure remained concealed from view as it approached him.

"I'll be back in a minute, Jerry. I gotta take a piss."

CHAPTER 4
BUT STILL SOMETHING'S MISSING

Beads of perspiration rolled down Jason's back. He felt the earth tremble as the Boeing 747 twin turbine engines grumbled overhead. High-pitched, metallic screeches rang out as the brakes toiled to slow down the massive hunk of metal. For a moment, it didn't look like the airplane would stop in time before careening off the tarmac and into the forest. Commotion from a hanger bay at the end of the terminal erupted. A group of Pharmakon men wearing orange reflective jackets scurried across the runway with a giant ladder. Jason walked towards the scene, hoping to get close enough to observe.

"You just keep doing what you were doing." A voice broke in over the receiver on Jason's helmet. When Jason tried to peek at the plane, the figures behind the window blurred. *"It's no use, you won't be able to see them. He won't let you."*

"Tracy? Is that you?" Jason asked. A response of interminable silence was all he got. "What's going on?"

"Get back to work." A soldier grabbed Jason by the shoulder. A finger dug into the meat of his deltoid. The excruciating pain was an exclamation point to the order.

Jason bent over at the knees and grabbed a leg. He decided to get back to work hauling the bodies off the runway. There was no point in trying to reason with anybody here. He had turned into their slave, waiting for his opportunity to slip away. The field was too open, and David Steele was up in that tower, his cold eyes gazing down at him. Resistance from the corpse forced a slight jolt through Jason's arm as he pulled back. Anger rose deep inside of him. He let it out with a forceful tug on the limb. For a moment, the undead freak clung to the bare pavement, the congealed blood beneath it frozen to the runway. Then, without warning, there was a sickening, wet explosion as the leg ripped loose from the hip. Jason tumbled backwards with the immediate release of pressure. The leg fell out of his hands and into his lap. He landed hard on his backside, still clutching onto the foot as a jolt of pain raced up his tailbone. A trail of blood stretched over the pavement, blackened fluids emptying from the massive wound. Yellowed bone jutted from the ragged wound; rotted strands of flesh and muscles, stretched out from the tear, dangled over it.

"You will clean that up." A Pharmakon soldier threw a shovel at Jason, the metal head clanging off the pavement. "We can't have this runway getting ruined. When you're finished scraping it up, get back to dragging the bodies away. Once you're done, we will come out and get you." The soldier turned around and walked away. "Come on, boys, Mr. Cook volunteered to finish the job."

Jason sat alone with his head slumped over the severed leg. "Goddammit," he cursed as he tossed the leg back at the frozen carcass. The sun was going down now;

he could see it retiring behind the mountains.

Not wanting to get stuck outside in the cold, Jason wasted little time. He set his mind to his task. The scraping of the metal shovel over the pavement turned his stomach. The frozen corpse tore from the tarmac with a long, drawn out ripping noise. Strands of blood, filthy cloth and ribbons of flesh clung to the ground, not wanting to let go. Jason eased the body down, giving him room to wrench the zombie upwards. Tearing from the torso, the cotton shirt remained on the ground, frozen in a puddle of blackened blood. Jason carried the bulk of the cadaver away, having to come back and scrape up the rest. It was hard, tiring work. He had to continue scraping the shovel against the mess—morsels of flesh and disintegrated clothing peeling off the pavement. Frozen slivers of blood curled off the ground until the strands got too long and broke off. He gathered the revolting mess into tiny piles, scooping it away with the shovel, flinging it off to the side of the runway.

Dead corpses littered the runway. They ushered the passengers from the plane through the maze. Jason tried to glimpse what was happening, but every time he tried his visor scrambled his vision. The blurred images gave him a headache, which combined with the revolting task, was making him sick to his stomach. His arms were heavy, his shoulders burned, and his neck ached. Cramps in his forearms made it challenging to maintain his grasp on the lifeless bodies, dropping them several times. Knots in his backside threatened to immobilize him. Now, with the last zombie in his clutch, he staggered backwards, dragging the creature across the asphalt. Bumps from the built-up ice jostled the lifeless head around, its teeth chattering with the motion.

Crunching footprints approached him from behind. Jason pulled off his helmet. The bitter wind nipped at his sweat-soaked skin. "Excellent work."

Jason ignored the compliment, letting the fresh air fill his lungs. With the sunlight fading away, the darkness of the evening crept in. Snow was falling at an alarming rate. Fierce winds swept across the boundless stretch of open runway, blowing swirls of white powder in every direction. A hand settled on his shoulder, offering to turn him around but never forcing him. Too tired to resist it, he allowed the stranger to guide him around. Tracy stood in front of him, her blond hair whipping around her face, concealing her expression. Thoughts of escaping developed into ideas, which grew into elaborate plans. "We have to get out of here." Jason reached out for Tracy's arm.

She avoided it, taking a deliberate step backward, standing just out of reach. "Get inside and eat. You wouldn't survive a day out there in this condition."

Jason snorted. "I've survived far longer on much less," he spat. "We can leave together. The dead won't bother us."

Tracy glared at him. A disappointed, scolding stare that made Jason shrink. "It's not the dead you need to worry about." She spoke to him as if he were a child. "David is observing us, so I suggest you do as I say. You do not understand how much convincing it took to allow him to talk to you alone without our helmets on. Now if you ever want to get out of this nightmare, trust me."

Jason craned his neck back to peer up at the tower. David leaned against the window sill, glaring down at them with malice. "All right, I'll head inside." Jason hesitated, holding the hatred inside, his blood boiling at the sight of David. "When it's time for us to leave, I'll be ready."

"Jason, it will not be easy." Tracy turned her neck to glance back at David, nodding her head when he matched her gaze. "We probably won't make it. Are you willing to take that risk?"

Jason locked eyes with David. "Anything worth fighting for is never easy."

"One of you will have to die." Tracy sounded disheartened. "That's the only way out of this for you, isn't it?"

"You don't think I'll win?" His wife's lack of faith hurt Jason.

"If it was a fair fight." Tracey looked back at Jason. "It will never be a fair exchange with him. He'll do whatever it takes to tilt the scale in his favor."

Jason realized she was right. There was only one advantage Jason had: the element of surprise. "I'll do whatever it takes. I have more to lose."

"You don't understand, Jason. He's a certifiable maniac. His ego means more to him than anything else you could possibly imagine." Tracey said in a hushed tone. "Now come inside, get some food in your belly and rest. If we don't do this tonight, we won't get another chance."

"You think there will be an opportunity tonight?" Hope, along with the wind, carried Jason's voice a little too far. If anyone were outside, his voice would have reached their ears.

"We are heading to Grand Falls. There is a girl in the area they need to find." Tracey held her helmet to her chest, looking down at it. Green light cast a glow across her face, the whites of her eyes mirroring a delicate emerald hue.

"What's so special about this girl?" A sinking sense of dread crossed Jason's mind. What if his wife had left on her microphone, trying to lure Jason into a trap?

"She has natural immunity to the zombie virus," Tracey said before placing the helmet back over her head. "Now let's go inside. We have to move soon if we will make it there on time."

Jason followed Tracey towards the airport terminal. A pleasant aroma of food was a welcoming replacement for the stench of the dead he had grown accustomed to; his mouth watered at the aroma of maple baked beans. Even though he knew they were from a can, he realized that this may be his last meal. The lengthy walk towards the door allowed him to reflect on all the potential scenarios the night could bring.

"Maple baked beans, my favorite," Jason quipped. No one paid him any attention. He dragged out a chair and sat down. Tracy sauntered past two guards and retired upstairs, heading into the radar tower with David. He wished they had discussed escaping before she took off.

Everyone minded their own business, attending to their lunch, absent minded of their surroundings. Jason couldn't believe such discord would exist amongst a group of survivors during the apocalypse. The incessant drone of chewing provided the background music for this evening's meal. Metal forks and spoons clanked off the sides of bowls or scrapped along the bottom, adding to the beat. Having lost his appetite, Jason's spoon lingered in the beans, swirling them around. Instinct forced him to grab a slice of bread from the centre of the dinner table, his hands going through the motion of buttering it. He realized that he was holding onto a knife. No one recognized, so Jason slipped the blade into a large pocket on the thigh of his pants.

"So, what do we know about this girl we are after?" Jason asked the man sitting next to him.

Perturbed, the man swallowed a mouthful of beans and wiped his face. "Why should I tell you anything?" He glared at Jason with a vacant expression. Large, black pupils filled his eyes. Only a thin ring of brown iris showed.

"Aren't I supposed to be part of the team?" Jason sighed, dragging out the last word. This elicited laughter from everyone seated at the table.

"You are a foot soldier, same as the rest of us." He gestured around the table, his finger stopping at the head of the dinner table. "Except for Samuel. He's the only one of us with any actual knowledge. I doubt that he will suffer the need to inform us grunts of any superfluous details to accomplish our mission."

"Hey, Samuel," Jason called out, "what's the deal with the girl."

Samuel looked up from his plate, brown sauce smeared on his chin. "You have your orders. You are to kill her on sight."

"Isn't that a bit extreme? Pharmakon terrified of some teenage girl." Laughter erupted from deep in Jason's gut, making his ribs hurt. No one else found his statement amusing. Everyone stopped what they were doing, gawking at him.

"You are trying to trick me into talking about it." Samuel said, returning to his meal. "Try again."

The others followed his lead. Soon, the room filled with the low, droning sounds of chewing and utensils clanging off glass dinner ware. Jason looked down at his bowl and spooned a mouthful of beans; his mouth watered with the flavor of maple, his appetite returning. He dipped his bread into the sauce, broke off insignificant pieces and chewed on them, savouring the butter. A chair scrapped across the floor. Jason glanced up and observed Samuel walk away from the table, leaving behind his dishes. "How rude," Jason muttered to himself, thinking no one would have been paying attention.

The soldier sitting next to him reached over and snatched away Jason's beans. "You will learn your place, the hard way if required."

Defiantly, Jason took a bite of his bread, chomping with his mouth open. He watched with joy as the soldier's face filled with spite, his face turning red with anger. "You must be hungry?"

"Don't push your luck." He stood up tall, dropping the bowl. It shattered against the table, shards of glass flying in all directions like a bomb had detonated. Flecks of brown sauce landed on Jason's suit. "Another peep from you and we will make you do the dishes."

"I've never been so fucking scared in all my life," Jason mocked him, pushing his boundaries.

A malevolent smile crept over the man's face. "Derrick, would you be kind enough to boil the water for Mr. Cook? He's volunteered to do the dishes for us. What a sweetie."

"I don't take orders from you, Sid," Derrick grumbled.

"Just do it, Derrick. Trust me, you will enjoy this," Sid chuckled. The brown ring around his pupils disappeared. His eyes looked like two drops of oil. "You three with me. The rest of you head up and prepare the vehicle. We shouldn't be long."

Three soldiers held Jason against the industrial-sized sink, shoving him against the metal edge. Cold steel dug into his stomach. Derrick stood in front of an oven, waiting for an enormous, stainless steel pot to boil. "A watched pot never boils," Jason scoffed.

"Ignorant prick." Sid thrust his fist into Jason's kidney. A jarring pain dropped Jason to his knees. His throat came dangerously close to striking the corner. "Stand him up!" Sid barked. The others obeyed without hesitation.

They hoisted Jason to his feet, accompanied by the struggling groans of the men lifting him. The florescent light above him shined off the grimy metal surface of the sink. Sid placed the plug in the drain, preparing for the water. The water churned, lazily at first, before shifting into a rolling boil. Loud, gurgling bubbles rose to the surface and exploded. Derrick let the pot boil for what seemed like an eternity before removing it. When the pot passed by Jason's face, waves of heat radiating from the steel poured over him. Derrick dumped the water into the sink. A large waft of steam ascended, leaving beads of water on Jason's forehead.

"Time to put the dishes in the sink." Sid pointed his finger in Jason's face, a vicious snarl on his face.

Jason strained against the force that began pushing his face down into the sink. He watched the bubbles rising in the water, a sinking feeling in his chest. Heat struck his face like a harsh slap. Jason struggled to free his arms, avoiding the scalding water. His right hand came free first, allowing him to grasp the sink and swing his shoulder. The unlucky soldier who had been holding his left hand launched over Jason's back, landing on the tap with a sickening crack.

"FFFFUUUCCCKKKKKKK!!!!!" A horrified screech erupted from the soldier's mouth as his backside slipped into the boiling water.

Sid launched a jab at Jason. His blow missed its mark, his knuckles driving into the flesh of the man clinging to Jason for dear life. Jason turned to face Sid, driving him backward into the sink. A shuddering gasp escaped the man's throat as it forced the wind from his lungs. A sickening pop echoed as his spine snapped in half. Jason noticed his arms go limp as he collapsed on the floor in a heap.

Four white knuckles appeared out of the corner of Jason's view, smashing across his cheek bone. Absorbing the blow, Jason caught Sid's wrist as he drew it back. Jason drove his shoulder into Sid's armpit, buckling his elbow the wrong way. Sid cried out in misery, doubling over, grasping at the dangling limb.

Derrick smashed a large metal plate over Jason's face, glass shards slicing into the top of his bald head. Warm blood trickled down his forehead. Jason stumbled backwards, choreographing Derrick's next movement. He caught the incoming fist in has palm, capitalizing on the momentum, sending Derrick sprawling head first into the metal sink. A sickening thud rang out. Jason spun around, smashing his fist into Sid's nose. The soft flesh squished beneath the force of his blow, a blossom of blood erupting from both nostrils. Jason pounced on Derrick's back, grabbing the knife from his pocket. A surge of endorphins exploded into his bloodstream. A sense of power grew, separating Jason from his sense of humanity.

The knife dug deep into the soft flesh with little effort. Jason enjoyed the man's agonized cry. It got easier with every thrust. Then he returned his attention to Sid, slashing the knife in between his ribs and deep into his lungs. A bubbling gurgle escaped Sid's throat. He tried to spit out the blood, but it was flooding in faster than he could bail it out. The soldier in the sink had first-degree burns all over his arms and face. His limp body dangled from the sink. Beneath the sink, the crippled soldier moaned.

Jason grabbed his helmet and took off for the exit. He edged it open, peeked outside, and found the runway covered in inky shadows. The light of the radar tower didn't reach the terminal. If he managed to find a way out of the dull lights of the cafeteria, he would make it into the woods unseen. Before he had time to think things through, Jason ran away from the radar tower. His footfall echoed in the snow. It only took a moment to escape the influence of the light, finding himself entombed in the darkness. At the edge of the runway, the flicker of a flashlight bounced up and down. It must have been a soldier on patrol, doing his rounds. He wasn't close enough yet to see anything except the halo of the flashlight which was pointing right at him now.

"Hey, what's wrong?" the hidden voice called out. "Wait a second, who goes there?"

Jason continued to rush towards the soldier, the blade of the knife hidden against his forearm. His breathing was laboured, rapidly losing steam, Jason drew on his remaining energy stores. "He's getting away!" Jason called out in between gasping breaths, trying to fool the guard.

"Down on your knees, Mr. Cook." The voice barked. A flash of gunmetal moved through the light, aimed towards Jason.

Jason stopped dead in his tracks. The soldier had picked up his ID on the screen readout. "Hey, everything is cool, man." Jason dropped to his knees. "I surrender." He maneuvered the knife behind his back, gripping the handle. The muscles in his arm tensed, ready to unleash a killing blow when the soldier approached.

The soldier inched closer, the snow crunching underneath his boots, approaching with his weapon raised to the ready. "Get those hands where I can see him."

Jason shifted the knife in his hand, doing his best to tuck the blade beneath his sleeve.

"Drop it, Jason." Tracy's voice preceded the chilling cold metal pressed against the back of his head. "Put the fucking knife down." Jason breathed heavily, his chest burning with pain. Tracy pushed the barrel of the assault rifle against his head. He could sense it slipping to the side. "Trust me, Jason, it's for the best. Drop it now, before this gets any worse."

Jason felt the weight of the knife slip from his grip; his confidence disappeared into the darkness with it. He was so close to escaping. "I trusted you," he said.

His captor removed his helmet, revealing his youth and innocence. His tanned skin shimmered with acne grease. Pupils as dark as the night sky studied Jason with caution, a lack of experience on his behalf making him second guess himself with every motion. The soldier reached behind his back, pulling out a pair of handcuffs from beneath his parka, and strode towards Jason. Warm breath, sweetly scented by the aroma of beans, spilled from his lips and over Jason. "This will on—"

Bang

Muffled by the silencer, a bullet grazed past Jason's ear and nestled into the skull of the soldier. The softness of his eye offered little resistance. An explosion ripped apart the back of his head, sending a wet splatter across the snow behind him. Dazed and confused, red tears ran down his check. The poor boy teetered on wobbly legs.

"We have to get far away from here if we are going to live." Tracy grabbed Jason's arm and hustled him towards the trees. An array of lights sprang to life behind them, all pointing towards the source of the gunfire. Jason and Tracy's shadows fell into the blackness. They scrambled to catch up.

CHAPTER 5
WILL I WALK THE LONG ROAD

Tires gripped the pavement where the wind had cleared the snow, leaving behind large drifts in other places. Mark Smith used every opportunity he got to gain speed, urging the jeep through the vast drifts on momentum alone. Tina slumped in the passenger seat, snoring away. Bowers and Edwards slumbered in the back, grunting and groaning in their sleep, lulled there by the codeine pills they'd discovered in a first aid kit. Bowers' arm wobbled inside the makeshift sling, his face grimacing in anguish with every bump. They piled the rear of the jeep with assault rifles and one lethal light machine gun. Boxes of ammunition rested on the floor, shifting back and forth. There were two crates stuffed with the remaining canned food from the armouries, all covered by several warm blankets Tina had insisted they take.

The wind whooped and howled on the open road, rattling the jeep back and forth. All the extra weight did an admirable job of keeping the jeep grounded in the treacherous conditions. Darkness dominated the horizon, the last dying amber of light a distant memory. The wipers squeaked across the windshield, the heat from the cab melting all the snow thrown at it. Mark turned the high beams off, the bright light catching in the falling snow. Under normal circumstances, they would have made it to Grand Falls by now. If his memory was correct, they would soon be at the bridge just outside of Badger. They were in danger of being late for the fireworks.

Everything was so tranquil—just the croon of the engine to keep him company. Static buzzed from the speakers. Smith fussed with the dial, searching for anything to listen to. A tower in Grand Falls broadcast a sermon by a man calling himself Preacher Willis. Tina turned it off, saying it terrified her. Turning up the volume, Smith strained to hear over the growl of the engine.

"*Job 28:28.*"

The preacher's voice filled the jeep with his almighty tone. Smith turned the volume down, hoping that it wouldn't wake Tina. He watched her stir for a moment. Her mouth twitched in the corner before she fell back into a deep sleep.

"*And unto man he said, 'Behold, the fear of the Lord, that is wisdom.'*"

Smith already loathed the self-absorbed, holier-than-thou speech.

"*And to depart from evil is understanding.*"

"*Now, folks, what does this mean? I appreciate you are all frightened. These are dreadful times. So, let me recite another verse that may shed some light on our problem.*"

The sermon tempted Smith to shut the radio off. He considered listening to the rhythmic grumbling of the engine, but its mechanical purring as they drove down the highway threatened to lull him to sleep. So, he kept listening. They were almost there anyway.

"*Matthew 10:28. 'And fear not them which kill the body, but are not able to kill the soul. But rather fear him, which is able to destroy both soul and body in hell.' Now, while those zombies may rip us to shreds and feast upon our mortal flesh, they cannot destroy your soul. As long as you keep faith in the lord, I can assure your ascension to the heavens. Keep your faith in the Highway Hangman's ability to keep us safe and you will stay on this earth. All plagues end. Stick with me and we will see you through this. The Egyptians, those heathens, survived the great plagues and we will too.*"

"What a crock of shit," Smith muttered back to the jeep, patting the dashboard of his prized possession. "Don't worry, we won't have to listen to him for much longer."

"Please, can you turn that off." Muddled by sleep, Tina's speech was slurred, her eyes still shut.

"I will make a deal with you," Smith offered, "you keep me company so I don't fall asleep or this stays on."

"Deal." Tina sat up, yawning into her palm. "Anything to shut him up."

"You don't like religion all that much," Smith chuckled as the preacher rattled on in the background.

"It's that man's voice. He's a rat." Tina leaned on her elbow, resting it against the door. "I pray that I will be the one to kill him."

"I thought you wanted to be the one who killed Ted?" Smith asked.

"I do," Tina spat out the words with hate.

"Good, my child, use your anger to make you stronger." Smith did his best Palpatine impression. When he saw the perplexed expression on Tina's face, he realized she didn't get the *Star Wars* reference. "Let the hate flow through you," he said, for his own indulgence.

"Now, I am sure you are all aware of the sinners who escaped from our flock."

Tina reached out to turn off the radio, Smith smacked her hand away, putting more force than he intended into the blow. "I want to hear this."

"I told you, the guy gives me the creeps," she sulked.

"He's talking about us." Smith pointed to the radio. "Maybe we need to hear this?" Tina slumped into her seat, crossing her arms across her chest.

"In conversations with the elders and the Highway Hangmen, we will organize work parties. We will pull some of you from your work, but those left behind will pick up the slack. Those of you who fortunate enough to be called upon will work long and hard looking for those filthy sinners. They are NOT to be slaughtered on site. No, they WILL NOT be getting the mercy of a quick death." Preacher Willis was working himself into a religious frenzy, raising his voice to the heavens. *"THEY WILL BE JUDGED, oh lord you better BELIEVE. The wicked have sinned and they WILL ATONE FOR THEIR SINS."*

"Turn it off." Tina turned her head to look out the window, staring off into the darkness.

"Aren't you the least bit curios?" Smith said to no response. The preacher proceeded to drone on.

"Anyone able to find them and bring them back ALIVE will be relieved of their duties and receive a lifetime of rations. Folks, I know this may take a miracle, but this is the season of miracles. Why, tonight is Christmas Eve of all days. At the Christmas

*service tonight, those of you selected will begin your noble jour-
ney.*"

"See, I told you it would be worth listening to," Smith
proclaimed.

"What, you're going to shoot up a church during
Christmas mass?" Tina said, snarling at Smith.

Smith roared, turning off the radio. "We won't have
to. I got a fantastic idea." Smith felt the jeep's tires leave
the ground as they drifted through a snow bank. Seconds
later, the jeep's tires bite into the pavement and barrelled
down the highway, passing the twenty-kilometer marker.

CHAPTER 6
CANNOT STAY

"There isn't time to move her," Dana said matter-of-factly.

"We can't stay here," Hank responded, "there are too many of them." After the tedious trek to get here, they needed rest but found none. Thrust into a situation neither could walk away from with a clear conscious, a child was about to be born into this dying world. It should be cherished and nurtured at all costs. Hank realized Dana needed to experience that it was possible. He watched Dana rub her belly. She wasn't showing yet, but was mindful of the life growing inside of her.

Upstairs, anguished cries rang out. Deafening, the shrill noise cut through the air like a sharpened blade through paper, tearing and ripping as it passed. Contractions crippled the suffering woman, with nothing to dull the pain except an effort to expel it from her belly with animalistic screams. Minutes passed without a break from the painful wailing. It ended as suddenly as it had begun.

"Two minutes apart now." A worried sigh escaped

Dana's lips, the exhaustion weighing on her. "It will happen soon, I think?"

"Goddammit." Hank balled his fingers into fists in frustration. "We have to move her now."

"She is too far dilated. If we head outside, there is a reasonable chance that the baby would be born in the snowstorm." Dana opened the bedroom door, then paused. "We need to move her to the bathroom." She yanked open the door and left without explaining.

"What?" Puzzled, Hank followed behind waiting for clarification. "Dana, we need to get her the hell out of here. Those screams will draw every undead from all around." A thought crossed Hank's mind, filling him with guilt. For a moment he weighed the dilemma in his head, bouncing the idea around inside his head. "We should leave before they realize."

"We can't leave her here."

"I can't stop them." The words fell from Hank's mouth. "There are too many of the—p"

Cries from upstairs cut him off. Hank watched Dana check her wristwatch. He didn't need her to tell him that the contractions were now less than two minutes apart.

"What are we going to do?" Hank asked.

"Get her into the bathroom and lay her in the tub. I remember reading that women stuck in remote locations could give birth to a baby all by themselves in a bath tub." Dana began striding towards the bedroom, continuing to talk as she walked towards the shrieking. "We can try to muffle her screams with towels." A soft, encouraging voice spoke, soothing the pregnant woman from the other side of the bedroom door. "I don't know what to do about the dead outside. I realize that we don't stand a chance fighting them off *here*." Dana emphasized the last word.

Hank didn't have to figure out what she meant. He nodded his head, acknowledging the unasked request. A tear formed in the corner of Dana's eye, pooling up in the bottom lid. "I'll come back for all of you once this is over," he said.

"Thank you." Dana leaned in to give Hank a hug. He felt her body trembling.

Hank cut the embrace short. "You get in there and make sure that the baby survives."

She paused in the doorway's threshold. The howl of the wind rattled the window. They braced the pregnant woman up with pillows, her husband standing by her side, caressing her hand. "I don't know what to say."

Hank just bowed his head, looking down at his feet, hoping that he would find something clever to say. Butterflies fluttered their wings in his stomach, glue sticking his legs in place. "I'll be back." Hesitant, he turned and ambled away. Beneath the nervousness lay a dreadful sense of doom. It bubbled in his stomach like heated asphalt. The sour essence of the dead greeted him as he opened the door, a revolting, fetid odour heavy in the air.

Hank banged the picaroon against the trunk of a tree, trying his best to lure the herd away from the cabin. An alpha zombie was working at keeping his pack on track, somehow knowing there was more to eat there than the scant meat on Hank's bones. "Come on, you dead bastards!" Hank called out, his tone hoarse. The racket that

he made caught their attention. The alpha zombie grunted, pacing back and forth, blocking the group's movement
and herding them back towards the cabin.

Soft, babbling water flowed behind Hank, buried
somewhere beneath the ice. He had been working to
get them to the river bank. Once they plunged in, they
wouldn't be able to get back over those steep banks, the
jagged ice formed along its edges serving as a barrier.
"You can't catch me!" Hank chuckled. The phrase left his
mouth before his mind comprehended, sounding ridicu-
lous, childish, and out of place. Every time Hank cried
out, he caught the alpha's attention, its almost human
eyes scowling at him. Hungry groaning encased him, the
ghoulish cries bouncing off the trees. When the wind blew,
it brought their decaying stench with it, burying Hank in
a disgusting fog. With another loud grunt, the alpha put
the herd back on course.

No matter how much effort Hank put into redirecting
the herd, he knew that the alpha zombie would thwart every attempt. There was only one thing left for Hank to do.
He needed to kill that abomination before it was too late.
Without swift action, the pack of undead would trample
through the cabin and massacre everyone inside without
remorse. He balanced the picaroon in his palm, sliding
it back and forth until he found the right position. With
great concentration, he gathered all the energy he could
muster into his legs and abdominals. His training during
filming the Greek epic guided his actions.

"Hey, ugly!" Hank called out, catching a glimmer of
moonlight in the alpha's eye. To build momentum, he
took a few steps backward before thrusting forward. The

picaroon left his hand with finesse and power, the metal tip racing across the open tundra. Muscle memory was a tremendous attribute. Even over the constant moaning, the wet popping sound echoed as the metal tip pierced through the skull. One final defiant grunt escaped his lips. The alpha quivered, his muscles twitching as he slumped backward. Held up by the spear, the alpha's body crumpled into an awkward hunch with crooked knees and a twisted hip.

"Come on, this way!" Hank rallied the herd. Without their leader, they staggered towards him. The rhythm of rushing water grew louder as Hank reached the river's edge. He peered into the black chasm lying in front of him. The river snaked its course through the forest, trees lining up along both sides of the river banks. He kept hollering out to the swarm, their footsteps following him.

The water roared just ahead. Impeded by the ice built up along its path, the water sloshed around, its current interrupted by tiny islands growing amongst the rocks. Hank caught his breath. He looked over the edge; the water was pure darkness, absorbing the moonlight above. Moans drew nearer, their decrepit footfalls lurching through the crust of snow. He looked along the river bend, making sure there was nowhere for the zombies to climb out. Now that he was sure, he gathered his strength and sprinted. Below his feet, the snow became hollow as he neared the edge.

With a giant leap, Hank noticed gravity yanking at his feet, trying to drag him down into the river. A wall of frigid, chilled air rose from the wintery water. The cold sucked the air from his lungs, driving the energy from his kicking legs as he came back down to earth. He closed his eyes, afraid to look down. His knees jammed into his rib cage as he touched down on solid ground. He tumbled face first into the snow before rolling to his feet with practiced grace. Giddy, Hank laughed emphatically, the sound drawing the zombies straight for the edge. He observed with glee as the decrepit forms approached the bank. Blackened by frost bite, and missing fingers, disfigured hands reached out for him across the gap.

The first zombie toppled over the edge of the bank. A splash of water exploded outward from the impact, washing over the snowy banks. Then, more and more zombies took the plunge. The sound of bones cracking as the bodies smashed into the frozen river bed was like music to Hank's ears. He sat on the edge, watching the clumsy bodies fall like a morbid waterfall into the freezing waters below. They piled on top of each other in their fruitless efforts to reach him. If he had a cigar in his pocket, he would have smoked it in celebration. Hell, if he had one, he'd bring them back to Clarence in honour of his new baby.

Could this be the first child born since the outbreak began?

The thought crossed his mind when he heard the ice splitting beneath him. A loud crack ruptured below him. He fell into the icy waters below, the shock seizing his muscles, holding him in place in the shallow water. Shivering, he struggled to his feet, his hands unable to gain any traction on the icy wall. Jaws snapped at his flesh. He shivered as the stubs and decrepit fingers tugged at his jacket. With nowhere to go, he felt himself being dragged backwards into the growing pile. Jagged teeth tore into his legs, shredding off a strip of flesh. Greedy hands pulled in him all directions. Jarring pain rang out all over his body as his flesh was ripped apart, torn from his arms, legs, backside, and cheeks. Icy water washed away the blood that drained beneath him as the dead feasted on his scrawny figure. Hank tried to scream, but the gargled cry caught in his throat, his airway blocked off by the festering mouth of a zombie.

CHAPTER 7
THERE'S NO NEED TO SAY GOODBYE

A spatter of hot fluids sprayed over Eric's face. Harry's eyes bulged out as the shock wave rippled through his cranium, the bullet erupting out of the top. With an uncontrollable shudder, Harry dropped to his knees, his weight toppling onto Eric. Knocked backwards, Eric tumbled into the snow as the wind rushed out of his lungs. Helen screamed, firing three bullets that all missed their mark. The last bullet sent snow and dirt exploding into Eric's eyes as he endeavored to haul himself out from underneath the deceased man. Eric returned fire, the bullet ricocheting off the windshield of the snowmobile, sending Helen diving for shelter. Shattered plastic shards fell over the bonnet of the snowmobile.

All the commotion rallied the undead, their hungry cries now a feverish state. He heard them drooling, their wet mouths snapping open and shut. Eric fired towards Helen, his bullets tearing through the bonnet of the snowmobile. A hydropic hiss sprayed fluids into the snow. Eric flicked open his revolver, reloading the three empty slots. He made a frantic lunge for Harry's snowmobile, seizing advantage of Helen's indecisiveness. Eric gained the edge. Then she made a catastrophic mistake. Ignoring Eric, she hopped into the seat of the snowmobile, fumbling for the keys. The engine wouldn't turn over. It whined and grumbled. Black smoke billowed beneath the hood, but it wouldn't start. A mechanical clicking punctuated her every attempt, the metal keys clanging off the dashboard.

Eric wasted no time. He took precise aim and only fired once. A crimson explosion sent a shower of blood sailing into the wind. Helen toppled off the seat, lifeless, her body smashed into the ground full force. A loud grunt caught Eric's attention. Near the edge of the blackness, he saw the alpha zombie. Its skin was ghastly white, frozen over from being outside in the elements, blending into the environment the way his deceased brethren never could. From a distance, he looked like another living being that had wandered off into the storm. Behind him, an army of decaying bodies followed with pack mentality. The alpha looked up at the moon, letting out another blood-curdling scream, then pointed at Eric. Fingers unable to coordinate pointed in several directions, but the hand pointed at him. The undead didn't need clarification. They moved with purpose. The noxious scent of blood wafted to them, energizing them.

A flash of moonlight reflected towards Eric. The alabaster glow of the key acted like a beacon, drawing him to Harry's machine. Eric turned the engine over. It rumbled to life beneath him. With a squeeze of the throttle, the machine glided forward over the snow. He made a sharp turn and followed the tracks back towards the town of Grand Falls. The wind tugged at him, the frigid blasts nipping at his exposed face. The early manifestations of frostbite were long past. Heat belching from the vents reminded Eric of that fact. The pain was unbearable as his toes and fingers thawed. A thousand needles pricked his nerves all at once as the heat drained into his body. He only looked back once. What he saw wasn't a shock. Members of the herd had circled the lifeless bodies, bloodied hands wrenching at the flesh of Harry and Helen Cooper. They held body parts torn from the torso up to feast upon like trophies. Only the alpha zombie didn't stop to take part. He continued his mission, leading the stragglers in the back onward.

Eric cursed at the snowmobile. The engine sputtered and choked on the last remaining fuel. A glance over his shoulder assured him that there was enough distance between himself and the relentless herd to feel safe. The crest of the hill was just ahead; the glow of the lights below glowed. He swore the hum of city life ahead buzzed in his ear. Behind him, the endless babbling of the undead loomed. They were ravenous for flesh, setting their migration towards Grand Falls, the town laying in their path of destruction. Eric turned to look back one last time at the ruthless herd, content to leave them behind. If his luck lasted, he would get in and out of Grand Falls before they fell upon the city like a plague.

Grey clouds of smoke spewed from underneath the bonnet. The engine knocked inside the frame as it died out. One last sputter of the pistons churning as the motor shut down, dragged out in a low, mechanical hissing. The snowmobile died in its tracks, ceasing to a stop just a few feet from the top. The last stretch of the journey would have to be on foot.

So much for his streak of luck. The heavy reek of oil and grease hung in the surrounding air. The dense smoke washed over him as it drifted back down the hillside. Eric flung his legs over the side of the seat, careful to keep his feet on the hardened, packed snowmobile trail.

Once he reached the top, he was close enough to recognize the bright, fluorescent sign of an old Irving station nestled at the entrance into the city. The red, blue, and white light stood out against the pale glow of the city behind it. Eric admired the surreal buzz of activity within the city limits. Since the first night of the outbreak, most nights were bare of human existence. No one dared allow the lights outside in fear of attracting the dead. Grand Falls defied them with its shameless display of civilization. Hubris would be the downfall of mankind once again. The haunting march of the dead would lay waste to everything that the Highway Hangman built. No matter the outcome of tonight, the city would lie in ruin. Either the dead would be triumphant, or the living would prevail, suffering tremendous losses in the Herculean struggle.

A horrifying thought crossed Eric's mind. He peered back at the creeping shadow and shuddered in fear at the size of the herd. The blackness of the dead would eclipse the light of the city below. Blood would flow tonight. More blood than society could spare. If they survived the night, it would take years to recover from the devastation slithering towards town.

Eric looked up at the swollen silver moon lurking behind the blustery December clouds. Hidden in the shadows below, the poisoned arms of a thousand dead souls reached out. They would stop at nothing to drag him into the horde. All they wanted was to taste his blood, have it run cold between their fingers, his organs turned into a fine paste. In the hushing dark, hungry cries rang out, desperate for a taste of flesh. Relentless, the darkness swept up the mountainside like a virus, wiping out everything in its path.

Eric looked down at the city lights of Grand Falls. Raising the flare gun above his head, he fired off the signal flare. Bright orange light lit up the sky like the smouldering embers of dying sunlight. The flare rocketed upwards with a sharp whistle, the piercing sound fizzling out at the apex of its arc. Eric trotted towards town, distracted, but whirled around when he heard crunching snow. Rapid bursts echoed in the cold night air, approaching Eric from below. He stared into the darkness with his weapon drawn, ready to fire at one of the alpha zombies. Emerging from the shadows, escaping from the midst of the pack, a shadowy figure raced up the hill. Beneath the sullen clothes and filthy appearance, a set of lively eyes looked towards him. Eric took careful aim and cocked back the hammer.

"Don't shoot!" a woman's voice hollered at him.

CHAPTER 8
AND I SAW THE DEAD

Aliyah peered over her laptop, watching as the cars raced down Prince Phillip Drive. Rain battered the glass windows that overlooked the restless street. Droplets of water streaked across the window with the powerful winds. Slipping beneath the black rain clouds, the setting sun reflected orange off the wet asphalt, the blazing ball of light fading away. The street lights flickered on, their pale glow growing stronger against the darkening sky, but failed to compare to the sun's powerful glare. Her stomach grumbled; Aliyah couldn't recall the last time she ate. She had spent the entire afternoon editing her English paper, wanting it to be perfect before she handed in to her professor, Mr. LeDrew.

Aliyah listened to the giant splashes of water as cars cruised through the forming puddles, gathering in the ruts of the well-worn road. She found it distracting. The boisterous chatter of students would drown out the ambient noise. She glanced around the food court; she found herself surrounded by empty tables and a few other students with their heads buried in their homework. It was the Thanksgiving holiday, and most of the student body was absent during the long weekend. Aliyah wore a grey hooded sweatshirt, the words Memorial in burgundy emblazoned across the chest. Faded blue jeans with a giant tattered hole over the right knee exposed her ebony skin. With her chestnut brown hair tied into a messy bun, she continually brushed away stray strands away from her emerald-green eyes.

A whiff of chocolate mixed with cinnamon and vanilla caught her attention. Aliyah turned towards Treats as the worker pulled a tray of cookies out of the oven. The sound of chairs scrapping across the linoleum echoed in the empty food court as students wandered towards the delicious aroma. Aliyah joined them and stood in line, waiting for her turn to order.

"Hey, Aliyah, did you have any fun this weekend?" Mallory startled her.

Aliyah turned around to greet her friend, who was dressed head to toe in black and royal purple. Silver chains dangled from her pockets; studded black wrist bands covered up her left wrist; and her nose, lip, and ears were all pierced multiple times. Mallory wore her hair short and dyed pitch black, streaked with burgundy highlights. Her pastel blue eyes stood out against the deep violet eye shadow, and her long black false eyelashes batted like a bird's wing as she blinked her eyes.

"No, I wanted to get caught up on my school work. Did you just get back from the skate park?" Aliyah laughed.

"You're such a square," Mallory chuckled at her friend. The two looked like opposites but bonded over their love of heavy metal music. "Were you speaking to Tina?"

Aliyah shook her head. "No, I didn't realize she was back yet?"

"Oh, so you don't know?" A sly grin crossed her face, her merlot-shaded lips curling into her wrinkled cheek. "Tina told the police she discovered a dead body while out for a walk, but they never recovered any corpse. Just a lot of blood. I gathered she's all fucked up now, headed straight to the loony bin," Mallory guffawed.

"That's appalling, how can you laugh at that?" Aliyah asked, disturbed by Mallory's malice. "It will scare her for life. I should call her."

The line staggered forward; an elderly man working the cash was in no rush. "She isn't coming back," Mallory replied, "going to miss the rest of the semester."

Aliyah watched the employee count back the customers' change; it was agonizing to watch him fumble with the change. "You seem suspiciously"—the cashier called her over, "I'll have a medium two milk, one sweetener, and a chocolate chip muffin." She turned back to Mallory as the cash register sang, calculating the cost of her order—"joyful about that."

"That will be three fifty." The clerk placed his hand on the counter, watching for her to pass him the money. Aliyah placed a five-dollar bill in his palm. Having worked retail before, she despised when people threw money at her. The drawer clanged open; the cashier scattered her change across the counter.

"Well, you know that Evan won't want to wait for her to come back," Mallory said with a smirk that lit up her face, her cheeks blushing to match her lipstick. "That boy only cares about one thing," Mallory winked, "and I intend to be the one to give it to him."

Aliyah picked up the paper bag that her muffin came in. It crinkled underneath her touch. Heat radiated up to her forearm as soon as she picked up the coffee. She expected Mallory to order, but her friend accompanied her back to the desk and sat with her. "You're not getting anything?"

"I don't drink coffee before liquor." Mallory fussed with her hair. "Doesn't go well together. Gives me a horrendous hangover. Strange, huh?"

Aliyah wanted to explain to her all the reasons it wasn't extraordinary. She could have explained how the caffeine affects her body's ability to process the alcohol. "That is weird." Now wasn't the time. Aliyah was still thinking about Tina Caines. She unlocked her phone and went through her text messages, finding the last one from Tina that she hadn't responded to yet. A strange sense of guilt washed over her. Maybe she would text her friend later once she had time to figure out something worthwhile to say.

"So do you plan on studying the rest of the night?" Mallory asked as she adjusted her top, making sure that just enough cleavage was showing.

"Why," Aliyah didn't like where this was going, "you make plans to go to the bar with Evan already?" She said it more harshly than she meant to, feeling remorseful over her tone.

"Actually," Mallory rolled her eyes, "he's working tonight. I thought he could use a friend to talk too."

"Jesus Christ, Mallory." This time Aliyah meant it. "I don't even know what to think about that. Don't you think you should back off a little?"

"Why?" Mallory stood up. "It's not like they're dating. At least, it's nothing serious."

Aliyah looked up at her friend, the steam from her coffee rising over her face. "Listen, I'm sorry. It's none of my business. Forgive me?"

"On one condition."

Aliyah let out a protracted sigh, knowing without having to ask. She gathered her books, sweeping them into her bookbag. "Let's go."

Walking down the extensive collection of stairs, the music pounded beneath them. The base boomed, overpowering the music as they approached. Aliyah could detect that stagnant, yeasty smell of the campus bar. People stumbled outside to have a smoke, raucous laughter providing background noise to the throbbing base. An icy gust of wind swept up the stairs. Fall had set in with the frigid winter weather looming in the imminent future. Aliyah shivered, cramming her hands into the front pouch of her sweatshirt. She dreaded the night life. Forced to take part, the ritual was as much a part of the university experience as the classes themselves.

"Look, there he is." Mallory pointed to the front door. Evan stood there in his T-shirt, holding the exit open for a group leaving, a brawny arm extending from the black sleeve. A pack of Export As stuck out of the pocket of his dull blue jeans. Once the last person left, he followed behind.

Aliyah saw the telltale yellow spark of a lighter as

Evan lit the cigarette. The wind drove the smoke away. "I suppose you want to go say hi." Here came the worst part, standing out in the cold, waiting for two people to flirt, while she stood between them.

"We could grab a drink first." Mallory didn't take her eyes off Evan. Aliyah knew she had no intentions of going anywhere else; she didn't bother to accept the hollow offer.

They strolled over to the door, Mallory's high heels clicking off the tile floor as she pressed ahead of Aliyah. A gust of frigid air hit them in the face like an unexpected slap. "Hey, ladies," Evan glanced up when he heard the door open, "what are you doing here tonight?"

"I should ask you the same thing," Mallory said.

"Uhmm," Evan tried to soften the embarrassing blow by lowering his voice, "I'm working."

Aliyah let out a cordial laugh. She felt bad for her friend, but this was too funny to ignore. Not wanting to surrender the comforting warmth of the bar, Aliyah stood in the doorway. Heat soothed her back, making the fall chill barrable.

Mallory produced a fake chuckle, struggling to cover up her own fumbling words. "I guess you can call what you do work."

Evan took one last long drag of his cigarette before throwing the butt at his feet. The orange spark flared as it struck the cement walkway. He stamped it out with his boot diligently. "Shall we head back inside?" Before Aliyah turned around, the sounds of a man cursing caught Evan's attention. "Damn it, I'd better go check that out. You guys can head inside, I shouldn't be long."

With a quick step, Aliyah lunged back into the heated lobby. Stale beer, and the sweet, sickly scent of mixed drinks welcomed her. Mallory stood in the doorway for a moment, hesitating just long enough to watch Evan fade into the shadows beyond the street lights. A concerned expression passed over her face. Aliyah shivered, resting her hands in the crook of her armpits, letting her body heat warm them up. "He won't be long." She tried to sound reassuring. "Probably some drunken fool."

"Yeah," Mallory's eyes lingered on the edge of the darkness, "I'm sure your right." She stepped backwards, letting the door ease shut, never losing track of where Evan had vanished. Cars drove down the road sporadically, the faint sound of splashing water as tires drove through the puddles amplified by the dead silence.

Music from the speakers faded away as the song ended. In that momentary lapse, all sounds ceased. Rain fell heavily, the bitter drops splattering against the giant glass window of the lobby. Wind blew the street lamps, and the soft yellow light teetered into the darkness revealing a little of the gloomy alley where Evan had disappeared. Murmurs rose in the alley, the voice too low to pick out. The intensity escalated, the whispers turning into arguing. After a few seconds, Aliyah realized that the conversation was one sided. Evan's voice boomed, his words muffled by the pouring rain.

"I'm sure Evan is…"

A horrific shriek cut off her thought in mid sentence.

Mallory sprang from the building and rushed off into

the shadows. "Hey, wait up a second," Aliyah called out to her friend, panic settling in now. That terrified scream ended abruptly. "Let's get help." Something was wrong; she didn't have the courage to run out there alone. Her feet felt stuck in quicksand. Wanting to run into the bar and grab one of Evan's coworkers, her stiff legs froze. "Help!" she screamed and banged her fist against the metal frame. "Please help!"

The door to the bar swung open, a security guard wearing a black T-shirt and a distressed expression on his face rushed out. "What's going on?" He sprinted towards the narrow corridor. A few bystanders followed.

Aliyah pointed outside. "Something's happened to Evan." The bouncer brushed past her without waiting for an explanation. Forced outside by the curious mob, Aliyah begrudgingly left the comfort of the bright lights. Rumors and excited chatter ran rampant through the swelling crowd, urging her into the darkness.

"We need an ambulance!" Mallory shrieked.

A bright white light emerged out of thin air, the glow of the bouncer's cellphone casting just enough glare to offer a view of the nightmarish scene. Mallory was holding her shirt over Evan's face, the purple fabric stained a deep maroon. Scarlet tears rolled down his face. The heavy rain diluted the blood, allowing it to flow like a river. A large jumble of clothing lay at Evan's feet, crumbled into an unrecognizable form. Even in the darkness, the puddle of blood flowing from beneath the shape was unmistakable, pooling beneath the victim's head. Aliyah's gaze was glued to the man's rib cage. It wasn't moving. His right leg was tucked beneath him, his foot digging into his own backside. The other leg sprawled out straight towards Evan.

"What the hell happened?" Aliyah said out loud. No one acknowledged her.

The bouncer was talking to the 911 operator. "I need an ambulance to the front entrance of the Breezeway." He paused as the voice on the other end asked questions. "I'm not sure what happened. One person has a severe head laceration and the other one has a vicious cut on his face. Hold on, I'll check." He tucked the phone into his chest. "Check his pulse."

A sense of dread washed over Aliyah as she watched the finger settle on her. "He isn't breathing."

"Please, just check for me." The bouncer raised the phone to the side of his face. "They need to know."

Deep, gasping sobs escaped Mallory's throat. Panic had taken hold; her hands shook as she struggled to hold the T-shirt against the deep gash on Evan's cheek. Evan stared off into the distance. Shock had drained all the colour from his face. Soaked with blood and drained of all colour, Evan looked like a dead man, his vacant stare a mile long.

Aliyah turned her attention to the man at Evan's feet. The rain had washed most of the blood away, and his matted hair concealed the savage wound. Underneath the mop of black, a thin sliver of white ran from the crown of his head to the back of his neck, exposing his skull. "Jesus Christ," she muttered to herself. "There's no way he has a pulse." Red flaps of flesh edged the wound, a brown fluid spilling out from beneath the torn scalp. The muscles in her stomach clenched, sending up a wave of nausea. Bile raced up her throat and filled her mouth with its bitter taste. Aliyah bent over at the waist and covered her mouth. Vomit filled her hand. Yellow liquid spewed from between her fingers, splattering onto the pavement, splashing into a pool of rain water and blood.

Aliyah could visualize the events that took place in her mind's eye. Her mother called it a gift; her father called it a nightmare. She had the ability to recreate, with pin-point accuracy, any occurrence based on a few visual keys. Evan and the outsider argued. Then, without warning, the man attacked Evan, catching him off guard, and bit his face. A retaliatory blow knocked the man unconscious, and his legs buckled beneath him. Then he smashed the back of his head against the pavement. Fueled by alcohol and adrenaline, his heart pumped too much blood out of the gnarly wound. White as a ghost, Evan was in shock. Not from the attack, but from the fact that he had played a part in the man's death.

"Goddammit," the bouncer said, angered by the situation. "Could someone check that man for a pulse?" He waved his phone in concentric circles, the LED display luring a man out of the crowd.

A man from the crowd rushed heroically towards the crumpled body, his boots splashing into the forming puddles. Once he got closer to the horrific scene, his movement slowed to a timid approach. They exchanged glances, acknowledging the horrendous ordeal, an understanding between them. He knelt down next to the man and placed his fingers on his neck. "The guy doesn't have a pulse." When he pulled his fingers away, they ran with blood.

"Yeah, he doesn't have a pulse," the bouncer relayed to the operator. "How long?" His voice overflowed with dismay. "I understand that, but this is an emergency. Hello?" He stuffed his phone back into his jean pocket. "It will be quicker if we walk to the Health Sciences Centre."

"You have got to be kidding me," Mallory burst out. "Evan needs medical attention right now."

"I've got my car around back," a voice from the crowd offered. Strangers rushed forward to help guide Evan towards the parking lot. Mallory, her stature made much smaller by Evan's exceptional size, refused to part from his side. Aliyah tried to grab her attention to no avail. The bouncer announced he was heading back inside to get more help. Feet shuffled in different directions; the murmur of the crowd dissipated. The world seemed to pass by Aliyah in a blur. Before she knew what was happening, she had somehow been left with the grave obligation of watching over the corpse until the ambulance arrived.

Rain poured from the pitch-black night sky in heavy sheets. Wind swept the falling drops over her like a blanket, engulfing her. Electricity hummed from the streetlights above. Aliyah shivered, first with the cold, then with the settling fear. All she wanted was to be anywhere else. Sirens wailed in the background, too far away to bring her any sense of hope. She was alone with the corpse. Everyone had abandoned her, not willing to suffer the weather for this stranger. But, bound by a sense of moral obligation, Aliyah waited with him. He deserved that much, at least. Soaking wet from head to toe and miserable out here alone, if she knew who this was, if the outsider had an identity, it would give her some form of comfort. She crouched at the hip, refusing to kneel into the bloody puddle, and went through his pockets for his wallet. Luckily for her, he kept it in his jacket pocket and not his jeans. His license was the first thing she saw when she opened it. Nestled behind see-through plastic, his license provided her with everything she needed. Jimmy Boone, age thirty-two from Stephenville Crossing, suffered a vicious fall and subsequently bled out in the street like a drowned rat. Ironically, he was an organ donor, but that fact wouldn't make her laugh until much later.

Pity filled Aliyah, forcing out the dread. She embraced it, even though it made her ashamed. Any emotion was better than the one she had been experiencing. Now that she learned his identity, she fumbled his wallet back into its resting place. Her hand inadvertently pressed against the man's stomach, and she swore she saw it grumbling. Her hand sprang back, as if a volt of electricity had jolted it. Something deep inside was begging her to run away. To get as far away from Jimmy Boone as her legs would carry her, but they wouldn't cooperate.

A low, guttural growl spilled from the man's pressed lips. Aliyah stumbled back and fell on her backside. She gawked at the man's chest. It was moving up and down in shallow breaths, his raspy groans drowned in his throat. "Are you okay, mister?" Aliyah half whispered, terrified she would get a response. The man's arm twitched. His finger nails scrapped across the pavement as he struggled to get up. His head, rolling back and forth, battled to lift. The blare of sirens approached as the red and white lights lit up the sidewalk. A strangled cry rang out from deep within his chest; it was a wet, clicking noise. When she looked towards the man, she saw his opaque eyes, rimmed with red rivers, gazing at her. Aware that her feet were within his grasp, she scurried backwards.

Anguished moans escaped his parted lips. His fingers stretched out, reaching out for her. Glazed eyes that hid behind the murky white film that covered the iris followed her movements. The metallic squeal of brakes wasn't enough to divert the man's attention. Ambulance doors opened and slammed shut, their boots splashing in the puddles as the paramedics jumped down. A shriek escaped Aliyah's throat.

"Sir, you need to stop moving," a tired voice ordered. A female paramedic reached out and tried to steady the man's neck. "Sir, you may have suffered a spinal fracture."

The man only responded with a hungry growl and snapping jaws. A male paramedic rolled a stretcher from the back of the ambulance. The florescent orange board stood out in the dull surroundings. Aliyah's heart fluttered in her chest; she wanted to warn the paramedic that something was wrong here. The man thrashed back and forth while the paramedic held his head in place. "Sir, you will hurt yourself. You need to calm down."

"Hold him steady, Jane. I'll get the sedative ready."

"Thanks, Adam." Her voice was haggard.

Aliyah fumbled her way to her feet. She wanted to turn and run. "There's something wrong with him." Her voice trembled. The man's movements were uncoordinated. It reminded Aliyah of watching her younger brother learning to crawl. His arms and legs moved out of sync, unable to generate enough force to push off the much smaller woman who had him pinned to the ground. With his neck held in place, his jaws snapped at the bitter night air.

"There's something wrong with half of this city." Adam held up his arm, rolling back the sleeve to expose a blood-stained bandage. "Last guy bit me." He tapped the syringe. "That's what this is for. I'll let the doctors handle him when he comes to." Adam yanked the guy's collar to one side. A festering wound spilled brown puss and blood all over the man's chest. "Damn." Adam recoiled from the wound as if someone had slapped him. "That smells worse than death." He found a meaty part of the shoulder and plunged the needle in. The man's struggled against the sedative, and the metal tip snapped off in his shoulder. Tendons stood out on his neck as his jaw snarled into a scream, but no sound came out.

"Christ sakes," Jane grunted as she struggled to hold his head in place.

"That won't help." Aliyah backed away, retreating into the darkness.

"Just takes a minute." Adam knelt down on the other side of the sedated man. "He'll go to sleep soon." Random muscles spasms contracted various body parts as the man's fidgeting died down. His lip was bleeding profusely. In his rage he had gnawed on the soft flesh until it smeared his face like gore-coloured lipstick. "There." Adam wiped his brow. "Let's get him loaded onto the stretcher and get him in."

"They'll run out of beds soon," Jane complained as she bent down to help Adam. She cupped her hands behind the man's knee, the strain of a long shift settling into her joints.

The two paramedics grunted as they hoisted the man, his limbs dangling below his body. Adam was burning up. Drenched with sweat, the salty discharge stung his eyes. They got the man onto the stretcher after much effort. Jane placed her hand into the small of her back, rubbing out a knot. Bothered by the stinging, Adam was constantly rubbing his eyes. He hacked into his sleeve, bringing something up from his chest. He spat a wad of yellow mucus. It landed in a puddle near his feet, an audible splat preceding it. When he glanced up at Aliyah, she saw the flaming ring outlining his eyes.

"Do you know the man? Does he have any health concerns?" Adam looked ready to vomit. He placed his hand over his mouth to camouflage a belch.

Aliyah shook her head back and forth before she remembered his wallet. "I checked his wallet. His name is Jimmy Boone. That's all I know."

"You haven't seen him around campus before."

She shook her head. "Not that I can remember. It's an enormous campus, but, no, I haven't seen him before."

"All right, we'll take it from here," Jane said, a thin smile on her face. "You should get inside now. You'll freeze to death out here."

Aliyah shivered but not from the cold and dampness. A chill traveled up her spine at the word "death." She tucked her head into her chin and headed back towards the Breezeway. Once she stepped inside, she realized that the sounds of the bar had vanished. An eerie silence filled the lobby. Everyone gone home early for the night.

She could see the workers cleaning up inside as the door swung open. The bouncer walked over with a beer in each of his hands. "Thanks for staying with him." He offered Aliyah the beer. "It'll help with the nerves."

Normally, Aliyah would have refused but not tonight. She took a giant swig from the brown bottle; it made her gag a little. "Black Horse?" For a moment she thought she would be sick, but she craved the warming sensation that flooded through her system.

"Yeah, sorry but the boss doesn't mind if we take the stuff that doesn't sell." He apologized. "I called Evan, but he's not picking up. Have you heard from Mallory?"

Aliyah checked her phone. There was a message from Mallory. She opened up her phone and skimmed her text. "They are at the emergency room now. She said it's over crowded, they will be there all night."

"You want to go check on them? Maybe they need something."

Aliyah thought that was a splendid idea. She was going to ask Mallory if she needed anything when she realized she didn't remember the bouncer's name. "I'm sorry, I know we have meet before, but I can't remember your name."

"Jacob," he laughed. "It's okay. I'm used to it. Most people don't notice me, I'm always overshadowed by Evan, anyway."

A flush of blood turned her cheeks an embarrassed red. "I'm sorry." She returned him a brisk glance and couldn't argue with him. Next to Evan, he was very forgettable. Raven black hair sat in a tangled mess on top of his head. His nose was too small for his face; it made the distance between his eyes appear comically far apart. With chubby cheeks and a round face, he looked much too young to be working in a bar. Muscles, if he had any, hid beneath his loose black work shirt. Baggy jeans rested too high on his hips with his belt buckle just above his belly button. Even with his shirt tucked in, the fabric drooped over his belt.

Jacob emptied his drink with one large gulp. "Want another?" He shook his bottle, making sure that he had emptied it.

"Sure." Aliyah felt like she would need a hand getting to sleep tonight. "That would be great, Jacob." She said his name out loud, hoping that would help her remember it. He disappeared back inside the double doors. She stood outside in the middle of the lobby and sent a text message to Mallory.

Do you need anything? Me and Jacob could bring you whatever you need. How's Evan doing?

It didn't take Mallory long to respond. Jacob still hadn't returned with the beers when she heard the notification.

We could use something to eat. Evan is complaining he has a fever. He's burning up.

Sure thing, we will grab you something and be right over. Are you still in the waiting room?

Yeah, we'll be here a while by the looks of things.

"Here you are." Jacob handed Aliyah another Black Horse.

Aliyah took a long sip from her first beer, sitting the half empty bottle on the coat check counter. "I'm not much of a drinker." Aliyah sensed the embarrassment in her own voice, hoping that he hadn't noticed. "They could use some food. We can grab some from the shops upstairs if they're still open."

"I think they'll be closed." He picked up her beer and drank the rest. "It's standard whenever the cops get involved. At least that is what my boss said."

Outside, there was nothing but the pitter-patter of rain against the gigantic glass window. There were no more sirens, no cars passing by. "I guess we can grab them something from my dorm room. I can run and grab a few snack bars or something."

"I'll come with you." Jacob tilted his head back and poured the rest of his beer down his throat.

Normally, Aliyah wouldn't be comfortable bringing a stranger back to her dorm room. Tonight, she didn't feel comfortable walking through those tunnels alone. "We should get going?" Aliyah drank as much of her beer as she could then handed the rest to Jacob. He drank it with practiced ease.

"All right, let's go."

CHAPTER 9
SMALL AND GREAT

Much to Aliyah's delight, Jacob never stepped inside of her dorm room. He didn't even ask if it would be okay; he just stood outside of the door and waited. She gathered several granola bars and a half-empty bag of rice cakes then stuffed them into her purse. Next, she went to the fridge and opened it. A refreshing burst of frigid air seeped over her, making her quiver. There was only one full bottle of water and a can of ginger ale; she crammed them into her purse. Music from the adjacent room carried in through silence. The "November Rain" guitar riff brought a well of tears into the corner of her eye; that song always got to her.

"Are you going to be much longer?" Jacob called out from the threshold.

"I'll be a second." Aliyah wiped her tears away with the sleeve of her sweatshirt. "Just got to change my sweater." Walking over to her closet, she picked out a black sweater that could have fit the both of them within, a warm cocoon for those blustery St. John's winter nights; a sweater knitted by her roommates' grandmother. Confirmed with a peek over her shoulder, Aliyah found the door closed over. Half expecting to see Jacob poke his head in at any moment, she changed. The wet sweater landed into the laundry basket with a heavy thunk. It wobbled backwards against the impact. "Do you need a sweater?"

The door squeaked open, Jacob leaned in, keeping his eyes fixed on his boots. Aliyah thought it was adorable. Most boys his age would have snuck a peek by now. "I'd appreciate that, the rain is getting cold."

Luckily for Jacob, Aliyah chose comfort over style. A large, black Element hoodie hung in the back. She'd bought it in the men's department at Winners. Too heavy to wear underneath her rain jacket, she yanked it down from the hanger and headed back outside. "Here you go." She offered Jacob the sweater. "This should fit you."

"Thanks," Jacob mumbled as he pulled it on over his head. "It's my style."

Aliyah agreed that it suited him; black seemed to be his colour. His frail frame was hidden underneath the sweatshirt. "I have money to call a cab."

Jacob held up his phone. "I already called, there will be a ninety-minute delay."

"It'd be quicker if we walked," Aliyah sighed, sounding a little impatient. "Hopefully, the rain will let up a little."

A thin smile crept over Jacob's face. "That won't happen tonight."

They walked down the hallway towards the exit. Axl Rose sang about the cold November rain as Jacob pushed the door open. Frigid drops of water pelted their faces. Deep down inside, Aliyah wanted to burst out laughing at the irony. The wind whooped and hollered in the darkness, and the echoes of sirens in the distance were drowned out by the boisterous racket of drunken fools and rowdy friends; laughter punctuating the good time inside, mocking the terrible tragedy of the evenings events...

The rain refused to let up, the intensity only growing. Greeted by chilling winds and ice-cold droplets, the fifteen-minute walk dragged on for an eternity. A starless sky hung overhead. Enormous rivers of water gushed alongside of them in the gutters, torrents of water cutting across the sidewalks to join them. They walked side by side in miserable silence. Several ambulances passed them on the way, their blaring sirens startling them. Aliyah's jeans clung to her skin. With every step she took, her pants pulled tighter against her thighs. The bright lights of the hospital stood before them, the red sign pointing towards the emergency department, which guided them towards a burgeoning crowd.

Parents carried their children through the sliding doors. Angry faces stood under the overhang while cigarette smoke gathered into a haze underneath the awning. Bloody bandages wrapped around various body parts was the next great fashion trend. Almost everyone was wearing one tonight. "This place looks like something out of a horror flick," Jacob observed, breaking the silence between them. "If I didn't know any better, I'd say there was a terrible pile up on the highway."

Aliyah noticed her stomach muscles clench. Something about the scene unfolding in front of them was screaming at her to run away. The leather strap of her purse dug into her neck. "Let's get out as fast as we can."

"I can run it in." Jacob must have seen the look on her face. "You can wait out here."

Aliyah considered his offer and after careful deliberation, she got out of the rain. "I'll go in with you. It can't be that bad in there. Besides, it's not like we have to wait there."

"Okay, come on then." He stepped out and took the lead.

Reaching out for his hand, Aliyah didn't want to get separated in the crowd. A mob of people crammed themselves into the triage section, standing shoulder to shoulder. Impatient family members banged on the glass window that separated the crowd from the nurse. An exhausted, helpless face stared at them from behind the partition. Angry voices implored her to hurry. The number 112 flashed red in the black box that hung over her window. A man shoved his way forward, gripping the stub as if it were the winning lottery ticket, brandishing it above his head. Every seat in the waiting room was full. People sat against the wall along the corridor. Jacob pulled her along at a brisk pace. A few angry people took notice, snarling as they passed.

People lined the corridor. Some of them were standing, while others had given up, laying down on the floor. A group of individuals gathered around a television in the next waiting room. *Hockey Night in Canada* was on, the sportscasters discussing the highlights of the evening's games during the second intermission. Pale, ghostly faces peppered throughout the room. Mallory's burgundy-streaked hair stood out in the room. She was standing over Evan who was slouched against the wall. His skin gave off an alabaster glow underneath the fluorescent lights, shinning in the gleam of sweat coating his face. He held a fresh, white gauze pad to his cheek. Crimson stains splattered over his jeans and fresh blood seeped from the bite mark.

"Aliyah, you're here. Thank goodness." Mallory's voice was dry. "I hope you brought us a drink." Her eyes were sunk deep in the sockets. Her smudged mascara exaggerated her expression.

Aliyah unzipped her purse and dug out the water. "Here you go." She passed the bottle to Mallory.

Evan was sweating profusely; it ran down his face in beads. A slight haze formed over his irises, distorting the colour of his eyes. He was staring off into the distance, a million miles away. She could tell that he was in pain. His lips curled into a grimace every time somebody bumped him. Mallory sucked at the water bottle, the plastic sides caving in as she gulped mouthfuls of water. She offered the bottle to Evan, but he didn't seem to notice her waving it in front of his face. "Drink up, you're dehydrated."

A dry moan caught in his throat. Evan tilted his head to look at Mallory with an expression that Aliyah had never witnessed before. It made her uncomfortable. An evil grin parted his lips just enough to reveal bloodied gums.

"Dude," Jacob said, "do you need me to go grab you a doctor?"

Evan ignored his friend. Trapped somewhere inside of himself, he opened his mouth, spittle and blood staining his teeth a bright red. Ropes of saliva dribbled from the corner of his mouth. Mallory reached out, a dirty cloth wrapped in her hand, and wiped it away. She didn't seem to notice that Evan was sniffing at her arm, his nostrils flaring open every time a finger got close enough.

CRASH

A deafening bang startled everyone in the room. Aliyah spun around to glimpse the commotion. An elderly man collapsed into the bathroom, the door wedged open by his hip. His upper body disappeared inside, leaving only the sight of his twitching legs. People screamed for help. Two junior nurses rushed to his side from a hidden door across the hallway. One nurse was still wearing her blue smocks. Her long, flowing blond hair fell far below her shoulders. The other was in a black tank top and her blue work pants. Fiery red hair dangled around her neck in thick curls. They called out for people to stay back. "Give the man some space, please!" the nurse in the tank top pleaded with the gathering crowd.

"Does anyone know this man?" the other nurse called out as she began giving the man chest compressions.

Jacob crept towards the commotion, standing on his tiptoes to get a better view. Aliyah felt claustrophobic as the flock of people grew. She backpedalled away. The commotion grew into pandemonium. Nurses screamed, the door crashed open, and people pushed and shoved. Backed into a corner, Aliyah appeared small and trapped. Drawn in by the boisterous noise, injured people in triage made their way down the corridor. Body odour and other foul scents oozed from the sickness that was spreading. At the end of the hallway, the double doors burst open. A doctor, holding his blood-soaked arm, cried out for help as he attempted to seal the door.

"They've gone mad!" the doctor shrieked. "I need help!" His white smock was covered in gore. Blood spewed from an artery on his arm, drops splattering against the tiled floor like rain. Several injured patients ambled down the hallway. They shuffled their feet along with their arms stretched out in front of them. Jacob raced over to help the doctor slam the door shut. A resounding clang echoed in the corridor.

The doctor turned to run away when Jacob snatched a handful of his shirt. "What the hell is going on here?" Before the doctor responded, the door swelled outwards, pushed to the limits. Twisting his arm, the doctor slipped from Jacob's grasp and took off down the hallway. He sprinted past the nurses trying to resuscitate the elderly man without offering help. A trail of blood was all that remained as the doctor darted around the corner.

Bangs rattled the door; it convulsed in and out, the hinges screaming in protest.

Evan fell out of his chair, crashing into Mallory, who stumbled backward and smacked her head off the floor. Aliyah rushed to her side, helping her back to her feet. Mallory winced as she touched the back of her hand; blood highlighted the tips of her fingers. "Damn it, that hurt."

"You'll be fine." Aliyah avoided looking at the rattling door. "But I think we need to get out of here."

"And leave Evan?" The suggestion offended Mallory. "No way, he needs our help."

Aliyah shook her head in concession. "He needs help, but there's nothing we can do for him."

Mallory shoved Aliyah away, a disgusted scowl on her face. "You go on then, I'm not leaving without him." She knelt over Evan and tried to sit him up.

Aliyah conceded, helping Mallory get Evan into a sitting position. He didn't want to cooperate, his body slumping towards the ground. Both girls dragged him into a corner, propping him up between the adjacent row of seats. They were breathing heavily now, fighting to catch their breath. The doors rattled as people beat their fists against the metal surface. Jacob was doing his best to keep the door shut. Random jolts threatened to send him crashing into the floor face first.

"I need to get Jacob, maybe he can help us carry Evan out of here." Aliyah stood up, gathering the courage to follow through.

Mallory just glanced at her, not speaking a single word. Barely acknowledging Aliyah's existence. Mallory fixated on Evan, placing her hand on her chest. "I can't tell if he's breathing." Her voice was timid.

Aliyah turned to walk away, trying to think of something, anything, to say. There was nothing she could say to console her friend. Survival instinct had taken over Aliyah's brain. A feeling buried deep inside her subconscious was brought to the surface. Her inner voice was hollering at her. *You need to leave now. Just get out of here and get as far away from here as possible. Terrible things are happening.*

Aliyah could see the two nurses slumped over the elderly man. She heard their conversation faintly, the loud thumping at the door drowning out the noise. The nurse with the fiery red hair reached out, running her hand down the man's face to close his eyelids. she had a defeated, exhausted expression on her face. Her partner pressed her back into the doorframe, resting her elbows against her knees and burying her head into her chest. The man lay motionless, his legs jutting out of the doorway. Bright lights from the bathroom reflected sharply off the floor, casting tall shadows.

Several people joined Jacob. Their blockade was only a temporary solution. Jacob locked eyes with Aliyah. A trembling lip and wide eyes displayed his terror. "We need to leave!" Aliyah called out. "You have to help us carry Evan." The look in his eye told her everything she needed to know. He wanted to leave, but he couldn't.

A stifling, gargled breath caught Aliyah's attention. She turned to see the nurses rushing to the elderly man's side. The curly-haired nurse leaned in, lowering her face near the man's chest. "I think he's breathing," she said astonished. "I hear something wet on his chest." A flicker of hope energized her speech. She leaned closer, tangled locks of her hair resting on the man's chest. The nurse was facing Aliyah, her bright blue eyes filled with terror. A blood-curdling scream erupted from her throat. She wrenched her head back as a waterfall of blood spilt from her neck and splattered over the man's face. His neck craned upwards, and a mouthful of shredded flesh filled his mouth. The blonde nurse jolted to her feet and held her hand over the gaping wound on her friend's neck. Blood flooded out from between her fingers, running down her arm. The man moved with the grace of a drunk, stumbling his hands around, trying to force himself on his victim. He wasn't trying to get up; all he wanted was another taste of flesh. Teeth clamped down on the red head's leg. Her blue pants turned purple as blood cascaded from the gash.

Aliyah froze, her eyes fixed to the gruesome sight. She watched the blond-haired nurse kick the man in the jaw. His neck snapped grotesquely to one side as teeth clattered across the floor. The man twisted his head back towards them, a diabolical smile smeared with blood plastered on his face.

A thunderous crash erupted behind Aliyah as the double doors smashed down. The crowd rushed away from the terrors concealed behind the door. Somebody bumped Aliyah. She collapsed forward, landing inches away from the mischievous smirk. Slick with blood, her hand slipped across the tiled floor. Stiff fingers snatched her forearm like a vice and yanked her hand into his mouth. Aliyah shrieked in pain as his jaw clenched shut. Sharpened edges pierced the webbing between her thumb and finger. Her arm recoiled, freeing her bloodied hand from his evil clutches.

A black shoe whistled past her face, smashing into the man's nose. A bloom of blood spewed from his nostrils as his head jerked back. The blond-haired nurse pulled Aliyah to her feet, dragging her away. Drawn to the agonized cries of the dying woman, the old man dragged himself on top of the red head. He embedded his face into her bosom. Another pair of hands grabbed Aliyah around the waist, pulling her away from her saviour.

"Come on." Jacob appeared out of thin air. "We are getting the fuck out of here."

Aliyah was in shock. Her legs didn't want to cooperate. She stumbled alongside Jacob, his shoulder support-ing most of her weight. Mallory somehow dragged Evan to his feet, her legs buckling beneath his weight. "Can you walk?"

Lost in a trance, Jacob shook her, trying to pull her away from the pandemonium. Men and woman scram-bled around in a mad dash, doing their best to avoid the sick people. Nurses, doctors, and security guards were trying to calm people down, reassuring them that every-thing was okay. The security guards pinned down the sick. Nurses and doctors ushered away the injured. A sense of stability was establishing itself.

"Aliyah, we're leaving." Mallory grabbed her by the hand, guiding her towards the exit. They passed the triage room, forcing their way past the throng of patients rush-ing into the waiting room.

Evan's feet dragged across the floor as Jacob struggled to keep his friend upright. A gust of frigid air washed over them as the automatic doors slid open. An elderly couple was getting out of a taxi just outside the entrance to the emergency department. The woman was coughing into a white handkerchief soiled with all forms of disgusting fluids. Mallory raced forward, launching herself into the backseat of the cab before the driver left. "Please we need a ride."

"Lady, I'm swamped," a gruff voice answered. "I got a dozen fares to pick up."

"It's just across the way, please help." Pleading with the driver, Mallory held the door open. Jacob laid Evan into the back seat, his head falling into Mallory's lap.

"You ain't leaving me much choice, are you?" the cab

driver snarled. "Where you headed?"

"Just over to the dorms, thank you so much." Relief filled Mallory's voice.

Drool oozed from Evan's jaw and spilled over into Mallory's crotch. His chest rose with shallow breaths then deflated as a gargled sounds escaped his lungs. The blood from his wound was dried up now. Flakes of red fell from his cheeks like dandruff. Producing heat like a furnace, perspiration flowed from Evan's pores. Every bump in the road sent a jolt of pain through his entire body; he groaned at even the slightest disturbance. The cab pulled up in front of the dorm. The driver sighed, waiting for them to get out.

Aliyah pulled out a ten-dollar bill and offered it to him. "Keep the change."

An angry grunt rumbled out of his throat. He snatched the bill out of her hand with his sticky, stubby, calloused fingers. Jacob was the first to exit the cab; he struggled to help Evan out of the back. Mallory slid out from beneath him, the tears in her eyes washed away by the rain. Once they were all out, the driver wasted no time leaving; the tires spun out on the pavement and screeched into the night air.

"What was that guy's problem?" Mallory muttered to herself.

Aliyah helped Jacob drag Evan inside. Most of the windows were black. Light spilled from a few scattered dorm rooms. Fake ivy clung to the weathered red brick building, the greenery stretching all the way up the northward face of the dormitory.

"What's *his* problem?" Mallory repeated.

Jacob pushed the door glass door open, leading them into the lobby and out of the elements. "Yeah, the guy was a jerk for no reason." Mallory followed close behind, treading on his heels.

"I'm sure they have stretched him ragged tonight," Aliyah responded.

"Aren't we going to talk about what happened at the hospital?" Mallory questioned.

"Whose apartment is closest?" Jacob asked, the strain heavy on his voice. The tendons in his neck bulged. A large vein throbbed with the rapid beat of his heart.

Aliyah couldn't take her eyes off Jacob's vein. She regarded the blood pulsate through it, understanding that the slightest cut would unleash a gushing torrent of vital fluids everywhere. "I think Mallory's place."

"It definitely is." Mallory brushed past Aliyah and sprinted towards her dorm room. She lifted her shirt, exposing a metal key ring hanging from her belt. There was only one key on the loop; she used it to open her door. "You can put him on my couch."

The doorframe wasn't big enough for the three of them to fit through, and it was too awkward to drag Evan side by side. "I'll get him the rest of the way." Jacob shouldered the brunt of his weight, dragging him to the couch by himself.

Posters of heavy metal bands and skulls lined Mallory's side of the dorm. Her roommate was much more conservative. A few family pictures stood on her shelves, the walls bare. The pale white paint was peeling, in desperate need of a fresh coat. "My roommate went home for the weekend. She'll be back tomorrow, but I don't think she will mind if Evan stays the night. I'll watch him, make sure he's okay."

"If you want," Aliyah said, "I can stay with you."

"Sure, we can take turns watching over him." Mallory agreed. "I'll take the first shift. You can have my bed." She turned to Jacob. "Thanks so much for your help, I wouldn't have been able to get him out of there by myself."

"No problem." He nodded his head. "Call me if you need anything. I'll keep my phone close."

"Thanks." Aliyah smiled at Jacob from the bed, her cheeks flushed red. Embarrassed that he had seen her in bed, he smiled back briefly before turning his gaze towards Mallory. Exhausted, she struggled to keep her eyes open. The door closed as her head hit the pillow. Aliyah fell into a deep, restless sleep.

CHAPTER 10
STAND BEFORE GOD

A horrifying screech startled Aliyah out of her restless sleep and in to a seated position. Disoriented, her mind couldn't grasp what was happening. A flood of grotesque images from the hospital raced through her mind: milky eyes, snapping jaws, blood spewing from wounds. Aliyah pulled the blankets up to her chin, believing the bedsheet would defend her. Evan's teeth sank into the meat of Mallory's shoulder, his heavy frame threatening to collapse on top of her.

Aliyah sprang out of bed, kicking her foot into Evan's crotch with a swift, deliberate motion. She expected him to collapse to his knees. He didn't even take notice. His lifeless eyes peered back at her over Mallory's shoulder. Confusion froze Aliyah; she stood there paralyzed and afraid.

Mallory dropped to her knees, crimson streaks staining her shirt. She yanked herself free of Evan's grip. "Help me!" she howled.

Aliyah thrust her arm in a wide, swinging arc. Her fist collided violently with Evan's jaw. She felt his teeth rattle against the impact. A numb sensation raced up the length of her arm. Mallory flailed her limbs. Drunk with panic, she tried to pull herself up using Aliyah as leverage. The force of the punch threw her off balance. She tumbled over Mallory and collapsed into Evan. His jaw clenched shut on the tender flesh of her chest just below her collarbone. Aliyah pushed him back with all her might. She observed as her flesh stretched then tore in a barbaric display of gore. A pained yell escaped her lips. She doubled her efforts to push Evan off. Putrid, sour breath poured from his open maw, his chin smeared with blood, eyes wide with anticipation. Out of the corner of Aliyah's vision, a desk lamp swung in a high arc and smashed down over Evan's head. Orange plastic splintered and cracked as it smashed into Evan's skull. He stumbled backwards into the couch. His legs collapsed beneath him, sending him careening into the arm of the sofa; he toppled over the edge and crashed into a heap.

"Come on, let's get out of here." Mallory tugged at Aliyah's arm.

Both girls raced towards the door. In a confused state, they both reached for the handle at the same time. Aliyah's hand reached first. She yanked the door open and spilled out into the hallway. Groans and exaggerated growls echoed behind them, Evan's awkward foot falls giving chase.

"Help!" Aliyah screamed at the top of her lungs.

Evan emerged from the door, his neck moving in jerky movements, his glazed eyes finding them. A door opened between them. Wandering into the corridor, a teenage girl stood there in a sleepy daze, scratching her tangled hair.

She studied Mallory and Aliyah, her eyes waking up before the rest of her body. Wide eyed, she froze in place,
unable to comprehend the sight of blood. Evan trudged
down the hallway, his gazing eyes no longer locked on
Mallory and Aliyah. The stranger turned around too late.
Evan collided full force into her, his colossal frame concealing her from view.

Aliyah took a step towards them to help, Mallory
grasped her around the waist. "We have to get out of
here." Her voice was filled with terror. "There's nothing
we can do." Aliyah struggled against her grip. Powerless
to free herself, she watched hopelessly.

Evan tore into the flesh of his victim's shoulder, vital
fluids spilling from the vicious wound. His weight sent
her toppling to the floor; uncoordinated, Evan collapsed
at her feet in a heap, smashing his face into a bloodied
mess. When he glanced up, his nose shifted to the right,
sitting flat against the side of his face. Shrill cries pierced
the silence of the sleeping dorm. She flailed her arms and
legs to drag herself out. Evan mounted her like a starved
dog angry at its master. He burrowed his fists into the
gaping hole, hauling out an extensive section of her small
intestines. The acidic burn of vomit filled Aliyah's mouth
as Evan stuffed the delicate organs into his mouth and
chomped down.

Mallory dragged her away. Doors opened along the
hallway as terrified screams curdled the night. Brave students rushed towards the animalistic scene, not aware of
the brutality taking place. Aliyah screamed to warn them,
but her message was lost in translation, blending into the
dying, anguished wails of the dying girl.

Mallory tugged on Aliyah's arm. "Come on, we have to get help." She guided her towards the entrance to the tunnels.

"There's no way I'm going back to the emergency room," Aliyah cried.

"Listen," Mallory didn't stop pulling on Aliyah's arm, "if we can make it to the Administration Building, they can save us. They could stop Evan and call the police. They will even have medical supplies."

Aliyah didn't argue, allowing her friend to manipulate her. She looked over her shoulder one last time before heading down into the labyrinth that passed underneath the entire university. A sense of panic narrowed her vision, dulling her ability to pick up the approaching sirens. Campus enforcement, with the local police department, were placing the school on lock down. Aliyah noticed the door close behind. A vortex of wind tugged at her back as the air rushed outside. They ran down the old cement tunnel, their own footsteps drowning out the approaching security guards. Faintly, Aliyah thought she heard the metallic *thud* of a deadbolt slamming shut.

Aged and corroded by neglect, the stone that lined the tunnels was in a state of decay. Moisture from the ground seeped through the walls, forming small tributaries and puddles over the cracked cement floor. Leading the way, Mallory followed the signs towards campus enforcement and the Administration Building. Aliyah's chest was burning. Stagnant air filled her lungs, giving her a headache. Pain flared from the wound on her chest. She watched blood exude from the wound on Mallory's shoulder, her beating heart thinning her blood. They came to an intersection. The black and white sign was difficult to read in the waning light from the dying florescent bulbs.

"We can get there quicker if we move outside—cut between a few buildings." Mallory slowed as the intersection approached. "Or we can just go straight."

Aliyah was getting claustrophobic down here. "I think some fresh air would do us good." They headed up the tight staircase, split in half by a black handrail. Mallory reached out to push the door open and halted. Her body crumpled like an accordion. If Aliyah wasn't behind her friend, Mallory would have tumbled down the stairs. The force of the impact knocked her backwards into Aliyah.

"What the fuck?" She pushed the door again.

"Let me try." Aliyah stepped forward. "It's just jammed." The steel bar folded down, but the door didn't budge. "Do they lock the doors at night?"

"I didn't think so?" Mallory responded with frustration. "Let's try together." They tried to force the door open, smashing their shoulders into the door with the latch pushed down. It didn't budge. "Come on, we should be able to get into the Administration Building."

They turned around and headed back towards the intersection. They heard someone cursing ahead. "Hello?" Aliyah's meagre voice echoed in the tunnel. Her call was meet with sudden silence. She glanced at Mallory, trying to calculate her next course of action. "Is anybody down there?"

"Did you come in through the door up there?" A man's voice boomed.

Mallory took a tentative step down. Aliyah followed suit, sticking close to her friend. She placed a compassionate hand on Mallory's uninjured shoulder, careful to avoid the wound on the other side. "The door's locked up here," Aliyah answered the stranger.

"You have got to be kidding me." Once they reached the bottom, the stranger was waiting for them, his burly arms crossed over his broad chest. Chestnut brown hair spilled out beneath a Fox Racing ball cap, the shadow from the brim concealing his eyes.

"Did you try the Administration Building?" Mallory asked.

"I just came from that direction." He paused, impatience heavy on his voice. "And that way too." He pointed down the other hallway. "I've been wandering around down here for thirty minutes. These doors have never been closed before."

"We entered over by the dormitory." Aliyah was trying her best to be friendly. "We didn't check any of the exits on the way over. Maybe some of them are still open."

Mallory nodded her head in agreement. "It's worth a shot. Will you come with us?"

The man took off his hat and wiped his brow. Aliyah couldn't help but notice a deep, purple scar just above his left eye. "I got nowhere else to be." A shocked expression bulged his eyes. "Holy shit, you're bleeding." A concerned grimace on his face.

"I'm fine, it's just a little sore." Aliyah was trying to convince herself. "It looks worse than it is." But it wasn't. It seemed much worse than it looked. A burning sensation coursed throughout her entire body. It was like having a fever that you could feel making its way around her body. What began in her chest now dispersed over every inch of her. Something warm was crawling through her, trying to overtake her body. Sweat soaked Mallory, droplets rolling down her face. She was burning up with the same fever trying to take over Aliyah's body.

"Jesus Christ, what happened to the both of you," he said with a sense of wonder.

"Same guy attacked both of us," Mallory interjected.

"Sounds like a wild night gone wrong," he laughed.

"Not the kinda night you're imagining." Mallory furrowed her brow. "What's your name?"

"Sorry, where are my manners. I'm Wendell, and who are you?" Wendell offered his hand, his stubby arm laden with thick muscle, his biceps out of his sleeves.

"I'm Mallory, and this is Aliyah." Mallory took his hand, which disappeared into his.

"The pleasure is all mine." Wendell took Aliyah's hand. For a moment she thought he would kiss it. His gaze lingered on hers for a little too long.

"So where should we start?" Aliyah pulled her hand back. There was something about the way he was staring at her that creeped her out.

Wendell took out his phone and looked disheartened. "Do you have a signal? I can't get any," he grumbled.

Aliyah didn't expect to have one; she could never get one down here. Much to her surprise, she had two bars. "I got one."

Mallory and Wendell leapt with joy, relief relaxing their worried expression. "Make the call," Mallory said with enthusiasm.

Aliyah dialed 911, and the call reached through. The first ring sent a ripple of excitement coursing throughout her body, pushing back the fever. After the fourth ring without a response, her spirit plummeted. She shook her head. "Nobody's answering."

"That makes sense." Mallory coughed into her palm. "You saw how hectic the hospital was. They're over-whelmed with calls. Try campus security, they could let us out."

"Do you know the number?" Aliyah asked.

"I don't." Mallory let out a slow, defeated sigh. Red circles rimmed her eyes, and black bags formed beneath them. "We have to call someone."

"I can call my mother," Wendell interjected. "She works for campus security. She's off tonight, but she can make the call for us. Here, hand me your phone." He held out his hand, his glare demanding it. Cautiously, she handed it over to him. "What did you do to it?" he grunt-ed. "There's no fucking signal."

Aliyah shrunk, intimidated by his aggressive behav-iour. "It was working a second ago." Her voice trembled. Wendell stormed down the corridor, holding Aliyah's phone out, searching for a signal. Aliyah glanced over at Mallory, hoping that her friend would offer guidance. A coughing fit buckled Mallory over. She was clutching her stomach and spitting up something foul onto the cement floor. Aliyah rushed to her aid. She noticed that the wound on Mallory's shoulder was festering, oozing blackened puss. "Wendell!" Aliyah cried out for help. "Don't leave me here!" Her voice echoed in the underground tunnels. It went unanswered. Wendell disappeared into the labyrinth, his angry growls fading.

Aliyah watched Mallory grow pale, her skin turning translucent, providing her an ethereal presence. Mallory's back slumped into the corner, her chin fixed to her chest. Puddles of sweat formed beneath, splashing onto the pavement, turning it dark all around her. Gargled coughs escaped her lungs, the fluids building in her chest. Each breath was an arduous labour. Aliyah wanted to chase after Wendell, but she was afraid of two things. What would happen to Mallory if they left her alone? And would she turn into a deranged maniac like Evan? She didn't want to speculate about why Evan acted so aggressively, or what had caused it. Was the man Evan first encountered infected with some foreign plague? An unusual strain of virus that caused psychosis? It seemed to be catching. After what she witnessed at the hospital, the disease was spreading fast. Her heart fluttered as the theory set her mind to race. If Mallory caught the disease from Evan, that meant she had it too. Pain spread from her feet to the small of her back. She took a seat next to her friend and reached out to comfort Mallory, her fingers tracing her cheek. Mallory's head snapped upwards away from the touch. Aliyah thought Mallory would speak. Then the expression dissolved into the vacant stare once more.

She rubbed her hand over the edge of the bite mark on her own chest. The torn flesh was tender. Her skin crawled as waves of heat crashed over her, white stars dancing in her vision. Aliyah looked down at her forearms, expecting to see beads of perspiration coating them. Signs of the fever didn't show; it wasn't advanced far enough to burn her up.

Mallory's body gave off heat like a furnace, setting her insides to a boil, all the fluids in her body evaporating out. Foot steps approached them. Aliyah assumed that it was Wendell.

"Mallory?" Wendell's growling voice demanded. "Aliyah, where are you?"

For a moment, Aliyah weighed her options. She might have been able to hide from him until help arrived. Her eyes settled on Mallory. That's when she realized that she could not move her by herself. There was no chance she would leave her friend alone now, no matter how much Wendell frightened her. "We're over here," Aliyah answered.

He stormed towards them, his shoes slapping off the concrete floor in a hurried rush. A long shadow swept across the wall before he appeared. "There you are!" he barked. "You hiding from me?"

"No way." Aliyah felt her blood pressure rising. "We're right where you left us."

Wendell took a threatening posture in front of them, towering over them. He peered down at them with hatred in his eyes. "I couldn't get a signal anywhere down here." The phone flew out of his hand and landed in Aliyah's lap with a hard thump.

"I don't know what you want me to do." Aliyah stared back up at him defiantly. "If you haven't realized, my friend is sick."

Wendell knelt down, one knee striking the ground, the other tucked into his chest. He examined Mallory with contempt. "Leave her here, she won't be any help."

"I'm not leaving her alone," Aliyah spat. Anger sparked a suppressed level of bravery, "You're a big boy, go get us some fucking help." Her chest heaved, drawing in deep breaths, attempting to calm herself down. She astonished herself with the sudden outburst.

It didn't surprise him. "I checked all the doors, and they're all sealed. I thought I heard people doing rounds." His response was mechanical, void of any emotion. "It would be best if we all picked an entrance. Maybe we'll get lucky."

Aliyah glared back at him, her heart thrashing against her ribcage. Flares of spite burst out of her mouth without control. "Does she look like she can stand watch? Are you fucking stupid?" Aliyah watched the scowl cross his face with delight. "What the hell is wrong with you? Get the hell away from us." Wendell didn't move. His unblinking eyes glared at Aliyah, his forehead turning crimson. Saying nothing, he sat down in front of the girls and crossed his legs Indian style. "Are you deaf? I said get out of here."

Mallory coughed. A splattering noise proceeded the deep, wet sound. A glob of blood landed next to Wendell's left knee. Some red drops stained his jeans. Mallory collapsed face first, her head falling into his lap. He caressed her hair, running his fingers into her matted hair. "You will be just fine," he swooned.

Uncomfortable, Aliyah tried to figure out something to say to get Wendell to leave. "Shouldn't you go wait by that door so we can get out of here?"

"I don't think that's necessary." His voice was distant,

trailing off into a void. "They'll be down to check on us when this is all over."

Mallory growled. It was a rumble in her throat, low and saturated with phlegm. Her legs twitched in a jerky spasm. "Wendell," Aliyah whispered, afraid if she spoke to loud it would speed up the process, "you need to get up."

"What are you talking about?" Unaware of what Mallory became, he didn't budge.

Aliyah leapt to her feet, grabbed a fistful of sweaty hair and yanked Mallory's head back. Wendell scurried away from her, grinding his ass along the cement floor, his powerful legs churning. A horrified cry spilled from his lips, his hands trying to keep sound from getting out. "What the fuck is wrong with her?"

Mallory's jaw was cutting the air around her mouth.

CHAPTER 11
AND THE BOOKS WERE OPENED

Springing to her feet, Aliyah tightened her grasp on Mallory's hair, struggling to prevent her from twisting her neck. Mallory flailed her arms and legs in an unco-ordinated endeavour to reach Wendell. With a forceful thrust, Aliyah sent Mallory face first into the cement. The echo of her teeth smashing on impact thundered in the tight corridor. A spout of blood spewed from Mallory's mouth in a brutal pattern. Her head jerked back, writhing her neck into an unnatural position. Glossy eyes glared at Aliyah from her blood-spattered face. A malevolent smile bared her teeth.

"Get out of here!" Aliyah screamed at Wendell. Her feet were moving before she realized it. Rushing past them, her hand reached out to snatch his elbow.

"What is going on?" Confusion muddled his words, blurring them together.

They raced down the hallway, Mallory's hungry groans giving chase. Lights flickered overhead as their shadows wavered on the bricked walls. They turned left and then proceeded straight down the lengthy corridor.

Aliyah didn't recognize where they were; she just understood they needed to be far away from Mallory right now. Feet scuffled along the cement at a steady paced behind them. At the end of the hallway, a broad, metal double door waited for them. The red paint stood out against the pale walls like a gaping wound.

Wendell threw his shoulder into the door with barbarous ferocity. A cry of anguish spilled out of him as he bounced back. "Now where are we going to go?" he asked. As he rubbed his shoulder with one hand, he rapped his fist against the tiny glass window with the other.

Grunts carried far in the silence as Mallory followed the scent like a wolf stalking her prey. Her relentless pursuit had driven them into a corner. With their backs against the wall, Aliyah's mind raced. "We need to go back, try another door." She needed time to think, a commodity she was running very short on.

"One of the other doors could be open now." Wendell didn't sound convinced.

At every turn, trudging down the hallway, Mallory's shadow reached the far wall. "If we run, we can beat her to the intersection and make our way to the far end," Aliya said.

They scampered down the hallway, their laboured breaths growing heavier with every fleeting moment. Mallory stumbled into view ten feet before the junction. Aliyah and Wendell made it there just in time; Mallory's outstretched arms remained empty. They rushed through the intersection and down the passageway, putting a safe distance between them. Wendell was huffing and puffing. Aliyah slowed the pace. But Mallory still pursued. There was nowhere they could hide, no safety. They wandered through the hallways, trying the doors along the way, finding all the entrances they stumbled across locked. No matter where they went, Mallory shadowed them.

Exhausted, Aliyah leaned against the locked door. Her head seemed heavy, and lactic acid filled every muscle in her leg. "What are we going to do?" Aliyah questioned God.

Pacing back and forth, Wendell searched for answers. "Take off your belt."

"What are you planning to do with that?" She didn't like his expression. "Are you going to beat her to death with it?"

Diabolical laughter erupted from Wendell. "That wasn't my intention," he replied with a glazed look, "but if that's what it comes down too, I won't hesitate."

"Then what do you plan to do with it?"

"I'll hold her down," Wendell began, his hands pantomiming his plan. "Then I'll pin her against the pole. You wrap your belt around her and fasten it as tight as you can get it." He turned his head towards the chasing groans. "We can't keep running anymore. If we don't do this now, I'll lose the strength to do it later."

Aliyah nodded her head in understanding. Her energy reserves were running on empty. "Okay but try not to hurt her."

"I'll do my best." Wendell turned around at the sound of scuffling feet, his voice trailing off.

Mallory stumbled into view, moving in a series of

jerky motions. Her neck craned towards them, and her nostrils flared wide open, her jaw snapping at the space in front of her.

Aliyah tugged her belt through the loops, the strap of leather slapping off the floor as she yanked it free. "Here." She held it out Wendell. "I can't do this." Sobs choked off her words.

Wendell grasped her tight, his hands squeezing her shoulders together. "I can't do this alone." A gentle finger lifted her chin. "I need you." He stared deep into her eyes, forcing her to understand, daring her to disobey him. "If you don't help me, I will hurt her. You don't want that, do you?"

"How can you put this on me?" Aliyah cried. Her legs trembled beneath her, struggling to withstand her own weight. All she wanted to do was collapse onto the floor—for tonight to end. There had been so many things she wished she would have done differently. Murderous intent poured out of Wendell's wide eyes. He would not search hard for a reason to open the flood gates. "Fine, I'll help you." Her voice fell from her mouth delicately. "Just don't hurt her, please?"

"I can't make any promises." He peered over his shoulder towards Mallory. "I'll do whatever it takes."

Before Mallory got too close, Wendell forced Aliyah backwards, giving them some distance to react.

Mallory's feet scuffed across the cement floor, her arms stretching out for them. Low, pained growls rumbled in her throat. Milky eyes, brimmed with crimson tracks, followed her prey across the corridor as they backed away. Spittle spewed from her clacking jaws while froth formed in the corner of her lips. Whatever was stalking them, it wasn't human. The essence of Mallory had vanished, the very substance of her soul replaced with something else. Demonic possession, poltergeist, ghoul, something evil now used the undead corpse of her friend for its own sinister intentions.

Wendell stepped forward, taking a moment to examine the awkward movements, not wanting to get too close. His entire body was shaking. Sweat pooled at the small of his back. He took another step back, remaining out of arm's reach. This beastly man physically towered over Mallory. Something held him back, and Aliyah felt it too. Fear dulled the edges of reason, making them irrational.

Without warning, Mallory lurched forward, her outstretched hands failing to get a grasp of Wendell's clothes. Her jaw smashed into the cement floor with a sickening thud. A piece of bloodied tongue flew out of mouth from the impact, fragments of her remaining teeth jangling across the floor. Agonized cries, muffled by a gush of blood cascading down her esophagus, rang out. Her hands seized a fistful of Wendell's jeans, and she dragged herself forward. Determined to sink what shards of teeth remained in her jaw into his legs, her fingers tightened their grip, pulling herself on top. He thrashed his legs into her, his foot entwined into her arms, sending him crashing to the floor. Just managing to get his arms up in time to brace his fall. Caught off guard by the sudden sequence of events, Aliyah watched in horror as Mallory's jaw inched closer to Wendell's calf muscle.

"Help!" Wendell cried out. Terror rattled his voice. "She's lost her fucking mind."

Snapped back to the gravity of the situation by the hellish wail, Aliyah lunged to the ground. She landed in arm's reach of Mallory, who didn't register Aliyah's actions. Every effort exerted was an attempt to grasp hold of Wendell, even though Aliyah would have been easier prey. Aliyah stuck her arms out, her hands plunging into the velvety soft strands of Mallory's hair. It felt like satin against her palms. She tightened her hands into fists then pulled back with all of her might, snapping Mallory's face towards her. A gushing torrent of blood spat from Mallory's gaping jaw. Her thin lips peeled back to reveal the jagged shards of teeth, slicing the soft flesh around her gums.

Wendell took advantage of the distraction, jumped to his feet, and maneuvered himself into a dominant position. He clutched Mallory tightly against his chest in a bear hug, yanking her off the ground. Not taking any risks, he slammed her into the black pole full force. Bones cracked and fractured, the impact breaking Mallory's rib cage into pieces like a shattered vase.

"Tie her up."

Propelled by instinct, Aliyah wrapped the loop of her leather belt around the pole, enclosing her friend's arms within. She planted her leg against the wall, tugging with all of her might to make the loop as tight as possible, pinning Mallory's forearms to the pole. Her friend fought against the restraints, blood oozing from her jaw, spraying in front of her face as she snapped at them.

"Do you think that will hold her?" Aliyah spit out the word in between gulps of air. Her lungs burned as her heart galloped in her chest.

Wendell stared at Mallory. "I think she should be dead." He shook his head in disbelief.

"You don't think…"

Wendell cut her off before she finished. "That's she's a zombie?" he snorted. "Like in the movies you mean?"

Aliyah didn't know what to think. After everything that occurred tonight, could there be any other explanation? Mallory continued to flail her limbs and snap her jaw. Gurgled groans escaping her larynx. "I can't stay here with that." Aliyah pointed at her friend. "Whatever that is. It isn't my friend Mallory anymore. We need to get away from that foul creature."

Gasping for breath, Wendell's chest rose and deflated. "You know the rules, we've all seen the movies."

Aliyah choked back a frightened gasp. "What do you mean?" Her entire body shuddered. An icy chill shot down her spine as her mind's eye conjured up scenes from every zombie flick ever made.

"You know exactly what I mean." He turned towards Mallory. "This could be my only chance to survive." He turned his gaze back towards Aliyah.

"What are you going to do?" She resisted the urge to turn and run, not liking the way Wendell was glaring at her. His eyes were fixated on something with a thousand-mile stare. He didn't say another word, going about his business methodically.

From Aliyah's point of view, she couldn't see what he was reaching for, but she heard it. The distinct scratching of rock over cement drowned out the hallowed groans of Mallory. His hand rose above his head, his fingers curled around a chunk of crumbled brick. In an act of furious violence, his arm pumped like a piston, thrusting his fist into the top of Mallory's skull. Each motion started with a nauseating blow, a grotesque thunk as the brick crushed her cranium. At the culmination of every strike, a splatter of blood coated the walls all around them. Then the action would begin anew, a repeated process that grew more sadistic with each blow. Horrified but unable to draw her gaze away, Aliyah couldn't do anything except close her eyes to escape this harsh existence. Those sickening noises wouldn't allow her any peace.

Unsure how many blows Wendell had landed, time continued to drag on for an eternity. Finally, it grew silent; the only sound was Wendell's winded breathing and the soft dripping of blood falling from the brick against the cement floor. Aliyah forced her eyes to open, exposing the horrendous scene, Mallory's head was pulverized beyond recognition. Scraps of flesh dangled from broken fragments of her skull.

Vomit raced past her teeth, splashing off the floor and splattering over her shoes. The sudden acidic discharge irritated her throat. She spat out thick, yellowish brown liquid; it hung from her lips in long ropes before she wiped it away with the back of her sleeve.

"Come here." There was no sympathy in his voice.

"I don't want…."

"I'm not asking!" Rage fueled Wendell's roar.

Aliyah found the courage to focus. Wendell tore Mallory's sweater, revealing a savage bite mark at the top of her shoulder. "Who bit her?" Blood trickled down her chest, staining her white cotton bra crimson. His eyes wandered downwards, his face flushing red with lust. His fingers traced the trail of blood from the wound all the way to the cotton fabric.

"Stop that." Aliyah took a step forward. "What the fuck is wrong with you?" His actions disgusted her. Before she acted, he held up his palm, gesturing for her to stop. "I won't ask you again." She fought back the tears welling up in her eyes.

"Was it the same guy who bit you?" he challenged her.

She stopped dead in her tracks. "What does that have to do with anything?"

A long, whistling sigh escaped his lips. "Show me your chest, I need to see if he bit you."

"You already know I was." Aliyah spat at him, beginning to backpedal.

For a moment, it seemed as if he would let her leave. Too focused on Mallory's exposed cleavage to worry about anything else. "Take off your shirt." His head snapped towards Aliyah, his eyes smoldering with lunacy.

"No way." Adrenaline flooded her system and her voice shook with contempt. "Why? So you can molest me?"

Wendell reached out, his fingers fumbling over the blood-stained brick. "Where do you think you're going?"

Aliyah thought about outrunning him, but how long could she keep it up? They were both exhausted. "I'm not sick. Mallory was burning up. I don't have the slightest fever." She tried to reason with him.

"Liar!" Wendell roared at the top of his lungs.

He hurled the brick at the ground. It skittered across the cement floor twice before smashing into Aliyah's shin bone. A jolt of pain raced up her leg and she felt the skin split open from the impact. Warm blood trickled down her leg.

"You'll turn into one of those meatheads," he bellowed. "Unless I prevent that from happening."

There was a faint creaking noise, like the sound of a heavy metal door opening in the distance. "Hello, is everyone okay down here?" a lady's voice called out. They both paused, trying to determine if the voice was real, or a hallucination. Aliyah knew it was real because Wendell heard it too. "If you're down here, answer me."

"We're down here." Aliyah answered. She turned just in time to see Wendell make his move. He coiled into a tight ball, making a lunge for her. She pivoted to the right. His fingers grazed the fabric of her hoodie, but not enough for him to get a grip. He stumbled forward, his shoulder slamming hard into the hand rail. Aliyah sprinted towards the voice. Mysterious footsteps chased after her. "Help me!" she shrieked. Realizing she would not get far before Wendell captured her, she spent her energy in one last burst.

CHAPTER 12
AND ANOTHER BOOK WAS OPENED

Wendell's laboured breath rumbled behind her; he was gaining on her—and fast.

"Please, he's trying to kill me!" Aliyah shrieked, scared for her life. Her lungs burned like someone had lit them on fire. She drew in shallow gasps of air, risking hyperventilating.

"Shut the fuck up, you stupid bitch," he growled. A warning, not just for her but for whoever was foolish enough to stand in his way.

"You leave her alone." The voice was much closer now, but it came back panicked.

Aliyah pumped her legs, afraid that her muscles would seize up at any moment. Depletion of oxygen wreaked havoc on the human body. It affects motor functions, vision, vital organs, and worst of all, thought processes. Stars danced in her vision. At first, they were tiny dots in her line of sight, fluttering around like a swarm of mosquitos. Now, they'd multiplied and grown into the size of bumblebees, obscuring her vision. She didn't see the crack in the floor. Just before she reached the corner, her toe snagged the crease, sending her hurtling into the ground at full force. Any wind remaining in her lungs rushed out of her body in a long whoosh. Her chin smacked off the ground and her mouth flooded with the metallic taste of blood. Those stars in her vision were now two giant globes, shining intensely white in the middle, rimmed by a moving yellow around the periphery.

A hand grazed her back. A defeated sob choked her throat. At any moment, she expected to be thrown around like a rag doll. A forearm lodged into her gut and pulled her tight. A hot breath fell on the back of her neck. "I gotcha now," Wendell whispered into her ear, wrapping her into a bear hug. Aliyah's blood pressure sky rocketed as Wendell compressed her lungs. She flailed her legs, driving her heels into his quad.

"Put her down." A woman rounded the corner. She worked for campus security. A double yellow strip ran up the length of her black pants on both sides. Her black parka, which was much too long, puffed out as she raised her hand above her head, a black billy club clutched in her hands.

"You have..." Aliyah tried to speak, but Wendell squeezed the rest of the sentence out. It spilled through her pressed lips in a rush of air.

"Don't say another word." Wendell snarled into her ear, the gruff sound piercing her eardrum. "Don't come any closer." He pointed his finger at the woman. "I'll hurt her if you do."

The stranger held up her hand and paused. "You don't want to do this."

"I have to," Wendell spat back as if it was common

knowledge. "She's turning into one of them."

Aliyah tried to pry her hands beneath his grip, hopelessly trying to get some relief from his death-like vice grip. His brawny forearms didn't budge an inch. Her lungs burned, still not recovered from running. She squirmed and wiggled, trying anything to free herself.

"One of them?" A confused look crossed the woman's face, her eyes wide with confusion.

"She's infected," Wendell stated.

If the woman could have seen Mallory, maybe it would have been obvious. But she didn't, and Wendell's remark tickled her funny bone. She snickered, sending him into a raging inferno. Wendell's grasp tightened up, drawing her closer. The bones in her rib cage were pushed to the point just before they would splinter and crack beneath the pressure. Now was her last chance. With savage ferocity, she dug her finger nails into Wendell's forearm and clawed the length of his arm. His skin split open and three long tears of the skin seeped blood. He yelped in pain and relinquished his grip on her. Aliyah sprinted forwards, towards the stranger, reaching out her hand for help. The woman stepped forward, the black head of the club swung past Aliyah's face, the breeze tossed her hair. She stumbled at the woman's feet. A loud crack echoed behind her as the club struck Wendell in the face.

"You bitch." Wendell's voice was gravelly. "You broke my nose." He held his hands to his face while blood oozed between his fingers, his eyes wet with tears.

The security guard bent down to help Aliyah to her feet. "You're safe now," she spoke, her voice calming. Aliyah couldn't help but notice the wrinkles around the woman's eyes. They spoke of a long life even if the rest of her features didn't.

Wendell screamed, stomping his feet like a scold-ed child as he paced back and forth. "You'll regret do-ing that." A deafening bang rang out like a gunshot as the woman banged the club against the railing. Wendell shrunk at the resounding noise, his eyes signalling defeat. He edged back a few steps, refusing to look the woman in the eye, but never taking his eyes off her.

"Listen, mister," the security guard spoke as she tapped the club into the meat of her palm. "With every-thing that's going on at the hospital it will be hours before they have time to deal with your shattered nose. So, un-less you want me to move you to the top of the list," she banged the billy off the rail to emphasize her point, "stay right where you are." Tears of joy, relief, and pain flooded Aliyah. She buried her head in the woman's chest and sobbed, her eyes burning as tears wet her cheeks and fell onto the woman's jacket. She felt the stranger pat the back of her head, assuring her that everything would be okay. "It will be all right, sweetheart. My name is Anita and I work for the university. I'll take you back to my office now and we'll take care of you."

"You'll regret that." Wendell sounded frightened. "She'll turn into a brain dead, flesh-eating monster."

"The only monster down here is you," Anita said with contempt. "I don't have time to deal with you, so I'll lock you down here until you cool off. I'll come back for you when I have reinforcements." She guided Aliyah away from Wendell. Neither of them took their eyes of him. He disappeared from view as they turned the corner. "Come on, we need to hurry before he makes his move." Anita's voice was hushed but strong. They picked up the pace. Aliyah could see Wendell's shadow following them.

Heavy breathing dogged them every step of the way down the corridor, Wendell's shadow lurking around every corner. Anita turned and headed down the corridor towards the Administration Building. She fumbled the key ring off her belt, thumbing through the keys as they picked up the pace. The reverberations from Wendell's footsteps picked up to keep pace, his shadow bounding up and down on the wall. "Do you think you can run?" Anita asked.

"Is that the right key?" Aliyah would not run only to get stuck in a dead end.

"Yes," Anita sounded sure of herself, "I'm positive. I've used it a thousand times. When things calm down, I can tell you which key opens what door just by touching them." Looking into her eyes, Aliyah saw trust. With a nod of her head, they made a silent agreement to make a run for it. Aliyah could see the doors from here. It was only a two-hundred-foot sprint to the doors.

In sync, they both took off running. Aliyah's feet scuffed the cement, her legs heavy like lead. She had difficulty keeping up with Anita. At first, she didn't hear Wendell chasing after them. She didn't know how much time remained before he'd catch them. She glanced over her shoulder. His shadow disappeared, replaced by his physical form as it materialized from thin air. He screamed like a banshee. Anita rammed into the doors and they shut-tered against the impact. Aliyah found herself trapped in the middle, praying that those doors would open just as she reached them. Heavy footsteps pounded off the ground behind them. His wild screams cried for blood, gone completely insane by having killed a rotting corpse brought back to life by some cruel twist of fate.

Anita threw the door open before Aliyah crashed into them. The girls dashed through and slammed the door closed behind them. They braced their shoulders against the door. Anita fumbled with the key, frantically attempting to lock it. There was a loud click as the door locked just in time. Wendell rammed the door, knocking both girls backwards from the impact. The keys fell to the floor with a jangle.

"You open this door!" Wendell pounded his fists against the door. It rattled loud metal thumps each time he forced the door open, just enough to see the light from the other side, before slamming shut. "You can't leave me down here to die!" he cried out in fear and frustration.

"You need to calm down," Anita spoke up. "I'll be back for you, I promise you." Then, before Aliyah objected, Anita had slid the key off the ring.

"What are you doing?" Aliyah trembled.

"Show me your wound, was he telling the truth?" The wrinkles around Anita's eyes darkened, her eyebrows furled into her nose. "Did you get bitten?"

Aliyah didn't feel threatened. It was something about the way Anita spoke; she trusted her. She pulled down the collar of her shirt, the impressions of Evan's teeth visible below her collar bone. "It happened hours ago." Aliyah replayed the sequence of events in her mind. "But I'm not sick, I swear." She turned her hand over, remembering getting bitten in the hospital. "And this was over three hours ago. It took my friend less than an hour to turn."

Anita took a cautious step forward, placing the back of her hand against Aliyah's forehead. "That's strange, you don't have a fever." Perplexed, she used her other hand to verify her diagnosis. "I observed an older student burn up with this fever. He turned into some kind of," she searched for the politically correct term, "unstable individual."

"What do you mean, you witnessed him turn into a zombie?" Aliyah couldn't believe her own words. Even after everything she witnessed, the term *zombie* sounded foreign in her mouth, almost dirty. "That's what you mean, right?"

Without hesitation, Anita nodded her head in agreement, but she refused to say that dirty word out loud, as if acknowledging it would somehow make things worse. Wendell continued to pound relentlessly against the door. At some point his screams had turned hysterical.

"My car is parked outside those doors. I'll go start the car and make sure it's running so we can escape. Give me five minutes." Anita peered down at her wristwatch. "If I don't come back, get out of here. Run away, don't trust anybody. I don't know what's happening out there, but I think it's only getting worse. You need to isolate yourself from people you don't trust." Anita handed Aliyah the key to tunnels. "Before you leave, slide the key under the door if you think he deserves it. If not, you can do whatever you want with it."

Aliyah looked down at her watch as Anita walked

away. The digital display on her wristwatch read 2:30 am. She held the key in her trembling hand, trying to decide what she wanted to do. The power of judge, jury, and executioner frightened her.

The university had situated the door leading to the tunnel just off to the side of the central foyer of the Administration Building. Somehow, it didn't belong there. An entryway to such a dank, unrefined passageway was a disgrace to the beautiful architecture of this building. Tiny flecks of moonlight glistened on the marbled floor. Throughout the room, pillars held busts of former presidents and other prominent literary figures. Magnificent paintings adorned the walls and exquisite moldings accented every doorway. While there weren't many classrooms in this building, or any other actual reason for the undergraduates to visit, this grand entrance was a favored hangout. Artists, poets, painters, and just about anybody searching for inspiration, would relax on a bench or on the stone ledges below each window.

Aliyah checked her wristwatch: 2:33 am. Two minutes from now she would have to make a tough decision. The key held a significant weight. Wendell had given up hitting the door, but he still lashed out, sometimes savagely. Other times he pleaded for forgiveness. Walking away from the tunnels, closer to the front entrance, Wendell's pleas grew muffled and distorted. Unable to pick out the words, she could tell from his tone right now that he was begging. The main doors swung open. The hinges creaked as a gust of chilly air filtered into the lobby. "Anita?" Aliyah sang out.

Her heart plunged into the pit of her stomach. Three men wearing SWAT gear entered, their faces veiled from view by the black glass on their helmets. Bullet-proof vests, lined with pouches, were pulled over their black fleece jackets. Each man was armed with automatic rifles. Aliyah couldn't be sure, but if she had to guess, they were AK-47s. Handcuff's dangled from their utility belts. Their black cargo pants blended into the combat boots. "Halt!" a thundering voice ordered when he saw her. The other men swung around, pointing their weapons at her as if she were a hazard to contain.

"Please, she's not infected." Anita ran in behind them. The SWAT team ignored her. They gestured for Aliyah to get down on the ground, brandishing their rifles at her and snarling at her. "You can't hurt her."

Aliyah sobbed into her chest and bowed down, placing her palms on the marbled floor. It was as cold as the midnight air. "Listen," Aliyah fumbled for the words, "I'm not infected."

The first man to reach her placed his hand on her shoulder, guiding her down. Aliyah didn't struggle, she allowed herself to lie on the floor. She craned her neck up, trying to monitor what was going on. A logo on the man's vest caught her eye. She had seen it before. The Pharmakon logo emblazoned over a pouch on the right side, just below the collar.

Why would a pharmaceutical company need a SWAT team?

Her mind raced. Something wasn't right. She felt the immediate compulsion to make a break for it. Aliyah noticed that one of the team members had confronted Anita, holding her back. "Three one Tango, this is Omega team lead," the other guard spoke into a radio. "We have contacted two individuals. One appears to be a high-value target." A burst of static echoed in the sizeable space.

"What value does the target contain?" a voice on the other end of the line asked.

"It would appear she has immunity. Advise on what action needs to be taken."

They knew what was happening. Aliyah's tried to get to her feet, but the hand on her shoulder held her in place. In the commotion, they had placed Anita on her knees. A man held his rifle to her head.

"Bring her in, we can't have her fall into the wrong hands," the man on the radio responded.

"Where are you bringing me?" Aliyah asked. No one answered her.

"What do you want us to do with the other target?"

"Expendable." The voice responded. *"We can't have anyone knowing there is a cure."*

Anita raised her hand to protect herself. A barking roar ripped through the silence as the muzzle flashed bright yellow. There was the sound of a sickening impact as the bullet ripped through Anita's hand and tore open a void in her forehead. Fragments of skull flared outwards. A wet splat hit the floor as a gush of blood spilled out of the gaping exit wound. Anita teetered on her knees for a moment before collapsing forward into a heap at the foot of the soldier.

A dreadful moan that escaped Aliyah's throat was stifled by the man covering her mouth with his fist. He

yanked her to her feet and dragged her out of the Administration Building kicking and screaming.

Clattering chains restrained Aliyah's arms and legs
against the side of SWAT van. Her escort refused to ac-
knowledge her hoarse cries. He was just perched there,
leaning against the wall, hands between his legs with his
fingers intertwined. With his helmet still on, she couldn't
tell if he was gawking at her or not, but deep down inside
she knew he was. Why else would he back here with her?
They weren't taking any chances with their high valued
target.

A tiny slit, offering her a veiled view of the streets,
ran the length of the van on both sides. The hole was just
big enough to fit the barrels of their rifles out, as the man
had done several times throughout the trip. Street lights
flashed by at a steady interval. The van raced through the
streets at a fast pace, swerving every so often to avoid
some obstruction. There were so many noises outside,
fusing together into a symphony of destruction. Sirens,
anguished cries, metal crunching, and, worst of all, a
sound that Aliyah wished she never learned. The sickening sound of flesh being battered and beaten. It was a dull
thunk from soft flesh striking hard metal, the disturbing
percussion of bones shattering against the impact. There
were more than a few times that sound rattled the entire
van as the driver struck someone alongside the road. If
Aliyah's stomach weren't empty, she would have thrown
up by now. Now, all she could do was dry heave. Her
stomach ached and her head throbbed from dehydration.

She asked the guard for a drink of water, pleaded for one, never once getting a response.

The van zigzagged its way up a steep road. At first, Aliyah couldn't be sure, but after several minutes it became evident where they were. There was no mistaking this route. Anyone who lived in St. John's knew it well. The van was heading up towards Cabot Tower on Signal Hill. "Excuse me, sir, why are we going to Signal Hill?"

That grabbed the man's attention. He slanted his head towards her, observing her as the van slowed to make the last turn. "You'll find out soon enough." He broke his silence. "You'll be safe here." Something about the way he said it made her feel uncomfortable.

"Why does a pharmaceutical company have a SWAT team running around?" Aliyah pressed her luck.

Silence grabbed hold of the man's tongue once more. The brakes screeched that high-pitched, metallic squeal as the van slowed to a stop. Bright, white light filled the small window. Aliyah shut her eyes, unable to look straight into the light. She dropped her gaze to the floor, trying to find relief. The back door swung open, flooding the van with the brilliant light. She heard the guard unlocking the cage, the chain link jangling as he opened the door. He snatched the chain holding her left arm, taking the slack out of it before releasing the cuff, then did the same for the rest of her constraints. He spoke a simple warning to her: "Don't do anything stupid."

Aliyah wanted to scream but thought better of that. If she would escape from here, now wasn't the time. That guard wouldn't hesitate to shoot her in the back; he was distant, a man following orders. She opened her eyes, allowing the pupils to adjust to the harsh light. Three shadowy figures walked towards her. They strode with a purpose. "Is this the girl?" a ghostly figure asked, getting straight to business.

"She is the woman we discovered at the university," the guard responded.

"Bring her to Level Two for examination," the man demanded. "Make sure you restrain her. I wouldn't want her to spread the virus if she has it."

"You're more concerned about her hurting you?" the guard replied.

"What we worry about," a woman stepped out of the shadows, "is far beyond your intellectual grasp." Her white lab coat hung down to her knees, hugging her form. "You just make sure you do your job. Or you'll find yourself stripped of your position here and sent out there to survive."

"I presume we both recognize the odds of someone surviving out there on their own." The male remained secluded in the shadow, refusing to step forward. "I understand it's less than two percent, isn't that right?"

"Yes, I expect you are rounding up, but yes. Two percent rings a bell." The woman grinned. She stepped back into the shadows. The three figures disappeared somewhere into the luminous white lights.

"Listen, just do as I say, and this will be over before you know it," the guard grunted, tugging on Aliyah's arm, guiding her forward.

"Please, you can let me go," Aliyah said in a hushed tone in case someone was prowling in the shadows.

He let out a hearty laugh. "They'll kill me for sure. Or

send me out there with the biters. That would be a worse fate than death."

"What are they going to do to me?" Aliyah asked.

"They will run some tests on you." They approached a door and the guard held up his arm. A light on the side panel changed from red to green. The door opened with a mechanical whoosh.

"What tests?" Aliyah thought about trying to run. She didn't understand where she was, or where the remaining members of the SWAT team were.

The guard forced her into the elevator. The surface, made from stainless steel, had a glossy finish, their reflection as clear as day on each wall. "It's best not to think about it." He removed his helmet, and a mop of brown hair fell over his eyes. Brushing away his hair with a gloved hand, he leaned in towards a camera. It emitted a red laser that scanned his eye. The door swooshed shut and the panel lit up. He pressed the button for floor two. They were on floor seven if the display up top was accurate. The elevator descended, riding smoothly and without a sound. "It's not that bad of a place to be right now."

"What do you mean." Aliyah trembled, her knees weak.

"Stage one of the outbreak has begun."

CHAPTER 13
WHICH IS THE BOOK OF LIFE

Alone with her thoughts, Aliyah tried her best to push the disturbing images from her mind. Her arms and legs were restrained to a hospital bed with a waist strap pinning her in place, forcing her to stare at the same wall. At least the white linens were crisp and clean, which soothed her. A vent, concealed somewhere close by, belched frigid air into the room. Before the guard departed on his rounds, she didn't realize how loud it was in the corridor, but now, with the door shut, all those sounds vanished.

Bright lights hung from the ceiling from cone-shaped shades, funnelling the light on top of her. She twisted her neck to get a look at the room. There wasn't much to see except for a few shelving units and a countertop along the far wall. Aliyah lost track of the concept of time. Unable to reach her phone, it remained in her back pocket.

Somebody had recently disinfected the room; the heavy, chemical scent of lemon lingered in the air. The burning sensation clogged her nostrils and followed the track to the back of her throat. She was on the verge of sneezing, but at least it suppressed the smell of fear—and her repellent body odour. Sweat, blood, and vomit stained her sweatshirt, which was damp from the rain.

The door handle rattled as the door swung open, revealing the female scientist from earlier. She was alone, closing the door behind her with a resounding click as the lock latched. "Good evening, miss," she paused, waiting for Aliyah to respond with her name.

"Aliyah," she answered, not wanting to reveal her last name. Already, she felt like she'd said too much.

"Well, isn't that a..." the woman searched for something clever to say, "...unique name," she said after a lengthy pause. "You're not from here, are you?" Her white lab coat, embroidered with the Pharmakon logo, was buttoned up all the way to the neck. Pens stuck out of the top of her breast pocket, the blue, red, and green tops in order. She carried a clipboard; the papers fluttered as she wandered to the far counter. With the small of her back pressed against the edge, she thumbed through the pages, licking her fingers every so often.

"What gave it away? Was it my name or the colour of my skin?" No matter how many times she faced that question, she never got used to it. Somehow, it still bothered her every time. Even when the person didn't mean any offence, it still irritated her.

"You just don't hear that name often here." She sounded interested. "It's Greek if I'm not mistaken? I couldn't find anything on you. Do you need any prescription medications that you left in your residence, anything of significant importance?"

"Yeah, my parents hail from Mykonos. I was born there, but I remember little about it." The woman impressed Aliyah, even if she terrified and intimidated her. She tried to think of something, anything that she left behind. Her only thoughts drifted back to Mallory. "I don't need anything right now. At least, not that I can think of."

"It's nice to meet you, Aliyah. My name is Jasmine. If you can think of anything, let me know. We will do our best to make sure you get it." She hovered over Aliyah now, focusing on her blood-stained sweater. "How did you get that?"

Aliyah didn't want to answer. She hesitated. "A man bit me."

Jasmine smiled, dimples forming in her cheek as she did. "Do you know if the person was infected?"

"What do you mean by 'infected?'"

"Don't play stupid," Jasmine snapped, a scowl on her face. "You know what I mean." She reached out and tugged at the collar of Aliyah's sweater, yanking it down to expose the wound. "Whoever bit you couldn't have been. There's no decayed skin around the bite, no signs of infection."

"He was infected," Aliyah snapped back. "Trust me, I'm telling you the truth."

Jasmine looked down at Aliyah with disbelief. "Listen, no one has been immune to this virus. So please, try to understand my skepticism and understand why I will take some samples. If you possess a natural immunity, we will deal with that."

"Guessing you don't want to get your hopes up." Aliyah was understanding the high security protocols. It was possible she held the key to curing this virus. "For a vaccine, I mean."

Jasmine walked over to counter and began rummaging through jars until she found what she was looking for. "If you have a natural immunity, we will make our decision on whether to let you live. We already developed a cure," she chuckled. "I mean, we created this virus."

"Why would you do that?" Aliyah yelled, her blood boiling. "What's wrong with you people?" She had lost her best friend tonight to the pathogen. Her entire body trembled, a sense of rage making it difficult for her to think straight.

"I just work here, honey," Jasmine replied, her tone void of any emotion. "They pay me extraordinarily well. I have a job to do." She approached Aliyah holding out a swab and pulled her sweater down. "They keep me and my family safe."

A jolt of pain shot through Aliyah's chest as the head of the swab dug into the wound. It burned her flesh as howls of pain escaped her body. "What have you done to me?"

"It's a chemical reactant we use to determine if the virus is present." Jasmine stared into Aliyah's eyes. "It would appear you have come in contact with the virus."

"So, what does that mean? I'll turn into one of those mindless freaks?"

Jasmine shook her head. "There's no sign of infection. You don't have a fever." She sounded excited, almost breathless. "You have natural immunity."

Jasmine took out her cell phone, dialing a number as she stepped outside. She didn't pull the door completely closed. Aliyah overheard a muffled conversation taking place outside the room. Her wound still burned and her skin smoldered like it would melt off. Tears rolled down her cheek. Powerless to contain the pain, she cried out in anguish, screaming for help.

After several minutes, Jasmine wandered back into the room, her eyes wide with excitement. "The others will be here. In the meantime, there's so much I want to ask you." She held two mugs in her hand. Aliyah couldn't tell what was in them from here.

Aliyah wasn't in the mood to answer questions. She glared at Jasmine, hoping that she would get the hint. Oblivious, Jasmine walked closer to Aliyah. The toasty aroma of coffee drifted up to Aliyah's nostrils, the delightful odor warming her heart a little. "Is that"—Aliyah's mouth watered—"for me?"

Jasmine walked over to the counter, placing both cups down, the ceramic clinking off the stainless-steel top. "If you can promise me you won't do anything foolish." Jasmine pointed to the door. "Your friend Keith, from the back of the SWAT van, has volunteered to remain watch outside. So, if I were you, I'd keep that promise and enjoy a coffee. We can chat about what will happen next like civilized people. I believe you'll find me very reasonable if you participate. So, what do you say?"

"That sounds fine to me." Aliyah didn't have the energy to attempt an escape. The scent rising from the coffee did two things: first, it boosted her spirits—she couldn't wait for a taste; second, something much worse, it made her realize how ravenous she was. Her stomach growled, her throat burned, and she was dangerously dehydrated.

"I promise, I won't try anything."

"I'm glad. For a moment I expected you would make this more burdensome on yourself." Jasmine walked over then fumbled beneath the mattress for something out of Aliyah's view. After a minute, the bed jerked with a mechanical hum and was raised to a seated position. Now, Aliyah had a better view of the room, even if there wasn't anything exciting to stare at. If she were going to be here long she would need a television or something to pass the time. The only detail that she'd missed earlier was a modest door tucked away in the chamber's corner, propped open just enough for Aliyah to realize it was the bathroom. Relief flooded over Aliyah as her restraints loosened, the leather strap falling against the bed.

When Jasmine handed her the cup of coffee, a sudden compulsion to cry grasped her, took a hold of her, and forced hot tears to well up in the corners of her eyes. "Thank you," was all Aliyah got out. Her emotions were as strong as the coffee smelt. She pressed the warmth of the mug against her chest, allowing wave after crashing wave to soothe her soul. Before she enjoyed her fist sip, she blew on her coffee. Swirls and bubbles danced around on the black surface. Aliyah brought the mug to her lips with both hands, with her fingers interlaced. It was bitter, acidic, and precisely what she needed right now. A jolt of caffeine jump started her system, and that phenomenon of light-headedness was embraced with open arms.

"So, I hope you don't mind, but I have a few personal questions I want to ask you." Jasmine sipped her coffee, peering at Aliyah over the top of her mug. Aliyah just nodded her head in agreement. "Who bit you? Was it someone close to you?"

Aliyah shook her head. "No, a friend of a friend."

"Do you know his name?" Jasmine demanded.

"It was Evan." Images of his blood-spattered face buried into Mallory's neck, his milky eye's gawking at Aliyah through wisps of her hair, flashed in Aliyah's mind. "I wasn't his only victim." Aliyah rubbed her temples, trying to vanish the hideous sight from her mind's eye.

"And do you know how he contracted the virus?" Jasmine continued with the line of questions.

Evan's image stood in the room with them, his ghastly pale skin turned translucent by the brilliant lights. Underneath his skin, she could see a river of darkness coursing through his veins. "He got it from a man in the streets." Aliyah couldn't think straight. She took another mouthful of coffee, hoping for another wave of euphoria.

"And where did this happen?" Jasmine was interrogating her, acting like a detective investigating a suspect.

"It happened outside of the university." Aliyah tried to recall, but everything seemed like a daydream to her now. Evan stood next to Jasmine, trying to speak to Aliyah, trying to warn her. She strained to listen, but his words came out gargled. As his lips moved, bubbles of blood spurt out from the back of his throat, the crimson drops blurring her vision.

"Did it work?" Evan vanished, standing in his place was another man. His voice was familiar. He wore tiny, round spectacles that rested on the bridge of his nose, making his small eyes appear far apart. Thin, silvery hair combed over to one side did its best to hide his balding scalp.

"I think so," Jasmine responded. "Aliyah, tell me about your parents."

Aliyah felt compelled to tell them even as she fought the urge to divulge their life story. It was a losing battle. Without an argument, she spoke about them. "Both are former professors. They're retired now, but they taught classics at the university."

"Okay, I think that's a yes, doctor," Jasmine said to the man, ignoring the rest of the details spilling out of Aliyah's mouth. Startled, Aliyah jumped as a clammy, stiff hand fell on her shoulder. Evan stood behind her bed, his jaw mouthing the words, tendrils of blood spewing from his mouth. When Jasmine and the doctor continued their conversation without acknowledging the brainless corpse behind her, she realized she was hallucinating.

"Excellent, the drug worked," the man sneered, peering down at Aliyah as if she was a side-show attraction. "Aliyah, have you ever heard your parents speak about any hereditary diseases that they may have passed down to you?"

Outraged, Aliyah wanted to scream. When she opened her mouth, words tumbled out instead. "My parents told me that my father carried Thalassemia, and that I may have it too. But we never got it tested." Aliyah didn't even remember that conversation until she spoke it out loud. The words jogging her memory already in a full sprint towards the finish line.

"Have you ever heard of that before?" the man asked Jasmine.

Mallory let out a chuckle, showing up out of thin air at the foot of her bed. Evan sat beside her, nuzzling his head into her chest. "Doesn't take much for you to put out," Mallory spoke, her face animated and full of life, her glistening red lips the colour of blood.

"No, I must look that up," Jasmine responded with a concerned expression twisting her lips into a tight pressed frown.

"Now you've done it." Mallory kissed the top of Evan's head, pulling him closer. "They'll know what makes you special and realize," she cackled, "you aren't that exceptional."

The two doctors left the room, leaving Aliyah with her guests. Before the door closed, the room spun out of control. Aliyah squinted tightly, trying to settle the room. Her eyes grew heavier as the rotations gained speed. With the effects of the drugs knocking her out, Aliyah drifted into a nightmarish fueled sleep.

CHAPTER 14
AND THE DEAD WERE JUDGED

Aliyah awoke, her head in a foggy daze, her body soaked in cold sweat. At least the visions had dissipated, succeeded by a pounding headache. Someone had dimmed the lights, but they were still on, the dull glow encouraging the throbbing. Still suffering the side effects of the medicine, her muscles were bogged down by some unbearable weight. She noticed her arms bound by the restraints. The bed, still in the seated position, kept the rush of blood out of her head. A painful pressure in her bladder had built up, and she needed to relieve herself before she burst. "Is anyone out there? I need to use the bathroom. Please?"

The door opened and Keith stepped in, his rifle slung over his shoulder, resting below his chest. His hazel-brown eyes studied her, sizing up the options. "Listen, if I let you out of those restraints to let you use the washroom, you climb back into bed right after." He drummed his hand off the barrel of his rifle.

"Do I have any other alternative?"

"I suppose you don't," Keith said, closing the door.

The shaving scars on his face from the morning had crusted over with dry, flaky skin now. A day's growth didn't amount to much for him, his five o'clock shadow still a few days away from coming in. He removed the restraints with practiced ease, his fingers deftly handling the buckles. "I'll wait for you by that door. If anyone tries to get in, I'll stall them. You rush straight back to bed. I don't care if you got to pinch one off."

Aliyah swung her legs out over the side of the bed. "Wait." Her legs felt like lead weights. "I think I need your help to get to the bathroom."

An inaudible sigh escaped through his nostrils. "Fine, make it quick." Keith propped Aliyah up, placing his shoulder into her armpit. A shock of cold tickled her feet when she touched the floor.

Once they made it to the doorway, Aliyah reached out and grasped the side of the wall to support herself. "I'll take it from here." She scuffed her feet across the cold linoleum. The toilet and sink were a matching porcelain white. There was a stand-up shower situated in the corner, with its flimsy curtain pulled open to reveal all the safety bars and rails you'd expect in a retirement home. Almost as if it were an afterthought, a sink sat in the opposite corner, next to the door. Not wanting to waste time, or get caught out of bed, Aliyah did her business and a half-assed job washing her hands. In dire need of a shower, she considered jumping in as her hand fell upon the door handle but thought better of risking it. "Okay, I'm done," Aliyah said as she nudged open the door. Keith stood in the entryway to the door, his back turned to her when she stepped out of the bathroom. Her legs wobbled when she let go of the frame. Keith rushed over to support her. He reached her just as she crumpled into a heap, her legs buckling beneath her.

"Easy now," Keith reassured her. "Let's get you back to bed." He ushered her back to bed, trying his best to be a gentleman while rushing at the same time.

"Can you help me get out of here?" Aliyah asked in a hushed tone. "Please."

"Listen," Keith went about the restraints, "even if I wanted to, I can't. They are always watching."

"Is your family here too?" Aliyah dragged out the last word, making the word sound foreign, rolling off her tongue.

Keith laughed out loud as if Aliyah told the funniest joke he had ever heard. "No, my mom and dad live out in Paradise. I was an only child and I'm not important enough to bring anyone here with me."

"So, you can't…" Aliyah's hope was rising, "…you can't let them manipulate you." He shook his head no, but his eyes betrayed him. Aliyah could see something hidden behind them. "You know what they will do to me, right?"

"I know as much as you." Keith finished buckling the last restraint. Refusing to look at her, he walked away.

"Please don't leave me here," Aliyah sobbed as the door slammed shut behind him.

When Aliyah came to, her eyes burned from crying herself to sleep. Dazed and confused, she wondered what time it was. She didn't feel rested and suspected she wouldn't for a very long time. Her stomach was empty, hunger pains tying knots in her intestines. The door opened. Jasmine tried to slip into the room, thinking Aliyah would be asleep. "I need something to eat," Aliyah demanded.

"Oh, you're awake. Good morning," Jasmine stood at the foot of Aliyah's bed, "I'll have breakfast served."

"Is it drugged?" Aliyah snapped.

"I guess I deserve that," Jasmine added. "We don't need to drug you anymore. We got everything we needed the first time. While we are waiting, I have a few more questions for you. After you're finished eating, we want to run some experiments."

"Go ahead," Aliyah groaned.

"How many people did you meet with this disease?" Jasmine held the clipboard at chest height, a blue pen hovering over the paperwork.

"I wouldn't be able to say," Aliyah tried to concentrate. "I couldn't be certain. The emergency room was crowded with them. I don't know how many people there were sick with the virus, or how many of them were there for something else."

Jasmine tapped the pen off the edge of the clipboard. "How many did you have close contact with?"

Aliyah counted silently in her head. "Four or five that I'm positive about." She wasn't sure why she was bothering to answer Jasmine's questions, because deep down inside she knew people like her didn't count favours.

"That's interesting." Her voice was flat and monotonous. She scribbled something on her papers. "Did all of them attack you?"

"Yes," Aliyah answered automatically. Then a memory flashed inside her mind. Mallory never attacked her, choosing instead to chase after Wendell. "But how much do you know about their behaviour?" Now Aliyah sparked intrigue in Jasmine; she saw it in her smirk.

"We have run a lot of tests of the subjects, gathered a lot of information on their individual versus group behaviours," Jasmine gloated. "What we have never encountered before, after the hundreds of tests we've run, is someone with immunity to their bite. Sorry, I'm just so fascinated by these facts. I love explaining them to people. But what I love is showing them. So, before we get to that, you had a question?"

"Do they have the ability to choose?"

Jasmine let out a sarcastic snort. "What do you mean by that?"

Aliyah wondered if Jasmine would have the answer. "I mean, can they make their own decisions? Like, choosing to eat one person instead of another?"

Jasmine hummed a melancholy tune. "From all of our studies we conducted, the temporary answer is no."

"And the long answer?"

"Definitely not the zombies you've come across," Jasmine answered. "They are thoughtless eating machines. They will attack everything that moves. First come, first served. They are not prejudiced, if that's what you're thinking?"

That wasn't what Aliyah was thinking at all, it never even crossed her mind. "One of those," Aliyah still didn't like the word *zombie*, "creatures, they chose someone else, even though it would have been easier to get to me."

Before Jasmine could respond, an orderly entered the room, pushing a trolly. The man wore a blue smock with the Pharmakon logo over his heart and his name over the pocket on the right. His black jeans fit a little too tight, and his excessive gut spilled out over them when he bent down to fetch a tray. "Here you go, enjoy." He handed the meal to Aliyah. His mustache wiggled like a worm riding a wave when he spoke.

"I've never heard of that before." Jasmine wrote on the papers, the pen scratching the board as it scribbled across the board. "We took a sample of your blood while you were sleeping."

Aliyah felt violated. "Why would you do that?" she snapped.

"We did you a favor," Jasmine added. "We confirmed that you carry the Thalassemia gene."

"So what?" Outraged and frustrated, Aliyah's temper boiled over, scorching her internal filter. "What gives you the right to do something like that?"

Jasmine ignored the outburst, glaring down at her clipboard. "From what we can tell," she glanced up, "and keep in mind that his is only a theory, but, if I'm correct, your condition somehow allows you to carry the virus without turning you. Isn't that remarkable?"

"I won the sweepstakes," Aliyah said sarcastically. "My lucky fucking day."

"You don't understand," Jasmine lectured Aliyah. "This virus will turn the bravest and strongest into mindless freaks. They will prowl the earth in an unrelenting pursuit of flesh, never being satiated. There's no capacity for them to think, no capability for emotion. A simple purpose. All they can do is feed. Count yourself grateful you are amongst the living. You are safe here as long as we allow it."

Aliyah didn't like being lectured, but it would do her no good to get angry. She allowed her mind to drift elsewhere. A growing warmth in her lap grabbed her attention. She spied her meal and her mouth watered at the prospect of food. Her stomach growled, demanding food. Jasmine muttered something, but Aliyah didn't pay her any attention. The scent of food lulled her away from the conversation. Two poached eggs, the peel already removed, sat in a Styrofoam cup. "Can you free my arms, or feed me?" Jasmine finished jotting down her note before releasing Aliyah's arm restraints.

With her hands free, she grabbed the tiny packets of salt and pepper, applying both, and inhaled the eggs in two bites each. Now she was voracious, the food igniting the furnace in her stomach. She gobbled down the dry toast in between sips of her tea, not noticing the container of margarine until it was all gone. Aliyah noticed Jasmine staring at her, but she didn't care. Her stomach craved more food, but an orange peel was all that survived. "Can you get me more?"

Astonished, Jasmine stared at Aliyah. "I suppose I could. If you're still hungry after our experiments, you can have whatever you want."

"I can't wait that long." Aliyah bit into the orange, not bothering to separate it into segments. The juices trickled down her chin.

"This won't take very long at all," Jasmine laughed, "I promise." She walked to the door, nudging it open. "Keith, we are ready. Please hurry, Aliyah is in a rush to meet her new visitor." She cackled like a witch as she joined Keith in the hallway, letting the door close behind her.

Aliyah finished the orange, licking her lips, savouring the aromatic flavour. She wiped her chin with the sleeve of her sweater. Disappointed, she stared down at her empty tray. Her stomach rumbled as it seemed to digest and process it faster than she could stuff it into her mouth.

She realized that Jasmine had slipped out, leaving her alone in the room, without her arm restraints. The leather strap hung off either side of the bed. This was her only chance to escape. It was now or never.

Aliyah loosened the constraint that pinned her waist down. The heavy leather strap slapped off the floor when she tossed it aside. Next, she freed her legs and bolted out of bed. For the first time since being brought here, she wondered where her shoes were. She rushed to the cabinets, tossing open the doors, searching frantically for her clothes. An Internal clock was ticking, the hands racing towards its final countdown. Her heart fluttered, beating too fast and more alarmingly, skipping several beats. She cursed. Every time she opened an empty cabinet, the end of the fuse drew nearer.

Tick, tock, tick, tock

Her mother's voice echoed in her head: *"If you're heading outside, you need your shoes."* She raced across the room towards the bathroom door. When the door opened to reveal a bare floor and a sink with no cabinet, she wanted to scream. All she wanted to do was get out of here. She'd find another pair of shoes once she escaped this hellish place. It took a considerable amount of convincing, but she gave up her search for shoes and worried about discovering a way out of this infirmary.

Tick tock tick tock

The internal clock sped up, the hands racing feverishly around in circles, winding down to the inevitable. As she turned to run towards the exit, she spotted her shoes poking out underneath her bed. Racing over, she slid across the floor on her knees, not wasting any movements. Not bothering to untie them, she crammed her feet into them instead then bounced to her feet. It took a few steps before they settled on her feet.

Ticktockticktocktick

Aliyah reached for the handle and it turned underneath her grip as she touched it. She recoiled, sliding out of view and behind the door as it swung open, crushing her. Snarls and wet grunts entered the room first, foreshadowing the decrepit creature. A man, who had been dead for a long time, shuffled into the room. His skin was ashen grey, withering and decaying folds of skin sagged grotesquely around his jowls. Stray strands of yellowish white hair sprouted from his bald scalp. Ominous red scars and blotches riddled his complexion. A collar cinched around its neck with a pole attached to it forced the vile creature into the room. Keith held on to the pole, guiding the zombie towards Aliyah's bed. Jasmine heeled him.

"Where the fuck is she?" Jasmine was the first to notice she wasn't in her bed. "Christ, I must have forgotten her restraints."

"What do you want me to do with this?" Keith asked as he struggled to control the corpse. Its limbs flailed around, working to reach out for him. Its cloudy eyes meandered over Aliyah, paying no attention to her.

"Bring it back to..." Before Jasmine finished, Aliyah threw her weight into the door, the edge clipping her shoulder.

The impact rattled the door, sending Jasmine crashing to the floor. This would be her best chance. The staggering corpse occupied Keith's absolute attention. Aliyah slammed the door and pounced on Jasmine. She rained her fists down on her captor. Each blow striking Jasmine's outstretched arms as she attempted to defend herself. Aliyah's hands throbbed with pain, each blow striking the bone in Jasmine's forearm. The zombie snapped his jaw at them, spittle flying out of his mouth in beads of thick, white slobber. Keith struggled to keep control, unable to do anything to help Jasmine. That left Aliyah free to impose her will against Jasmine. The first blow that landed on Jasmine's face surprised Aliyah. Jasmine blocked a few more blows before the pain was too much to bear, her defences falling to her sides. Aliyah's next strike landed squarely against Jasmine's jaw. It made her sick to her stomach. She could feel Jasmine's soft lips peel back against the impact, flesh giving way to the teeth below. Saliva greeted Aliyah's fist as a gush of blood splashed over Jasmine's lips.

"Had enough?" Aliyah asked, wheezing. She didn't want this to go any further.

Jasmine sobbed. A trickle of blood spilled from the corner of her mouth. "You'll never get out of here."

Aliyah looked at Keith, finding him occupied with the undead freak. Sweat beaded on his forehead, exhausted from the creature's relentless movement. A plan formulated inside her head. She saw her way out of here, and it didn't have a single thought in its head. "I'll get out of here. The question that should concern you is will you?"

"Shit!" Keith screamed as he tripped in his own feet, stumbling backwards for a moment before losing his footing. Once the zombie found itself free, it lurched forward. His stiff hand smacked off Aliyah's back as he thrust forward. He should have landed on her back, but he attempted to avoid Aliyah and attacked Jasmine. Surprised, Aliyah didn't have enough time to save Jasmine from the jagged teeth. The zombie buried his face into Jasmine's neck. Hot blood gushed from the jugular, spraying over the creature's face. Jasmine cried out in horror, her glazed eyes begging Aliyah for help.

A boisterous *thunk* echoed in Aliyah's ears. Keith drove the pole into the base of the creature's skull, the blow sending the creature spiraling forward. It collapsed into the floor, its teeth cracking off the floor. Aliyah watched helplessly as Jasmine tried to stop the flow of blood. It was too late. Her life force flowed through her clenched fingers and onto the floor like a bursting dam. In an awkward sequence of movements, the zombie spun around to face the girls again. Keith whirled the handle in a downward arc, snapping the hardened plastic handle in half. The creature groaned from the impact, the guttural sound a primal cry. Its clawed hand dug into Jasmin's shoulder. The creature's filed teeth cut through the soft flesh just below her ear.

Keith yanked Aliyah to her feet. "We are getting the fuck out of here." His voice shook with fear. Aliyah watched the creature crane its neck towards Keith. Somehow, she knew the creature didn't have eyes for her.

CHAPTER 15
OUT OF THOSE THINGS

They sprinted down the corridor, Keith dragging her by the hand towards the elevator. "Come on," Keith wheezed, "we have little time." The door was wide open. The stainless-steel interior shined like a beacon, inviting them in. Keith reached the elevator first, letting the retina scanner go about its business as Aliyah tried to catch her breath in the far corner. The panel lit up and he pressed the button for the seventh floor repeatedly, as if doing so would make it work faster. "Come on, you son of a bitch." He directed his anger towards the elevator, thumping his free hand against the far wall. The door closed with a mechanical whoosh.

Aliyah's stomach rose with the elevator as it ascended towards the ground floor. "What are we going to do?" Aliyah sobbed into her hands.

"We'll walk to the van." Keith responded.

"That's it?"

A worried look aged Keith's face. "And pray that no one notices."

The elevator beeped, signalling they had reached their

destination. With a loud swoosh, the door slid open, allowing a brisk gust of air poured into the elevator, washing over them. Aliyah sucked in mouthfuls of fresh air, amazed at how satisfying it tasted. They stepped into the underground tunnel. A trickle of sunlight lit up the entrance like a glowing ember. "There's our ticket out of here." Keith pointed towards the SWAT van parked in line with seven identical vehicles, which somehow Keith knew was his.

Wandering around the tunnels, the employees went about their business. Some of them wore SWAT suits, others were dressed up in coveralls, ignoring Keith and Aliyah as they dashed across the tunnel. An eighteen-wheeler, parked at the receiving doors, was being unloaded by a forklift. Two men wearing hardhats oversaw the driver, giving him conflicting orders about where to store the equipment and supplies. The lights of the van flashed twice after Keith unlocked it and the doors creaked on their hinges as they opened.

"I can't believe we're leaving this place. I never thought I'd enjoy the sunshine against my skin again," Aliyah said, her voice wavering with emotions.

"This seems too easy." Keith's voice trembled. When he turned the ignition, the motor rumbled to life, deafening in the confined space. No one appeared to pay them any attention. "They don't know what's going on yet. We have to get as far away as possible before they discover what you've done." Without saying another word, he put the van in drive, allowing it to roll out of its parking space.

"You're part of this too now," Aliyah reminded him.

"Once they realize that you helped me escape, they'll be after you too."

"Don't you think I realize that?" Keith yelled. "I felt sorry for you, you didn't deserve what they were doing to you." The van sped up as he pressed the gas. People drifted past the window as they drove down the tunnel. Aliyah expected the garage door to slam shut at any moment and hundreds of armed guards would open fire on them. They were fugitives, trying to break out of prison like Snake Plissken from those awful movies her father worshipped. Dull daylight awaited them. If Keith wanted, they could have rushed out before they'd shut the door. They were close enough to see freedom. Aliyah spotted a small pond next to a square parking lot, the road forking into two directions just off it. The road snaked up and down Signal Hill. Aliyah recognized where they were. Just above them, Cabot Tower stood a silent vigilance over the harbour.

As they crossed the threshold of the underground entrance, low-hanging clouds greeted them. A fine mist showered the windshield, a gentle breeze carrying it in from the ocean. The salt sea air filled the cab. Freedom awaited them; it sprawled out before them on a dreadful canvas. A sequence of flashing lights caught her attention in the passenger side mirror. Keith had noticed too, adjusting the rear-view mirror.

"Crap." The word stuck in Keith's mouth.

"What is it?" Aliyah sank into the soft cushioned seat as Keith pressed down on the gas pedal. The tires squealed across the wet asphalt. Keith approached the turn too fast. The tires drifted off the pavement and skidded over the soft dirt on the shoulder. The tires dug deep into the soft-ened dirt, pulling the van off the road. The suspension handled the rough terrain with ease. They bounced over ruts and rocks as Keith struggled to pull the van back onto the road.

"They're after us," he stammered. "They'll kill us." He eased off the gas as the road twisted into the decline, the tires holding an unyielding grasp on the pavement.

As the thunder of engines grumbled overhead, a sink-ing feeling took root in the pit of her stomach. Aliyah twisted in her seat, peering out through the window of the cab. It was difficult to see anything through the cage in the back. The double windows on the door narrowed her line of sight. When she couldn't see anything, she still knew they were in danger. They were being chased by the security detail. Aliyah could hear the screech of tires and roar of engines getting closer. She looked back at the cage. The chains rattled off the plexiglass, swinging back and forth like a pendulum.

Tick tock tick tock

The van bounced up, rocking the cab as they vaulted over a curb. They approached the bottom of Signal Hill, pursued by the other SWAT team members through the narrow streets of old St. John's. A sign for a local restau-rant exploded into a shower of wooden splinters as the grill crashed into it. Slivers of timber advertising the daily special ricocheted off the windshield. Aliyah threw up her arms, expecting a deluge of glass fragments. Keith re-gained control. The van rocked as the tires bounced back over the curb, tearing through the desolate streets.

"Can you see them?" Keith screamed as he navigated another sharp turn, avoiding the metal pole of a stop sign at the corner of an intersection by an inch.

Aliyah checked her mirror to see a single pair of headlights keeping up with them. "They're still on our tail."

With an abrupt turn, Keith drifted the van into a tight ally between two homes, blindly navigating through the congested streets. "Goddammit." He slammed his foot on the gas. Shrubs filled the cramped alley, the branches clawing at the van's undercarriage. Metal garbage cans left in the alley banged against the bumper, crashing up and over the van, landing with an emphatic bang behind them as the van burst into the adjacent avenue. Lined with colourful houses, the street ran down a steep slope. From their point of view, it looked like the street emptied into the harbour.

Discarded garbage littered the roads, the wind sweeping it down towards the water. The streets abnormally bare even for an early Sunday morning. Aliyah noticed that a pack of dogs prowled the streets. In the distance, church bells chimed, set on an automatic timer. People had left their doors wide open, abandoning their cars in the midst of the road. "Oh god, what's happening?"

"The apocalypse has advanced to phase two." Keith swerved the van around a parked car, "Pharmakon's plan is ahead of schedule." Debris cluttering the road crunched beneath the tires. Doors torn from their hinges and the remnants of shattered glass scattered the streets. "We would have been safer where we were."

"You would have been," Aliyah snapped. "Not me. I

would've been Pharmakon's newest lab rat."

"Christ." Keith slammed on the brakes, sending the van into a sideways skid. The seatbelt pulled against Aliyah's shoulder, agitating the bite mark beneath her collar bone. Hundreds of undead corpses shuffled through the intersection. They shifted their attention towards the raucous screech of tires and the howl of brakes.

"Get us out of here," Aliyah almost whispered, her voice trembling.

"You don't have to tell me twice." Keith slammed the gearshift into reverse. He put his arm behind his headrest, craning his neck out the window to guide himself back up the roadway. A black van emerged from the alley, cutting their escape route off. "Crap, there's no where to go." Above them, at the breast of the hill, three black vans sped into view, their brakes screeching to a halt. The swarm of zombies groaned impatiently, staggering up the hill. Somehow, they realized they had cornered their prey, their hungry groans growing with anticipation.

"What are we going to do?" The pale, dead eyes hypnotized Aliyah—wicked smiles, teeth stained with blood, and blackened gums showing their sinister resolve.

A loud thump of metal boomed behind them. Keith peered down at the driver's side window. His arm darted out, finding the top of Aliyah's shoulder blade. "Get down!" he shouted as he shoved her head down between her knees.

A hail of gunfire erupted behind them. Glass rained down around them, shattering into a thousand fragments as bullets tore through the back window. Errant rounds destroyed the mirrors as the front windshield imploded into itself. Without looking, Keith jammed the gearshift into drive and pressed his foot down on the gas. The van bucked forward, speeding down the hill. A solid thunk, followed immediately by a wet crack, caused the van to shudder. The next bang sent a corpse careening over the hood. Its snapping jaws dangled just out of reach of Keith's flesh. Its hands reaching out for him, getting entangled in the steering wheel. The van teetered out of control. Keith screamed, unable to lift his head up to see where they were going.

Aliyah reached her hand over calmly. The zombie didn't bat an eye as her fingers crossed the foul creature's mouth. She clutched the undead corpse by the shoulders and thrust it backwards. The creature's limbs didn't prevent its fall by grabbing on to the side of the window or the steering wheel. Instead, it reached for Keith. With a final push, the zombie rolled off the hood of the van, its spine cracking in half as its back smashed into a light pole. Keith popped his head up just in time to avoid crashing into a derelict truck, the sharp turn threatening to tip the van over. The grill ate up cadavers, sending spurts of blood and bodily fluids over them through the broken windshield. Bones cracked and popped as corpses got caught under the tires. Loose body parts jammed into the drive shaft.

Keith tried to make the turn before crashing through the living room window of the home at the bottom of the hill. "It won't turn!" Keith cried out. He slammed on the brakes too late as the van veered to the right. It collided with the garden gnomes, the terracotta ornaments bursting into a thousand pieces. The van crashed into the window. Glass and splinters of wood swept through the living room like a tidal wave.

When Aliyah came to, her head throbbed.

As she struggled to unbuckle her belt, she discovered her lap filled with debris.

A ringing in her ears drowned out the surrounding noises.

She rested a hand on her thigh; she peered over and saw Keith's face was a bloodied mess. "What happened?" Dazed, Aliyah stared into the living room.

"We have to get out of here." Keith rushed his words. His hand fumbled into Aliyah's lap. She tried to push it away but didn't have the strength. He unbuckled the seat belt. Not expecting it, she collapsed face first into the dashboard.

As the outside world crept back in, her senses switched back on, one at a time, making sure they didn't overload her system. Tires rolled to a halt just outside the house, the rubber crushing pebbles beneath the considerable weight of the SWAT van. The hungry howls approached from all angles, enveloping them. Next, the pain in her back flared, sending radiating waves of heat through her spine. She tasted blood in her mouth, inhaling the coppery tinge in the air. Her muscles struggled to move, her joints seized and locked in place.

"Please," Keith's pleaded, "you have to get up. I can't carry you." Aliyah pushed her door open and it groaned a high-pitched, metallic grind. Doors slammed shut outside the household. Footsteps approached the front door.

An assault rifle barked, the metal casings clattering off the front porch. The hollow moans grew louder. "This is our chance, while it distracts them. We can slip through the back door." Keith motioned towards an exit at the back of the kitchen.

Aliyah slipped out of the passenger's side, stumbling forward into the sofa. Blasts of automatic fire resounded outside, accompanied by angry yells and dull thumps. A family picture lay shattered on the floor of the destroyed living room. Aliyah stifled a scream at the gruesome sight, covering her mouth with her hands. A body lay on top of a broken table, one of the wooden legs planted into the top of the man's head like a fence post. Beside him, blood pooled beneath a woman's head, a yellowish puss oozing from her skull, a screaming smile frozen on her face.

"Come on." Keith put his arm around Aliyah's shoulder. "We have to leave."

They raced through the living room and into the kitchen towards a sliding patio door. Keith tripped on an arm that jutted out from behind the kitchen island. He pulled Aliyah down with him. They crashed into the floor. Aliyah's hand slid through a cold, congealed puddle of blood. Keith grabbed a handful of sweater and yanked Aliyah back to her feet. A wooden block, filled with kitchen knives, rested on the center island. She reached out and slid a butcher knife from the block, the weight of the blade balanced in her hands.

"Just through here," Keith slid the patio door open. They rushed into the tiny backyard, just big enough for a small wooden landing. Enclosed by a fence, they searched for a gate. "Christ." Keith was growing frustrated. "There's no way out of here."

Aliyah scanned the fence. There was only one way out of this yard: up and over. "I don't know if I can climb it," she said to herself. The front door to the house swung open, crashing into the wall. She heard footsteps walking through the house, searching for them.

Keith knelt by the side of the fence, clasping his hands together. "I'll give you a lift."

Aliyah rushed over, knowing that they were running out of time. With her left foot, she stepped into the make-shift stool, her hands finding a spot to hold on to at the top. Keith stood up, nearly sending Aliyah careening over the top. Her hip swung over first, her weight yanking at her hands as gravity pulled her down on the other side. Splinters embedded into her palms, slivers of weathered wood tearing into the soft flesh, compelling her to let go. She fell feet first, her knees buckling upon impact, and toppled backward. The fence rattled as Keith jumped up, swinging his leg over the top, his butt resting on a support post. He glanced over his shoulders as they threw the patio door open, demanding his attention.

As the first shot missed low and wide right, the bullet penetrated the wooden board with ease. The wood blew outwards and split in half. Another shot missed wide, sailing over the fence and colliding into the siding of the next house. Aliyah watched the third round hit its mark. A gory shower of blood and cranial fluids burst from Keith's skull like an overripe tomato. Somehow, Keith held himself upright on top of the fence, teetering back and forth. A stiff breeze would be enough to send him toppling in either direction. He seemed to look at her through a gaping, black hole where his right eye should have been. His lips parted to scream, but his tongue blocked off his throat, preventing any sounds from escaping. Then a gloved hand reached up, yanking Keith from his perch. His body collapsed into the yard with a thunderous thump.

Aliyah jumped to her feet and ran in between the two houses towards the next street. As she reached the paved driveway, she heard the fence rattle as the Pharmakon SWAT team leapt over, landing on the ground with a loud thump. Without turning around, she scurried past a red jeep, her feet slapping off the paved driveway. The street, lined with rainbow-coloured houses, sprawled out before her. Not knowing which way to turn, she ran towards the harbour.

CHAPTER 16
WHICH WERE WRITTEN IN THE BOOKS

A herd of corpses gathered on the street just below, attracted to the commotion. Their feet shuffled across the asphalt aimlessly, searching for their next meal. Behind her, the SWAT team was in close pursuit, hounding her at every turn, expecting them to open fire at any moment. With everything happening all around her, she did her best to use the abandoned vehicles to her advantage for cover. It was slowing her down, but it also placed her out of their line of fire.

Bang

The initial shot fired missed her, sending a shower of dust over her as the bullet struck a street pole. Before they locked in on her, Aliyah dashed into a driveway, hiding behind a parked truck. Then another outburst of automatic fire peppered the rig. Tires hissed as the rounds chewed up the Ford Ranger. Shielding her eyes with her hands, Aliyah felt shards of glass sprinkle over her. With her back pressed against the Ford, she scouted for her next hiding place, trying to determine the safest path. The adjoining driveway was empty, but the bank dropped off just after it. Not wasting anymore time, she got to her knees, trying to stay as low as possible as she scampered across the asphalt on her hands and feet.

A volley of slugs tore up the earth at the edge of the driveway as she leapt over the bank. Bursts of earth exploded into the air as she tumbled down the embankment. At the bottom of the bank, she spilled into the next driveway, her shoulder colliding with a grey Kia Rio. The car rocked on its suspension, the impact leaving a dent in the driver's side door and an immense pain in her shoulder. Her chest crumpled like an accordion. When her shoulder struck the pavement, she grimaced in anguish, rolling underneath the vehicle, sliding her way across the pavement to the other side.

There was nothing between her and the swarm of undead as the pack was lured towards her by the gunfire. Hundreds of scuffling feet veered up the hill towards the SWAT unit. Aliyah didn't see any other way out of this. She gathered her courage and dashed straight towards the zombies. The decaying scent of flesh poured out of their pores, mingling with the shit and piss in their clothes. It forced Aliyah to pull her sweater up over her nose to block it out. She ran forwards blindly with her head sunk into her chest.

For a moment, Aliyah thought she would get eaten alive. All at once, several heads snapped towards her, sensing her presence amongst their ranks, their dead eyes falling on her. They followed her, allowing her to walk amongst them, never giving her more than a second glance. She walked past the rotting corpses. Their injuries looked fresh on some; others looked like they'd suffered their wounds ages ago. Overwhelmed, Aliyah stumbled into one of the more decrepit creatures on the street. A wound opened a second smile just below the creature's chin with dried blood crusted along the edge of the gnarled gash. Flaps of decaying flesh had pulled back from the red hole, revealing a bobbing Adam's apple in the zombie's throat. It rose high into the creature's throat as it let out a gruff growl. The odor was foul; it turned Aliyah's stomach, the bile in her throat dampening her scream. Terrified, she drove the butcher knife into the zombie's skull; the creature fell backwards, yanking the blade from her hand. Suddenly, a gunshot burst the head of the undead to her right, the skull scattering like pieces of a ripe melon. Brain matter showered the street. Aliyah backed away from the grotesque creature at her feet, leaving the butcher knife behind. She crawled through the awkward, shuffling legs, not wanting to get hit by a stray bullet. Bodies collapsed into the surrounding road, body parts slapping off the pavement. The resonant bark of gunfire erupted from above, the SWAT soldiers forced to fall back. Swarms of undead marched forward without fear—the perfect soldiers. Bullets ripped through flesh as blood and flecks of shredded flesh sprayed into the air in a vaporizing mist. Most of the shots missed their mark. Bodies twitched and shuddered, pressing forward relentlessly. Aliyah found her way through the bulk of the horde and turned to watch the zombies in pursuit of flesh. A tiny smile crept over her face as she watched the SWAT team backpedal.

Aliyah heard the fearful screams. The security team barked orders amidst the chaos, never getting organized.

As she watched, the horde slithered up the hillside. It was a sea of undead corpses flooding through the streets, the rising tide headed towards the SWAT team. One soldier broke rank, racing back towards the vans, pushing past his fellow team members. Not waiting, he hopped into the driver's seat, turning over the engine. Muzzle flashes sparked. The approaching corpses were close enough for the expended rounds to find their targets. With a sickening thump, heads burst open, cranial fluids and blood carried backwards by gusts of wind. The zombies kept coming, stepping over fallen corpses to reach their prey.

One of the rifles jammed at the worst imaginable time. Fumbling to fix it, the soldier accidentally dumped the magazine. Shells scattered over the street as it smashed against the pavement. The undead reached out, their hands tugging at his arms as he tried to reload. He swung his arms in a violent arc, freeing himself from their clutches, turning to run towards cover. After three strides, his foot slipped on the magazine, sending him tumbling to the ground. A pile of zombies piled on top of him before he could react. Their fingers burrowed into his flesh, tearing it from his face and neck.

The undeads' next casualty was foolish. Aliyah chuckled as the man hurried towards his friend to save him. When he grasped onto a hand, he wrenched it back forcefully, only to find it already severed from the torso. Not expecting the task to be so easy, he tripped over his own feet, falling backwards. Unable to control his actions, his finger pulled the trigger, burying a round into his upper thigh. A geyser of blood spewed from the severed femoral artery. He withered in pain, rolling onto his chest to squirm away. Before he could get away, rotted hands reached out, seized his ankle, dragging him towards their gnashing teeth.

The van cruised down the hill, coming to a halt just before the security team. All the members loaded into one van. A single man laid suppressing fire, covering them as they made their escape. Stiff hands reached out for him, pulling him into a feeding frenzy. His anguished cries rang out in the downtown streets. A bright yellow flash sparked from the open door, the rifle firing on automatic. A few of the zombies spasmed and twitched before collapsing to the road, but not enough. With the magazine spent, the van door slammed shut. The driver turned back up the hill, showing its exhaust pipe to the horde, speeding out of sight as it crested the hill.

Left to watch the horde feast upon the forgotten employee of Pharmakon, Aliyah caught her breath. Then, she wandered into the heart of the swarm so she could get a better view of his face as they tore him into pieces. A gurgled scream erupted from his throat. Aliyah saw a bubble of blood burst from the man's lips. Bloodied hands pulled sections of intestines from a gaping wound, stuffing the innards into their faces. A sloppy cacophony played in the street, fluids and organs splashing against the pavement. With his eyes frozen open in a state of unmitigated shock, it appeared he was gawking at Aliyah. She let out shrill laughter, strolling amongst the herd.

Now, without something to feast upon, they appeared to follow her. She continued up the street, looking at the damaged houses and littered streets. There were blotches of blood in the street, staining the pavement and stone steps leading up to the doors of the giant cathedral. Bloodied handprints and claw marks riddled the doors. Stray zombies shuffled out of their hiding spots, joining the swelling swarm of corpses. Aliyah was at the head of the pack, wandering through downtown St. John's with nowhere to go. Everything was closed or abandoned. She walked past the Rooms and avoided the Sobeys. Then the hushed murmur of the undead grew louder as she approached. Countless numbers of rotting corpses roamed the parking lot and surrounding areas, shambling towards Aliyah, merging into her pack of the undead.

Countless storefronts showed the signs of looters. Broken windows and damaged doors lay strewn about the sidewalks in front of the buildings. When she passed a convenience store, she saw bare shelves toppled over and picked clean of the essentials, counters covered in blood, bodies slumped over chairs, and vital organs on exhibit, torn from their victims, left behind to rot. Corpses lay in pools of blood, their heads bashed in to destroy the brains.

What had begun as a faint whisper bloomed into an orchestra of hungry groans. She peeked over her shoulder, and found the horde had grown broader, more than doubled since she first trekked into the midst of the pack. Her lips spread into a devilish grin. A terrible idea formed in her head. She didn't want to live in this world anymore. There was one last thing she wanted to do before checking out. She craned her neck back to look up towards Signal Hill and laughed.

CHAPTER 17
ACCORDING TO THEIR WORKS

Aliyah slowed her pace, making sure she didn't get too far ahead of the pack. They accompanied her up the Hill O'Chips, through the narrow streets, and towards the secret underground Pharmakon laboratory. A wicked wind swept the clouds across the sky. The road heading towards Cabot Tower up Signal Hill sprawled out before her like a winding serpent. Aliyah detected movement above: guards completing their security detail. It would only be a matter of time before they noticed the looming shadow creeping up the hill. Hungry growls kept pace behind her. The cacophony of the dead rang loudly, as if someone had rung their dinner bell. They must have picked up a trace of the living, carried down from above on the breeze like an offering to the devil himself.

Partially covered in shadows, the fall sun wasn't powerful enough to dispel the darkness on this side of Signal Hill. Above the symphony of the dead behind her, Aliyah could hear the commotion above. Voices shouting, the pounding of boots across the asphalt, a sense of dread accompanied the increasing clamor. When someone had

discovered the herd; a deafening siren blared its warning.
Aliyah was close enough now that pack of undead would
pick up the lingering aroma of flesh wafting down the hillside. She stayed in the middle of the street, allowing the
corpses to scuffle past. The overpowering stench of death
washed over her like a sinuous wave, making her gag.

Watching the throng of undead pass by, Aliyah prayed
she wouldn't see a face she recognized. Then an elderly
woman bumped into her, her white, knitted shawl, covered in grime, draped over her shoulder. Her parched lips
had yet to savor blood, her eyes glazed over by a faint
mist. Pink slippers, shrouded in muck and caked with
dried blood, scrapped across the pavement, wearing
holes into the soles. Then, a little boy, hardly ten years old,
caught her attention. He was missing a leg, dragging himself up the hill. Red blisters oozed puss from his torn-off
fingernails. A brownish white thigh bone stuck out of the
mangled wreck that used to be his kneecap. Surrounded
by torn flesh and muscle fibers, the bone scrapped over
the pavement. There was so much gore, Aliyah found herself mesmerized by the gruesome wounds.

The rumble of engines boomed overhead like thunder. With a grinding mechanical groan, the entire mountainside shook. Aliyah looked up. Two giant metal doors
emerged from the rock, gliding towards each other to seal
the entrance. The base was going into lockdown. It was a
simplistic barricade, enough to keep the dead out. They
would pound their fists into dust against that door before they'd ever get through, no matter how many of them
there were. Aliyah would have to lead them into building
herself if her plan would work.

Birds circled overhead, gawking down at the chaos on Signal Hill. A murder of crows flocked together, gathering on the craggy cliff side, waiting for a free meal. The boisterous clamor of gunfire couldn't deter them, merely keeping them at a distance.

War raged on the hillside.

The living fought the dead strategically; the dead pursued the living relentlessly. Rounds ripped through dead flesh and teeth savoured the taste of fresh meat. Enlistment into the undead army increased as the number of living souls diminished. The living couldn't replace their members as efficiently as the dead.

Aliyah crept through the deceased, unseen by both sides. With the soldiers' attention drawn to the dead and their magazines running empty, they were too occupied to notice Aliyah's fluent movement through the awkward shuffling. With the growling roar of automatic gunfire, heavy thumps echoed all around her. The corpses shuddered and collapsed to the ground in a heap. Well-aimed shots struck their mark, biting through the softened skulls, the undead finding their ultimate resting place. Blood and fluids splattered over the blacktop, spilling from chest wounds and ruptured arteries. The Pharmakon soldiers grew fatigued, their distressed cries growing haggard. As the battle progressed, the mistakes piled up. Jagged teeth found a sample of human flesh wherever it was possible. Aliyah made her way to the edge of the pack, finding herself running over the rugged terrain at the shoulder of the road.

Then a man took charge over the security team. Overrun, he barked the order to fall back. Following his command, they ran way from the zombies. With a momentary lapse in gunfire, it allowed the horde to secure more ground, no longer having to trample over fallen bodies. Aliyah found a dying man, a trio of dead feasting on his abdomen, tearing him apart. With his weapon laying at his side, Aliyah tugged at it, the harness fixed around his shoulder. "Help me!" His cries gurgled through a throat clogged with blood. Guilt washed over her as she stared down at him. Searching his eyes, she saw his immense suffering and took pity.

"I wish it didn't have to be like this." Aliyah angled the muzzle of the rifle underneath the adolescent man's chin. She applied pressure to the trigger. It seemed to repel her force, warning her that there would be no turning back from this act.

A resounding boom echoed as a yellow muzzle flash gave birth to a crimson explosion. Bursting through the top of the man's cranium, the bullet tore his eye outwards. Blood gushed from his ears. The feasting corpses hardly noticed. Aliyah stomped her foot into the dead man's chest, yanking the rifle off his shoulder. His upper body raised with her effort while the dead held his lower half down. A sickening pop echoed as the upper half tore free. Whatever remained in the mans chest cavity flooded over the dead, and they feasted upon the organs.

Aliyah turned back towards the entrance as the bark of gunfire erupted once more. The men took position on raised platforms and catwalks built into the mountainside. Yellow ladders rose high into the sky. The zombies gathered below them. Rounds rained down on them, several of the undead collapsing into a heap. The pile grew high, allowing the taller zombies to reach their hands out to the metal frames. Screams rose and metal clanged as the men banged their feet into the fingers. Severed digits fell into the heap of lifeless carcasses.

"Preserve your rounds!" the leader called out, his voice shaking. "If the pile grows much larger they'll walk right up here." He smashed the butt end of his rifle into the nearest zombie, sending it plummeting down over the jumble of undead.

Aliyah maneuvered close enough so she could see the fear in the leader's eyes. She couldn't get a clean shot at him. The only clear shot she had from this angle was at the guard closet to her. Hidden amongst the zombies, she took aim and squeezed the trigger. A deafening bang startled the SWAT team. The bullet opened a flowing red wound in his chest. Shock filled his face and tears cascaded from his eyes. His hands reached up, drawing back to reveal the red stain on his fingertips. He slumped against the rail, which snagged his armpit, keeping him on his feet, blood dripping from his wound.

"What the fuck was that?" one guard screamed, wrenching his friend back from the edge.

"Find the shooter!" the leader snarled.

Aliyah slipped back into the midst of the pack, remaining low to the ground to avoid detection. The horde continued to press forward, their outstretched arms reaching for the metal facing of the catwalk. She found a clear shot, sending a quick cluster of rounds towards the men before ducking back into the crowd. Not wanting to get caught, she weaved her way between the shuffling legs on her hands and knees. The anguished cries from the SWAT team were enough to know that Aliyah hit her target. When she peeked up again, the leader was scouring the crowd, his gun swinging back and forth. Members of his team fired into the crowd at random. A few rounds landed near Aliyah, sending a shower of asphalt and dirt over her. The swarm of zombies thinned out and there weren't many hiding spots left. She stayed amid a tiny pack, waiting for her next opportunity.

"Do you see anything?" the man taking charge barked. "If you have eyes on the target, call it out. If not, hold your fucking fire." Distracted eyes saw movements all around and itchy trigger fingers couldn't hold back. They spent more ammunition into random zombies. The leader charged across the catwalk. His hand reached out and grabbed someone by the collar, dumping them over the side. "Next person who wastes ammo will join him."

"Who put you in charge?" a guard demanded, turning to face him.

"Your foolishness put me in charge," he growled. "Pull yourselves together."

"I'm out of ammo," someone added.

Aliyah used the distraction to fade back into the herd, buying herself cover and a better firing position. As the men bickered amongst themselves, ignoring everything down below, Aliyah disappeared from view. Then they started shoving, throwing high arcing punches, and kicking. The catwalk rattled, the hinges grinding against the rock face, sending a miniature avalanche of pebble cascading down and piling in front of the door. One man toppled over the rail, landing at an awkward angle, the fall breaking his neck with a sickening snap. More bullets wasted were on those shuffling corpses. A few zombies twitched violently, collapsing into a heap. Without hesitation, Aliyah took aim, firing several shots. Most of her rounds missed. None of them were fatal, but they produced more confusion amongst the surviving guards. Only two men remained alive, and they were both wounded from the errant gunfire. One man rolled onto his side, curling into the fetal position. Aliyah spent the rest of her magazine peppering shells into the man's backside. He shuddered and convulsed, blood oozing from multiple holes in his back.

Now, the last man standing leaned against the rail, panting, exhausted and suffering. Aliyah walked with a purpose towards him. He attempted to raise his rifle, but the muzzle clanged off the metal railing, causing him to drop it. A grimace, saturated with pain, distorted the man's face as he leaned down to retrieve his weapon. He slumped to one knee, his other hand locked on the railing, preventing him from falling. Aliyah stood just below him now. She watched his fingers fumble over the weapon. More zombies reached the top of the pile, their hands rocking the catwalk. Then the man slouched against the back rail of the catwalk, giving up trying to reach his weapon, content to bleed out.

Aliyah picked up a rifle from one of the fallen soldiers. "Do you want to turn, or do you want me to put you out of your misery?"

"Please," a choked plea escaped his dry lips, "don't sh—"

She fired three rounds towards him. With his last breath, and his eyes glazed over, he stared off into the horizon. Aliyah wasn't sure what he was looking at. Maybe God? Somehow, it didn't matter anymore. Aliyah had come with a purpose. She remembered that Keith had used a key card to unlock the security door. A fallen soldier, with his limbs torn off, was just a bloody stump. She found his arm and picked it up. It felt much heavier than she thought it would. Dead weight. She checked a zippered pocket and found the man's security card in the same place that Keith had kept his. Aliyah headed towards a small door along the rock face. She scanned the card. The panel lit up and the door unlocked with a metallic click.

Aliyah left the door open behind her, allowing the zombies to file in behind her. A narrow corridor led to a single door at the end with another security check on a side panel built into the cinder block wall. She flashed the card. The panel lit up green and the door clicked open, exposing the enormous cargo bay. The room was eerily calm, a barren space settling into the hillside. Metal girders groaned against the weight of the mountain. She searched for the controls, wanting to open the cargo bay doors. A small stream of undead ghouls trickled in from the side door. Aliyah wanted to open the floodgates.

It didn't take long to find the control room. A woman wearing a yellow hard hat cowered beneath a desk. Aliyah raced towards the door, thrusting her boot into the flimsy wood, splitting it down the middle with a resounding crack. Her knee buckled back. A sharp pain in her hamstring seemed to tug at every muscle fibre. Each chord of sinew and tendon burned hot. Zombies shuffled towards her, drawn to the lively aroma of the worker. The lock held the door shut; a superficial crack in the door was visible.

"Open the cargo bay door." Aliyah smashed through a glass window with the muzzle of her rifle. The woman sobbed beneath her desk, absorbed in her own world of fear. "Hey!" Aliyah barked, trying to capture her attention. She swept the glass away from the windowsill, the fragments breaking into smaller fragments as they shattered against the floor.

"Go away," the woman bawled. "You've killed us all." Locks of golden hair fell from beneath her helmet in tight curls, resting on her shoulders.

"I wasn't the one who brought them back to life," Aliyah snapped. "You deserve this."

"I just work here," she got to her feet. "A lot of the people here had nothing to do with this. We are just trying to survive." She waved her hand over her desk towards a framed picture of her and an adolescent girl, both with shining curls shimmering in the sunlight, giant smiles pasted on their faces. They were standing at the edge of a boat, the swells of the ocean providing the backdrop, a crystal blue skyline above. "There are families here. You've doomed us all."

"Then this is your last chance to be with them." Aliyah lowered her rifle. A sense of dread and regret fell on her like a heavy blanket. "There must be another way out of here?" Aliyah asked. "An emergency exit?"

The woman bowed her head. "If you open that door, there won't be enough time."

"Go now. I'll give you thirty minutes before I open it." Aliyah stood out of the way.

The door creaked open. The woman slipped out, her dark blue eyes fixated on the rifle, trying to hold it in place with her gaze. "Thirty minutes isn't enough time," she spoke in a hushed voice.

"You should hurry, those zombies will be here any second." Scuffling feet added an exclamation point to her sentence. "I hope you can save your daughter. But I can't let Pharmakon get away with this."

The woman stood still, frozen in place by the words on her lips. She needed to force them out, their burden too great. "There's another base on the island." The words tumbled out of her mouth. Before Aliyah could ask her another question she sprinted away, narrowly escaping the outstretched arms of a decrepit corpse. They shifted to follow her as she ran towards the elevator. She was fast, her legs carrying her in long strides, putting enough distance between the zombies and herself to wait safely for the doors to slide open.

Out of the corner of her eye, Aliyah noticed a red exit sign hanging over a door next to the elevator shaft, it would lead to the stairwell. She took out her phone, disappointed to discover the battery had died. With nothing else for her, she wandered into control booth. Inside, computer screens with a security camera's view of the base stretched the length of the far wall. There were six of them in total. On the desk, a locked computer locked displayed the time in the lower right corner. She slumped into the chair and spun back and forth, waiting for the time to pass. Once the thirty minutes elapsed, she would start opening the stairwell doors, leading the zombies down into the bowels of the Pharmakon base.

When she first started this journey, she had expected it to end with her own death. Now, knowing that there was another base here on the island, her job wasn't over yet. She would have to be careful. Not wanting to get into a gunfight in the tight corridors, she gave the people below more time to evacuate. With the base destroyed and nowhere to run, Aliyah had defeated them. Let them fend for themselves, like everybody else. If she were lucky, she could follow the tracks of the Pharmakon employees to their other base.

Then Aliyah noticed a row of lockers in the room's corner. One door was ajar, giving her a hint of what they stored inside. It was the belongings of the woman who had just raced off to warn everyone of the swarm. Aliyah walked over, pulling the door open, a bright smile lit up her face. "My lucky day." She looked down at a clean change of clothes hung on the hooks. There was a black bag full of shower gear on the top shelf and an extra pair of shoes next to it. When she looked at the bottom, there was a beige bookbag. Not wasting any time, she unzipped it, discovering two pairs of socks and underwear stuffed inside. Aliyah couldn't wait to get out of these filthy clothes and realized that she would soon enjoy a warm shower. The only thing that bothered her was the thought of those dead eyes, cramming into the room with her, glaring at her. Somehow, she would deal with their hungry groans asking what to do next.

With the base built into Signal Hill evacuated, Aliyah showered and changed into clean clothes. Then she determined it was time to carry on. If the survivors had left through an emergency exit on the bottom floor near the battery, there was no sign of them when she walked out. A dull, dying fall sun drifted towards the horizon as a biting wind swept through the abandoned streets. There were footprints, but they weren't clear enough to follow. Aliyah wandered the streets for hours. Once day turned to midnight, she roamed the city. A silvery moon hung overhead and the night sky was decorated by the milky way. The survivors she found ran from her. Those that got away disappeared into the shadows. Most weren't so lucky— swarmed by the zombie herd and ripped to pieces.

As Aliyah roamed the roads, her cult of the undead followed her without question towards the city limits. She wanted to leave the chaos behind. The herd swelled into the tens of thousands over night. She didn't want to stop anymore. Every time she did, they would go on a feeding frenzy. The city fell in a matter of hours; the virus ravaged the living. Too congested, the zombies fed on the living, recruiting members into its undead army at an alarming rate.

When the sun rose on another day, its pink aurora lingered in the clouds, warning of danger. Aliyah grew accustomed to the groans of the undead. Her feet ached as blisters developed on her heels and the pads of her feet. She was hungry, but she didn't have any appetite. The rotten smell of decomposing flesh turned her stomach. Completely exhausted, Aliyah wandered into a house, the door left wide open. She scoured the cupboards, finding plenty to eat, settling on some crackers and peanut butter, not wanting to upset her stomach. The undead roamed through the living room while most of the swarm were content to wait for Aliyah in the streets. She wandered upstairs and found a bedroom. Laying in bed, she decided to head west across the island then drifted into a restless sleep.

CHAPTER 18
RED GLARE

A glaring, red star lit up the sky followed by crimson tail, which hovered amid the clouds then drifted listlessly towards the ground. The snow briefly disappeared in its intense radiance then reappeared, striking the windshield. "There," Smith exclaimed, waking the others. Tina jerked out of a sound sleep, startled by the commotion. There was a rustling from the backseat, accompanied by confused grumbles. "We are late to our own party."

"What's going on?" Tina mumbled, still waking up.

The town of Grand Falls was coated in a faint, maroon glow, the silhouette of buildings forming from the shadows. "Eric shot the flare," Smith declared. "The herd must be close." He strained to pick up the gunfire as the roar of wind howled against the jeep, drowning out any outside noises. "We're just in time." He pointed towards the side road that would lead them to the ambush site. He pulled over, the tires crunching the snow beneath them, dragging the jeep through the fallen snow.

"Do you think we'll have enough time to get the ammo to the front lines?" Bowers spoke up from the back.

"I need you to stay with me. Edwards," Smith glanced over his shoulder, "I want you to run ahead. Grab a few people from the front lines and bring them back to help." The jeep rolled to a halt, the motor sputtering, guzzling the remaining fuel in its tank. Smith turned it off, took the keys out of the ignition and stuffed them overhead in the visor.

"What do you want me to do?" Tina yawned, stretching her arms out over her head. "I'm not staying here."

"No, you're not. I need you to stay with me. You'll help us carry the weapons." The hinges creaked and groaned as Smith pushed his door open and stepped outside. An icy wind cut through the jeep, vanquishing the heated air that took hours to build up in an instant.

"Do I get to pick which weapon I use?" Tina questioned.

"Sure." Smith realized they would need every able body firing a weapon if they would win this fight. More than once Tina had acted heroically, demonstrating her worth. "You can have whatever you want."

Tina reached out, placing her hand on Smith's arm. "I want you to promise me one thing." Her eyes caught his.

"What would that be?" Smith already knew what the request would be; he and vengeance went way back— they were old acquaintances.

"I want to be the one to kill Ted." Tina spoke with clarity and conviction. He could read in her voice that she wouldn't second guess herself when the opportunity present itself.

"If he's still alive by the time we get to him," he locked eyes with her, "Ted is all yours."

With a brisk nod, she expressed her approval. She opened her door, allowing the frigid winter winds to sweep through the jeep. Bowers and Edwards jumped out of the back, leaving Smith alone in the jeep. He placed his hand on the dashboard. "I'll be back for you." With a deep breath, he inhaled the musky scent: worn leather, caked mud, tobacco, and the lingering aroma of diesel. Before he left, he tapped the skull and crossbones decal sticker, earned from his days in Afghanistan. Treating it like a religious symbol, his fingers traced the outline of his rosemary.

The night was frigid, forming a faint crust over the snow. His boots crunching with every step, striding towards the back of the jeep. He unlocked the trunk, the gate opening in a wide arc to the left. "Isn't that beautiful?" Edwards and Bowers both agreed. Tina said nothing, fixated on the assault rifles. "Have you ever used one of those?"

"I've shot a gun," Tina replied, never shifting her glance.

"That's not what I meant." Smith reached out, taking up the rifle with a familiarity, the weight balanced in his grip. "This isn't just another herd of zombies we are facing." He pulled the bolt action and examined the chamber.

"I can handle it. Point and shoot." Tina held out her palm. "I can pull the trigger." Bowers chuckled, knowing that Smith was getting ready to give his lecture. Every soldier from their regiment received it.

"When you pull the trigger"—Smith aimed the muzzle at the ground, squeezing the trigger. A sharp, metallic click thudded from the rifle—"that is only the beginning. What you just heard was the firing pin striking out for the primer. If the chamber weren't empty, a spark would have ignited the gunpowder. This causes the gas in the chamber to expand before exploding, forcing the round through the barrel at a high velocity."

"Great, so now I understand how the magic works," Tina added. "I didn't think magicians revealed their secrets?"

Smith placed the assault rifle in her hands. "Do you know how to load it? Reloading when someone is shooting at you is altogether different."

"I'll learn," Tina snarled. "All that matters is that I'll fight with the Republic." She held the rifle in an awkward stance.

Smith reached into an ammo box, taking out a loaded magazine, feeling its weight. He handed it to her, placing it in her palm, but never let go. "It's heavy, much heavier than you'd expect," he said then let go. Tina fumbled with the magazine. It slipped out of her palm, her fingers snagging it just before gravity took hold. Her cheeks flushed with embarrassment. "Happens to everyone," Smith chuckled.

"Maybe you could give me a few tips," Tina whispered. "Before it's too late."

Smith bowed his head, knowing what she meant. "Bowers, change of plans. I will stay behind with the weapons. Tina will watch my back. You and Edwards find Wade. Bring back what help you can." A single, resonating gunshot boomed in the distance. Then, as if awoken from a deep sleep, the thunderous bark of automatic fire sparked to life. "One of you stay in the trenches and help cover the lines. I think we're running out of time."

"Do you think it's started?" Edwards asked, his voice quivering with anticipation.

"Not yet, we need those rounds for the dead. Whoever is shooting is much further away than where we are." Smith estimated that they'd fired the shots from the other side of town. If they were lucky, the Highway Hangman would make a stand on the other side of town, giving them the time they needed.

"Hurry, you clowns."

Gunfire rang out, mimicking thunder as it rolled over the hills. Tina was a quick study, catching on to everything Smith taught her with ease. The shooting, which grew more intense, still sounded far away from the ambush site. "Hey!" a voice called out from the forest. "The ammo is just over here, in the back of the jeep. I hope we can carry it all. We're running out of time to get prepared." Bowers emerged from the blackness with three inexperienced men Smith didn't recognize. They were all members of the Republic of Newfoundland, and if he lived long enough, he'd learn their names.

"Did you speak with Wade?" Smith asked as he walked towards the jeep. Tina followed close behind. He could only hope she'd picked up enough in the short time that they trained together to keep her alive. At least, long enough to kill Ted.

Bowers shook his head. "Not exactly."

Smith knew what he meant; a smile pressed his lips

against his teeth. "I guess he told you what he wanted done," he laughed.

"Not before ripping me a new one," Bowers sighed. "He wasn't too happy about giving me men from the line."

Eager, the first man reached for two boxes of ammo, sliding them out of the back of the jeep and nearly dropping both into the snow. "Jesus, that's heavy," The man grumbled, his cheeks flush with embarrassment. He handed one box to the next man. "One at a time I guess." They headed back into the woods, the third stranger grabbing a box and rushing to catch up to them.

"I guess it's that time." Bowers slid a box into his hand. "You coming now?"

"Yeah." Smith glanced over at Tina. "We're ready."

Tina nodded her head, gripping the rifle in her hand the way he taught her. "Thank you," she whispered.

Smith noticed that there were still several weapons left in the jeep along with three boxes of ammo. "Before you go, grab an extra weapon, Bowers." He looked over at Tina. "You too if you think you can handle it." He waited for Bowers to come back, placing the sling over his neck. Tina lined up behind him. He fixed one on the opposite shoulder, tightening the strap so it wouldn't bounce around too much, then handed her ammo box. Her face strained with exertion. "You going to be okay with all of that?"

"I got this," Tina responded with some effort.

Smith slung two rifles over his shoulder, leaving three in the trunk—they may come in handy if they needed to retreat. He wished there were a way to transport the light machine gun; the beast took up most of the back trunk. If there was more time, he would have dragged it to the front lines himself. He let out a long, disappointed sigh then took the remaining two ammo boxes, the handles cutting into his hands through his gloves. "Let's get a move on." Smith's boots sank deeper into the snow. If he came across a drift, he'd drop in a heap, breaking his ankle.

"You going to be all right?" Tina asked over her shoulder.

"I'll be fine," Smith laughed, "don't worry about me." The moonlight all but vanished once they entered the forest, the canopy of branches overhead blotting it out. Glow sticks hung from the lower branches, guiding them along the path. Once they entered the trail, the snow was hard packed, making it easier to walk. "How you doing up there, Bowers?"

"Embracing the suck," Bowers responded without hesitation.

The trail wound back and forth at unequal lengths, navigating the safest path through the clusters of trees. Overhead, snow fell relentlessly from the sky, weaving its way through the branches, dusting the pine needles in sparkling white. Smith felt his shoulders pulling out of their sockets. Under normal circumstances, he would have carried one container at a time, shifting the weight back and forth between his hands. If the numbers reported were accurate, the size of the herd was well over one hundred thousand. Even with all their ammo, and if by some miracle the dead killed every one of the bikers, they would still be woefully short on rounds. A flicker of white-hot blue flames just ahead caught his eye. It was the burner of a Coleman's stove. They had reached the rear lines. Bustling movements and chatter sprang to life.

"Would you like a coffee now?" A woman offered a mug to Bowers as he approached the tiny gathering.

"If I have time?" Bowers turned, asking permission from Smith.

He placed the heavy containers on the ground. "Sure, I'm sure we could all use a coffee. Drop the ammo here for now."

"The water just boiled." The girl poured two more mugs, passing them both to Tina to distribute.

Smith took a long sip. The water burned his lips and tongue, igniting a fire in his stomach. "Tina, stay here on the rear lines for now. I'm going to find Wade." Then he continued down the path, stopping for a moment, craning his neck over his shoulder. "Make sure the ammo gets to the front lines, Bowers." Smith had no intentions on coming back.

CHAPTER 19
PROOF

"Please don't shoot!" a woman's voice hollered at Eric.

Confused, he tried to respond, his voice caught in his throat in a bubble. His finger trembled on the trigger. Tension pressed back; it was at the point right before there was no turning back. The girl raced at him, her legs pumping up and down, her hands fluttering over her head. "I'm not a rotter!" she pleaded, her voice wavering, sucking in deep gasps of air.

Eric backpedalled, his mind demanding more time to decide. His eyes studied the stranger. She acted alive, even if she blended in with the undead. The flare hovered high in the sky, its red glare illuminating the girl. Covered in grime, gore, and tattered clothes, she footed the bill of a corpse.

"Please, point that gun away from my face," she called out again.

At the last moment, Eric's finger slipped from the trigger, allowing the hammer to fall back as he lowered his arm. If she were a zombie, he would soon find out the

hard way. "What the fuck are you?" He demanded answers from the speechless species, leveling the barrel at
her head, speaking the universal language of lead.

"I'm just like you." She reached out for his hand. "My
blood is warm just like yours."

Hesitantly, Eric took the hand, feeling the warmth
in his own. "How is that possible?" A million questions
coursed through his mind. First and foremost, he wanted to ask her how she walked amongst the dead unno-
ticed. Tired, his mind must be playing dirty tricks on him.
"Where did you come from?"

"Down there." She gestured towards the herd. "You
shouldn't be here."

"From," Eric glanced over her shoulder "down there?"
The swarm was slithering up the hillside, a black mass
coating everything like oil. "That's not possible."

"I don't have time to explain." She tried to push him
away. "I can't steer them away from your city. Especially
since you fired that flare. I can try to delay them while you
get your people out of there."

Eric couldn't believe a word she was saying. "You can
walk amongst the dead?" he chuckled, approaching the
point of hysteria.

"Just get out of here," her voice faltered, "please. I
don't need those people down there to die." Weary and
tired, she didn't look capable of taking another stride.

"They need to die." Eric couldn't risk her diverting the
horde, even if he didn't believe a single word she said.
"It's the only way the Republic of Newfoundland can survive."

"What are you trying to say?"

"I'm saying I can't let you stop them. Our plan is already set in motion. If those bikers survive, we can never defeat Pharmakon." Eric noticed a spark ignite behind the girl's eyes. "They stand in our way of the underground base."

The girl snatched Eric's collar, tugging him forward. "Tell me where it is," she demanded.

Eric pushed her hands away. "Come with me. We have a little time." The herd was upon them. An overpowering stench of death reached out for them ahead of the pack. Eric led her down the hill, running towards the flickering light falling in the sky. For the first time, as they scrambled down the hill, Eric heard the bark of gunfire. Zombies crested the breast of the hill, stumbling, following the road towards Grand Falls. Eric didn't know what they directed the gunfire towards. He feared that the battle had already begun without him, that the swarm of undead would arrive too late. If the bikers discovered members of the Republic of Newfoundland, they would mow them down where they stood in their trenches.

Exhaustion forced Eric to slow the pace. It astonished him that the woman kept pace with him. She looked utterly spent. It looked like she had been through hell, and now it was nipping at her heels. "Can you keep up?"

"It's not me you should worry about," she replied. "I'm not in danger."

Eric suppressed the growing desire to burst out laughing. "Have you ever seen that many zombies in one place? Do you know what a herd that size is capable of?"

"I know better than you," she snapped. "I've seen more death than you can imagine. The only thing keeping me going is destroying Pharmakon." She reached out, her hand grabbing Eric's shoulder, spinning him around. "Tell me where the base is now." She asked, showing little patience.

Eric pulled his shoulder free, resisting the urge to throw a punch. "I'll take you there myself if I survive through the night. But I need those zombies to win this fight."

"You're fucking crazy." Disgusted, her lips curled into a snarl.

"Me?" Eric retorted. "I'm not the one claiming to walk amongst the dead."

"Do you want me to prove it to you?" She turned around, walking towards the zombies. "You keep your eye on me, just watch your distance."

Eric watched in disbelief as she strolled back up the hill, his feet backpedalling through the freshly fallen snow. She approached the front of the pack and they filed past her as if she was a tree. They bumped into her, pushing past her, always focused on Eric and beyond. "What the fuck?" Eric mumbled to himself, maintaining his distance. The woman reached out, snatching a tattered scrap of clothing right off the back of a rather decrepit corpse, forcing the creature to fall flat on its backside. Then, miraculously, she strolled out of the midst of the herd, jogging to catch up.

"Come on." The girl flung the soiled cloth at him. "Let's talk about what happens next."

The swatch of cotton was soaking wet, gritty with grime, and smeared in bodily fluids. Eric tossed it aside. It spoiled the pristine snow, leaving behind an oily smudge behind in its wake. The wind howled, kicking up a whirl of snowflakes all around him. Whiteout conditions cut Eric off from the world, disorienting him for a moment, leaving him alone with his thoughts. Frigid wind cut through to his bones like a thin razor blade. Above, the flare was all but extinguished, falling gracefully across the horizon. Its illuminating glow died and the blackness surrounding it was reborn, stronger than ever now after the glimmer of light.

Eric could smell the noxious stench of rotting skin and shit. He searched for the woman, glimpsing movement at the edge of darkness, disappearing into the blackness ahead. A deep, exhausted sigh rolled over Eric's tongue, his breath coming out in a burst of steam that rose over his face. There was only one option. Needing to trust the stranger, he raced off towards her.

"Hey," Eric called out, trying to catch up to the youthful girl. The hollow noises of the dead chasing after them. Slowly, the boisterous roar of gunfire ahead replaced the hungry groans. "What's your name?"

"Aliyah," she called back over her shoulder, keeping her pace.

"Aliyah, wait up." Eric panted like a dog, his tongue hanging out of his mouth. She paused, allowing Eric to reach her. "How did you do that?" Aliyah matched his pace. It wasn't enough to put any distance between them and the herd, but they kept ahead of it, matching the tedious march.

"So, do you believe me now?" Aliyah asked.

"I trust you." Eric felt like he was apologizing. "How?"

"I'm immune to the disease," Aliyah explained as the thunderous booming of the guns stopped as unexpectedly as it had started. "Something in my genetics, a condition that makes me undesirable to the flesh eaters."

"A double-edged sword."

"Not exactly. The disease I have lies dormant, or at least I think it does. I have no major symptoms, perfectly healthy as far as I can tell." Aliyah turned to stare at Eric. "Where is the Pharmakon base?"

"If I told you, you wouldn't help me." Eric wasn't prepared to divulge that information; it was the only thing keeping the herd on its current trajectory.

"If you die, I won't know where to go," Aliyah grumbled. "Whatever war you're fighting, it isn't as important as stopping Pharmakon."

"That's not true," Eric answered back sharply. "Destroying Pharmakon won't reverse what they've done. No matter what, the only thing we can do is survive. There's a group of people, The Republic of Newfoundland, that can make this island habitable. We can start over here, rebuild society without interference from the outside world."

"Pharmakon needs to pay for what they did. Just tell me where they are and I'll help you," Aliyah pleaded.

"They are," Eric hesitated, not sure if he should trust her, "in the old Millertown Mines, just past Buchan's junction."

"I don't even know where that is," Aliyah griped.

"Typical townie," Eric grumbled. "Like I said, I'll show you myself." Street lights, starting out as tiny sparkles of dull light, took shape and developed into spheres of yel-low. Grand Falls was just ahead. The highway divided the town in half. It looked like a dark void, slicing through the scattered street lamps, averting their glow. "This will be dangerous."

"I've been through worse." Flashes of being trapped back in the Pharmakon base under Cabot Tower played in the back of her mind. She'd lost her sense of humanity a long time ago. It died along with Mallory, Anita, and Keith.

"Just stick by me. We have to make it through the cen-tre of town with no one noticing us." Eric searched the horizon, trying to locate any movement. He didn't want to get caught here out in the open with limited ammo, his pockets light. His only concern now was keeping Aliyah safe. If what she said was true, if she could control the herd, force it to move from Grand Falls when this was all over, she would play a vital role. Up to this point, they didn't have a strategy to deal with the countless undead, whose numbers far exceeded their initial estimates.

Rushing up the middle of the street, Eric wanted to put as much distance between them as possible before they needed to sneak between the buildings to avoid con-frontation. "Listen, before anything happens. If we get separated, keep moving west along the highway. Once you reach Badger, you'll find a turnoff for Buchan's. Just follow the road and you'll come across the Millertown mines. They built the Pharmakon base into the old mine shaft. You can't miss it." Eric was hoping to gain her trust by divulging this information.

Aliyah said nothing. She just kept pushing forward

down the street, running under the dim yellow glow of the street lights. As if the low, electrical hum of the lamp hypnotized her, she stared up at them, her jaw wide open in an awed gape. It took Eric a moment to catch up. He grabbed hold of her and shook her. "Hey, we can't stand under the light like that." Underneath the grime, beneath her weathered clothes, Aliyah was scrawny, like a skeleton to Eric. His fingers wrapped around her upper arm, almost reaching his thumb beneath her bicep. In the heat of the moment, he dragged her out of the light, forcing them both to hide behind a parked car. Even though he felt awful shaking her, afraid she would snap in half, they couldn't afford to be spotted here. On the wrong side of town, far away from help, Eric didn't have enough bullets to get them out of a jam. What they needed was a stealthy approach.

"I haven't seen a working light," Aliyah sounded dazed, like the losing boxer after a twelve-round fight, "since I can't remember." A tear sparkled in the corner of her eye.

"This isn't the time to stick around and admire it. We need to get out of here." Eric tried to get her moving, her body not responding to his guidance.

"I thought the entire planet had reverted to the stone age." Aliyah wouldn't take her eyes off the street light. Mesmerized, she tried to walk back towards the light like a moth towards the flame. Eric yanked on her arm, practically pulling her to the ground. "I didn't think there was anything to live for anymore. Once this was all over, I was going to…"

"We don't have time for this," Eric cut her off. Echoes

of footsteps approached from the street ahead. A bright white halo bobbed, casting a thin ray of light towards them, the beam bouncing off the shiny surface of the vehicle. Between the house and a snow bank, a shovelled driveway rolled all the way into the back yard and disappeared beneath a garage door. "This way," Eric pointed, "keep low." Bent over at the waist, his quad muscles wobbled and threatened to collapse as they shuffled across the pavement, keeping close to the house for cover. It was hardly ten feet, but Eric doubted his legs would hold out long enough.

Aliyah reached the edge first, waiting for Eric to slink towards her. She reached out her hand and pulled him forwards. A swatch of light caught the edge of the house, casting a sharp angled shadow across the driveway. "Samuel, you know that curfew is in effect. It's too late to be out poking around. I told you before, get back inside," a woman's voice called out.

"Where are we going to go?" Aliyah's head spun, her eyes scouring the landscape for an escape route.

Eric led Aliyah by the hand, towards the back steps. They charged up a flight of stairs. The staircase swayed against the side of the house, rattling the siding. A deck that spanned the length of the backyard waited for them as they reached the top step. With a trembling hand, he reached out, turning the handle. It twisted and the door fell inwards much to Eric's relief. He pulled Aliyah in, closing the door behind them, just loud enough for it to echo. They ducked beneath the window, their backs against the door, praying the woman wouldn't try to enter the house after them.

CHAPTER 20
LOVERS IN THE NIGHT

Tree branches scratched and clawed at them from all angles. The overpowering bouquet of pine needles washed over them in waves as they hurried through the forest. Where the trees allowed, moonlight cast a silvery aura over the snow-covered ground, its glimmering light reflecting brilliantly at them. It was just enough light to avoid stumbling into any major holes or running into a trunk. Beneath their feet, the slick, treacherous, wet ground threatened to spill them onto their back. Hidden out of view, rocks buried beneath a thin veil of white stubbed their toes. Gnarled roots and decayed branches awaited them, hidden from view, threatening to trip them up, or roll an ankle. A half-frozen, marshy surface sometimes gave way in some places to icy water below. Jagged edges of ice cut into the shin bones as the opened holes ate up the boot.

As lights chased them relentlessly, flashlight beams cut through the darkness behind them, nipping at their heels. Breathing heavily, the pursuit through the dense forest stretched on for hours. Every time they thought they'd lost them, a snapped branch would betray their location. Rays of light would cast them in dancing shadows, forcing them to continue running blindly through the woods. The forest stretched on endlessly, enveloping them. Tangles of tree branches reached out for them, tugging at their clothes and clawing at their faces. They climbed rolling hills, cut across wide open plains and crossed countless streams. Icy water chilled their feet, the dampness loosening the skin, blisters forming and rupturing, far beyond sore. Questions lingered in their minds, distracting them. Afraid of being heard, they pushed them aside, remaining silent until they were safely away from their pursuers.

When they broke through the edge of the forest, a precipitous slope sent them plummeting down the steep bank, spilling onto an ordinary stretch of highway. There were no distinguishing features that they could use to pinpoint their location. A single set of tire tracks rested in the middle, the falling snow filling them in. They followed the tracks, picking the direction that felt right. The lights that chased them faded away like a distant memory left behind. Frigid wind whipped snow into their faces, chilling them to the bone. It cut right through them. Exhausted breath was whisked away in the breeze. The clouds vanquished the moon and stars from view, trying to hide all hope away. A desolate stretch of road rolled out in front of them. Twists and turns wound into the woods and around mountainsides.

They walked hand in hand down the highway without saying a word, only trying to catch their breath, waiting for the chase to begin anew. Deep down inside, they both realized that this horrible night was far from being over. In the distance, a single headlight crested over the mountain. A thunderous grumble roared and approached them, the engine guzzling gas and spitting out carbon monoxide behind. Too tired to run away, they waited in ambush alongside the shoulder of the road.

CHAPTER 21
COFFIN NAILS

Approaching footfalls echoed amid the crisp snow, coming to a stop just a few feet away. After a moment, a relieved gasp immediately proceeded the indistinguishable rip of a zipper opening. The powerful splashing noises of a healthy man voiding his bladder rang out as he relieved himself into the snowbank. Then the stink of piss stood out in stark contrast to the fresh air. The man groaned, struggling to pull up his pants, grunting and grumbling until the zipper yanked up. "That's better," he announced with much relief.

Byrne could see the man's shadowy figure obscured by the driving snow, lumbering just a few feet away. He was lying face down in the snowbank, his stomach cramping with the cold and twisting with fear. If the man weren't so preoccupied with emptying his bladder, he would have spotted him. He held the rifle off to the side in his right hand, doing his best to keep the muzzle out of the snow. The guard didn't seem to be in a hurry to leave, his shadow lurking just beyond the curtain of white. Once the wind died down, Byrne would be in plain sight. His hand fumbled into his pocket, searching for the multi-purpose tool he kept in there for emergencies. He opened it up to the corkscrew, angry at himself for having cracked the blade off, whittling away at a block of wood one day. When the wind hollered, building in intensity as it swept down over the mountain side, it drove snow over his back and into the man's face.

This was his best chance. Byrne leapt to his feet and bounded across the snow, coving the distance in three strides. Before the stranger could react, Byrne pounced on him, knocking them both to the ground. The twisted spike of the corkscrew punctured the man's windpipe. A choked cry gurgled through the blood, his hands frantically grasping at his throat. Byrne yanked his hand away, the corkscrew tearing away a strip of flesh, revealing the grotesque flesh of the man's larynx.

"Hey, Freddy?" another voice called out. "Everything all right over there?"

Byrne rolled off the dying man, dashing away, seeking to find a place to hide in the wide-open field. "Shit," Byrne mumbled under his breath. With the wind winding down, the howl changed to an indistinct murmur. Stuck in the middle of nowhere, Byrne dived into the snow. The world around him emerged from the shell of white, bursting into view.

"Jesus Christ, I need help over here!" the stranger barked into the wind, a rustle of footsteps answering his plea.

There was no where to go. The tree line was too far away and didn't provide suitable cover from gunfire. Closer, but not close enough, the old gas station would provide the necessary cover. It was his only option, but it would drag him further into the enemy lines. The only way to get there was to run towards the approaching bikers. He flipped the safety switch off, putting the gun on full auto. The element of surprise was his best chance at survival. He could see their lumbering forms taking shape, emerging from the corner of the building and racing across the open ground towards the anguished cries.

"What happened to him?" a worried voice asked.

"It looks like a biter got 'em."

"So where's the corpse?"

"Hey look, footprints heading off in that direction."

A crimson sun exploded to life overhead, the intense glare of a flare reflecting off the blackened winter clouds, changing the sky into an open wound. Distracted by the sudden outburst, the bikers stared off, looking at the sky in a bewildered wonder like a child witnessing fireworks for the first time. Momentarily, they forgot about their dying friend, trying to understand what just happened, not realizing the dangers awaiting them.

Byrne did not squander this opportunity.

Yellow flashes sparked from the muzzle, spitting out rounds in short, measured bursts. The bikers scattered for shelter. Most of his rounds missed as the majority off his magazine sailed harmlessly into the darkness beyond. Nonetheless, there were tangible results despite the poor execution. Rounds tore through flesh with frightening efficiency, producing sprays of blood, which were carried away by the wind, coating the white surface in exaggerated arcs of maroon.

He didn't know if any of the wounds were fatal and

didn't stick around long enough to find out. With the clip spent in a matter of seconds, he flipped the toggle to semi-automatic and took off running for cover before the group recovered their wits. He took shelter behind the corner of the building to reload. By then the bikers regrouped, taking aim at their assailant, and riddling the cement wall of the gas station. A shower of dust and rock lashed out at Byrne. He tucked his head between his legs for cover. Their rifles barked into the night, shredding away the silence that had settled over Grand Falls. After what seemed like an eternity, the gunfire seized.

"Did you get him?"

"Do you think he ran around the other side?"

"You two go check round back. The rest of you, go see if he went the other way. I'll cover you all from here."

Byrne used the confusion to spy around the corner, observing the bikers as they scattered. Three of them ran out of view towards the other side. Two of them approached him, their eyes scanning for any signs of their attacker. He held his breath, taking careful aim through the scope, then fired off two rounds into the kneecap of the closest man. A dreadful shriek cried out as the man crashed into a crumpled heap. He languished on the ground, clutching at the pulpy mess that used to be his knee. His partner, hysterical, dove into the snow next to him. Byrne raced towards the road. Puffs of snow erupted from the ground all around him as bullets thudded around his feet. Rounds whistled past his ear as he dove for cover behind a snow bank. He tumbled down the tiny hill of snow, jumped to his feet, and raced towards a house on the outskirts of town.

Footsteps pounded against the pavement behind him. The wind howled, chasing after him as he cut across the desolate stretch of lawn. His ears expected an eruption of gunfire at any moment. The house appeared to be out of reach. Caught in the open, he could hear screaming voices behind him, catching up to him. There wasn't enough time to get behind cover. Byrne dove to the ground and faced towards where he thought they would crest the hill.

A masked biker's head popped over the snowbank. Byrne took deliberate aim, held his breath, and squeezed the trigger. His aim was deadly. The man shook violently, rattled by the bullet, convulsing as it tore through his heart. A deep, red stain blossomed on his vest. He collapsed face first into the snow, and the next man moving over the bank tripped over his legs and fell on top, driving him deep into the accumulated snow. Byrne fired another three shots. Blood sprayed into the breeze, rounds digging into the flesh of both fallen bikers. Anguished cries screamed for help.

Three more bikers crested the hill, all from different angles, diving for cover before Byrne could take aim. He fired wildly in their direction. Bullets whizzed through the air, whistling a high-pitched hiss as they sailed aimlessly into the midnight air. The bikers ducked for cover, burying their heads in the snow, giving Byrne an opportunity to line up his next shots. His reticle fell over the silver skull bandana shrouding a biker's face. When he pulled the trigger, all that escaped the rifle was a dull clunk as the hammer landed on an empty magazine. Byrne dumped the magazine in the snow, yanking another from his vest, slamming it into place. It didn't take him long to do this, but in that brief time, the cartel members got organized.

"There he is."

Byrne rolled to the side just in time as bullets hammered the snow, sending up puffs of white powder. The bullets tore into the frozen ground with a low thud. Then, escaping the hail of bullets, he laid down cover fire, but there were too many of them. He sprayed the shots in a wide arc, watching them scatter in different directions as he lunged to his feet. This time, he counted his shots, making sure he didn't find himself on empty when it mattered. None of his shots found their mark, but they did the trick. The bikers disoriented and separated from each other, Byrne used this window of opportunity to make a break for the house again. He fired over his shoulder as he raced towards the building.

The cartel fired at him, bullets flying past from three different angles as they reclaimed the upper hand. It took a few leading shots until one biker found their aim and got a bead on him. As he reached cover, Byrne felt his stomach catch fire. Then he tumbled to the ground, a puff of snow scattering around his body. The next few shots missed, striking the side of the house, the cold plastic siding shattering into fragments. Byrne reached out and grasped the gutter's downspout. It groaned and creaked as he hauled himself to safety. He reached down, pulled open his parka and touched a damp spot forming on his tunic. "Shit." Byrne looked down at the exit wound and saw a trail of intestines torn out along with the round.

Giant drops of blood splattered into the snow, staining

into the shovelled patio blocks beneath him. As he sought to shove his intestine back into the shredded wound, the pain was too much to bear. They squished and slithered in his grip. When he pressed against the flesh around the exit wound, he grimaced in pain. The bullet burnt the surrounding flesh, making it tender. Footfalls echoed in the dark recesses of his mind. The world was shutting down around him. Suddenly tired, he fought the urge to fall asleep. Dragging the rifle into his grasp, he leaned his back against the house. His heavy head pivoted up and down on his neck as he struggled to stay awake, jerking in and out of consciousness.

A flutter of movement flashed at the edge of his vision. His finger tensed, controlled by muscle memory. Startled by the raw power, the rifle flew out of his hands as the round exited the muzzle. As his target grasped at his crotch, withering in agony just in front of him, shrill screams slipped from the biker's clenched jaw. Then Byrne broke into hysterical laugher, realizing that he shot the man in the balls. Even if he didn't die tonight, the man's life as he knew it was over. The next cartel member appeared, his face leaning cautiously around the corner.

"He's here, go around the other side."

Byrne fired off a round. It crashed into the side of the house, well short of the corner.

"We will kill you, mother fucker!" the biker boomed.

"Go fuck yourself." Byrne reached into his pocket, pulled out a pack of Macdonald Original and his lighter. He placed a cigarette in the corner of his mouth. With a trembling hand, he snapped his zippo open, holding it in a cusped hand to protect the flickering flame. Lighting the cigarette, he enjoyed a long drag, holding the smoke in his mouth, savouring it before letting it drift over his face.

"Big talk for a dead guy," the man laughed thinly.

"Face me, you coward," Byrne spoke with the cigarette dangling in the corner of his mouth. He picked up his rifle with his right hand and pinned it in the nook of his armpit, holding towards the corner with his finger on the trigger. "I dare you."

The biker stepped from around the corner, his blue jeans spattered with blood. It took a second examination for Byrne to realize that it belonged to one of his deceased buddies. "I hope this was worth it." He pulled down his silver skull bandana, "You're gonna die here." His thin lips pressed against his teeth in a devious smirk. "What did you think would happen? Who are you here to rescue? Some friend or hot piece of ass no doubt," he snickered.

"I came here to kill all of you." Byrne tried to aim the rifle, but it rattled in his grasp, his strength fleeing his body.

"You've failed miserably, kid." The biker reached out and snatched the muzzle, yanking it from Byrne's fleeting grip. "I'll give you credit, you got three of my friends. I'll have to make quick work of you—I gotta go back and put them out of their misery."

"Do you hear that?" Byrne cocked his head to the side, a trail of smoke wafting over the side of his face. An ill wind swept over the town, carrying the voices of the undead with its bitter chill.

The biker shook his head, oblivious to the creeping noises, his black wool toque pulled down over his ears to prevent frost bite. "I hear nothing except for my friend coming around the other side of the house." He waved his gloved hand. "So, any last requests?"

"Just let me finish my last smoke."

"I can respect that." The biker knelt in front of Byrne. "You want to seal your fate with one last coffin nail, be my guest." His brown eyes searched Byrne for a concealed weapon, not taking any chances. He opened up the pouches on Byrne's vest, taking the last two magazines and his pack of smokes. "Do you mind? No sense letting those nails go to waste."

"I wouldn't want them to go to waste," Byrne chuckled, "help yourself." The groaning moans grew louder. Byrne could see that the man had discovered it but didn't realize what it was yet. "You'll probably have just enough time to enjoy your last dart."

A fist smashed into Byrne's face. Stars danced in his vision as a warm trickle flowed from his nostrils, leaving a bitter coppery taste on his lips. Somehow, Byrne kept the cancer stick nestled in the corner of his jaw. He spat a wad of blood into the snow behind him. "Looks like your last coffin nail too. That's proven to be a remarkably productive pack."

"Don't press your luck." The biker lit his own fag, sucking at the filter in quick gasps. The tip flared orange then back to ashen grey. A tiny stalk of smoke drifted away in the same wind as the hollowed growls. This time, his eyes widened with realization. "Hey, go gather the boys," he shouted at one biker. "Looks like we got some biters in town." Footsteps faded behind him. "You dragged some dead towards town, good for you."

"It's more than you can handle," Byrne taunted him.

"There's over a hundred of my cartel brothers here, armed to the teeth. And don't forget about the Highway Hangman, they outnumber us. We can handle a few undead creeps."

Byrne wished he had killed more members of the Silver Skulls Cartel. The Republic's scouts underestimated their numbers, but that throng of rotters would still swallow them whole regardless. "You will die."

"No," the biker stood up, "you failed." He stomped on Byrne's stomach.

The pain flared and burned hot, forcing him to scream. It was a guttural, defiant roar. His cigarette fell from his lips, landing in his lap. His vision filled with black leather as his head snapped back, the impact crushing his orbital bone. Pressure built up behind his eye, forcing it to swell out in excruciating pain. "You're a dead man," Byrne choked out the last word as a left hook unhinged his jaw. He collapsed onto his side. Then a boot drove the wind from his gut. Gasping for air, he felt like he was drowning. Another blow struck his ribs. The brittle bones fractured and shards of bone sliced into his lungs. His body shuddered with each thundering blow. Gilbert Byrne lay shivering in the cold, suffocating on the blood flooding his throat. Unable to draw another breath, the last image he saw was the burning orange glow of the man's cigarette as he took a long drag.

CHAPTER 22
THE HITCHER

"Do you think they can track me?" Jason asked in a hushed tone. Tracy laid next to him on the downward slope of the ditch, keeping a vigilant eye on the approaching headlamp.

"For some reason, I don't think it's Pharmakon." She didn't bother to whisper. The choking, rough grumble of the approaching motorcycle drowned out their voices. Then the bright light swelled, approaching across a lengthy, straight stretch of road. "A lone biker is not their style."

"Must be a member of the Highway Hangman." Jason thought about the last time he saw Eric. Somehow, that seemed like an eternity ago now. He could picture Nick standing there with him as they expressed their goodbyes. Eric had left to follow his mother's trail to Grand Falls.

"Yeah, they are on a night run." Tracy crept up towards the edge of the snowbank.

"You know about them?" Jason asked, astonished.

"Pharmakon's been keeping track of them and the Silver Skull Cartel. We've also been watching the massive

East Coast herd migrate across the Avalon towards central." As the bike approached, she said something beneath the bike's engine, the booming and rumbling drowning her out. "Wait here." She jumped over the edge of the bank before Jason could protest.

Silhouetted by the intense light, she flagged the driver down, waving her hands over her head. Jason crawled forward, getting himself into a better position to see what was happening. The bike slowed to a stop and the engine grumbled on idle. Now that the bike was halted, the chains on the tires rattled as the bike rested, the links clanking against the spokes. A glistening white cyclops eye peered ahead from beneath the cherry red fender. The words *Harley Davidson* were scrawled across the black body in flaming letters.

"Hey, what's going on?" a frightened voice rattled out from beneath the helmet.

"Please, help me." Tracy rushed towards the man, waving her arms hysterically.

Not taking any chances, the biker pulled a pistol from his belt, the silver barrel shaking in his hand. "Stop there, don't come any closer," he demanded in a trembling voice.

"They chased me from the woods, please help me," Tracy begged, taking deliberate steps forward.

Without warning, the biker held the gun towards Tracy, his arm struggling to hold his hand steady. Gusts of wind got under his vest, the leather flapping off his jacket beneath. "Who chased you?"

"Those things," Tracy gasped, burying her face in her hands, whimpering.

"Hop on." He lowered his gun, inserting it back into his pants. "I'll give you a ride to Grand Falls." His voice had settled. He flipped up his visor, revealing a thin strip of pale flesh. His eyes looked like two drops of oil.

Tracy raced towards the back of the bike, swinging her leg over the back wheel. The springs gave as she squatted down. "Thank you." Tracy threw her arms around the man's chest. Before the man could balance the bike, Tracy slipped her hands onto the man's helmet and wrenched his neck to a grotesque angle. Jason heard the bone in his neck snap. Tracy held the biker's body upright as his head pivoted loosely on his chin, digging into his chest. "Help me take him off the bike. I don't want his dead weight to tip it over."

Jason couldn't believe what he'd witnessed. Never in a million years would he have imagined Tracy being able to hurt a person in that way, even with the undead roaming the earth. He stumbled down over the bank, his feet slipping, drifting through the loose snow blanketing the hardened surface beneath. A bitter gust swept over the road, hissing over the bank with a fierce wail. By the time Jason reached the dead man, Tracy was losing her grasp on him. Slumped to the right, the bike was propped against the kick stand, the metal bar straining at the hinge as the back tire lifted off the ground. Jason wrapped his arms around the body, taking the burden from the bike and transferring it to the pavement below.

As the lights swept the tree line above them, casting long shadows over the hill that spilled over onto the highway, Jason opened the throttle. "They're on our tail—they must have tracked our footprints. Unless they can track me?" Jason realized he was putting his wife in mortal danger. David Steele wouldn't rest until one of them remained victorious, standing over the defeated corpse in triumph.

"They can track this." Tracy held out the remote that controlled Jason's vision. "David won't let this go."

"Let's break it." Jason reached out for the black controller, but Tracy's arm recoiled. "Hey, what's wrong with you? Do you want them to find us?"

"Don't you realize that if they find us, they will kill me too now? I risked everything for you."

"What's stopping me from breaking that?"

"I'm afraid."

"What are you scared of?" Jason responded with frustration, not knowing if he wanted to scream or laugh.

"What if when that breaks," Tracy stared at him, her light blue eyes trying to hold his, "you lose your eyesight. I don't know if that is how it will work, but I'm nervous to find out. I can't drag you through the wasteland, taking care of you like an infant." Voices shouted at the edge of the clearing, the halo of light shining just out of reach. "Come on, we have to go before they find us."

"Where can we go?" Jason took the handle bars, easing himself into the driver's seat. Tracy didn't care much for driving before the apocalypse, and he assumed that hadn't changed.

"Head towards Grand Falls." Tracy tapped his shoulder. "I'll explain once we get close. If the herd is there, I have a plan."

Jason let the throttle out, giving the bike a steady supply of gas. The engine guzzled the fuel greedily, rumbling in a deep, gurgled boom as they gained speed, the chains rattling. Gunfire erupted from atop the bank as bullets whizzed past them, tossing up pieces of pavement and a burst of snow. A loud, metallic bang rang out as a bullet grazed the tailpipe. Jason felt the vibration beneath him as it rumbled through the frame. He weaved left and right, feeling the tires slipping across the snowy surface, threatening to dump them into the road. The bike wobbled on its tires. Jason fought with the handle bars to keep them steady. Bullets scattered across the road and the bark of automatic fire roared over the wind. Jason opened up the throttle and the engine growled, pushed to its limits. They accelerated out of range, rounds biting the asphalt just behind them.

Narrowly escaping the spray of bullets, Jason maneuvered the Harley down the straight road, reaching a twist. The bike's headlight guided them along the road, which wound down a steep hill, cutting into the mountainside. Stone walls stretching towards the sky on either side protected them from the hail of bullets. Jason righted the bike, easing off the throttle, riding the brake down the winding road. The road emptied into a flat valley below like a river feeding into a bog. Long stretches of pristine white fields stretched on either side with thorny, dead branches. A small pond on the left fed water though a culvert that ran beneath the road just ahead. Jason coasted towards a white sign poking up through the snow, resting on an angled board on the shoulder of the road. He turned off the ignition. The engine choked and died with a defeated rumble.

"What are we doing?" Tracy demanded.

Jason kicked his heel against the stand, letting the bike tilt to the side. "It's a fresh spring, I'm thirsty."

"They're going to catch up to us." Tracy slid off the back of the seat, landing in the snow, her feet crashing through the crust with a resounding crunch.

"I don't think they'll be chasing us on foot." Jason placed his feet on the ground and stood up, the suspension groaning a sigh of relief. "They'll head back and report to David Steele. Then they'll get into their vehicles and chase after us." He sidestepped down the bank.

Water cascaded from a blue pipe sticking out of a snowbank, splashing into a tickling brook. Jason took his gloves off then cupped his hand to catch the water. It was numbing, making him want to pull back with shock, but he forced the water to his lips. It sent shivers coursing through every inch of his body, satisfying his thirst and waking him up a little. "What are you doing up there?" he called out to Tracy. He could hear rattling and banging behind him.

"I'm looking for a bottle or something," she called back then added with triumphant satisfaction: "Here we go." "Heads up." The warning came a little too late.

Jason turned just as the sheep skin pouch thumped against his chest. His hands fumbled to catch it. "Thanks," he sighed. He held it beneath the pipe, filling it with the ice-cold water. It took much longer than he would have preferred; most of the water splashed over his exposed skin, filling the pouch with a slow trickle. "So, what's your plan?"

"We find a stray zombie from the edge of that herd," Tracy said, "then we stuff this remote in its pocket and let the Pharmakon soldiers chase after it. If we're lucky, they'll be eaten alive by the swarms of undead."

"What if they find the remote?" Jason asked.

"We'll have disappeared by the time they discover it," Tracy answered. "We just have to hope that I'm mistaken about your eyesight."

"What are we going to do after we ditch the remote?"

"We head back to the Pharmakon base. They have vials of the cure. I was given a dose a long time ago. It prevents you from turning when you die or even if you're bitten." Tracy spoke with her head lowered into her chest, afraid someone else might overhear her.

"Is it worth it to go back just for that?" Jason took three giant gulps of water then placed the bottle under the flow to fill it back up.

"We can also rig the base to explode." Tracy grinned, revealing her teeth. "They put it in place in case they ever needed to abandon it."

CHAPTER 23
COOPER

"Congratulations, it's a boy."

Dana swaddled the baby in a grey wool blanket, handing the bundle over to Janet. Clarence leaned over her shoulder, a giant smile on his face, folding back the blanket to get a better view. The baby's powerful lungs produced a high-pitched screech. His arms and legs flailed in uncoordinated, jerky movements.

"He's handsome," Janet swooned, her face flushed in an incandescent brilliance. Hair clung to her forehead in clumps. "Isn't he, Clarence?"

"He looks like his momma." Clarence swelled with pride, his eyes wet with tears.

Through the window, a vivid red glare lit up the sky. It hovered there like a nightlight, casting a fiery glow across the top of the pine trees. From the window, Dana glimpsed the outline of buildings beyond the forest. Eric was just on the outskirts of town now, the great East Coast herd shambling behind him. At that moment, she missed him fiercely. She rubbed her belly, a flutter of soft kicks as the baby became active. Dana suspected the baby sensed her excitement, her own emotions getting their child worked up. At that moment she was both afraid and relieved that Eric had made it this far and was still alive. Her head spun with mixed feelings.

Dana backed away from the bed, wanting the new parents to share this moment privately. She didn't want to be there when they realized something was wrong. Worse than that, there was nothing to be done about it. "I will give you guys some privacy."

"No, please stay," Clarence insisted. "I expect I'd be more comfortable with you close by."

"I'm not a doctor." Dana eased her way towards the door. The floor boards groaned in protest, as if they were on the parents' side.

"You just delivered a baby." Janet's throat was sore from the screaming, her voice raw and hoarse. "I guess in this day and age, that makes you as close as we will get."

Clarence nodded his head, humming his agreement. "I'd be awful thankful if you'd stay."

Defeated, Dana nodded her head in agreement. "If you insist." She spoke more delicately than she had intended, scarcely more than a whisper. She watched the new parents, their glossy gaze glued to their newborn.

"What should we name him?" Clarence held his boy in his arms, looking down at him with love in his eyes. Love was blinding both of them. They couldn't look past it to identify the problem.

"I'm too tired to think," Janet rasped. The endorphins wearing off, her eyelids drooped, scarcely able keep them open.

"Is everything okay?" Clarence asked, concerned.

"I'm sure it's just her body's reaction to what happened," Dana spoke for Janet, who was half way to sleep now, her head rolling towards the window. "She's exhausted, and I'm sure she's in pain. We didn't have much to offer her for it."

Clarence nuzzled the baby into the crook between his arm and chest. "Well, I'm just going to call you Cooper for now. Do you like that, little man?" Cooper seemed to pump his fist in joy. Or was it objection? "He's heavy, I'd say ten pounds or more. What do you think?"

Inclined to agree, Dana nodded her head. The boy was a healthy size, but something was wrong. Why couldn't they see it? "At least ten pounds." She wanted Clarence to recognize it for himself; she would not be the one to break the news to him. For all she knew, the baby was healthy, and its condition didn't matter. But it did. Deep down inside, she knew it mattered. "You must be very proud."

"Oh, I am. Seeing his little face, scrunched up but still smiling, makes all of this worth it. I'm glad we escaped Pharmakon. I'm just afraid they will find us one day." Clarence sat at the edge of the bed, rocking Cooper back and forth.

"You expect they'll come find you?"

"I know they will. They'll show up for Cooper," Clarence said matter-of-factly.

"Why would they come for him?" Curiosity got the better of her, even if she was hesitant to learn the answer.

"Because he's the first baby born where the parents were both immune to the virus." He shook his head as if it disgusted him. "I mean, look at him. Can't you tell he's different?"

"I didn't want to say anything—I didn't think you noticed," Dana said, not sure what response she would get.

Clarence laughed. "I get it, not every day you see an albino baby delivered." He peered down at his swaddled child. "They told us that there would be side effect, but they weren't sure of the full effects. The plan was to monitor the newborn. I didn't want my child to be a lab rat, that's why we ran." He gazed over at his wife, who was sawing wood now. "Here, can you hold Cooper for a minute? I need to go get something from downstairs."

"Uh, sure." Surprised, Dana fumbled for words, "No problem." When Dana took the baby, she realized the blanket was a little too course. "If you can find a nicer blanket, I believe that would help soothe Cooper." Clarence winked at her over his shoulder and lumbered out of the bedroom and down the hallway. His footfalls heavy, the entire house creaked and groaned as he made his way down the staircase. Dana walked over to the windowsill, wondering where Eric was. The flare floated towards the ground, its blazing glow dying, the brilliant red fading to a pale pink. Something like thunder roared in the distance. It was the first shot of many tonight. The noise made Dana shudder. It tugged at her. An urge to find her husband flourished with each gunshot. "Where are you, Hank?" Dana mumbled to herself. Cooper cooed, as if he'd figured out the answer. Looking down at him, Dana thought maybe somehow he had. His pale skin, soft pink lips pressed together, and his scrunched-up face made it appear like he was receiving a message. The only way she could describe the shade of his light blue eye was man made, manufactured. They were eerily bright, as if there were two LED lights behind them, computerized and running an advanced diagnostic. Cooper appeared to be bald, but the hair on his head was transparent. She felt it there, like a smooth peach fuzz, his eyebrows the same complexion.

Wailing, Cooper demanded his mother's attention. His little arm broke free of the blanket, jerking forward and reaching for Dana's chest. "You must be hungry, Cooper. I'll get your mother." She carried him over, his cries waking her out of her deep sleep, an unbreakable connection between them.

"Cooper," Janet mumbled the words, her eyes still shut, her hands reaching out. Her subconscious attaching the name Clarence had said to her child. Dana put Cooper in her arms, and Janet instinctively fed her newborn child. Cooper's cries vanished, focused on his hunger. Janet breathed heavily, somewhere between awake and asleep, responsive only to Cooper's movements. "There you go, Coop, eat up."

Dana went back to the window to watch the flare fizzle out, the forest going back into hiding beneath the blanket of darkness pulled over it. The gunshots rang out more clearly now, as if the sound transmitted through the blackness easier. "Where are you Hank?"

Clarence's footsteps boomed down the hallway, announcing his arrival long before he passed through the doorframe. "How's the little guy doing?" he asked Janet. She remained silent, too exhausted to respond. Her slight reserve of energy on autopilot. "Is she okay?"

"I'm sure she's fine." Dana looked at the blue blanket dangling from Clarence's hand, it looked like something he'd use as a facecloth. "I'd wait until Cooper's done before you change his blanket."

In his other hand, Clarence held a cardboard box, a young child in diapers on the box. "I've never changed a diaper before." He sounded terrified.

Dana couldn't help but laugh.

"What's so funny?"

"Let Cooper finishing eating, then I'll show you." Dana felt sorry for Clarence, he looked terrified. His hands trembled, unsure what to do with them. "Everything will be just fine." Dana peered out the window, the resounding roar of gunfire thundering in the distance drawing her attention.

Restless, Dana noticed the oil lamps flicker. As the pump gurgled the reserves of propane, a choking guzzling noise rattled as it drank up the remaining fuel. In all the commotion during the birth and everything after, Dana had lost track of time. An hour, or four, could have passed by. She didn't understand why she was so nervous. As time ticked by agonizingly slow, her thoughts wandered. The midnight sky was pitch black, the wind howled against the cabin, and snow pelted the windows. "Where are you, Hank?" she asked the window. Earlier, she had guided Clarence through putting a diaper on Cooper. Then she helped him swaddle the newborn in a blanket and left them all upstairs to get some much-needed sleep. The fire cackled, scorching through the logs with a feverish ferocity. Not able to catch any sleep, she constantly got up to put another log in the fireplace. It was her only distraction.

Then a squall of wind rattled the door. It thumped against the doorframe and the window rattled in its frame. The tips of the flames reached up the chimney, drawn up by the tremendous force of rushing air over the roof. Cooper made a single, faint cry, then suddenly the house fell silent. The wind whooped and hollered outside, the windows and doors taking a beating from mother nature. The wind carried with it a subtle groan, dead voices yelling at the house. Without thinking, she walked into the kitchen, grabbing a package of salt-top crackers to munch on, anything to take her mind off the noises outside. Until she took a bite, she didn't realize just how hungry she was. Her mouth watered. The more she chewed the more she wanted, a vicious cycle when you needed to ration food.

The voices in the window grew rowdier, no longer transmitted to her by the wind. She could hear them just outside the cabin, or at least she assumed she could. There were no shuffling corpses outside the kitchen window. Silently, keeping her head down, she crept to the living room window, nudging the curtain open, peering through the tiny slit. A small pack of zombies, drawn to the soft flickering light from the house, shuffled through the thick tangle of pine trees just outside. Studying them, Dana concentrated on trying to determine how many of them there were lurking in the shadows. Their decrepit eyes measured the cabin as decaying smiles leered at the light spilling from the window into the darkness. She expected to see Hank any moment lunge from the shadows to deal with the pack. Zombies staggered from the tree line, flowing into the open, the deep snow slowing them down and tripping them up. Without intervention, they would reach the cabin in under two minutes. "Where are you?" she whispered to the curtains.

"How many of them are there?" Janet's voice startled Dana. She jumped back, knocking over an end table.

"You scared me," Dana said through gasping breaths.

"They are here, I can smell them." Janet stared beyond Dana, her eyes settling on some unseeable point.

"It's nothing to worry about." Dana tore her eyes from the window, trying to reassure Janet—and herself. "Hank will take care of them." There was an unmistakable lack of confidence in her tone.

"What if your friend didn't make it?" Janet suggested. "Clarence is in no condition to deal with those monsters."

Dana peered over her shoulders. The undead groaned, drawn towards the light from the window, their hands outstretched. "I'll take care of them. You need to get Clarence to board up the windows while I'm out there." Dana grabbed her jacket from the hook hanging in the closet. She reached for the handgun Hank gave her, feeling the grip poking out of the pocket. "I'll be back once I lure them away." Dana opened the door, greeted by a wintry gust of wind eager to get into the house. The zombies howled, sniffing at the air, their dead gaze burning a hole through Dana. They twisted and turned their heads, confused, not understanding why the decaying aroma of flesh wasn't there, carried away from them by the breeze.

The door slammed shut behind Dana and the latch locked behind her. She was all that stood between the cottage and the undead. That lock wouldn't hold off the dead for long; they would be relentless, pounding away at the door until it collapsed. She needed to lure them away. There were to many of them to mount a defence here.

Dana darted around the side of the cabin, screaming over the wind, luring the zombies away from Cooper. Her legs sank into the knee-deep snow as she searched for the path they had travelled to get here. It was barely visible. The snowstorm had all but filled it in now, just a slight indent remained. It was easier in the old path but not enough. Her leg muscles already burning, she laboured to pull her boots out of the deep snow with every step. She glanced over her shoulders, making sure the zombies were following her. A small swarm of rotting corpses shuffled through the snow, leaving behind a trail of blackened blood, their frost-bitten skin peeling off the bone and falling into the pristine snow.

"Come and get me," Dana screeched. Not wanting to lose the stragglers in the back, she kept uncomfortably close to the herd. The wind swept their putrid decaying stench over her. They lumbered towards her, growling, their lifeless eyes fixed on her. She pulled out the handgun, not wanting to fire it so close to the cabin, more to make sure it still existed. It made her feel better, not so alone in the woods. Then another thought raced through her mind, remembering who had given her the weapon. "Where are you, Hank?" Dana's plea was shrill, desperately needing to hear his voice. There was no response. Her insides twisted into tight knots. The zombies wouldn't give her a moment to think, pressing their ruthless pursuit.

Dana developed a plan in her head. She remembered a tactic Hank would often use when they lived at the cabin just outside Corner Brook. Zombies were dumb creatures, attracted to the closest distraction. She remembered Hank would lure them away from cabins as they rummaged for food, making a racket. Too stupid to realize that there was more flesh inside. If Dana could lure them away from the light of the cabin, they would discover the thundering claps of gunfire.

"Over here!" she announced as she turned towards Grand Falls. The resounding echo of gunfire made it easy to stay on course through the thickening woods. She looked back over her shoulder, noticing the zombies' heads angled towards the noise, attracted to it.

"Keep up, you bastards!"

Dana trudged through a dense cluster of branches at the edge of the clearing, the pine needles scratching at her jacket, poking at her tender flesh.

CHAPTER 24
GUTS

The footsteps made it as far as the first step. The boards creaked once, then the owner walked away investigating no further. Eric and Aliyah breathed a sigh of relief. Then, a soft silvery light filtered into the kitchen from the living room. At first, it reminded Eric of a television set, the way the shadows flitted and danced. It turned out to be the light from the halogen flashlight as the guard walked past the front window. They remained in silence for what seemed like an eternity, making sure the biker was long gone before standing. A lengthy sigh escaped Eric's lips; he wasn't aware that he'd been holding his breath.

"That was too close," Aliyah spoke first. "How did you know the door would be open?"

"Just a hunch."

Aliyah walked towards a stainless-steel fridge, yanking the door open. She leapt back when the light flipped on. "How the hell do they have electricity?" Her jaw drooped to her chin as stunned disbelief gave way to a sly smile. "Check this out." She reached into the fridge and hauled out a glass bottle filled with white, creamy liquid.

"Is that milk?" Eric asked, licking his lips.

Before giving her answer, Aliyah unscrewed the cap, and tilted her head way back, taking three large gulps before lowering the bottle. She belched loudly. "Better believe it."

"Don't drink it all." Eric reached out his hand.

"Do you think they put the empties on the doorstep every morning?" Aliyah mused as she passed Eric the glass bottle. She rummaged through the fridge, the bottles and cartons making an absurd amount of noise as they shifted across the glass shelf.

As Eric chugged the remaining half bottle of milk, a thin mustache was all that survived, "Anything to eat in there?" Eric's stomach growled with anticipation.

"There's not a lot—a few containers of leftovers." Aliyah slid the plastic containers out, dropping them onto the counter next to the fridge. She kept routing through the shelves on a mission to find hidden treasure. "Looks like fresh eggs in a carton."

Eric ripped off the lid and the gamey scent of moose meat wafted out. "Can you believe it?"

"And you want to destroy this?" The words came out muffled, Aliyah's head buried deep in the fridge.

"This isn't how everyone in this city lives." Eric needed to remind himself of why he was here. "They're holding people as slaves here."

"No shit?" Aliyah stood up, holding a plate with a wedge of apple pie, uninterested in anything else. She threw open a drawer, rummaging through the utensils until she located a fork. Before she dug in, she placed the plate on the counter and walked over to the sink. She turned on the tap, running the hot water over a cloth and placed a healthy amount of dish detergent on it. "It's been ages since I've washed up." Aliyah sounded like she would cry. Her hands trembled as she wiped her hands. Filthy brown water dripped into the sink, revealing ebony skin beneath the grime. Now with all that dirt washed off, vivid red cracks and dry skin stood out. She cringed in pain, layers of skin rubbing off as she scrubbed. Tears welled in her eyes, but she forced herself to keep going. Her face disappeared behind the dish towel. She rubbed gently. When her hands dropped from her face, red-rimmed eyes, large and wet, looked ready to bawl.

"Are you okay?" Eric asked.

Spots of blood and blackened dirt remained on her cheek, her eyelashes were glued together in clumps, and deep cracks split her trembling lip. "It feels so good to be clean. But it hurts so much." Aliyah fought back the tears. "Kinda bitter sweet, you know?"

"Yeah, I know what you mean." Eric felt a tinge of pity for Aliyah. With all that dirt removed, he could see she was a youthful woman, a college kid. Her tender, emerald eyes looked like she'd been sitting next to a campfire for too long, the smoke puffing them up.

"Well, we should get moving I guess." She didn't sound like she wanted to leave.

Eric shook his head. "We need to eat something first. We can share this moose?" Aliyah nodded her head in agreement. Eric opened the cupboard doors above the sink, finding it filled with grey plates and bowls. They didn't look like glass, but when Eric moved one, the weight startled him. The dish slipped out of his grasp and clanged against the plate beneath. The boisterous noise gave birth to a loud thump, accompanied by rustling movements upstairs.

"Shit." Aliyah's hand shot over her mouth too late, her glistening eyes wide with fright.

Eric took Aliyah's hand and dragged her towards the living room, his eyes searching for a hiding place. Deliberate foot steps thudded upstairs towards them as the staircase shifted and groaned. The room, sparsely furnished, consisted of a two seated chesterfield pushed against the far wall, just below the window, a leather recliner, and an oval wooden table. With no time remaining, Eric's fingers found the hilt of his revolver. Drawing it, he aimed it towards the staircase, the wooden railing obscuring his view. A white socked foot swung into view first, followed by another. His finger held against the trigger, waiting for a clear shot, only the meaty part of the calf muscle was in range.

"Mom?" a sleepy voice called out. Eric aimed the barrel towards the ceiling as a teenage boy, no older than fifteen, drifted down the stairs, rubbing his eyes. "What was that noise?" He asked in an alarmed but exhausted yawning tone. His multi-coloured striped pajamas were too small for him, a strip of flesh poking out between the top of his pants and the hem of his top. The boy's eyes shot wide open, frozen in terror, glued to Aliyah, drawn towards her bizarre appearance.

"Hey," Aliyah's voice remained hushed and calm, she held her hand out cautiously, "it's okay."

"My mom told me to stay away from strangers." The boys voice rattled with fear.

Eric feared that the boy would scream at any moment. He discreetly lowered his revolver, placing it back in his hip holster as Aliyah captured the boy's attention. "What's your name?" Eric tried to defuse the situation, recalling his youth trauma training from before the apocalypse. The boy didn't respond. He trembled, his eyes darting back and forth between the two strangers in his home. "It's okay, I'm a police officer. At least, I used to be. You know, before all the rotten people showed up."

"My name," the boy was stammering, "is Carl." He choked out his name.

"It's nice to meet you, Carl, I'm Officer Jones, and this is Aliyah." Eric used his police officer voice.

The boy took a deliberate step backward, his lip quivering. "Don't come any closer."

"Is your mom here?" Eric kept his tone mellow, but inside his blood pressure was rising. The teenager was a powder keg waiting to go off.

"No, my mom is out on patrol." Carl stared down at his feet, refusing to make eye contact, but maintaining an aware view of the intruders.

"She left you here alone?" Aliyah burst out, appalled by the situation.

"Please just leave." The little boy's voice was scarcely more than a thin whisper. "Get out of my house." The octane of his voice rising a few tones.

"It's okay, kid," Eric tried to reassure the boy. "We won't hurt you."

"Get OUT!" Carl screeched, stomping his foot against the floor. His cheeks turned bright red. He squinted his eyes shut and raised his chin towards the ceiling. "GET

OUT GET OUT GET OUT!"

"We need to shut him up." Aliyah stepped forward with her hands out in front, her thumbs pressed together, forming a triangle between her arms and chest, her fingers spread wide. Eric reached out for her elbow, his hand snatching a handful of her jacket for a moment. She yanked her arm away.

"HELP ME!" Carl screeched like a banshee.

A sliver of light swept over the living room window, giving it a ghoulish radiance. Eric wrapped his arms around Aliyah's waist, forcibly dragging her back into the kitchen. Carl threw the front door open, ran outside in his bare feet, screaming for help. Eric could hear voices calling back to him.

"It's too late, we need to get out of here now." Aliyah allowed her body to go limp, her stomach convulsing as she sobbed. All her pent-up emotions released at once. "Hey, Aliyah," Eric dragged her body and bones through the kitchen, "you need to snap out of this." Her boots scuffled across the floor as her limp legs wobbled and swayed back and forth. He threw the back door open and a gust of wind roared through the house, ruffling all the papers and curtains.

"What are we going to do now?" Aliyah found her feet beneath her and stood up. She wiped away a tear. A streak of grime smeared her face from the cuff of her jacket.

The melodies of chaos rang in the streets of Grand Falls. Automatic gunfire barked in the crisp night air. Men and woman yelled. Boots slapped off the pavement and crunched the snow beneath them. Engines rumbled to life. Houses sprang to life with the turmoil, lights flicked on in the windows. Doors opened and slammed. The boom of guns intensified into a continuous chorus of clapping thunder. Hungry growls added to this symphony of destruction, providing an eerie undertone.

"We'll sneak to the other side of town and join the Republic." Eric pushed his way outside onto the patio, scanning the backyard for movement. "Come on, now's our chance while they're distracted." They trudged through the snow in the backyard, running along the perimeter of backyards, lined by fences and aged oak trees. The streets swarmed with panicked crowds, all running in the opposite direction. The great East Coast herd had arrived in Grand Falls, falling on them with a savage hunger for flesh.

Eric led the way. It was difficult navigating the backyards; the snow was knee deep in most places. Fences slowed them down, and occasionally the trees were too tight together, forcing them to go around. They avoided the streets unless it was unavoidable to cut across the road. Too many people with too many eyes. The disastrous harmony grew stronger in the background, even as they distanced themselves from the herd. Gun shots boomed in deafening echoes. Voices carried shrilly on the wind. Cries of suffering, defeat, and anguish prevailed over the scattered outbursts of victory. The shuffling swarms of undead made the ground tremble beneath their advance.

"Wait," Aliyah called out from behind Eric, grabbing his jacket in between Eric's shoulder.

"What is it?" Eric snapped.

"Look," Aliyah pointed towards a van. Headlights poked out behind a modified grill made from the heavy iron bars from an old fence, the black spikes pointing outwards. "Do you know how to hot-wire a car?"

"Yes," Eric responded, investigating the street, "hold up." Two bright lights approached the curve in the road where the van was parked. The rough grumble of two motorcycle engines drowned out all the commotion behind them. They pulled their bikes into a driveway out of sight, hidden from view by the van.

"We could use that van," Aliyah suggested.

Eric heard the engines choking and dying as the clamorous roar of gunfire rose anew. "Wait here, I'll take care of this." He pulled his revolver in front of his face.

Aliyah meant to protest, but Eric sprang out of the bushes and rushed the bikers. The passenger door opened first, and a body lumbered into the seat, the van rattling on its suspension as he slammed the door shut. Eric crossed the lawn and was running through the driveway, drawing attention from the driver. The man fumbled for his pistol, lifting his leather jacket, revealing a black gripped handle sticking out of his pants.

Eric fired a round into the man's chest and the impact staggered him. His arm reached out for the hood of the car, an iron spike driving into his diaphragm. A yelping howl exited his throat in a sharp gasp moments before his body went limp, the iron spike holding him in place. Suspended in a permanent slump against the grill, his arms rested over the makeshift bumper, his fingers spread across on the hood. Eric was on the street now. The passenger tried to exit the van, but his arm was entangled in the seatbelt, suspending him in place. Another well-placed round found its mark. The bullet shattered the glass then buried deep into the man's skull. He slumped against the seatbelt and his free arm dangled out of the door, his face pointing towards the ground.

"Nice shooting, cowboy," Aliyah said with astonishment. "Now they'll know we are here."

"It's just another round fired," Eric explained, "it'll blend in with the rest. A stray zombie put down in a hurry." He walked around the front of the van. "Can you come give me a hand?" He noticed that three spears had impaled the biker. There was one poked into the soft flesh just above the pelvic bone, and another pierced through the man's stomach, intestines dangling from the hole and blowing with the breeze. The last one was lodged into the man's chest, the iron tangled in between the rib cage. As Eric placed his arm around the dead man's shoulder, he waited for Aliyah to do the same. "On the count of three, pull."

"One,"

"Two,"

"Three." They both pulled. A spiked iron head tore the man's stomach lining open with a sickening pop, unleashing a half-digested meal over the grill as the man collapsed onto the pavement. As the noisome spew filled Eric's nostrils, the spoiled air stung the hairs in his nose. Somehow, the foul odor reminded him of spoiled hamburger seasoned with too much garlic mixed with dry mustard. It was overpowering and acidic. Then his stomach betrayed him, returning the milk, which had soured in his stomach, up his throat. It splashed over the dead man's shoes. Aliyah laughed morbidly. "Are you kidding me?" Eric glanced up at Aliyah. "Doesn't that smell bother you?"

"I've walked amongst the dead for the better part of the apocalypse." As Aliyah stepped over to the passenger side, she unclipped the seatbelt. With a reverberating thud, the biker fell to the road unceremoniously. "This is only the third time I've left that herd." She pulled herself into the van. The door groaned on its hinges as she used it to hoist herself up. "Come on, before someone else comes searching for them."

With a tormented expression, Eric stumbled his way to the driver's seat, continuing past the open door towards to the deceased driver. His stomach slid out of the gaping wound, laying between his legs, ripped open and on display. A trail of intestines led back to the pulpy red mess. The disgusting scent lingered. Eric covered his mouth and nose with his left hand, pinching off his nose with his thumb and forefinger. With a deep sigh, he knelt beside the corpse. Rummaging through his pockets, he found the keys to the van stuffed into the inside pouch of the man's vest, which was slick with blood and stomach fluids. The keys jingled, the loop heavy with dangling skulls. Eric heard stories that members of the Silver Skulls Cartel added a skull made from pure silver for every soul they took.

"Hey," Aliyah shouted, "hurry up."

Eric jumped into the driver's seat and turned the key, the ignition turning with it. Surprisingly, the motor purred a low, gentle rumble. Eric rested his head against the steering wheel, drawing in deep breaths, allowing himself a moment's reprieve. "Okay, let's get out of here." Eric put the car in drive. He wasn't sure where he was, but he could see the highway that split the town of Grand Falls-Windsor in half. One of the side roads nearby would lead them there—he just needed to find the right one. He kept his eye out for a sign, and it didn't take long. They came to an intersection where a large green sign directed them to take a right turn. An old two-story motel stood on the corner, the lights shining out of the second and third-story windows. They'd boarded the first floor up with gigantic pieces of plyboard. Old cement barricades, once used as highway dividers, created a defensive perimeter, leaving enough space in between to walk the trenches. That made Eric think about what Smith was doing, if he was waiting in the trenches or still on his way back.

CHAPTER 25
TOLLERABLE LOSS

Smith hunkered down in the front-line trench, leaning his back against a frozen wall of earth. As they waited anxiously for the right time to spring the ambush, he sipped the last of his coffee. Tarps rustled in the wind behind them, the loose nylon slapping softly in the breeze. The concealment allowed them to keep the fires and stoves burning late into the night without being detected. In times of stress, Wade realized morale would suffer. So, he developed a plan to keep it high during this crucial stage. In a thankless task, runners brought coffee and soup to the front lines. Smith was warming his hands with his fourth cup, feeling a little jittery from the caffeine. The sounds of the battle raged on, inching closer as time crept along at a snail's pace.

"This is always the worst part," Wade spoke over his mug, "people get nervous waiting. Imagination starts playing tricks."

"That's why we try to teach discipline," Smith agreed. "It's the first thirty seconds of a gunfight that will determine who you can trust."

"You can't win a battle in thirty seconds," Wade poked his head over the breach, "but you can damn sure lose it."

Smith nodded his head. "How much longer before they get here?"

"If we can assume our runners can funnel them to us with no unforeseen issues," Wade considered the facts silently, his eyes wandering off to some unknown whiteboard, "I'd say thirty minutes, give or take ten minutes either way."

"They sound a lot farther away than that." Smith took his own look at the no man's land. "I'm surprised at how long this is taking, actually. They are holding their own much better than I would have imagined. They got to be getting close to running out of ammunition by now though."

"My guess is they have lots of ammo left. Otherwise, they would've fallen back a long time ago." Wade shook his head. "Once they realize they can't defeat the horde, the retreat will be fast and furious."

"How long have they been fighting?" Smith checked his wristwatch. He didn't take note of the exact time it started, but at least fifteen minutes had run off the clock since the shooting began.

Wade looked down at his wrist. A dim green glow lit up on his old Timex. "Thirty-seven minutes since the first shot rang out. Twenty-three since this constant rate really intensified."

BANG

A thunderous boom echoed over everything and shook the night sky. "The snipers are taking aim." Wade stood up. "Won't be long now. They'll lure them into the ambush any moment now."

Smith got to his feet, looking down the line to his right. The Republic of Newfoundland soldiers were standing too, the signal stirring them into action. "You expect those traps will work?" Smith aimed the barrel towards the ambush sight, looking for any signs of movement.

"If we're lucky," Wade sipped his coffee then set the mug in the snow in front of the trench, the heat melting the surrounding snow. "They won't be expecting it. When they get caught off guard, that sniper rifle is deadly accurate and will dismantle them. I've seen a man's head implode from one of those rounds." Wade chuckled. "It sent his friends standing nearby scurrying back into their holes."

Smith roared. "I guess these bikers are in for a rude awakening. What booby traps did you prepare to slow them down?"

"Just trenches with spears drove firmly into the ground. We covered up the holes with branches. When they step on them, they'll impale themselves. I doubt it'll kill them," Wade peered behind him towards a rustling noise, "but It'll take them out of the fight."

"Kebabs for the zombies," Smith chuckled, unable to help himself.

"Exactly what I was envisioning." Wade glanced over at Smith, a slanted grin on his face. "We soaked some pits in gasoline. When they fall in, we have it rigged to ignite."

"Do zombies like roasted meat?" Smith asked, trying his best to sound serious. "Anything else?"

A wide grin stretched Wade's lips. "We dug a few claymores out of storage."

"Where did you find those?" Smith asked, astonished. He couldn't remember the last time he saw a claymore.

"My basement," Wade responded matter-of-factly. "A retirement present from an old friend."

"That's so cool, I hope I get something exceptional when I hang up my boots."

Branches cracked behind them as a runner approached. Smith looked down at his coffee cup and it was empty. He would take a refill just for the warmth; he didn't think his body could handle any more caffeine. It sounded like someone was running in place towards them, the snow crunching beneath their boots in a consistent patter. After a brief, confusing moment, Smith realized there were two pairs of feet walking out of step making all that commotion. "Hey, how are things going back there?"

"I would ask you the same question?" a familiar voice countered.

"Who's that?" Smith inquired. "Please tell me you brought coffee?"

"Sorry, can't say I did." Eric's feet stood at the edge of the foxhole, sending a miniature avalanche of snow tumbling down the side.

"Eric, you made it back." Smith let out a sigh of relief. "It's great to hear your voice."

"Outstanding work out there," Wade interjected. "How big is that herd? Is it as large as they say it is?"

"It's bigger than you can imagine," Aliyah answered.

Wade and Smith stared wide eyed at the newcomer. "You found reinforcements?" Smith asked.

"I found something better." Eric shot Aliyah a sly glance, sharing a secret between them. "Where's Tina?"

"She's in the rear lines, in a trench with a stove." Smith turned his gaze back to no-man's-land. "She wanted to help."

"I realize you won't like this," Eric started, "but after you spring the initial ambush, there's been a change of plans."

"What's up?" Wade was interested in Eric's alternative strategy, leaning forward to make sure he heard every word. "Did you see something out there?"

"You'll never believe what I saw." Eric tilted his head towards Aliyah. "I am still having trouble comprehending what I saw out there in that swarm of undead."

"What was it?" Smith worried about the alpha zombies, wondering if they were natural evolution or if they'd been created in a lab.

"Meet the leader of the pack." Eric gestured towards Aliyah. "This is Aliyah. And she can walk amongst the dead."

Aliyah waved her hand like the queen, a foolish smirk plastered across her face. "Hey, guys."

"That's not possible," Smith argued. Wade nodded along, his throat making that *uh-huh* noise. "You're telling me she can manipulate the herd?"

"Yes," Aliyah defended herself, "I can. Once this is over, I'm taking the herd towards the underground Pharmakon base."

"Wouldn't that be splendid," Wade snickered. "A solution to all of our problems. Jesus walks amongst us."

"I've seen her walking amongst the ranks of the undead," Eric explained. "Listen, I know it's hard to believe, but you just have to trust me."

Smith stared into Eric's hazel brown eyes. "Your eyes might be the colour of shit, but I'll give you the benefit of the doubt."

"Besides," Wade interrupted, "if she's full of shit, those rotters will eat her up and we'll be in the same position as before. I say let her try." He looked at Aliyah, his eyes full of apprehension.

"It doesn't change the Republic's plans," Smith stated for the record. "The Republic will fall back with me and regroup. We won't be going off on any suicidal mission with you to destroy Pharmakon. These people will need a break."

"That's fine with me." Eric answered. "I'll take Tina into town."

"We need every capable person on the line!" Wade snapped.

"He's right," Smith added. "We could use you here."

"My mother is in there somewhere," Eric said, "and Tina is the only other person other than you that would know where to search."

"I don't know about this." Wade didn't sound impressed. "It's your call, Smith."

"We can spring a second ambush from behind." Eric pleaded his case. "I'm sure the others they have trapped there will fight with the Republic."

Smith looked between Eric and Wade, trying to evaluate both options. "Eric, you might be one of the best shots we have. I could employ you here, but I can't stop you. If you're going, take Bowers as backup. I can't afford to lose you on some fool's errand."

"Thanks, but you need him here." Eric extended his hand and Smith shook it. "I'll make sure you don't regret this."

"I parked my jeep…"

Eric cut him off. "On the road. I know. I'm parked next to it."

Smith placed the jeep keys back in his pocket. "I didn't want you driving it, anyway." Everyone laughed. "You go find Tina. I'll get Bowers to gather some ammunition and assault rifles." Eric nodded his head, leaving with the woman without saying another word.

"You sure that's the best plan?" Wade asked once they were out of ear shot.

"I've learned to trust Eric." Smith recalled the first time they met. Eric was a leader; people would follow him no matter what. "If he believes he can do it, I'll let him try."

The hungry growls of the undead pack were closing in on them now, enveloping them. Anguished cries and screams of terror, punctuated by the resounding blast of the sniper rifle, rang out in the distance. "Steady now!" Smith called out, confident that the symphony of undead would drown out his voice. "Take your time, make every round count."

The wind carried the decaying stench of rotten flesh as confused cries accented the revolting odor. Then an abrupt break in the storm offered an unobstructed view through the forest. Smith could make out shadowy figures running between the trees, darting in and out of view. Thunderous gunfire bellowed from the sniper rifle, the frequency of the shots intensifying like the maddening tick tock of a death clock. Automatic gunfire barked in rapid bursts. Branches rustled, roots snapped, and snow crunched beneath the fleeing feet. At any moment, the members of the Silver Skull Cartel and the Highway Hangman would spring the trap. Smith's heart thudded in his chest; every shadow sent his pulse racing.

Without prompting, a deafening explosion sounded off in the distance, giving birth to a series of pained screams. Tree trunks splintered and cracked as the claymore exploded, dispersing an array of scrap metal in a wide arc. The sound of branches bending and sliding into the trenches bellowed with deep *whomps*, followed by hard thumps as the hole swallowed them up. Surprised screams turned to pure agony, the wooden stakes impaling the unfortunate bikers who crashed into the traps. As shadows gave way to forms, features took shape: terrified faces, their mouths hanging open, lower jaws quivering with fear. The hollow groans of the undead nipping at their heals. Some unfortunate bikers, looking over their shoulders, plunged into the pits on top of their friends. A man tried to jump over the hole, landing awkwardly on the opposite side. His knees buckled and broke, sending him tumbling backward onto the spikes below. People maneuvered around the trenches, leaving behind their friends to die without a second thought. They spilled out of the thickened woods and into the open space.

No man's land.

It was Wade who fired the first shot. A carefully aimed round that collapsed a man's ribcage. His breath deflated from his lungs in a sharpened shriek. Smith pulled the trigger again, letting off a sequence of calculated shots. Thin plumes of smoke drifted over his face as rounds exited the chamber. All at once, the trenches barked automatic gunfire, yellow muzzle flashes going off like a sky full of fireworks. The rifle ate through a magazine of ammo greedily. The hollow thunk of empty rang in Smith's ears. "I got to reload," Smith informed Wade.

"I got you covered." Wade fired his rifle deliberately, not wasting a single round. He timed his reload almost in sync with Smith's first shot, only a few seconds off.

With no cover, the bikers found themselves trapped in the danger zone. They couldn't go backwards, the undead horde too much to handle. With no alternative options, they pressed forward, returning fire blindly. At first, it seemed like victory would be assured, but the bikers continued to spill into no man's land, sending a barrage of bullets in their direction. A few rounds kicked up snow in Smith's face, forcing him to duck into the foxhole for cover. Wade continued his methodical assault, empty casings falling from the rifle into the frozen dirt with a clattering jingle.

"We have to fall back," Smith said out loud to himself. "FALL BACK!" He growled the order as he got back up, firing rounds down range. "Fall back!" he repeated.

They carried the order down the line, from trench to trench, almost like a rolling echo. Smith observed the bikers racing towards them, the fear of what was coming behind them far more powerful than the prospect of death. Without faltering, he sent two well-placed rounds into the closest enemy. The body convulsed and shuddered, collapsing into the frozen ground with a loud thump. Boots pulverized his backside, breaking his limbs and ribcage, his fellow bikers scrambling out of the woods like rats from a burning building.

"Go, I'll cover you," Wade called out over the bark of gunfire.

A dreadful scream rang out from the trench beside them. It was the first casualty of the Republic. A man laid sprawled face first in the snow, blood spewing from his neck like a river. His partner, unable to see the vital fluids spilling out of the newly opened hole, tried to roll him over. A barrage of bullets riddled his torso. Convulsing, his blood turned into an aerosol spray. Smith emptied his magazine towards the bikers, bullets finding homes inside of chests and tearing through limbs.

"Go on," Wade urged, "get the fuck back there. They'll need you." Wade slapped a fresh magazine into the housing.

Smith was at a loss for words. His jaw hung open, a restrained sigh escaping his parted lips. "You fall back right after." Smith couldn't think of anything else to say. Wade nodded his head in agreement before turning his attention back to the task at hand. Smith knew that Wade wouldn't be talked out of staying, and time was running out. He leapt out of the trench. Keeping low to the ground, he scrambled towards the rear lines. Bullets whizzed past his head. Tree trunks exploded into splinters and slivers of wood. The ground exploded around his feet in puffs of snow and dirt. Men fell into the surrounding ground. Then, dying screams rang out amongst the Republic as the tides changed horrifyingly fast.

The soldiers in the rear line took cautious aim towards the bikers, making sure not to hit their own members. Return fire was slow, hardly enough to keep the pressing bikers heads down, but it bought Smith enough time to reach the rear lines. Now with the fleeing soldiers out of the line of fire, the rate of fire picked up to a feverish rate. Smith looked for Wade but couldn't spot him amongst the hail of bullets. The bikers reached the Republics front lines, using those trenches for cover. Their numbers were divided in two directions. One group fired at the Republic's rear lines, while a much larger group fired at the threatening throng of undead behind them.

The forest boomed and thundered, tree trunks creaking and groaning as they toppled over. It sounded like a bulldozer approaching. The ground trembled and shuddered beneath the stampeding horde. Smith recognized this would be their best chance to regroup.

"Fall back to the highway," Smith ordered, keeping his gun focused on the bikers aiming in their direction.

The rear line gave way to a steep slope, making their retreat much easier. Those who survived the first wave made their way down the bank, getting out of harm's way. The members of the Highway Hangman and Silver Skull Cartel made their last stand against the undead before their eventual retreat. Smith led the Republic, whose numbers had taken a considerable loss, through the woodlands. Dismayed cries of defeat rose from most of the survivors, not realizing that this was all part of Smith's plan. Although the losses were greater than he preferred, he'd expected them. It was a tolerable loss.

CHAPTER 26
RED MIST

Frigid winds cut through Jason's jacket, numbing his hands and feet. The bike's four-stroke engine grumbled and choked. Tracy had her arms wrapped around his chest with her hands buried in his pockets. His ears tingled as tiny daggers of pain pierced his earlobe. The headlights cast a narrow cone of light over the road, the snow dancing through its beam. Out of the corner of his eye, Jason saw the bright light reflecting in the chrome tailgate of a vehicle. He eased off the throttle as they neared the curve of the highway ahead. The light settled over an orange jeep with a tire mounted on the tailgate.

"Why are we stopping?" Tracy leaned her chin over Jason's shoulder, her breath hot on his neck.

"It looks like there's a number of tracks leading into the woods there." Jason pointed towards the jeep. "We might find some help there."

"You think it's worth stopping?" There was a hint of annoyance in her tone.

"We need food and a place to stay for the night." Jason guided the motorcycle into the ruts leading up the short bank towards the jeep. When they got closer, Jason recognized the camouflaged vehicles stored beneath a leafy canopy. "I expect we are in luck."

"I think stopping here is an awful idea." Tracy grumbled something else under her breath, but the breeze carried it away. "Pharmakon will be on our tails any minute. I don't want to get caught here."

"All right, let's just take a minute to check out the jeep." The front tire spun in place, digging itself further into the deepening snow. Not wanting to get stuck, Jason let the bike roll backward down the slope before parking it. He left the engine idling, the light pointed towards the jeep. "If you could keep your eye on the highway for Pharmakon, that would help."

"Jason," Tracy responded with a sense of urgency, "don't be too long."

"Relax, we are far ahead of them." Jason suspected that they had an excellent head start on them. He peered through the back window of the jeep. "Jackpot." A light machine gun rested across the length of the trunk, the barrel and stock touching the walls on either side. To Jason, it looked like a weapon wielded to combat a tank or shoot down aircraft. He tried to open the hatch, finding it locked in place. Too busy trying to find a way into the jeep, Jason ignored the roaring blare of approaching gunfire.

"Wait for me Jason," Tracy shouted, running up the hill.

Spinning around, he expected to see a convoy of lights rolling down the interminable stretch of highway. The road dissolved into the darkness, the looming hills behind them shrouded in a black blanket. He saw the terror in Tracy's wide eyes as she raced towards him, her feet slipping in the snow beneath, her hands clawing at the snow, dragging herself forward. Suddenly, as if a bomb went off, Jason heard the turmoil behind him. Gun shots thundered in the forest.

"Get back to the bike," Jason called out.

"Get down on your hands and knees." An authoritative voice boomed, emerging from the woodlands. "Who are you?"

Jason thought about running, but Tracy was already kneeling, her hands cupped behind her head. He stumbled a few steps forward and knelt beside her. "I'll get us out of this," he whispered to his wife.

"I told you it wasn't a good idea," she snapped at him.

"Now's not the fucking time, dear." Jason shook his head angrily. He watched as a group made their way out of the woods, recognizing the man in the lead. "Is that you, Smith?"

The man halted, "who's that?"

Jason recognized the voice. There was no doubt. "It's Jason Cook. Is Eric still with you?"

"Holy fuck," Smith replied with a gasp. "There's no time to explain. Get in the jeep, we got to get out of here."

"What's going on?" Tracy demanded.

"I'll explain on the way into town." Smith opened the jeep, unlocking the doors with the electronic remote.

"Is Eric alive?" Jason got to his feet, pulling Tracy up with an outstretch hand.

"I honestly don't know," Smith said, breathing heavily. "We'll find out soon enough. Get a move on." Smith jumped in the cab. The motor sputtered to life, choking on fumes. A woman sat in the passenger seat next to Smith with a rifle slung over her shoulder.

Jason dragged Tracy by the wrist, pushing her into the backseat. Before Jason got into the jeep, terrified screams rolled out of the forest, chased by the hungry growls of undead. He slammed the door shut as Smith shifted the gearstick into reverse, backing down the hill and spinning the jeep to the left to face town. In the rear-view mirrors headlights shined like stars. Jason glanced over his shoulder and saw a line of vehicles heading towards them. "Shit, we got company."

"You don't know the half of it." Smith shifted into first gear. The jeep lurched forward, the gears grinding.

Jason turned to Tracy. "We need to get rid of that remote."

"If we throw it out the window, they'll find it right away." Tracy held the black controller in her grasp. "We need to find that herd."

"You'll wish you never crossed its path," Smith said as he moved into second gear, a convoy of green trucks driving just behind him.

"Where is it?" Jason asked.

"You'll see it soon enough." The woman turned around. Jason recognized her.

"Is that you Sherry?" Jason shouldn't have been surprised to see her with Smith, but it astounded him all the same.

"Hey, long time no see." Sherry stared into the side mirror. "Friends of yours?"

"It's Pharmakon security," Jason explained. "They're after me."

"Aren't they the bastards who started all of this?" Smith asked with a mischievous smirk on his face.

"Yeah," Tracy responded, her hand covering up the logo embroidered on her breast pocket.

"Well, they're about to face off against their own creation."

A black mass shuffled through the headlights ahead. At first, Jason couldn't pick it out. It looked like a black tidal wave washing across the road. Then his jaw dropped to the floor. It took a moment before he realized that it was the massive herd crossing the highway, spanning across the bare strip of pavement and into the trees on either side. "How the fuck are you going to get past that?"

"Can you reach the assault rifle in the trunk?" Smith popped the canvas top of his jeep. Forced by the wind, it fluttered before it tore backwards, buckling in half and slapping off the trunk once before ripping off the hinges.

Jason reached behind the seat. The weapon weighed a ton. He struggled to lift it without the strength of his legs to back him up. Tracy helped him guide it over the seat, the wind whipping her hair around in a wild mess. "I got it." Jason strained his voice over the rustling gusts of air.

"You can rest the barrel on the top bar." Smith turned his glance to Sherry. "Get back there and open a way through."

Sherry maneuvered her way to the back seat, helping Jason balance the cumbersome machine gun on the metal bars that the roof used to rest on. The barrel jutted out over the front windshield. She cocked the action;

a loud metallic thunk seated the first round. "Cover your exposed skin," she peeked down at Tracy, "spent rounds can get extremely hot."

Tracy tucked her head into her chest, sheltering her face with her arms. Sherry pulled the trigger. The muzzle belched orange flames, jolting violently against the metal bar, rocking the entire jeep. The jeep's headlights caught the crimson mist as the zombies turned into a viscous pulp. A slight clearing in the road opened as the pavement burst into puffs of rock and debris. Zombies' heads exploded, cranial fluids spraying in all directions, corpses collapsing into heaps. Smith pressed down on the gas. The jeep sped through the closing opening. The suspension jostled as they drove over the fallen corpses. Bones shattered and fluids squished beneath the jeep's tires. Their convoy made it through the opening just in time before the herd filled the gap with more shuffling corpses staggering over the snow bank.

"That should slow down Pharmakon security," Smith laughed as they approached the city limits. Corpses roamed the streets. The living ran around firing off weapons and fending off the dead with whatever they could find. It was chaos, a living hell. The roads were clogged, laden with panic and frantic screams. "All right, aim for the bikers. I think it's time we put them down."

CHAPTER 27
METAMORPHASIS

"There are too many of them." Frightened, Aliyah searched for a path out for Tina and Eric. The van shuddered and rocked as the grill crunched the bones of the undead. The suspension bounced and bolted as the tires ran over unknown body parts, vibrating the dashboard with a nauseating consistency.

"We have to make it to the Mount Peyton." Tina held onto the back of the driver's headrest, hauling herself into the front. "I have to kill Ted and rescue the twins."

"I don't think he can survive this." Aliyah swerved the van, dodging a cluster of zombies. Then, the front bumper caught the hip of a haggard corpse, spinning it three hundred and sixty degrees. Its back smacked off the side of the van as the crushing blow sent the creature collapsing face first into the pavement.

"If anyone can survive this, it's that fucking rat," Tina snapped. "If you don't want to go on, let me out here."

"Don't be foolish," Eric broke his silence, "you'll never make it through this herd. Aliyah, please. We need to get to the hotel now. It's our best chance at surviving."

"What makes you believe it's still standing?" She swept her hand across the road, strewn with the shuffling corpses.

"Let's say I just know that it is. It's where they would have taken anyone not able to fight." Without another word, Tina sat back down in the backseat. There was no convincing her otherwise; her mind was made up.

"It's on the outskirts of town. Other than fleeing, it's the safest place to be." Eric rocked forwards as a head was ripped from its shoulders, rolling over the windshield like a bowling ball. "Goddammit," he mumbled. Blood smeared the fractured windshield, splintering outwards like a spiderweb. "There it is." Eric pointed his finger. Hidden beyond the treeline, the hotel rose above the forest.

"I see it," Aliyah replied, "how do I get there?"

"It'd be quickest if we cut through the trees on foot," Eric answered. "Maybe even the safest."

"If we get stuck in the streets, we won't survive." Tina spoke up from the backseat, eager to find Ted. "I say we go for it."

"What do you think Eric?" An oncoming motorcycle forced Aliyah to cut the wheel hard to the left, narrowly avoiding it. "Jesus Christ!" Aliyah cried out as they peppered the van with bullets. They all tucked their heads down by their legs, shattered fragments of glass raining over them. The van jerked over the curb, rocking them up and down as the wheels bounced onto the lawn.

"They figured out we aren't part of the Cartel." Eric kept his head down, gripping the rifle and cocking the action. A dull metal thunk echoed.

The tires were spinning in the snow over the lawn, losing traction and sinking through to the frozen ground beneath. Aliyah slammed on the brakes just before they smashed into the front steps. The van slid onto the paved walkway, providing the tires just enough traction to keep them spinning. She spun towards the driveway as a shower of bullets rattled off the side of the van.

"Keep your head down," Eric barked at Aliyah, grabbing hold of the wheel. "Just keep your foot on the gas."

Shards of glass fell into Aliyah's lap, getting tangled in her hair. She jammed her foot on the pedal. The van lurched and jostled, jerking forward as the tires caught the asphalt. Eric's arm spun the wheel and the van jolted forward. Aliyah pulled herself back up, finding the van facing another set of headlights. There wasn't enough space to avoid a collision this time, the grill colliding with the front tire of a motorcycle. The occupant was hurled from his seat and through where the windshield should have been. His neck ripped open from a jagged shard of glass, opening a gush of blood over the dashboard. The motorcycle crashed off the hood, crushing the biker's spine before falling off to the left. Aliyah screamed as blood dripped onto her knees, hot and steaming against her cold jeans. She lost control of the wheel as the body tumbled into the front seat, pinning Eric's arms beneath him. He struggled to free himself, but it was too late. The van smashed into a parked pickup. Jerking forward violently, the back tires lifted off the ground and crashed back down on the road. Aliyah heard the passenger door creak open. Groaning, Eric forced himself out, the hungry howling of the undead closing in on them. In the street, a lone pair of boots walked deliberately towards Aliyah's side.

Tina moaned in the backseat, mumbling incoherent-ly. Glass broke beneath heavy boots in the road. "What's going on?" Tina sounded far removed from reality. She reached out, grabbing a tuft of the biker's shaggy brown hair, lifting his face up, then let it fall with a thunk against the center console.

"Tina," Aliyah strained, "we need to get out of the van." The footsteps drew closer. She squinted into the rear-view mirror and saw a hulking figure approaching with a shotgun held across his chest.

"Tina..."

The sudden blast of a shotgun cut Aliyah off. She cov-ered her head with her arms to shield herself from the shot. Buck shot pelted the van, denting the panels and explod-ing the mirror. Wires, plastic, and glass dangled from the side-view mirror, the rest falling to the pavement below. Out of the corner of her eyes she saw a flash rush over the crumpled hood. The mangled metal crunched beneath Eric's weight as he slid across, the revolver drawn to his face. As he landed, he fired. The bullet whizzed past the window, colliding with a sickening thump behind Aliyah. A deep, pained scream accompanied another thunderous shotgun blast. Eric dove to the ground, out of sight.

The van door slid open. "Come on." The commotion outside brought Tina up to speed. Aliyah tried to open the door, but the twisted metal had jammed the door in place. She struggled to push it open with her shoulder, the latch mangled and stuck in place. "Tina, I need your help." There wasn't enough room for Aliyah to climb over the dead biker. A hand slapped the driver's side door, reaching for a handle, followed by a long, aching groan. Eric's head appeared in the side window, his face twisted in a grimace of pain. "Jesus Christ," Aliyah gasped in relief, "you're alive."

"No thanks to your driving." Eric coughed into his palm, leaving behind a splatter of blood.

"Let's get you out of there." Tina appeared next to Eric, ushering him aside. "I'll get that, cowboy." It took three hard yanks before the door opened, the hinges screeching.

Aliyah stumbled out of the van. "Over there." She pointed to a path that ran alongside the road. "That's probably the quickest path."

"All right, let's go." Tina took off, thrusting the butt end of her rifle into a zombie's face. A flower of blood blossomed from its nose as it tumbled backwards and collapsed with a hard whack. Eric raced off to join her, side stepping the fallen corpse as their hands reached out for him. Aliyah needed to catch her breath. She followed close behind, walking amongst a small congregation of the undead.

The Mount Peyton Hotel captured all the falling snow-flakes in its radiant glow. All the lights on the first floor remained off, but it seemed they occupied every room on the second and third floor. As the throngs of undead roamed the streets, they trudged towards the building like moths to a flame. Eric and Tina rushed towards the board-ed-up entrance, zigzagging in and out of trouble. Aliyah was trying to catch up to them, running straight through the pack without being recognized. Without dread of the horde, she screamed hoarsely at the top of her lungs, distracting the zombies, drawing their attention to her.

When Tina reached the front door first, she tried to pull it open, rattling the beams boarding it up. Even from twenty feet away, Aliyah could hear Tina's frightened holler. Then Eric yanked on the door. The crack opened enough to see the shadows inside, but the boards held firm. The scuffling corpses were practically on them now, and there wasn't enough time to muscle the doors open. "Get out of there!" Aliyah called out. "There's got to be another way in." She examined the perimeter, looking for a window they'd neglected to board up or with a loose plank. Her eyes scanned the side of the hotel and saw they'd sealed each window shut. Out of the corner of her eye, a rusty fire escape led up the side of the building all the way to the roof. "There!" Aliyah ran towards the ladder.

Not wasting any time, Eric and Tina rushed towards the fire escape. The lower rung hovered eight feet above the ground. They used the cement barricade to get leverage, hoisting themselves up just in time. As decrepit hands reached out for their legs, Eric leapt off the blockade, capturing the third rung under his armpit. Tina wasn't waiting for him, she was already on the second-floor landing, her hand stretched down for Eric. Now that they were out of danger, Aliyah breathed a sigh of relief, taking a moment to catch her breath. The vile stench of frozen meat and fetid shit soiled the air, stinging at her nostrils. No matter how much time she spent walking amongst the herd, she would never grow used to the rancid stench.

"Are you coming up?" Tina called out over the growls beneath. A small pack of zombies gathered at the barricade, reaching their hands up for their prey.

Aliyah didn't know what dangers lurked inside the suites at the Mount Peyton Hotel. Oddly, she felt safer amongst the undead; there was no chance she would catch an errant bullet from them. "I'll wait for you here." Aliyah cupped her hands to funnel her voice. "Once you're inside, I'll lure them away from here for when you're ready to escape." Aliyah watched Eric and Tina climb up the fire escape, disappearing behind the edge of the roof. Aliyah wandered along the perimeter of the inn, the stray zombies following her, drawn towards her presence. When she'd gathered most of the undead corpses, she meandered back towards the town, her followers shuffling close behind. They stumbled through the blizzard, their groans asking her questions. "I will feed you," Aliyah said, never knowing if they understood her, "just follow me." She waited as they stumbled past her, drawn to the smell of fear.

She observed a biker run across the street, firing a handgun into a crowd of zombies. Two bodies shuddered and convulsed, collapsing to the ground. The biker dumped an empty magazine. It clattered against the sidewalk, his tired hands fumbling to reload. "Goddammit," he croaked in frustration. He pistol-whipped a zombie with the butt-end of the handgun, embedding it into the creature's skull. When he tried to pull his hand back, his grip slipped off the bloodied handle, and the corpse tumbled into his legs, causing him to stagger backwards. He threw a wild left hook and dislocated a female zombie's jaw with a sickening crack. But she just kept coming, her mouth hanging wide open in a red snarl, rotted teeth lining her gums. He thrust his boot into another decrepit creature, bending the zombie in half like an accordion, buying himself enough time to stumble away. Aliyah watched him scramble between two homes, not willing to die without a fight.

The streets were littered with corpses, most of them recently deceased, their flesh still holding on to its last colour, growing pale and smeared with blood. Carnage enveloped her. Gun shots boomed from the remaining bikers, fighting desperately until the end, searching for a way through the crowded streets. Aliyah spotted a leg twitching and kicking at the pavement, trying to walk before it was standing. An inexperienced kid wearing a black and pink jacket was progressing through the transformation. Overwhelmed with a cruel sense of guilt, she laughed, thinking it was ludicrous that this was an easier transition than puberty would have been. She examined the kid's limbs jitter and shake, fumbling to its feet. It moved in the jerky movements of a newborn baby, stiffly standing up, incapable of coordinating its movements. Learning to operate its jaw, the kid's mouth snapped open and shut, rattling its teeth.

"Fuck this," Aliyah grumbled to herself. She turned around, unable to stomach the sight of the young child transforming anymore. Just beyond the tree line, the lights of the hotel shined like a beacon, pulling her back towards humanity.

She made the trek back towards the hotel when the rumble of a diesel engine caught her attention. Three sets of bright LED headlights lit up the streets as the thunderous roar of heavy machine gun fire drowned out the sounds of the herd. She dashed towards the trail in the woods, not wanting to get caught in a hail of bullets. When she reached the entrance, she peered over her shoulder at the source of the firepower. A modified tank, covered in sleek black armour, rolled through the streets. The treads crushed the asphalt beneath, tossing up the debris behind it. A man wearing a black Kevlar vest operated a mounted machine gun atop the tank with a large shield protecting him from the empty casings. None of the shooters paid any attention to Aliyah, too focused on the chaos in the streets. Their bullets mowed down the living and dead in one savage display of superiority.

Aliyah ducked into the trail, racing towards the hotel. She needed to warn Eric and Tina about this unknown threat. If they didn't deal with it, it could annihilate everything in their path.

CHAPTER 28
LIFE AND DEATH

"Are you positive she'll be here?" Eric whispered, his hushed voice carrying up the empty stairwell.

"If she's still alive." Tina crouched next to the entrance to the third floor, keeping below the tiny window in the large beige door. The light overhead buzzed and flickered, almost pulsing with life.

"Do you know what floor?" Eric asked.

"My guess would be the second floor." Tina peered through the window, checking the hallway for movement. When they opened the door a gust of wind ripped through the staircase. "The rooms on that floor aren't as nice—or as safe. If the zombies could gain access to the building, they could scramble their way to the second story. But you can only access the fire escape from the third floor; so it's possible to evacuate from there, but not the second floor; you'd be trapped...I wish I remembered that when we were by the door. If it weren't for Aliyah, we'd probably be dead right now."

"Don't beat yourself up about it." Eric noticed an iron gate on the landing between the second and third floor.

"They installed gates as added protection. That's re-sourceful."

"Keep it down." Tina held her index finger over her lips, ducking down. The hollow echo of footsteps approached. They paused just outside the door. She expected to see a face appear, but a door opened and gently closed in the hallway. "He must have been going back to his own room." Tina breathed a sigh of relief.

"How will I know where to look?" Eric wasn't letting up.

"Weren't you a cop?" Tina asked impatiently. "They patrol the second floor. If you can take him out quietly, bark out her name. She'll probably come to the door."

"Okay, thanks." Eric descended the first three steps silently before swinging back around. "Is there a guard on your floor?" Eric sounded concerned, leaning back up the stairs.

"No, it's a bit of freedom for the privileged members." Tina could still picture Father Willis standing in front of the white board, explaining the rules. His stubby little fingers tapping against the board to make sure she was following along.

"If you get into any trouble," Eric locked eyes with her, "call out for help. I'll be up in an instant."

Tina nodded her head, holding her assault rifle close to her chest. "Room 328 if you hear me."

Eric smiled. "I'll drop by when I'm finished. Then the three of us can leave."

"What about the rest of the people here?" Tina started down the stairs. "They're innocent. We can't just leave them here to die. And do you think your mother will survive out there?"

"I can't stay behind. They need me out there." Eric took a step forward. "We could use you, but so do these people. Would you be willing to protect them until Aliyah can lure the zombies out of town?"

"I can do that." Tina would not leave those people to fend for themselves. It wasn't fair what was happening to them. "Once you find your mother, bring her upstairs. I'll watch over her."

Eric mouthed the words *thank you* but no sound came out. He turned and headed down the staircase. Tina edged the door open, finding the hallway empty. A long brown carpet with black swirls ran the entire length of the corridor. There were eight doors on each side. The wallpaper was a yellowish cream colour, outdated and worn, peeling off the wall in some places. Overhead, long fluorescent lights, the shades decorated in a floral pattern, hummed the constant buzz of electricity. She didn't bother to creep down the hallway, instead choosing to walk as if she belonged there, hoping that if people discovered her, they wouldn't grow suspicious. Everything around her seemed to fade into the background as her vision tunnelled towards the numbers 316. She stood in front of the door, her hand resting on the handle. The push bar gave way when she applied pressure. Without resistance, the unlocked door swung open.

Locked by a bolt, Eric reached his hand through the iron bar, hunting for the release. Looking down, he noticed the latch was on his side; he let out a thin chuckle as he slid the bolt over with a dull clunk. The gate swung open as if it were spring loaded. Eric reached out, grasping the cold iron bar before it could smash against the wall behind it. He stepped through, allowing the door to rest against the wall because he didn't want to fumble with it in case Tina found herself in trouble. The door to the second floor didn't have a window. There was a push bar on this side. Eric applied pressure and the door swayed open.

A man wearing a Highway Hangman leather vest roamed the hall, a pistol dangling from his hip in its holster. He spun around. A baseball bat hanging loosely from his left fist scuffled across the carpeted floor. "Hey, Dennis, you're here early."

When he recognized it wasn't his relief, his jaw dropped wide open. Eric dashed down the hallway towards him. The man fumbled for his gun, dropping the bat to the floor. His fingers fumbled with the handle, forgetting to unbutton the holster. Eric drove his shoulder into the biker's gut. A rush of air escaped the man in an exaggerated gasp. The biker tangled his arms around Eric's waist.

They both tumbled into the wall. As Eric fell backward, the top of his head busted the gyprock, dust falling into his hair. Pinned against the wall, the biker freed an arm and thrust his fist into Eric's gut. The impact knocked the wind from him. There was only one place to go. He slumped to the ground and swiped at the back of the man's leg, dropping the biker to his knees. They rolled across the carpeted floor in a tangled embrace. Eric ended up at the bottom, looking up just in time to watch a fist blot out his vision. He felt the pressure building behind his eye, instantly swelling. Tears blurred his vision. Then he raised his forearms in front of his face just in time to shield the next blow. A third jab glanced off the side of his head, just below his ear. With each blow, the ringing pain radiated through his skull.

Eric rolled the biker off, sending him stumbling into an end table. The leg shattered, spilling the vase onto the biker's back. It smashed, sending a shower of sharp glass over the carpet. The biker grunted, straining to get to his feet. Eric rolled onto his side and stretched his arm out for the baseball bat. The glass nicked his fingers as they curled around the taped handle. He turned just in time to see the tread marks of the boot. When he ducked to avoid the vicious kick, the biker stumbled off balance, his legs spread apart. Without hesitation, Eric drove his forearm into the man's groin. Brought to his knees, the biker yelped in misery, crashing to the floor.

Doors opened along the hallway, drawn out by the excitement. Eric ignored it, focused on the biker as he squirmed and withered, his palms cupped over his crotch. He raised the bat over his head, smashing the shade over the light, and drove the barrel down with savage intent. Glass followed the head of the bat, colliding with the man's skull with a sickening smack. As the wood splintered, the man let out one disturbing scream. Blood spilled from the biker's ear, the left side of his skull caved in from the crushing blow. Now, breathing heavily, Eric noticed he was on display, strangers' eyes starting at him. Worried murmurs rippled through the hallway.

He looked around at the frightened faces. Most people

weren't brave enough to step into the hallway, peering out at him from the crack in their doors. Eric dropped the bat. It thumped against the floor, the carpet dulling the impact. "I'm looking for Pauline Jones." He spoke through laboured breathing. Not sure if anyone heard, he repeated himself.

"Eric?" Stella's voice rose behind him.

He turned around as his mother stepped into the corridor, an expression of disbelief plastered on her face. "Mom," Eric rushed down the hallway, "you're all right." He exhaled a sigh of relief. They embraced as people wandered into the hallway.

"Are you here to help us?"

"Will you save my baby?"

"Can you get me out of here?"

"Please don't let them hurt us anymore."

Eric stood in the hallway, everyone looking to him for help. "We're trying to free you, but you have to stay here for now. There are too many roamers in the streets."

A thunderous blast upstairs interrupted Eric's speech.

Ted slumped in the loveseat, his right ear touching his shoulder, drool running down his chin. He was wearing his soiled white robe, the waist drawn over a sullied wife beater covered with an assortment of stains. His right fist grasped a short glass filled with amber liquid, slanting towards the floor. His other arm dangled over the armrest, the remote control on the floor below. The end credits to an old movie scrawled over the screen, a familiar song winding down. His scrawny legs poked out beneath the bathrobe, a pair of open backed black sandals on his feet. He looked like a skeleton of his former self. Stubble grew dark over his face; he hadn't shaved since their confrontation. The bruises around his eye had turned yellowish blue around the edges. She could see where her nails had clawed his face, still not healed.

She experienced a pang of revulsion for ever having loved this man, waves of heat coursing through her body. Ted's head lolled to the left, his chin coming to rest on his breast bone, a delicate snore filling his throat. He hacked but didn't wake up. Tina noticed the girl's bedroom door drawn closed. They'd saved her the last time but wanted to make sure they weren't a part of what happened next. This would have to be silent; she didn't want them to wake up and rush out into trouble. She crept over to the couch, picked up a pillow, monitoring Ted the entire time. His chest rose and fell in a slow rhythm, drawing shallow, drunken breathes. She detected the sickly-sweet bourbon on his breath, could practically taste it. Not wanting to make too much noise, she unslung the assault rifle and concealed it beneath a pillow just in case he gained the upper hand.

The carpeted floor deadened the noise of her approach, allowing her to stand over Ted. She glared down at him, holding the pillow over his face, gathering her hatred for him. His eyelids fluttered open, as if weighed down, and a bewildered expression screwed up his face. Tina pressed the cushion down, driving her knee into his gut forcing the air from his lungs into the pillow. His arms flailed in the air and found her hair. He yanked violently, tugging her head down into the other side of the pillow. She let out a muffled shriek as he jerked his entire body. The sofa toppled over and they crashed to the floor, Tina landing on top. His eyes opened wide with hatred. Her knees dug into Ted's elbows, restraining his arms. He kicked his legs, unable to generate enough force in his intoxicated state to push her off. His heels scuffed over the carpet, searching for footing that wasn't there.

Ted screamed her name as her fingers found his throat. She watched with satisfaction as his skin turned purple. Froth formed at the corners of his mouth. The veins on his face swelled to where they were about to burst. She dug her thumbs into his windpipe, feeling it collapsing into itself. Ted's eyes bulged out of their sockets, blood red around the rim, and the whites turned a vivid shade of maroon. He clawed at the flesh on Tina's wrist, his finger-nails scratched the length of her forearm, drawing blood. She leaned all of her weight onto her wrists, feeling Ted's larynx crush beneath the pressure. His arms flopped to the floor with a lifeless thump. Tina refused to believe he was dead, continuing to apply the pressure long after he was deceased.

A loud creek as the bedroom door opened caught Tina's attention. She glimpsed Katie over the toppled chair, pausing in the doorway in her pink nightgown, her entire body shivering. She gawked at Ted's legs poking out from behind the loveseat.

"Are you okay, Katie?" Tina's voice quivered.

When the young girl didn't respond, Tina worried. Katie just stood there, shuddering. Tina looked down at Ted, his jaw hung wide open, thick, bloodied froth oozing and bubbling from the corner of his mouth. His face was an extreme shade of purplish blue, and his eyes were inhumanely wide, filled with broken blood vessels. "Everything will be just fine, Katie."

"Is my dad going to be okay?" Katie asked warily, tears wetting her eyes, rolling down her cheeks in a steady stream. Tina could see her sister, Jessica, fast asleep in the bed, sawing wood, with the blankets pulled up to her chin.

"Honey," Tina forced herself to sound calm, her tone coming out flat and hollow. "Your father turned." A wave of remorse washed over her with the audacious lie.

"Where did you go?" Katie said sleepily, the confusion compounding her condition. If Tina were lucky, this would all be a dream to Katie in the morning.

"I went to search for our friends." Tina monitored Ted, afraid that he would turn before she could get Katie back to bed.

"That's not what dad said, he told us you've been evil." Katie began to sob as the realization settled in over her. Tina watched her last shred of innocence shatter before her eyes.

"Listen, sweetie, I love you." Tina heard footsteps in the hallway. "Me and your dad were just in a big fight, and he said some words he didn't mean." She overheard someone just outside the door. "Do you remember Eric and Stella? They're here now." Tina remembered that Katie and Stella used to play games in the Jones' cabin.

"Is that," Katie glared at Tina's hands, "blood."

Tina held up her palms. Her forearms were riddled with rich crimson and clawed scrapes. There was flesh embedded beneath her fingernails. "Sweetie, it's not what you think."

"Did you kill my dad?" she demanded, not seeming to understand any part of the equation but knowing the answer, anyway.

"I had too." Tina stuttered.

"Father Willis is here." Katie rubbed her eyes, trying to wipe away the fatigue.

When the door swung open, Tina turned, her jaw dropped to the floor. Father Willis stood in the entrance with a Bible clutched against his chest. "Ted, I overheard a commotion…" His voice caught in his throat. He stared wide-eyed at Tina. "What have you done?" he asked in a trance.

"Listen to me, Katie, get inside your bedroom and close the door," Tina ordered. Katie tried to protest. "Now, honey. Just stay in there until I come to get you." Katie stomped away, slamming the bedroom door shut. Behind the closed door, Jessica complained about the noise to her sister.

Father Willis stood before her, his robes flapping open. The belt holding it closed had come unraveled. With a giant yellow stain covering his white boxers, it looked like he pissed himself. When he moved, his bare chest and flabby stomach jiggled. Suddenly, he leapt awkwardly, almost falling flat on his face. With nimble grace, Tina sidestepped the charge. Father Willis braced himself against the couch, his right hand brushing the cushion hiding the assault rifle. "You'll pay for what you've done here. Through my hands, God will strike you down." Every word jumbled together in a drunken gibberish.

Tina maneuvered herself into position, lining herself up to make a move for the concealed weapon. "Your days of being a false prophet are over."

"The end times are upon us, and only the chosen will survive." He slurred his speech, leaving sizeable gaps between each word.

"Fuck you." Tina provoked the preacher, wanting him to go back on the offensive. "And fuck your God," she hissed, letting out her rage.

When Father Willis stepped forward, his feet tangled into Ted's leg, and he lurched forward as Tina dodged his outstretched hands. She watched him smash into the wall on the other side, letting out a deep, pained grunt. Snatching up the rifle, she turned towards the preacher. Suppressed laughter rose, but Tina forced it back down. It was the sight of Father Willis curled into a lump against the baseboard that made her snicker. Along the far wall, a splatter of blood smeared the wallpaper from where he busted his nose open. Tina walked towards him with confidence, knowing he was defenceless. She checked the toggle, making sure it pointed towards semi-automatic. Without prompting, Father Willis rolled onto his back with a hard thud, his face wincing in pain, blood trickling from his nostrils.

"Where's your God now, preacher?"

Never one to back down, Father Will opened his mouth to reply.

BANG

As the back of his head burst open with a wet pop, cranial fluid and grey brain matter splattered across the floor and walls. Katie screamed in the bedroom. Both of the twins cried. Tina heard the bustle and commotion of footsteps outside in the hallway. Father Willis's gaze was glued towards the heavens with his eyes fixed towards the bright light of the ceiling. Tina pulled the barrel out of his mouth, his jaw full of burnt and pulped flesh. His tongue had turned into a gelled paste, filling in the bottom of his mouth.

Eric burst through the door, huffing. "Tina, are you okay?"

"I've never been better." Tina placed the assault rifle on the end table. "I'll check on the kids, make sure they're okay."

CHAPTER 29
FROZEN

Dana stumbled through the dense cluster of tree branches, shoving them aside as she squeezed past. With the roar of gunfire close and the herd nearby, she was besieged by danger. Drawn towards the sound, she found herself wedged between them and the town. Glowing against the pitch-black skyline, the radiant city lights hovered just beyond the trees, casting a dizzying array of shadows over the ground. Then Dana stumbled into a clearing. The wind had swept most of the snow away, leaving behind dead, yellowed grass poking up through the thin dusting of white. As her foot slipped on the ice, she caught her balance just before she fell. The ice creaked and groaned beneath her weight; she could see the fracture lines spreading out like a spider's web all around her boot.

Without realizing it, she'd found herself in the middle of a bog. It was a hundred metres across to the far side. There wasn't enough time to backtrack with the swarm of undead dangerously close. One misplaced step or fall would turn into a catastrophic mistake. Her only option was to push forward, hoping the ice would hold her weight. She tried her best to stay close to the tufts of grass, finding the ground soft in places. Water seeped up from the ground around her boots, sending a chill up her spine. The ice was thick in some spots, thin in others. Sometimes she'd break through, submerging her foot in the frigid waters below, landing in the mucky bottom. The mud tugged at her boots as she worked to pull them free. More than once she almost fell over.

When she heard the tree branches rustling, she peered over her shoulder. A decrepit corpse struggled his way through the thick tangle of branches, not smart enough to push them out of its way. Branches slashed at the frostbitten skin, shredding it from the bone in clumps. Coppery red blotches riddled its face and arms. Deep cuts had ripped a sinister grin on its face, exposing its rotten teeth. More of the undead made their way through the tree line, spilling into the bog that Dana was struggling to navigate. The first zombie to reach the ice took a hard tumble. Its feet slipped out from underneath it and up above its head, crushing the ice beneath its back as it landed hard. Water splashed out all around it. As the decaying creature sunk below the ice, half submerged into the shallow waters, its limbs flailed trying to pull itself out of the crater it created.

Dana did her best to keep her focus straight ahead, making certain she didn't take her eyes off the lights. She jumped from one patch of grass to the next, avoiding the ice wherever she could. Sometimes her feet crashed through the ice near the edge of grass, finding the ground in the shallow water. The roar of gunfire raged nearby,

drowning out the guttural growls of the undead behind her. She reached the other side of the bog without
too much trouble. Her feet were wet and cold, her legs
were scrapped up, and every muscle ached. There was no
doubt she would catch a cold when all of this was over.
She glanced over her shoulder and saw she'd put considerable distance between her and the pack of zombies.
Ahead, towering over the trees, in the breaks between the
falling snow, Dana studied the outline of a building. Light
spilled from many windows. It was as good a place as any
to search for Eric.

Like a tribute to the days before zombies roamed the
earth, the Mount Peyton Hotel towered before her, just
across the highway. Without taking her eyes off the building, she dashed across the street, avoiding treading on
the corpses buried beneath a thin shroud of freshly fallen
snow. Guns blared in the background as bright muzzle
flashes shined brightly like fire flies. All around her,
screams rang out as the battle raged in town. Focusing
ahead, Dana spotted a lone body shuffling towards the
hotel. With a sense of grace, it wandered with a deliberate
pace towards the edge of the building. Long coils of hair,
too filthy to recognize the original colour, rested midway
down the creature's back. Not wanting to deal with the
creature, she raised the pistol, her finger applying slight
pressure against the trigger as her mind weighed the options. If she fired, she'd risk the possibility of luring more
of the undead. Dana lowered Hank's weapon and con-
cluded that she would try to sneak up behind the creature

and take it out.

She moved lightly on her feet, the snow crunching beneath every stride. The noise caught the creature's attention. Its head jerked towards the sound but didn't bother to turn around. Dana kept low, slowing her pace as she approached. The zombie reached a concrete barrier and stepped onto the top, stretching its hands out for a ladder. "Hey!" Dana shouted out, realizing it wasn't a walking cadaver.

A girl spun around, her face marred by filth and deep lines. "What do you want?" she demanded accusingly.

"I'm searching for my husband," Dana explained, "I need your help."

"I don't care who your husband is," the woman hauled herself up the fire escape, her feet searching for the bottom rung. "Or why he would be here?"

"I don't know where he is." Dana climbed onto the concrete barricade, judging the distance between the ground and the ladder. "But he's somewhere in this town."

"What makes you think he's here?" The girl was already on the second landing, peering down over the rail at her.

"He brought these zombies here," Dana watched the girls eyes widen.

"Your husband is Eric," she declared matter-of-factly.

"Yes, are you part of the Republic?" Dana hoped so. If not, Eric would be in serious trouble.

"I suppose I am." The woman made her way down the ladder, holding out her hand for Dana. "Your husband is inside. My name is Aliyah."

Dana took Aliyah's hand, making the jump for the ladder. Her hands found the third rung as the bottom rung jammed into her hip. Aliyah yanked on her jacket until Dana's feet found the metal bar. "Thanks," Dana was breathing heavy, "lets go inside."

"Hold up," Aliyah said forcefully, "I don't think it's safe in there."

"What do you mean?" Dana sensed a surge of panic rise.

"Can you let me go first?" Aliyah asked.

"I'm coming with you," Dana insisted, "this isn't up for debate."

As Aliyah gauged Dana's stoic expression, she realized that there was no changing her mind. "Stay close and don't get in my way."

They ascended the fire escape, the metal frame rattling beneath their weight. When they reached the roof, the wind was relentless and bitter. A gale passed over them, unimpeded by any trees or buildings. Snow didn't build up in the roof except along the far edge where the wind piled it against the ledge and held it there. Dana braced herself against the powerful gusts so she wouldn't get swept off her feet. Aliyah reached the stairwell first. She struggled to pull it open, but the wind worked against her. Dana helped her yank the door open, and they both dashed inside as the wind slammed the door shut behind them.

There was a rising jumble of voices coming from below as they walked down the staircase to the third floor. Aliyah made her way in first then held the door for Dana. People lined the hallway along both sides, remaining in their doorways. They stood in their bathrobes and pajamas, chatting amongst each other about being rescued by a man and woman. "Eric?" Dana called out. Faces in the crowd turned towards her, but no one acknowledged her. There was a modest crowd gathered outside a room at the end of the hall, four residents were carrying something out. Dana couldn't see through the crowd. She followed behind Aliyah who was making her way through the clusters of people. When they got close enough, Dana realized they were carrying a body out of the room. They'd wrapped it in white sheets. A giant red blotch sullied the blankets where the man's head pressed against the cotton. "Eric," the words fell out of Dana's mouth onto dead ears. No one answered. She felt lost, helpless to fight back the atmosphere of dread.

"Dana?" Eric's voice called out to her from inside room 328.

Dana froze in place, not convinced she'd heard his voice, or if she imagined it. Aliyah disappeared inside the room, leaving her behind. The surrounding voices blended together, turning into white noise. An eternity passed by. Dana was frozen in time. Her mouth opened to call out, but all that came out was a silent gasp. Eric emerged from the room. "Is it really you?"

Eric rushed forward, pulling her close, holding her firmly against him. "What are you doing here?" His voice swelled with happiness tainted by frustration. "It's not safe here, they could have killed you."

"You too," Dana replied.

"Stay here with mom and Tina." Eric placed his hands on her shoulders, staring into her eyes. "They need you to help keep these people safe."

"Eric, we have to go," Aliyah said, tapping her foot impatiently.

"I'll meet you on the roof," Eric added. "I just need a minute."

Aliyah trudged through the crowd towards the end of the hall without another word spoken between them.

"Eric, I don't know if I can leave you again," Dana sobbed. "I'm afraid I won't see you again."

"If you stay here, I'll know where to find you when this is all over," Eric whispered, but there was a sense of desperation in his eyes. "If I don't warn Smith about Pharmakon, we won't be able to save everyone here. I need to go, but I'll be back. I promise."

Dana stared down at his feet, holding back her tears. "Okay, but I'll never forgive you if you don't come back."

Eric held her close, rubbing his hand on her pregnant belly. "I will be back. I love you." Dana stood silent, not returning the words. "Don't be mad."

"I won't say it until you come back."

"Fair enough." Eric hugged her once more, kissing her on the mouth. "I'll see you in the morning." Eric kissed her belly, then left without looking back.

Dana felt a hand on her shoulder. "He'll be back." Stella pulled Dana into an embrace. "We are all going to be okay."

CHAPTER 30
THE GAME BEGINS

Jason tossed the empty magazine into the snow then jammed another into his rifle. Empty casings spilled across the asphalt and around Tracy's boots. Smith and the other soldiers watched their backs, protecting them with well-placed shots. They established a defensive perimeter amongst the abandoned vehicles. The dead struggled to get around them while the living couldn't get a clear shot. All around them, bodies strewed the roads, piling up on top of each other in some places. The deceased didn't think twice about stomping over their fallen comrades. Jason ducked behind the van as a group of Silver Skull Cartel members wandered into the street from an alley, stumbling into a pack of zombies.

They fought heroically against the undead, taking down a dozen shuffling corpses in a hail of bullets, but the undead just kept coming. The bikers had depleted their ammo. Having nowhere to run, they fought back with brute force. The tallest biker wore brass knuckles, which made a wet sucking noise with every punch he landed. The group remained alive amidst the horde for a commendable amount of time, worthy of praise, but they ultimately fell to the dead. Bodies were littered around them in a tight circle. Their screams lasted an absurdly long time as the zombies repaid the favor with their rotten teeth.

To conserve ammunition, they hovered behind the cars, obscured from view, only firing when a group of corpses lurched towards them. Jason used a long, rusted piece of iron rebar to defend against the stray zombies, while Tracy wielded a giant machete Smith had given her. The others attached bayonets to their rifles, jabbing over the cars like spears over shields. All the muscles in Jason's arm felt like solid stone and every effort to aim his rifle hurt his shoulders. His eyes stung from being awake so long and his feet ached and throbbed. But if Tracy was feeling worn out, she wasn't showing any signs. She actively sought stray corpses, leaving the safety of the group to take down stray walkers.

A deafening, mechanical growl rang out as brilliant lights illuminated every shadow in the street. It forced Tracy to twist her head towards the commotion. "Shit."

"What is it?" Smith called out, turning to confront the disturbance.

"Pharmakon found us," Tracy ushered a thin whimper. She held the remote in her palm. "What do you want to do with it? If we keep it, they'll be on our tails forever."

"If they're on my tail," he snatched the remote, "I'll lead them away."

"Get down!" Smith barked, grabbing Tracy by the collar and yanking her to the pavement. Catching them by surprise, a barrage of automatic gun fire rained over their heads. With a savage ferocity, sharp metallic *clunks* rang out around them, the steel and aluminum twisting and breaking apart around them. Three light armoured vehicles drove up the street, all in a straight line, the first one laying down suppressing fire. "We need to move." Smith pulled Tracy up to her feet.

"Where are we going to go? We are fucking surrounded," Bowers said, his voice riddled with desperation.

The gunfire erupted again, except this time the bullets mowed through the shuffling corpses in the streets. Body parts disintegrated and heads vaporized into a fine mist. The large calibre rounds ripped through decrepit flesh with ease. With his head down, Jason searched the street for an escape route. The only suitable spot he found was a tight alley just behind them. "Over there." He pointed towards the alley.

"We'd be toast if we head into the open like that." Smith pressed his back into the turned over car. Gas was leaking from the tank, splashing onto the surrounding ground. "We need a distraction."

"It's me they're after." Jason looked over at Tracy. "You guys get out of here while I distract them." Smith didn't disagree, he just nodded his head at him. Not sure what to say next, Jason was hoping Smith would have a better strategy, but there wasn't one. An eerie calm fell over the street, the dead all but eviscerated from existence. Jason got to his feet and unslung his rifle, holding it in his right hand, the strap brushing against the road. He let out a lengthy sigh and stepped out from behind the destroyed vehicles.

"Wait," Tracy snatched Jason by the shoulder, yanking him backwards. "I have a better plan."

With an emphatic bang, the doors opened on the tanks. They could hear the heavy thud as boots landed on the road. Someone was giving commands, ordering them into formation to sweep the area. "The target's signal was last seen in this area. Do a sweep and find his body. David Steele wants proof of Mr. Cook's death," a sharp voice barked. The pitter patter of boots scuffled across the pavement towards them.

"Pretend to take me prisoner," Tracy said loud enough so the entire group could hear her. "When they're all distracted and concentrated on us, you guys ambush them. If we act swiftly, we can steal a tank when all of this is over."

"I can make that work," Smith agreed. "Excellent idea. We have little time, they're almost on us."

Tracy nodded at Jason. He smiled a stupid grin, grabbed her by the waist and spun her around, holding her against him with a gentle but convincing hold, his arm wrapped around her neck. "Let's do this." They walked around the edge of the discarded vehicles, a line of Pharmakon security aimed their weapons at them. Attached to their rifles were bright lights, narrowed to a straight beam that acted both to illuminate and guide their sights.

"Freeze!" a hidden voice boomed. "Let her go, Mr. Cook. This is over."

"It's over when I say it's over." Jason raised the gun above his head, holding it in one hand by the grip. "I want to talk to David Steele."

"I'll give you one piece of advice." A soldier strode

forward, lowering his weapon. The beam of light made a big circle over his black boot. "We don't need her. Either you give her up now and we let her live out the rest of her life in a cell. Or you can pretend you're fucking Rambo. I won't hesitate to kill you both. Dead or alive. Those were my orders for both of you."

Jason let Tracy go, she stumbled forward, keeping in the line of fire. "Oh, thank God you're here." Tracy produced a sharp, shrill cry. A shot from behind the car rang out and the soldier convulsed and dropped to the ground. The other members of the security team looked around, perplexed by the origin of the shot. Before they could re-group, Jason and Tracy opened fire. Bullets pounded into the Kevlar vests. Soldiers twitched and rocked as rounds riddled their bodies. It didn't take long for the rest of the Pharmakon security to fall, withering and dying horribly on the ground.

"All right, let's get out of here before the dead swarm in." Smith rallied everyone towards the sleek black tank.

A thunderous roar erupted from the second tank. Bowers screamed in agony as a round shredded his stomach. His hands dropped to the gushing wound, trying to hold his organs inside the gaping red hole. Fluids splashed onto the ground at his feet, sullying his pants and boots. He collapsed to his knees. Slippery segments of intestine squirmed between his clenched fingers.

"Hands up, fuckers!" a booming voice demanded from the darkness. "That was a good try, couldn't have done it better myself."

Jason recognized the voice. "Reveal yourself, David. This is between you and me."

Devilish laughter cackled from deep in David's stomach. "Yes, my friend, it will be between the two of us. A fight to the death." Twenty security guards emerged from the darkness. "Your friends are free to leave." David stepped forward into the light, his hulking frame as wide as two of his men. "Go on, leave now or you'll all be dead. This is between the three of us."

"Three of us?" Jason asked.

"Did I fucking stutter? Do you think I didn't know about your wife helping you out?" David said bluntly. "But don't worry. Once I'm finished with her it will be between you and me."

The Pharmakon security advanced on Smith and the Republic, greatly outnumbering them. A man barked at them to get a move on, that it wasn't worth it. Left with no other choice, Smith prepared to lead his men away. Making matters worse, the turret on top of the tank was pointed directly at them. There was no way out of this for the Republic. Smith refused to risk their lives. "All right, men, fall back," he said with deep regret in his voice, "Jason, I'll figure out a way to stop them."

"It'll be too late by the time you come up with a plan," David was enjoying this, his laughter jovial. The security team marched Smith and his men far away. Only a handful of security guards remained by David's side. They stepped forward and stripped the guns away from Jason and Tracy. "Well now, shall we begin?"

As Eric drove the blade of his recently acquired fire axe down, the entire skull imploded inwards from the blunt

force of the impact. Softened by decay, the bone splintered into several fragments as brain matter oozed from
the rotting skull. In a swift motion, he kicked his boot into
the limp creature's gut and the axe slid out with a wet,
sucking noise. Yellowish red cranial fluid dripped from
the blade, the viscous liquid forming into big beads before
falling into the snow. When another zombie approached,
Aliyah grabbed the shambling creature by the shoulder
and held it in place. Eric brought the axe down again, his
shoulder burning with exhaustion. The blade sunk into
the skull with a sick thunk. Blood splashed over Aliyah in
a wide arc, the blackened fluids congealing on her face.

"There has to be another way through this mess," Eric
panted. Exhausted and starving, he was having trouble
finding the energy to keep going. "Why do they ignore
you?"

"The best explanation I can offer is that I appear dead
to them." Aliyah swung the butt end of the rifle into a
zombie's skull. It cracked open with a sickening pop. The
bone rearranged beneath the putrid flesh, shifting grotesquely to one side.

"What if I stink like them?" Eric stared down at the
corpse. "I'd be able to walk…"

"Before you go any further, let me stop you," Aliyah
cut Eric off and her hand darted out to grab the handle
of the axe. "I had a friend try that. It works. He roamed
through the herd with me."

"So why are you trying to prevent me from doing
this?"

"Because my friend became sick and turned. Let's just
say that smearing your face with decaying guts and taint-

ed blood is an awful fucking idea. You realize how many bacteria and diseases are coursing through their body."

"Shit," Eric replied. If he weren't so fatigued, he would have never dreamed of attempting something so outrageous. "Can you find any signs of the Republic?"

"There." She pointed towards flashes in the distance. "If we're lucky, it's the Republic."

"Or it's the Cartel." Eric's frustration grew. He was freezing, chilled to the bone. The snow was falling much heavier now, filling in the boot prints around them, making it virtually impossible to track anyone. "There has to be a sign somewhere." Frozen body parts stuck out of the white blanket all over the streets. Crooked arms and bent legs showed a wide path of destruction. As the wind howled around them, it drowned out the battle raging throughout the city.

"We have to keep searching." Aliyah didn't sound convinced. "Unless you have a better suggestion."

"Get down." Eric grabbed Aliyah's arm and dragged her to the ground with him. A shot rang out as the bullet whizzed overhead. Eric yanked Aliyah beneath him, shielding her with his own body. Once it was safe, he looked up to see their attacker. The biker wore a silver skull decal on his leather jacket, his face concealed beneath a skull bandana. With a cowboy stance, a pistol dangled loosely from his fist. The next shot sent up a shower of snow over them both, followed by an empty clicking sound. Not having any other options, Eric didn't waste time getting to his feet, bull rushing their assailant. The man countered Eric's charge, side stepping him and driving the butt end of his handgun into the back of Eric's head. Stars danced in his vision, a radiating pain at the base of his head. The blow staggering Eric and the axe slipped from his hands. He fell to his knees, crashing into the biker's legs. With their limbs tangled up, Eric fell on top of the biker. A loud gush of wind escaped the man's lungs as he fell onto the curb.

Eric reached out for the man's jacket and pulled himself into position with a handful of leather. A primal instinct activated and Eric head-butted the biker, driving his own forehead into the bridge of the man's nose. A wet splat beneath the bandana spilled blood into the fabric, soaking it and making it impossible to breathe through. With his hands fidgeting to clear his airway, it gave Eric the time he needed to grab his revolver. He aimed it towards the man's face, but the biker swatted it away before Eric pulled the trigger. The gun flew out of his hands and landed in the snow. He tried to reach out for it just as the biker bucked his body. Eric lost his balance and his hands slipped, his trigger finger landing in the man's mouth.

"AAARRRGGGGHHHHH!!!"

An intense, burning pain pulled at every nerve receptor in Eric's brain. He jerked his arm away, hauling back a bloodied hand, holding it in front of his face, a monstrous gap between his thumb and middle finger. Eric screamed out in anguish, his entire arm trembling with horror. The biker spat Eric's trigger finger into the snow, growling at Eric with unbridled rage. Before Eric could react, the man threw Eric into the snow and scrambled to his feet. He drove a boot into Eric's rib cage, the brittle bones splintering. The biker drove his knee into Eric's gut, forcing the wind out of him and pinning him in place. A sinister smile curled on his lips as he drew a blade from beneath his jacket. Glimmering light caught in the four-inch steel blade. He rose the knife above his head with both hands, his eyes glaring madly at Eric's chest. Eric swerved his body enough to avoid the wild blow, the blade digging into the frozen ground. The biker struggled to pull the blade free. Eric rolled back over onto the handle of the blade, ripping it from his grasp.

The biker grunted a deep, animalistic growl, glaring at Eric with threatening eyes, focusing on nothing else. He didn't see the knee hurtling towards his face. His nose blossomed into a grisly mess as his head snapped back with a vicious crack. Eric rolled over, trying to catch his breath in giant gulps of air. Aliyah slashed at the biker's throat with her nails, opening three red ribbons across the soft flesh. Instinct drove the man's hands to his neck, his fingers probing the damage. He pulled his hand back to examine the smear of blood, looking between his hand and Aliyah with astonishment. "You bitch." His words came out choked and wet. A bubble of blood burst on his lips as he collapsed, tendrils of blood running down his throat.

"Thanks," Eric said as he regained his breath, sitting in the snow. He held his hand against his jacket to contain the flow of blood from his severed digit. The wind swept over him, blowing snow up his back and into his face.

"Are you going to be okay?" Aliyah asked, concerned. "You're looking a little pale."

"I'll be all right." Eric felt faint, his voice flat. He peered down at his trembling hand. "Goddammit, why'd it have to be my trigger finger." The biker had torn it off just below the first knuckle. The joint stuck out of the shaved flesh just below.

"Is it that much harder to shoot with your left?" Aliyah asked, offering her right hand to pull him up. Eric glared at her for a moment, then took her right hand awkwardly with his left. "Sorry, it's a force of habit."

"That about sums it up," Eric groaned, his ribs ached. "It's instinct that gives me my advantage. Now that I have to force it, I could be late on the draw."

"I see," Aliyah said. "Well, let's hope it doesn't come down to that."

"Fat fucking chance I don't need this again." Eric bent over to pick up his gun and it sent a shiver of pain through his ribcage. He examined the chamber of the revolver then counted the rounds in his jacket pocket. "I'm down to eight rounds." He loaded the chamber and pocketed the rest. "If I don't make it…"

"You'll be fine."

"Just listen to me." Eric holstered his revolver, and picked up the axe, grimacing in pain. "Make sure Dana makes it out of here. I don't care how you do it, just promise me you'll keep her alive."

"I'm going to the Pharmakon base," Aliyah responded. "After that I don't plan on backtracking here."

"Where will you go then?" Eric felt a flare of anger rise when she didn't grant him his wish.

"That herd will follow me wherever I go," Aliyah said with disdain. "I'll make sure I don't put anyone else in danger, because I'm not willing to risk anyone else's life. I've tried. It never works out for me."

Eric couldn't disagree with her; he didn't want Dana

around this herd. "Okay, I guess I understand what you mean."

"Let's just find Smith." Aliyah walked away. "Maybe he'll help."

"Yeah, you're probably right." Eric glanced around at the anarchy that was destroying Grand Falls. The streets were choked with bodies. For every zombie they put down, three or four dead bikers or innocent citizens took their place. The herd stretched the length of town, and was as wide as the city limits.

"Shit," Aliyah said sharply.

"What is it?"

"Look, over there." Aliyah pointed towards an alley. Smith and two members of the Republic were on their knees, their hands raised above their heads in surrender. Men wearing black Kevlar suits aimed guns at Smith and his men, getting ready to execute them.

"Give me the rifle," Eric held out his hand, demanding the weapon from her. "Follow me." Eric snuck forward, keeping low to the ground. If Aliyah got lost in the blizzard, she could follow Eric by the drops of blood staining his path.

The barrel of a rifle pressed against the side of Jason's head. Guards on either side forced him to his knees. Another man held his head up, making certain he could see what would happen next. Jason struggled against the guards, but his only reward was a hard smack on the back of the head. Stars danced in his vision.

"Now, doesn't this look familiar?" David cackled like

a hyena. "What do you think, Jason? Just like good ol' times or what?"

"Fuck you," Jason said bitterly. "You're a coward. Fight me."

"Now hold on a minute. I just want you to have something to fight for." He stepped in front of Tracy, towering over her. His finger lifted her chin up. "Was he worth it?" Tracy didn't say a word and didn't move a muscle. "I think I'd like to have a little fun this evening. What about you guys, are you interested?"

"Whatever you have planned just get it over with, David," Jason roared. "I'm not up for playing games with you."

"Mr. Cook, I insist. You've made it this far and now its time for the final showcase." With an authoritative gesture, David slapped his hand off a guard's back, knocking the man forward. "You will love the prize."

"You're a sick fuck, David." Jason glared at him with hatred burning in his eyes.

David smirked, the corner of his lip scrunching his cheek. With the city silhouetted behind him, muzzles sparked like camera flashes.

"I won't do whatever sick game you got planned," Jason announced.

"But I think you will, Mr. Cook." David yanked Tracy to her feet by her wrist, tossing her aside like a rag doll.

"Run, Tracy!" Jason screamed out as a fist pounded into his gut, forcing out her name in an exasperated whoosh. All he wanted to do was buckle over, but the guards held him upright. Another blow jarred his stomach.

"Let him go, boys," David ordered. "Here's your

chance to save her, hero."

Tracy stood up, a whirlwind of snow swirling around her. "I'm not running anymore," she said defiantly.

"Fair enough," David replied. "You heard her, boys, she isn't afraid of you."

"Get out of here, Tracy," Jason bellowed.

"No." Tracy was ready to make her last stand. "This ends tonight."

"My dear old friend, take my advice." David was on the verge of laughter, tickling his every word. "Happy wife, happy life."

"Fuck you," Jason growled, delivering a right hook at the guard in front of him. His knuckles clattered against the man's bared teeth. The man's neck jerked to the right as an arc of blood and teeth spewed from his gaping mouth. Jason lunged towards the guard on his left, not allowing him a chance to react, clenching him in a bear hug. They tumbled into the snow. A wheeze of air gushed out of the man as Jason landed on top of him. Tracy screamed behind him, out of view, but he realized she could take care of herself. He needed to keep his focus on the assault; this would be his last chance. A forearm dug under his chin, yanking his head backwards. Thick chords stood out on his neck as he strained against his assailant. His hands fumbled blindly behind him, searching for anything to grab. He found a strap on the man's vest. Grabbing hold of it and dropping to one knee, Jason flung the man over his shoulder. With a soft thump, the Pharmakon soldier landed on top of his teammate.

Jason could hear David's maniacal chortle and turned just in time to catch Tracy's assault. She leapt at the behemoth, her knee on a trajectory for his chest. When they collided, he stumbled backwards, absorbing the blow with glee. Tracy landed on her feet with bent knees, ready to spring again. Jason tried to join the fray, but someone swept his leg out from under him. He fell face first into the snow. A knee drove into Jason's back, pinning him on the ground. Tracy let out her war cry, swinging for David's groin with a pointed boot. David caught it in his meaty fist, his fingers curling around her calf muscle. With a sickening snap, he wrenched her leg until the kneecap ruptured. She cried out in agony. Rolling around on the ground, grasping at her knee helplessly, Tracy howled a feverish, high-pitched wail, the commotion drawing a throng of zombies. Pharmakon security went to work, taking them out with lethal precision, guards appeared out of thin air to join them.

"Let her go, David," Jason barked, struggling beneath the weight of a mercenary on top of him. Seven guards surrounded him now, forming a wide defensive perimeter. It was just four of them in the circle: Jason, Tracy, David, and an unknown Pharmakon employee. "This is between you and me."

"Have it your way," David snickered. A smile flared crookedly on his face. He reached into his back pocket, drawing out a machete from beneath his jacket. Light flickered and danced on the blade. He held it in front of his face, dividing it in half. Tracy withered on the ground in agony, too fixated on her knee to pay attention to David. He snatched a fistful of hair, yanking her to her feet. Tracy braced all of her weight on her good knee. "Say goodnight, my dear," David plunged the blade into her stomach. Blood gurgled in Tracy's throat as she screeched, creating a wet, phlegmy, bubbling noise. When he pulled the machete out, a flood of stomach fluids and blood poured into the snow. Steam rose from the viscous liquid, rising over her face, her eyes fluttering out of consciousness.

Jason screamed a dreadful cry into the night as the world closed in around him. Once the guard let him up, Jason bolted towards David, unleashing a devastating right hook. It clipped David cheekbone, and he staggered backwards and toppled over a leg half buried under the snow. Jason stared down at Tracey, her chest expanding and falling gently, still drawing shallow breaths. With Jason distracted, David retaliated with a vigorous left jab to Jason's gut, driving him back and giving himself room to get up. Jason felt a hard wrap against the back of his leg. His hamstring muscles were cramping, hobbling him. Another quick punch, this time to Jason's chest, followed by a wide arcing right hook sent Jason crashing into a heap of snow. A guard, carrying a baton, approached from behind, driving the hardened club into Jason's calf muscle.

"Fight me like a man, David." A radiating pain made it difficult for Jason to get to his feet. Another blow across the shoulder blades kept him down.

"Get up, Mr. Cook, lets finish this once and for all."

CHAPTER 32
THE NEXT MOVE

As he walked, Smith felt the handle of the handgun against his hip with every stride he took. Drawing on their training, the Pharmakon security team took their rifles from them and forced them to their knees in a darkened alley while the surrounding chaos continued to rage on. When members of the Silver Skull Cartel crossed their path on the way down, the guards slaughtered them with ease. They barely even put up a fight and were now a distant memory. Wind funnelled through the alleyway, the bitter cold cutting through them. Blankets of snow swirled in Smith's face. Not only well trained, the Pharmakon security guards had better equipment. But they made a fatal mistake. Not willing to give up yet, Smith peered to his left. An enormous metal dumpster rested against the brick building—able to provide them sufficient shelter to buy them enough time to determine their next move.

"Would you shoot an unarmed man in the back?" Smith taunted them. "What a bunch of cowards."

"If you want to face us, be my guest," a booming voice responded. "Turn around nice and easy. And no sudden movements or I'll make you suffer."

Smith turned to his left, gauging the distance to the dumpster, noticing there was a snow-covered door concealed behind it. All he needed was a distraction. He didn't think anyone who took aim at him would be quick enough on the draw.

"Do you have any last words before we execute you?" a concealed voice demanded. The wind howled, throwing up a wall of snow that whipped through the tight confines of the alley.

Not wasting the opportunity, Smith reached over and grabbed Humber, hauling her behind the dumpster with him. He pulled his handgun out and fired aimlessly into the whiteout. Screams of terror rose behind them, then swept away by the gale force wind. The Pharmakon soldiers retaliated with a barrage of bullets. From the veil of white, a hand reached out for help. Smith yanked Edwards from the darkness and into cover. The wind died down, gradually revealing the aftermath of the gunfight. A member of the Republic, whose name Smith didn't even learn, lay in the street, drowning in a pool of their own blood. Unable to assess the damage that he'd inflicted on the Pharmakon security, he listened as the anger swelled in their leader's voice. An enormous smile hurt his chapped lips. Smith angled the handgun around the corner of the dumpster, keeping his hand behind cover. It didn't take long for the guns to ring out, a hail of bullets kicking up puffs of snow and debris.

"They have us trapped here," Edwards groaned with disgust. His eyes darting back and forth, searching for a way out. Smith pointed to the door, disguised behind a drifting snowbank. Edwards turned the door knob slowly, the metal hinges squealing, in desperate need of lubrication. They dashed into the building as Smith took up the rear. Before he could slam the door shut behind him, the roar of gunfire erupted from outside the alley. He turned his head in time to watch Eric firing from the hip on fully automatic, spraying a hailstorm of rounds into the tight confines. The barrel billowed a blueish gray smoke the wind whisked immediately away. There was no return fire. Eric remained in the open and re-slung the weapon over his shoulder.

"It's over, guys!" Eric called out, motioning for them to come out.

"Thank God you're here Eric." Smith stepped back outside, leaving the safety of the brick building behind. Edwards and Humber hesitated. "Are you guys coming?"

"Yeah, just give me a second," Edwards grumbled beneath his breath.

"You son of a bitch!" Smith yelled. "You were almost late."

"Seems like you had it all under control." Eric held out his fist and Smith gripped it firmly. "It's good to see your still alive."

"You too." Truthfully, Smith had never expected to cross paths with him again. "Although you've seen better days my friend."

Eric chuckled and coughed at the same time. When he held up his hand Smith couldn't help but stare. "Don't worry. Just one of the Cartel members with a late-night craving." Eric was ghastly white. Beads of perspiration formed on his forehead even in the frigid weather.

"You had me worried for a moment." Smith patted Eric on the shoulder. "Glad to hear you're okay."

Aliyah snuck up behind them without being noticed, her voice startling them. "Well, I guess you discovered Pharmakon is in town."

"Yeah," Smith sighed, "and so is Mr. Steele." Aliyah looked puzzled, but Smith didn't have time to explain. "He has your friend too."

Eric stared at him for a moment, his lower jaw dangling on its hinge. "You mean Jason?"

"Yeah," Smith sighed regretfully, "the bastard has him and his wife."

"Tracy is still alive?" Eric said dumbfounded.

"Last time I saw her," Smith walked back through the alley. "If we don't hurry, they might not be for much longer."

They kept low in the underbrush, out of sight from the vigilant eyes of the Pharmakon security guards. Not letting any zombies get close, they put down the stray shuffling corpses. When they arrived at the edge of the clearing, Smith watched Eric sneak up, trying to find a way into the circle without being detected. He moved when the wind picked up, creating blizzard-like conditions. Every time the storm swelled, Smith would lose him in the veil of white then discover him closer to where David and Jason struggled against each other. Edwards, Humber, and Aliyah stayed behind, keeping a watchful eye on their backs so they wouldn't get overrun by the undead.

The last thing he needed was to get caught in a surprise ambush or drawn into a firefight he couldn't afford right now; Smith didn't have the time or bullets to spare.

Smith edged closer, getting a clearer picture of the battle below. It wasn't a fair fight. Every time Jason seized the upper hand, someone would intervene, allowing David to recapture control. Tracy was stirring, the snow stained red beneath her as she struggled to keep moving. Smith realized that it was a mortal wound, even from far away. It would simply be a matter of time before she slipped away, but she was not dead yet. He watched a wall of snow blow across the open field, Eric moving within it, getting dangerously close to a Pharmakon security guard. If he weren't careful, he'd get himself captured. With still too many guards to make a move, Smith needed to bide his time. He didn't know how much longer Jason could keep going. David jarred his head with a thunderous uppercut. Jason countered blindly as he stumbled backwards, his fists cutting through the space in front of David's ghoulish grin. Jason rolled out of the way as David stomped viciously at the ground, aiming for his legs, trying to cripple his opponent. David wasn't trying to kill Jason with one crushing blow, he was dragging this out as long as possible, enjoying every moment.

In the background, Tracy found her way to her hands and knees, holding her stomach, trying to keep the vital organs enclosed within. Her head hung at a painful angle, peering at the blood dripping from the wound, soiling the surrounding snow. With a strained grimace, she rocked herself onto her knees, waves of pain twisting the soft features of her face. The force of the wind was enough to knock her backwards, her jacket billowing in the breeze. She reached out and braced her hands against the ground just in time before she collapsed. If she went down, Smith didn't think she would make it back to her feet. With their focus on Jason, no one was paying attention to her. It allowed her to fidget in her pockets for something, searching with desperation.

Under the cover of a mighty gust of wind, Eric made his first move as the snow whirled around him. His hands wielded the axe above his head, slashing it straight across. The razor-sharp blade sliced through the soft flesh of its victim's neck. A geyser of blood erupted as the violent strike landed, blood spreading into a broad arc. His head lolled to one side, a flap of sinew and flesh still affixed it in place. The guard stood still, leaning into the wind but not falling, keeping a watch on the horizon. When the wind died out, the man collapsed in a heap. His head rolled away from his body, coming to a stand still perfectly upright. If it weren't for all the blood, Smith could have believed the man had simply fallen into a deep sinkhole.

"One down," Smith muttered to himself, "one to go." If Eric didn't move quicker, Jason would run out of time. Now, with the element of surprise on their side, Smith gave himself the advantage. Without that edge, the amount of gunfire on the other side would demolish them in a fair fight.

He lost sight of everything as the blizzard raged across the field, sweeping a heavy blanket of white over everything. The snowstorm whooped and hollered in his ears. All the trees around him came to life, dancing with the wind. Branches rattled, clicking together, as the bushes rattled boisterously around him. The strength left the wind, dying down to a gentle breeze, revealing the landscape again. Things were much the same, except for a few key differences: Tracy had something concealed in her fist, pressing it against her chest to make sure she didn't lose it; Eric appeared in position behind the furthest security guard, calculating his next move: David had Jason embraced in a bear hug, shaking him violently back and forth. Smith realized it was time to make his move, signalling for Edwards to rejoin him. Aliyah and Humber would keep a watchout for zombies.

CHAPTER 32
ROOK TAKES QUEEN

Jason's arms were constrained to his sides by David's suffocating clasp. With his blood pressure soaring, every vessel in his body was ready to burst. His lungs were on fire from oxygen deprivation and his ribcage was ready to collapse. Froth formed along his lips, which he spat at David's face. Discarded like a rag doll, a torrent of wintry air gushed into his lungs. David kicked Jason in the back. Immensely relieved by the sudden ability to breathe, he hardly noticed David kick him in the back.

Out of nowhere, Tracy lunged at David, wielding a short hunting knife in her grasp. The blade slipped between his ribs. He howled with rage, the back of his hand slamming into Tracy's face as he swung his arm. Then a sickening crack rang out as Tracy's nose shattered, blood splattering her face. The force of the blow forced her to stumble, backpedalling away from his wild, blindly aimed strikes. The blade slipped from his back, landing in the snow at David's feet. He trampled over it as he stalked Tracy. Before David could find the blade, Jason leapt for the green handle. The guard saw the same thing and raced towards Jason to stop him. Jason reached the knife before the guard reached him and thrust it at him as he left his feet. When the blade slashed into the guard's stomach, it slit open a wide gash. Hot fluids and wet organs splashed into Jason's lap, making him want to wretch.

Gunfire erupted in the background, generating enough commotion to distract the guards around the perimeter. This was Jason's chance to face David on a level playing field. He turned just in time to watch helplessly as David stomped his boot into Tracy face. Her eyes turned towards him, staring at him through a pained gaze. Jason boomed, charging at David, and jabbed the blade into the beast's chest. The steel clove through the flesh, but slipped out, turned away by the sternum. Jason dragged the knife down, cutting a deep crimson ribbon down his abdomen, tendrils of blood soaking his jacket. David cried out for help, but no one answered his plea. Jason stood over him, holding the knife in both hands, plunging the knife downwards. At the last second, David deflected the blow with one hand and threw a thundering right hook, toppling Jason into a heap. By the time Jason rolled over, David buried his boot buried into his midsection, sending him tumbling onto his side. David moved in, but Jason kept him at arm's length, swinging the blade towards his throat, missing by an eighth of an inch.

Jason swung the knife again, this time the blade tasted flesh, slashing open a gashing wound on David's thigh. Before Jason got the blade back around, David kicked it out of his hand, his boot crushing Jason's fingers. A gunshot boomed behind them. David's hand shot up to his neck. In an instant, a red pattern of blood blossomed beneath his jacket. There was a gory hole opened in the thick muscle covering his neck. It wasn't a fatal wound, but it was enough to send him stomping away, leaving behind a trail of blood in the snow down the hill.

"Jason," Eric scrambled to his side, "are you okay."

Jason pushed him aside. "Tracy." He spat out her name. His finger pointed towards his dying wife. She was lying on her back, choking on her own blood. She coughed ominous red spittle over her checks, a wet sucking sound caught on her chest. Eric rushed to her side, his hand lifting her chin up. He swept her mouth, trying to clear the blockage with his fingers. Tracy jolted back to consciousness, her last memory before passing out had been fighting for her life against David. Confused and disoriented, she lashed out at Eric, her jaws snapping at him, trying to taste his flesh. Saddened, Eric stared at Tracy, a tear tracked down his check, knowing he had failed her. Too late to help, Eric backed away from her and let Jason step in.

"Tracy, you're all right." Jason grabbed her by the shoulder and shook her, staring into her eyes. "You're still here with me." She tried to talk, but all that came out was a wet, clicking noise as her tongue stuck to the roof of her mouth. "Don't talk."

"I'm sorry I'm late," Eric groaned.

"All that matters is you're here now," Jason said, attempting to free Eric from his guilt. "Listen, buddy, there's an antidote for the virus. It's at the Pharmakon base. With it, you'd save a lot of people. Promise me you'll get it."

"I will, I promise. And you can come with me." Eric held his against his blood-stained jacket, trying to stop the flow of blood. "You'll be just fine."

"I have to kill David." Jason needed to slow his words, finding it difficult to catch his breath.

"You just stay put. I'll take care of that freak." Eric looked down at his friend. "If I don't make it back, keep Dana safe for me."

"I'll do my best, if I can hold on." Jason coughed into his hand, expecting to find blood. The spit was clear and frothy, but no major signs of blood.

"I'll get that bastard." Eric dashed off in David's direction before Jason could protest.

Jason searched around for a place to lay Tracy to rest. He refused to leave her to die alone in a field like this. But it didn't take long to realize he was in no state to burry her. Instead, he decided on a nice tree at the edge of the clearing. Carrying his dying wife across the field took more effort than Jason wanted to spend.

Eric stumbled forward through the deep snow on the outskirts of town. The raging wind whipped the snow in a vortex all around him, making it near impossible to stay focused. Every single muscle in his legs started convulsing all at once, painful knots forming, restricting his movement. Every breath felt laboured as his lungs burned from exhaustion. The surrounding noise drilled deeper into his muddled mind, making it harder to concentrate. Gunfire erupted all around him as the all-out war in Grand Falls continued to rage on just ahead.

The Republic's plan had gone smoothly until the agents from Pharmakon arrived unexpectedly and threw a wrench into it, hitting them hard. Eric didn't know if it was a planned ambush or if the herd had drawn them to the area, but they were better equipped to fight a war than the Republic. The events of the last two days should have taught Eric nothing ever goes as planned. A cruel twist of fate rendered every detail and trap that they'd placed ineffective. They were prepared to fight the Highway Hangmen once their bullets had run out fighting off the army of dead that he'd lured into Grand Falls. This would have been all over except David Steele and a group of soldiers arrived prepared and equipped to wage war against the Republic of Newfoundland.

Eric's head pounded fiercely, and bright spots floated in the air clouding his vision even when he closed his eyes. The stars burning into his sight stood out in stark contrast to the darkness that enclosed the surrounding woods. A cluster of storm clouds did their best to block out what little light the moon offered.

A powerful gust of wind caught Eric off guard and knocked him down into the freshly fallen snow, sending a burst of the light powder into the whirling cyclone. Eric strained his neck to lift his face out of the snow, but holding his head put a cumbersome strain on his spine. The terrible burden of having to save everyone that he carried with him was just as crushing as his physical fatigue. His muscles seemed to reject the impulses sent from his brain, and his actions were becoming clumsier with every passing moment. Through his convoluted vision, he tracked drops of crimson dripping from his broken nose into the snowfall. The taste of copper soiled his mouth as blood ran down the back of his throat, but Eric kept pushing forward. The war wasn't over yet, and he wouldn't allow this to be for nothing—he'd lost too much to give up now. He'd witnessed so much unnecessary blood spilled, but what bothered him even more was how much of that precious fluid he was responsible for. So many poor decisions had led to the bloodshed of people he believed to be evil, but it had cost him the lives of his loved ones.

Not ready to give up. he pushed himself back up, sending a searing pain into his abdomen, the warmth in his stomach nauseating. He felt the hot fluids in his stomach eating away at the lining. Eric kept throwing up, and when he wiped away the puke with a bloodied sleeve, a trickle of warm blood oozed from an open wound. Steam billowed from his body; he felt like his blood was boiling as it flowed through his veins.

A vivid flash in his mind of his recently lost loved one kept him pushing forward. It forced Eric to slow down and lean against a tree, struggling to catch his breath. His vision was fading away into obscurity. Eric realized that time was running out, but he wouldn't risk making another mistake.

More enemies than he could count stood in his way, both living and dead. They fought against him and with each other; the grim reaper was collecting souls without prejudice. His only allies belonged to the newly formed Republic of Newfoundland. And if Eric wanted to be remembered as a hero, he knew that they would have to be on the right side of history. Smith's words had haunted him ever since he explained to Eric that heroic acts are at the discretion of those that write the history books. If the Republic of Newfoundland lost this war, they would most likely become the villains in someone else's story. Eric didn't want to be remembered for all the ruthless and heinous acts he'd committed.

He'd spent every day avoiding the undead since they refused to depart from this world. They had proven themselves to be the apex predators in their shark-like pursuit of human flesh. And over the past several hours as the battle raged on one thing had become clear, the army of the dead would be the victor. The living may have triumphed over thousands of the undead tonight, but the numbers of the breathing had been dwindling all night and now were switching sides.

The thunderous booming of gunfire exploded just beyond the tree line, and Eric recognized the slight flashes from the muzzles of guns through the blizzard. Tiny sparks of light guided him towards his inevitable encounter with the Pelley brother's army.

The sour stench of the long dead mixed with the bitter odour of the freshly fallen into a bouquet of death, which poured forth from all angles. Eric trudged through the deep snow towards the chaos that continued to boil over on the streets of Grand Falls. Sweat rolled down his back and soaked his shirt, the wickedly cold winds piercing his body, making every movement complete agony. He knew his anger was only a shield for his pain, but it was all he had left now. He reached the edge of the forest and leaned against a tree trunk as he looked out over the bloodied streets. A swarm of shuffling corpses littered the battlefield. Dead bodies that had yet to turn lay slumped over in the street in heaps next to the soulless creatures that had met their ultimate resting place. Eric pulled his old service revolver out of its holster and opened the chamber and laughed. There was only one bullet left and that wasn't even his biggest concern. Still laughing, Eric held his hand up and stared at the blood flowing from the severed digit. He'd known that the end was near ever since his trigger finger had been bitten off earlier that night.

It took Eric a long time to realize that David's trail had changed directions. He thought it was disappearing beneath the snow, breaking off at the bottom of the hill. With the storm surging around him, he studied his surroundings. There were no other signs of David anywhere. Members of the Republic were following Smith out of the city, falling back to the hotel for safety, where they were making their last stand. They'd trapped the Silver Skull Cartel and Highway Hangman amongst the dead, the few remaining Pharmakon security scattered and separated. He stood in the middle of the blizzard, searching for any clue that would help him pick up David's trail.

Jason slumped against a tall pine tree, and the snow quickly buried him as a harsh wind drifted it against him. The sun rose, struggling to push through the dense clouds. The world around him slowly came to life. The trees were slumbering under a blanket of pure snow. There were no plows or salt trucks to dirty the pristine white flakes. It was what the ancestors of this island must have witnessed before the invention of cars and roads. This beauty must have been why they stayed here. During the breaks between gusts of wind, Jason could see grey jays fluttering back and forth between the trees. Their chirping calls drowned out by the gunfire in the streets behind him.

With a strained smile, Jason raised his bloodied hands. The scarlet red stood out against the vast white of the snow on the ground. He didn't know how much of the blood was his and how much belonged to the others. He'd extracted his revenge on David even though he'd lost the fight with the behemoth adversary who'd turned his life upside down. Still, while both men still roamed this earth, neither was long for it. Would they both be dead by the time the sun was high in the sky? Jason looked down at Tracy with a tear in his eye, her blank eyes frozen open for eternity. Covered in wounds, she was almost unrecognizable to him. Worse still was his knife buried between her ear and jawline. Even though it had pained him, he couldn't bare to watch her turn into a roaming corpse and he didn't want her wandering around, looking for her next meal. So, he'd done the merciful thing.

Jason was glad that he was sat with his back turned to the war zone taking place in the once quiet town of Grand Falls. The army of the dead had brought out the worst in humanity and were only a catalyst for the carnage that had befallen the entirety of the human race. This apocalypse had been on the verge of happening for years. The dead rising from the afterlife gave it the push it needed to begin. It was the corrupt politicians selling the rules and laws of the government to greedy businessmen who were the ones responsible for all this chaos. All Jason wanted to do was spend his last breaths alone and in peace, reflecting on his victory. He was coming to terms with departing from this world. He'd done his part in securing a better future for the Republic of Newfoundland.

Jason stared at where Eric's blood gushed from his hand and spilt over the ground. He wasn't sure if Eric would have enough time to save Dana, but he told him where to find the cure for the zombie virus that plagued the world. If Eric got it into the right hands, humanity would finally have a fighting chance against the dead.

When the wind and snow stopped without warning, one last thunderous roar of gunfire blared loudly before everything fell silent. The sun shone brilliantly through a break in the clouds, the golden glow pushing the clouds apart. What snow remained seemed to hang in the air, frozen in place against the background like white specks of paint on a canvas. A giant moose trotted out of the forest, holding its antlers up proudly as it knocked the snow from the branches. Its grey fur kept the animal warm and equipped for the rugged winters of Newfoundland. Its large black eyes turned to look at Jason. They locked eyes and the majestic beast turned and trotted towards him. Jason reached out his filthy hand towards the animal. The moose stopped just outside of Jason's reach, not getting close enough for him to touch. The moose's eyes were as black as the pure night sky and wet, as if it were crying. Jason admired the creature's antlers. They must have been six-feet wide, and the bones had remained unsoiled by the filthy creatures roaming the earth.

Jason didn't know why the moose had chosen this moment to come out of the woods. Or why it stood in front of him, staring down at him with its sad eyes. The mighty beast nodded its head up and down for some unknown reason before walking past Jason and heading towards the town. He looked over his shoulders and watched as the giant animal used its antlers to gore a shambling corpse that had wandered away from the city. The zombie's stomach tore open, the blackened organs flooding over the moose. The foul corpse's intestines hung from its stomach, swaying back and forth as the zombie lunged forward trying to bite the poor animal. Before the dead man could sink its teeth into the neck of the mighty moose, it flung the corpse head over heels into the sky. The zombie's head smashed hard into the frozen ground, its neck snapping on impact. A gush of blood and rotten grey brain matter spilled out of an enormous crack that had split the creature's head wide open.

Jason looked down at Tracy once more, stroking her blood-soaked hair with his hand. He wanted nothing more than to stay here with his wife and look off into the sunset, wondering what the unfamiliar world will become. Deep inside, he wished he didn't have to leave her here. But unfinished business lingered over him, compelling him. Even though he wished he could have lain here, letting the snow fall over him and Tracy, frozen together until the sun melted the white blanket in the spring, Jason wasn't done. So, he struggled to his feet and reached down to move Tracy's body towards the tree. He felt a sharp, burning pain in his chest from where David had crushed his ribs. He fought to get oxygen into his lungs, his breaths shallow and short. Jason realized that he would never rest knowing that David was alive. He knew Eric wouldn't be able to kill the behemoth; he had to be the one to deliver the killing blow.

It would be the last thing he did before he would draw his last breath. By the time he got to his feet, David was already in the clearing, waiting for him. "Well, isn't that sweet," David cackled. "Did you get to say goodbye?"

CHAPTER 33
BISHOP TAKES PAWN

Dana fought against sleep, a battle she wouldn't win; she considered admitting defeat. Afraid, her body shivered. Concerned that she would wake up to the news that Eric hadn't returned, she resisted the inevitable. Earlier, Stella had pulled the couch in front of the window for her, letting her keep a vigilant eye out for him. Now, Stella stood at the counter, preparing tea in the minuscule kitchen, humming a sweet tune as she waited for the kettle to boil. The wind rattled the windows, pelting a barrage of snowflakes off the glass. Outside, the light of the hotel died in the adjacent field, barely stretching across the parking lot. While peering into the blackness across the highway, she waited impatiently, knowing Eric was somewhere on the other side.

They were alone in Stella's room; it was essentially bare, a sharp contrast from Ted's room. All the furniture, which was vintage and worn, was scarce. The beige curtains were drawn back, exposing the second story view of a desolate parking lot. There wasn't a separate room for the bedroom, the bed arranged dead centre in the room.

Missing a television, Dana assumed they'd removed until she could have earned it. She didn't want to consider about what kind of work Stella would have to endure to get it back. Dirty, ashen grey industrial carpet covered the entire floor. It was a far cry from the luxurious style found upstairs in Ted's suite, which now, by default, belonged to Tina and the twins.

When the black kettle whistled, a hissing steam billowed from the spout towards the ceiling as the water boiled. Cups and plates rattled as Stella went about the important business of making tea. A metal spoon clanged off the edge of the mug, ringing loudly as she strained the tea bag. "There's a little milk and sugar left." Stella was halfway into the fridge, rummaging through it.

"I'll have a little of both," Dana yawned, struggling to keep her eyes open. She expected the sugar would wake her up a little, just long enough for Eric to get back.

Stella handed her a cup of tea on a saucer, a spoon and packet of sugar resting beside it. "Here you go." Stella didn't quite look sleepy. Exhausted would have been a better phrase—and not from an absence of sleep. Deep lines had formed in the corner of her mouth, the wrinkles in her forehead more defined now. Large black bags sat under her eyes, giving them the illusion of sinking into the skull. She sat at the edge of the bed, and the springs groaned beneath her frail frame. Now, at approximately three in the morning, according to the clock that hung on the wall, the tension was growing. Stella glanced over, then let out a sigh of relief. "I don't know why I'm still watching that thing. There won't be anyone to force me to work at dawn."

"I suppose not." Dana realized they had an abundance of work ahead of them if they wanted to survive here, but not tomorrow. "Are you going to sleep?"

"No," Stella sighed, "I'm too excited to sleep. For the first time in an extremely long time, since before this all happened, I'm hopeful for what tomorrow could bring." She needed the rest. Once the adrenaline wore off, she'd be sound asleep. But she continued fighting it, same as Dana.

"You have no idea," Dana laughed.

"You don't think I realized," Stella spoke with a knowing tone, "but I see it on your face." A smile swept across her face, momentarily wiping away the burdens of the past few months. For a fleeting moment, she didn't appear to have aged a day since the outbreak. The lines smoothed, and the colour returned to her cheek, her eyes radiant and alive. "Did you find out how far along you are?"

"If my math is right, slightly less than four months." Dana placed her hand on her stomach, that was still not showing.

"So, you've been pregnant since all of this started?" Stella's smile faded just enough to show Dana just how tired she was.

"I didn't know how to tell Eric." Dana remembered the sleepless nights in their old home. "I can't remember what I was so afraid of." She let herself laugh.

Stella placed her hands on Dana's knee. "You will be just fine."

Dana tried to suppress a yawn but couldn't help it. Her mouth hung wide open, her hand raising to hide it. Her eyelids seemed to gain weight from the yawn, barely able to keep them open now. "There's so much to do…" Finally overwhelmed, Dana fell asleep mid-sentence.

Dana jerked awake, surprised to discover herself beneath a blanket. Spilling in through the curtains, a delicate trace of daylight crept over the darkness, revealing a thin white glow outlining the mountainside. She craned her neck towards the bed, finding Stella fast asleep on top of the covers, the handle of a mug twisted horizontally in her grasp. At some point during her sleep, Stella had splashed tea over the white sheets. It was still dripping onto the floor, the pitter patter of drops continuing at a steady pace. Dana frantically jumped out of the chair, knocking it over with a loud thump. Terrified that Stella had suffered a heart attack, she shook her, shrieking.

Stella's eyes shot open. "What's wrong?" Her tone was full of concern.

"Are you okay?" Dana asked stupidly, sleep still tugging at her mind.

"I'm okay," Stella mumbled, her hand dragging the cup across the sheets. "Guess I must have fallen asleep." With a dazed expression, she ran her fingers through her tangled hair, scratching at her scalp. "You scared the life out of me."

Dana searched the room for any signs of Eric. She didn't see his boots, but maybe he'd kept them on and was still in the bathroom. Hope dragged her across the room towards the door against her better judgement. She eased it open. A hollow feeling of dread filled her at the sight of emptiness. "They still haven't come back." She glanced up at the clock but couldn't seem to focus long enough to tell the time.

"Not yet," Stella responded through a yawn, stretching it out. "What time is it?" It was her turn to look at the clock. "It will be sunrise soon," she stated.

Dana turned back towards the window, looking out over the town. Plumes of smoke, once hidden in the dusk, caught the faint light of day. Fires raged all over the city, buildings burning to the ground. Abandoned vehicles littered the streets. Even from a distance, the chaos left behind was on full display: bodies strewn over the asphalt, draped over the hoods of cars, and piled on top of each other. "Oh my god," she muttered. There were countless shuffling corpses still roaming the streets, passing through town, clustered together in groups of thousands or more. They seemed to be migrating out of town, but Dana couldn't be certain.

As tears streamed freely from her eyes, a surge of bitter emotion found its way out. Stella rubbed her back, trying to console her, but when her eyes wandered outside the window, her words floated away with hope. "He'll be okay," Stella said faintly. "They'll be back soon."

Neither one of them believed it.

CHAPTER 34
KNIGHT TAKES KING

"This ends now," Jason bellowed. His fingers curled into fists, drawing blood as his nails dug into the soft flesh of his palm. "Just you and me."

David approached as coppery red blood trickling from the wound on his thigh. He leered at Jason with a crooked grin on his lips, exposing his rotten teeth. "I can't wait," he announced. "I've been dreaming of this since Fox Island."

He raised his fists in front of his face in a boxer's stance, angling slightly to the right with his left foot forward. David's first jab designed to keep Jason off the offensive. His body twisted to the right then sprang forward, uncoiling with all his raw power, unleashing a vicious right hook. Jason ducked under the arching arm and dug his shoulder into David's ribcage. They toppled over into the snow, Jason landing on top. David twisted his hip, tossing Jason off, landing face first into the snow. Jason rolled over twice, putting some distance between them. He somehow got to his feet before David.

Now it was time for Jason to go on the offensive. He

thrust his boot into David's leg, reopening the deep gash on his thigh. Blood gushed over Jason's boot as David yelled in agony, his face contorted into an ugly grimace. Then, Jason threw an uppercut, his knuckles connecting with David's chin. His neck jerked backward. Another quick left hook glanced off David's cheek. The momentum spun Jason around and he staggered into the massive frame of his adversary. David recovered enough to tie his arms around Jason's shoulders, forcing them both to the ground. They rolled around the snow, each man wrestling for leverage, neither man willing to surrender. Finally coming to a stop, Jason found himself on his back, glaring up into the maddening glare. David worked to slide his hands to Jason's neck, his fingers pushing against his windpipe. Jason flexed his neck muscles, struggling to buy himself enough time to free himself from the death grip. His hands tangled up David's arms, but he couldn't pry them away. No matter how hard he tried he couldn't catch a breath. Slowly, his vision turned bright white, as if there were flames burning a hole in his cornea. Jason gathered every ounce of his remaining strength and twisted his hip, a last-ditch effort to buck David off balance. They crashed hard into the snow, Jason and David limbs entwined as they struggled to secure dominance. David refused to surrender the vice-like grip on Jason's neck the entire time. Jason ran out of steam. The world was spinning around him as he faded out of consciousness.

Just when Jason didn't think he could take it any more, David relinquished his grip and tumbled off. The icy air stung his lungs, but he inhaled it in large mouthfuls. He braced for David's retaliation, expecting a boot to the ribcage, but it didn't come. Ferocious screams barked out obscenities. Jason couldn't understand what was going on, his head still swimming. Gradually, the yelling took on two varied tones, with David's rage focused on somebody else.

"You're going to regret that," David bellowed, driving his knee into Jason's saviour. The man keeled over, gasping for breath as he fell into a crumpled heap. With one hand, David yanked the stranger to his feet, his chin pressed against his chest, concealing his face. David snatched the man by the wrist, a fire axe held tenaciously in the stranger's grasp. David squeezed until the bone fractured, and the axe fell harmlessly into the snow.

Eric wailed in misery, pain twisting and manipulating his ghastly facial features. David held him up by the wrist, like a toddler. Eric swayed back and forth, pivoting from his knees. Another savage knee to the chest sent Eric toppling over backwards, landing on his backside. David placed his boot on Eric's chest, driving him deeper into the snow. His balled his right fist into a club and slammed it down repeatedly. "You had enough yet?"

"Go fuck yourself," Eric spat out blood, his nose shifted all the way to the left. He barely lifted his head up, but somehow he kept eye contact with David.

"You defiant little shit." David spat a wad of yellowish brown spit at Eric. "I remember you now. You're that fucking cop from Fox Island." He leaned into his leg, applying more pressure on Eric, driving a gush of air from his lungs. David fumbled in his back pocket, reaching his right hand over to his left side. When he drew his hand back, a hunting knife protruded from his fist. "You will die slowly." He plunged the blade down into Eric's stomach and yanked back an empty hand. The handle stuck straight up from Eric's abdomen. Eric's arms fell to his side, his chest rising in shallow breaths.

Then Jason finally noticed why David was only using his right hand. Eric had severed his left arm clean off just below the elbow. The discarded limb lay next to Jason in the snow, a purplish red stream inching towards his face. As he struggled to his knees, the snow gave way and slid into the bloodied mess. Somehow, Jason found his feet. With one last defiant act remaining, he picked up the fire axe. The handle was slick with blood, the blade stained crimson. "Hey," Jason struggled to speak, his lungs still burning. "Why don't you pick on someone your own size?"

David laughed. "That's rich. You know, I'll miss you when you're gone."

"Can't say the same, asshole," Jason taunted. A thin smile pressed his lips against his teeth, suppressing his own urge to laugh.

David removed his boot from Eric's chest and eyed Jason, staring down at the weapon in his hand. "I thought you wanted an honorable fight?" The colour was draining from his skin along with the blood from his arm.

"Fuck that," Jason coughed, spitting up blood. He felt faint, fighting to remain on his feet, the axe tugged at his shoulder, dragging him down.

David growled, his eyes bulging with rage. "You're a dead man." With a surge of power, he sprinted forward like a bull, lowering his head. Jason swung the axe over his head. The weight caused him to stumble backwards, his arms falling behind him. David's shoulder crashed into Jason, buckling him in half. The axe flew out of his hands, landing far out of reach. Jason reached out, his hands groping at David's jacket. He leaned into the behemoth's chest. With tremendous force, David shoved Jason to the ground, driving the heel of his boot into Jason's groin.

"Here we are again, Mr. Cook," David laughed menacingly, "and I win again."

"Fuck you," Jason hawked, "you would never beat me in a fair fight."

"I grow tired of this," David snickered, smiling to rub salt in an old wound. With a callous grin, David raised both arms above his head, his meaty right hand mimicking a sledgehammer, his bloody stump along for the ride. No longer able to find the strength to defend himself, Jason was powerless to stop the blood thirsty animal. David was full of unrelenting violence to the bitter end. Without a reason to continue his fight, Jason closed his eyes in defeat, and waited for the final blow, his last words muddled by a hiccup of blood.

BANG!!!!!

CHAPTER 35
CHECKMATE

Eric's insides were on fire. His hand fumbled over the hilt of the blade sticking out of his abdomen. Somehow, the three-inch blade had miraculously missed his vital organs and arteries. He rolled onto his back, bracing himself on his elbows, his lips pressed together. A low whimper caught in his throat and was drowned out by the wind. A whirlwind of snow obscured his vision. In the background, he heard Jason grunting in pain, spitting up blood that gargled in his throat. The dull, sickening sound of flesh being struck repeatedly echoed behind the gusts of wintery winds. Two shadows struggled just beyond Eric's vision, a tangle of arms swinging violently. Eric realized he couldn't wait for the storm to die down to see the carnage; he needed to act now.

He rolled over onto his knees, and a flare of intense pain shot through his entire body. Blood seeped out of the sharp gash, running down the exposed blade and over the handle before dripping into the snow. His elbows dug into the snow, crawling towards the two fighting figures. Eric struggled to keep pressing forward, the shadows never appearing to get any closer.

"Here we are again, Mr. Cook," David laughed menacingly, "and I win again."

"Fuck you," Jason hawked, "you would never beat me in a fair fight."

Eric crawled closer, edging towards them at a painstakingly slow pace. His neck strained towards the sounds, hoping to glimpse David Steele.

"I grow tired of this," David boomed. His voice blared like thunder in triumph.

Jason mumbled something, but his words were made incoherent as they passed through the blood flooding his mouth. When the winds died down, the snow settled around Jason and David like a snow globe. David was standing over Jason, a bent knee driving down on Jason's chest. Then his right arm raised above his head, his hand clenched into a fist. He was facing Eric, his eyes glaring at Jason with rage, ignoring everything else. Eric drew the revolver with his left hand, his thumb fumbling to cock the action while his fingers fidgeted into place. The trigger felt foreign in his left hand, like a stranger bumping against his finger.

He held David in his sights, the iron aimed at the back of his skull, just like on Fox Island. A powerful sensation of deja vu washed over him, the eerie red light from that prison hallway replaced by a smoldering pink horizon. This was the last round in the chamber. It needed to count and time was running out. He closed one eye, drew in a deep breath, and pulled the trigger.

BANG!!!!!

An erupting burst of blood sprayed into the wind. David's ear was torn clean off, replaced by a gushing crimson mess. Angered by the wound, David spun around, snarling and growling, his right hand cupping the hole where his ear used to be. "I'm going to fucking kill you," David roared, his eyes wide with rage, thick ropes of blood seeped down the side of his face.

A deep, wet thunk changed David's expression into shock and confusion. Not understanding what happened, he stood silent, trying to determine the source of the noise. Something was dripping into the snow behind him, a substantial torrent of *drip-drop-drip*. He twisted his neck, trying to find the source of the sound. Then his hand found the blade of the axe, his fingers tracing up the handle. Jason stood before him, gripping the axe, using it to hold himself up. The head of the blade sank deeper into David's back, tearing open a broad gash along the way. Reaching out with his right hand, Jason wrapped his fingers around David's throat and squeezed, glaring into David's eyes. A trickle of blood seeped out between his fingers, the tips disappearing beneath the tender flesh. David choked and spat blood. His bloodied stump flailed towards his neck, his phantom hand working to pry Jason's fingers away. Buried to the knuckles, Jason's ripped his hand away, pulling out an arc of bright red blood. He tossed aside David's white, grizzled windpipe. Jason let the axe go and both men collapsed to the ground.

"Jason," Eric croaked, making his way past a bloodied David. Eric could see in his desolate eyes that he was dying slowly and painfully. Jason opened his mouth wide, trying to draw in oxygen, but his throat produced a gargled whistling cry. "Hang in there, I'll get you out of here," Eric called out as he knelt next to Jason.

Jason coughed and spat into his hand. "I don't think so. Not this time."

"You can't die out here alone," Eric said, opening his jacket and tearing off a swatch of cloth to impede the flow of blood. "You'll make it."

Jason shook his head. "I need you to bring me over there." A trembling finger pointed towards an aged oak tree.

"I can save you..." Eric's voice faltered, knowing the difference.

"Please," Jason groaned. "I just want to be with Tracy one last time." Eric nodded, not saying another word. There was nothing left to say. He toiled to haul Jason off the ground, but his dead weight was too much for Eric.

"Hey," a familiar voice called out from behind. "There you are."

CHAPTER 36
THIS IS MY SHIELD

Eric turned around, his eyes squinting against the blowing wind. Out of the blustery veil of white, Smith stepped forward with two others lagging behind him.

"I need help."

"Fuck sakes," Smith uttered as he raced forward. His eyes inspected the carnage, the settling snow doing little to mask the splattered gore. "Is he okay?"

With a sense of dread, Eric glanced down at Jason. His eyes were fluttering closed, just a thin slit filled with tears glaring back. "Help me carry him." Without hesitating, Smith and his friends rushed to Jason's side, taking their share of the weight. As they dragged him across the snow, a nasty trail of blood followed them. "Hang in there, Jason." Eric fought back tears, knowing Jason's time would soon be up. They laid him to rest in a seated position, his back slumped against the tree trunk.

Jason slid his hand across the snow, coming to rest over Tracy's, squeezing it gently. Then a thin smile appeared on his face and his eyes flickered open. "I killed her," Jason said regretfully. "If it wasn't for me, she'd still be alive."

"You rescued her," Eric replied, patting Jason's shoulder. "Without you, she would have died alone—and a monster. She loved you."

"Promise me you'll take care of the Pharmakon base." Jason struggled to spit the words out, catching his breath. "Find the cure, survive."

"We have to go," Smith said with a sense of purpose. "There's too many of them. We have to get back to the hotel. It's safe there."

"Not yet," Eric said defiantly. "We can save you."

"Go," Jason coughed. . His face twisted in discomfort, the pain too much to bear. "You have Dana to take care of. I'm at peace here."

"I'm not sure men like us have a chance to find peace." Eric's bottom lip quivered. "I'm sorry, Jason."

When a low croak escaped Jason's throat, his head bobbed down as if someone turned on the gravity. His chin landed on his breastbone and his arms fell against his sides. Smith grabbed Eric by the shoulder, tearing him away from Jason's side. "We need to bury him." Eric bellowed. "He deserves that much."

"You can't stay out here." With the help of Edwards, Smith pulled Eric away by the collar, the fabric bunched up in his clenched fist.

"We have to bring him back," Eric pleaded hysterically over the rumbling growl of approaching undead. Out of the blinding storm, corpses shambled into the clearing, drawn towards Jason and Tracy. "Get away from them!" Eric drew his revolver and pulled the trigger repeatedly. The hammer thudded against the empty chambers, producing a low, audible clicking.

"Calm the fuck down, Eric," Smith snarled as he dragged him into the tree line. "You're empty.

Zombies dropped to their knees in front of the couple, rapacious hands tearing into the flesh. They feasted on their bodies, stuffing hunks of bloodied meat into mouths, their teeth chomping into the defenceless prey. They removed lengths of entrails and other vital organs without caution, gnarled fingers shredding the stomach lining. Eric continued to pull the trigger as a maddening scream from deep inside spilled out of him in a tidal wave of emotions. The hammer thudded dryly over and over. There was no rationale behind his motives, just a sense of remorse and hatred. The tree branches closed around him like someone had drawn the curtains, shutting out the horrific spectacle.

"Listen to me, Eric." Smith rattled Eric back and forth. "We need to move on. There's still a lot we need to do before we are safe. We can rebuild, but not if we die in this goddamn field trying to dig a grave for a dead man. Let it go."

"But…"

Smith slapped Eric hard across the face, sending a wad of bloodied spittle flying out. "Do you want to fucking die?"

"No," Eric roared, his entire body trembling with fear.

"I promised Dana that I'd bring you back." Smith let go of Eric. A hungry growl drew closer just beyond the clearing. "If you want to go back out there you can explain that to her yourself. Now if you're done being fucking stupid, get a move on."

Eric let out a defeated cry, hunching his shoulders, staring at his feet. "All right, let's go." He didn't look back; he couldn't even if he wanted to. Tired and exhausted, he trudged through the forest, not paying attention to where he was going. He moved, essentially on automatic, following behind Smith, instinctively stepping into his footprints. "We're almost there."

"I need a doctor," Eric groaned, stumbling over a buried root.

"No kidding," Smith couldn't help himself. "Edwards, give me a hand." They both braced Eric, his arms draped over their shoulders. "Jesus Christ, you really have lost a lot of blood." Worry filled his voice. "Humber, make sure the path ahead is clear."

"No problem." She ran ahead, her feet thumping off the ground *thump-thud-thump*.

Daylight glared. An infinite field of tiny, brilliant sparkles reflected the sun's energy. Squinting against the rising sun, Eric tried to block out the harsh rays, the light burning through his eyelids. The warmth of the sunrays made him drowsy. A shadow loomed ahead, cutting across the highway, dampening the effects of the day. Eric lost the use of his legs; there wasn't enough energy in his body to keep them pumping. His feet dragged through the deep snow. He could hear Edwards and Smith grunting through the laborious task.

Gunfire erupted ahead on the path, followed by a soft *thump*. A distant voice called out: "Clear!" It was the last thing Eric remembered before passing out.

A harsh, florescent light shone into Eric's eyes, burning a hole into his brain. He opened his mouth, discovering it abnormally dry, his tongue glued to the roof of his mouth. Everything ached, knots twisted his stomach, and a pounding pain pulsated in his temples. "Where am I?" Eric choked on his words.

"You're awake." Dana's voice sprang up from beside him, her hand caressing his own.

Eric rolled his head to the right. She was sitting in an armchair next to his bed, a gigantic window behind her. To his left, the wispy white curtains did little to prevent the daylight from spilling into the room. A blue sky spanned the length of the horizon without a cloud to blemish it. "How long have I been asleep?"

"You need to get some rest." She was standing now, checking him over. First, she flung back the sheets, placing her hand on his stomach. A worried looked weighed down her face. Then, drawing her hand back, she glared at the traces of blood on her fingertips.

When Eric glanced down, he discovered his stomach wrapped in soaked gauzes. The fabric clung to his body, stuck there by the sticky secretions. The gruesome, sour stench of infection was heavy, wafting from his wound. The fetid scent turned his stomach. "Goddammit," Eric muttered to himself.

"Try not to worry about it," Dana tried to reassure him. "And don't move around too much. You must have torn your stitches in your sleep." She walked around the bed and headed towards the bathroom. When she disappeared inside the room, he could hear her rattling through the medicine cabinet followed by the rush of running water. She trudged back towards Eric, a plastic cup filled with water in one hand and two red and yellow capsules in the other. "Take these for the infection."

Eric tossed a pill in his mouth, it stuck to his parched tongue. He took a generous mouthful of water and gagged down the first dose. The second went down easier. "Thanks." Eric started taking small sips of water, trying to moisten his mouth.

"Do you want more water?"

Eric chugged the last half of the cup and passed it back. "Yes, please." His stomach was boiling with pain; every movement he made sent a ripple of pain coursing through it. He flinched in agony. "Is there anything for the pain?"

Dana disappeared without another word. Eric heard the tap run again. He recognized the rattle of bottles as she thumbed through the shelves. When she came back out, she carried a red-labelled bottle in her hand. "Humber said you can have two of these every six hours. She said they won't do much, but they'll take the edge off." Dana poured the oval red caplets into her palm, picking out two and placing the rest back inside the container.

Eric swallowed both pills with a large swig of water. "My stomach is killing me." Dana cried, her hand tenting over her eyes. "What is it?"

"Your stomach *is* killing you." Tears rolled down Dana's cheek. "She's hoping that they'll find something at the Pharmakon labs to help you, but she didn't sound very confident they'd make it back in time."

"What do you mean?" Puzzled, Eric still didn't comprehend how long he had been out. "They took off without me?"

Dana glared at Eric. "Do you realize how close you are to death? You don't have to do everything," she scolded him.

"How long have I been out?"

"You've been in and out of consciousness for four days now." Dana dabbed at the corner of her eyes with a tissue she took out of her pants pocket. "You've had a fever ever since, and the infection is getting worse, even with the pills we've given you."

"When did they leave?"

"This morning at dawn. Aliyah left two days ago after she rounded up the herd." Dana shook her head, refusing to look at Eric. "Do you need to be the hero? Smith and the other members of the Republic are perfectly capable of handling it from here."

"I can still catch them." Eric tried to swing his legs out of bed, but a jolt of pain pinned him down and cut him off mid sentence.

"Goddammit, Eric," As Dana placed her hand on his shoulder with a firm grip, she threw back the covers. "Christ, I will change your bandages right now. We are running out of gauze and you're not the only person here that needs them." She was furious. "I had to fight with Humber to get extra, and they don't expect to be back for another two days. If you keep this up, you will use them all up."

"Okay," Eric relented, "I'm sorry."

"I need you to sit up." To help, Dana put her hands on Eric's shoulders, gently guiding him to a seated position.

His face grimaced in pain, and he let out an anguished whimper. "I know you still think you're a cop." Dana unraveled the bandage. "I guess that part of you will never go away, but you need to understand that not everything needs to fall on your shoulders. You run off every time there's any sign of danger, which is great, but do you have any idea how hard that is on me?"

Eric stiffened as the bandage tugged at his skin as Dana unwrapped the last layer. "I know," Eric squeezed out between a series of quick breaths. "I appreciate it must be hard to deal with—the waiting. It tears me up every time you're alone. Even when I think you're safe, I still worry."

A foul, rotting stench filled the room. Dana covered her mouth and gagged, nearly throwing up. Eric sensed a hot fluid ooze down his side. When he looked down, bile raced up his throat at the sight of the festering wound. Brownish yellow puss coated the bright red gash, laying over it in a thin film. "Jesus Christ, Eric," Dana stared down at him with wet eyes, tears tracking down her cheek. "It's worse than the last time. The antibiotics aren't working at all, and the wound isn't healing either."

Warm waves of pain crashed over Eric, the sour, noxious odour making his head spin. "I'll be okay." He didn't believe himself, and he could tell by the look on Dana's face that she didn't either. Fading into obscurity, Eric collapsed onto his back, his vision fading to black.

"I need help!" Dana screamed out shrilly.

CHAPTER 37
I BARE IT

"Girls, you will be okay. Just stay here with the door locked and don't open it for strangers." Tina knelt in front of the twins. They both shuddered, gawking out the door. Dana's cry for help was horrifying, eliciting a fear of the unknown in them. "I'll be right back. I just want to make sure everything is okay."

Katie nodded her head, clutching a teddy bear in her arms. Jessica stared down at her shoes, her lower lip trembling. "Come on, Katie, let's go play." Her voice was timid and shaky. Jessica leading Katie towards the bedroom by the hand. As the door clicked shut behind them, Tina heard Katie sobbing.

Tina rushed out into the corridor, her feet stomping down the hallway, *clud-clomp-clud* in a maddening echo. Other people wandered into the corridor, but none of them recognized the shrill scream except for Tina and Stella, who just disappeared into the room. By the time Tina got there, Stella was scrambling out. With no time to avoid Stella, they bumped into each other. In a tangle of limbs, they somehow managed to hold each other up.

"Do you know which room the doctor is staying?" Stella asked, her voice frantic with panic. Tina nodded her head. "Can you please go get her and tell her to hurry?"

"Is everything okay?" Tina sensed the dread.

"Just hurry." Stella fled back into the room, leaving the door wide open. Tina saw Dana leaning over Eric. A frightening amount of blood was spattered over the white bed sheets, crimson drops dripping onto the carpet. Eric's head was rolling back and forth, his hair matted against his head. A sheen of perspiration glazed his skin, beading on his forehead. Stella rushed over with a handful of towels. Dana removed a filthy towel from Eric's mid section, tossing it to the floor with a wet *plop*. A dark reddish black slime saturated the formerly white hand towel. As the revolting odour reached Tina, it made her want to wretch. Stella turned her head, finding Tina frozen in place. "Hurry!" she barked.

Tina spun around, disoriented with fear, afflicted with a sudden case of amnesia. She couldn't remember where Humber's suite was or even which floor. "We need help!" Tina cried out to the crowd of gathering onlookers, curious what was taking place behind her.

"Is everything okay?"

"Are we in danger?"

"What's that stench?"

"What's going on here?"

In a confusing blur, all the voices blended into a single, piercing noise that bore into Tina's head. Overwhelmed and intimidated, Tina felt a panic attack developing. The walls closed in on her, the lights suddenly too bright. She thought that they'd build a peaceful home here. The sudden shift back to reality was crippling. To help fend off the anxiety, Tina cupped her hands over her ears, blocking out the voices in the crowd. The first hand that touched her pushed her into a frenzied state. Pushing her way through the crowd, Tina raced down the hallway back to the security of her room. If she had concentrated, she would have seen Dr. Humber as she bumped her aside. Tina ran into her room, slamming the door shut behind her. Then she pressed her back against the door and slid down, tucking her head between her knees, trying to calm herself down. Deep breaths, she reminded herself, trying to get herself back in control.

"Are you okay?" Jessica asked with a lock of her blond hair twirled around her fingers.

Tina raised her head. "Yes, sorry." The girls were still holding hands, the teddy bear dangling from Katie's hand. With a terrified shudder, she saw the dread painted on their faces, their eyes wide and scared. "I didn't mean to scare you." Tina regained control. She needed to act brave for the girls; she wouldn't fail them. They were all alone now, their father's corpse dragged outside and burnt with the rest of the dead, thanks to her. Even if he deserved what he got, the girls would never understand.

They missed their dad, devastated by his untimely death. She couldn't imagine how that affected them. He had been their entire life, even during his worst moments. Deep down they must have known Tina killed him. All they had left were each other, and Tina was responsible for them. In a cruel twist of fate, this world had forced them into this situation. "Come here." She held out her arms. The twins walked into her embrace. They huddled against the door. Somehow, they would get through this horrible ordeal together. Her sole obligation was to keep them alive. The courage once again grew inside of Tina, only held back by the dread of raising the twins alone in this rotten world.

The fever was near unbearable, the vile stench worse. Dana pressed a clean towel against the wound, and he watched a crimson rose blossom through, turning black as the puss drained out. "Fuck," was all he managed through clenched teeth.

"Here," Stella passed Eric a rolled-up facecloth, "bite down on this."

Eric chomped down on the cloth, the cotton an alien sensation in his mouth. He screamed through it, the agonized yell muffled by the facecloth. A bitter, coppery taste of blood filled his mouth. But at least it helped dull the pain, or at least gave it an avenue for release.

"Jesus Christ," a stranger's voice gasped at the sight of Eric. He rolled his head towards the visitor as she pushed Stella and Dana aside. The doctor had her blond hair pulled into a tight bun on top of her head. Beneath her eyes, giant bags formed black circles, crow's feet aging her youthful complexion. There was a black bag draped over her shoulder, the strap standing out against her floral-patterned blouse, the radiant colours insultingly cheerful. "Can you tell me your name?"

"Eric Jones," he fit it in between his strained cries. "Do you need to see my fucking medical insurance?"

"That could be an encouraging sign," she said to

Dana, ignoring Eric's outburst. "He's not delirious. Maybe there's still time."

"Do you think he can hold on until they get back?" Dana asked.

The stranger furrowed her brow, shaking her head back and forth. "If I can get that infection under control and keep his fever down. I don't know if I can spare the resources. There are a number of people who will need it. And it's not like I can just swing by the drugstore and pick up some more. It will be years before we can manufacture it ourselves."

"Do whatever you can." Dana rubbed her stomach. "You can't let him die doctor Humber."

"I haven't seen anyone this far gone come back," she said without emotion, showing no compassion for Dana's situation. "I don't want to waste these drugs on him. The amount he'll need will deplete all of my antibiotics."

Dana's face dropped, shocked by the doctor's bluntness. "Is there anything I can do to persuade you? I'll do whatever it takes. Please, just help him."

"This is basic battlefield triage. I can save five lives or maybe save his life." Humber emphasized the word maybe, her gaze unwavering. "The risks aren't worth the reward."

"They will find more at the Pharmakon base," Dana argued, not willing to let her walk away without a fight.

"What if they don't?" Humber turned to walk away. Stella stood between her and the door. "Unless you plan on taking the drugs from me, get out of my way."

"Not until you treat him." Stella refused to back down.

Dana reached out and grabbed Humber's wrist, spinning her around. "Look at him, you can't just leave him to suffer like this." She was vehement. "He deserves better after all he's done."

"She's right," Eric spoke through the pain. All at once, they all turned to gawk at him, stunned that he was lucid enough to speak. "I can't put myself ahead of the many. This isn't what I wanted."

"What is it you want, Eric?" Dana spat, the chords in her neck stood out. "Are you trying to atone for some horrendous act?"

"When I set out to do this, I did it to keep you safe," Eric said, the words still blurring into each other as his voice faltered.

"I'm safe!" Dana shouted back.

"What if you need the antibiotics during the pregnancy? Or the baby needs them after? What then?" Eric forced the words out as fast as he could. He could feel the wave of darkness rising over him, crashing down over him, threatening to drown him.

"They'll discover more at the base," Dana said. "You know they stocked up for years. It's not even that big of a risk. It's as close to a safe bet as you can make."

Humber rummaged through her pouch, pulling out a green vial. "I'm only giving you a half dozen of these." She rattled the red and black capsules inside. "If he doesn't show any signs of improvement by tomorrow morning, you won't get another capsule."

"Thank you." Dana let out a lengthy sigh of relief, a single tear tracked down her cheek.

"I can offer him something for the pain." With a sudden change in her tone, Humber spoke with compassion. It was the first time she'd let her emotions cloud her judgement. "It's the best I can do. You might not like it, but you must understand I have to keep as many people safe as possible."

"We already gave him acetaminophen for the pain," Stella said, speaking up for the first time since Eric woke up.

"Those bikers were running a drug lab," Humber reached into her bag, pulling out a baggy full of bright orange tablets. "It will help with the pain and help him sleep."

"You'll make him high?" Dana laughed uncomfortably. "Is that even safe?"

"He needs his rest." Humber handed Dana the bag. "I'll let you make the call. It's what they give terminal patients."

CHAPTER 38
BEFORE ME

"Where the fuck did they go?" Edwards asked, scratching his head.

"I don't know," Smith growled, kicking over a computer chair in frustration. Toppling over on its side, the wheels spun and rattled in the silence. "Turn this place upside down. I want to pinpoint where they went before they get too far," he ordered, slamming his fist down on the desk. The laptop leapt off the table and crashed back down.

"What are we searching for?" Edwards asked Smith, adding to his increasing frustration.

"I don't fucking know!" Smith barked, losing control. "Just start looking around. And get the others to help you. I'll investigate this room." Edwards fled the room, his feet thumping down the hallway, the door swaying in. Smith frowned at the nameplate. "Where are you, Mr. Purchase?" He yanked on the desk drawer, only to find it locked. Then he checked filing cabinets to no avail. Everything in the office was in its place. All the papers had been taken when they left or locked away. Determined to find out, he smashed the butt end of his rifle into the deck drawer until the latch snapped. It fell open, gliding out on the smooth track. "Why the fuck would you lock it if it's fucking empty?" Smith pounded his fist against the desk again.

He picked the chair up, setting it right side up in front of the laptop. "What are the odds?" Smith muttered to himself as he opened the computer. The screen flicked on. With a radiating glow, the screensaver displayed an aerial view of an island. "Now, this looks familiar. Where have I seen this before?" He couldn't place his finger on the location's name. With the identify of the island on the tip of his tongue, his mind raced. Smith powered the laptop down, then unplugged the power cord and placed it on top of the computer to take when he left. Even in his rage, he allowed his better judgement to prevail. Someone back in Grand Falls might hack into the laptop later. The thought crossed his mind that the memory had already been wiped clean, but still it was worth a shot.

Before he left, Smith noticed the picture on the wall hung crooked, the frame slanting down towards the left. It was out of place, and that bothered Smith, so it must have bothered Gordon Purchase—unless there was a reason for it. Smith traced his fingers over the canvas. It was portrait of a craggy shoreline, the waves lapping over the rocks. Seafoam rolled with the tips of the waves. It was calming and full of rage at the same time. His fingers felt a hollow spot behind the center. He lifted the frame, discovering the painting was hinging on the wall. It swung out to the right. A hidden safe, concealed behind the painting, revealed itself. They'd sealed it with an electronic lock, fingerprint scanner included. "I guess we will break into this the old-fashioned way." Smith closed the hinged painting, then took notice of the words scrawled on the gold plaque on the bottom of the frame.

Shoreline of Scenic Fox Island

"We found nothing." Edwards appeared in the doorway. "Do you want us to keep searching."

"Not here," Smith grinned. "Get topside and radio Aliyah."

"What do you want me to tell her?"

"That we won't be here waiting for her when she marches the zombies inside."

"Where are we going?"

"We are going to Fox Island." Smith stared at the painting, enthralled by the sheer beauty.

Tink   Tink   Tink

"Do you hear that?" Edwards asked, turning towards the source of the noise.

"Must be the heaters," Smith said. Uncertain, he leaned towards the persistent, metallic droning. But it wasn't the heat. The rhythm—a feeble attempt at *SOS* for help.

"We need to find the source of that sound. I think there's people trapped inside this building."

Eric's insides were on fire, rejecting everything they forced fed him. Even water would stir his stomach, forcing bitter acidic bile up into the back of his throat. The sickly taste lingered in his mouth, nauseating him. His breath was rancid, like rotting meat. It came out hot and moist. Now, a gurgled rattle had developed. His lungs saturated with fluids, a wad of phlegm sat on his chest. With these sensations mixed, his head was a muddled mess, hungover from the drugs they'd given him. When the pills wore off, the creeping pain pushed away the euphoria. To his right, resting in the chair next to him, Dana was in a deep, tortured slumber. Unable to concentrate, his vision swirled and the room spun out of control. Images of the past and future fluttered through his mind's eye. Everything terrified him. His muscles knotted up and tensed with every shocking image, his body trying to run away from his mind. He couldn't block anything out, forced to watch the horrible events play out.

In an abandoned cabin, Dana stood alone, pressing her hands against her stomach, blood oozing through her fingers, dripping bright red against the pristine white blanket of snow. She reached into her stomach, pulling out fragments of the shotgun shell, throwing them at Eric, screeching that this was all his fault. Then she plunged her hand back inside her stomach, rummaging through her belly. Eric cried for her to stop, but he couldn't move, his eyes glued to the horrific sight. She yanked her hand out, her fingers clasped tightly around a bloodied hunk of flesh. Her fingers unravelled, revealing a tiny hand within her own.

Suddenly everything blurred, and Eric found himself in a strange room. There was a baby crying in its crib, Dana stood over it, exhausted. Enormous bags formed by sleepless nights hid her eyes within. She picked up the baby, cradling it into her shoulder, massaging its back. "You must be hungry again," Dana cooed, trying to settle the baby. She put the baby to her breast; the child latched on greedily. Loud, wet sucking noises filled Eric's head. When Dana took the baby away, blood flowed from her nipple, dripping over her nightgown, pouring onto the floor like spilt milk. When the baby stooped feeding, it turned its head revealing a face smudged with blood.

An abrupt change of scenery found Eric standing in a room filled with flickering shadows. The spectres transformed from blackness to images of people he knew and back again. Calvin reached out for him, cursing Eric for murdering him. Springing from the gunshot wound in his chest, gushing rivers of blood flowed, splashing over Eric's feet. The red drips turned black with the flickering transformation. From the shadows, Craig crawled along the ground towards him, his busted knee leaving a trail behind him, his lips curled into a savage snarl. Jarvik stood between them, defending Eric from their advances until his head exploded, an explosion sending a shower of crimson over everything.

When the flood of blood ceased, Stella stood watch over a blank tombstone, the sour stench of wet earth fresh in the air. The soil freshly turned, sods of grass piled up beside the grave. She put them into place, struggling to lift the tufts of grass. "Let me help," Eric said. His mother frowned at him with hate in her eyes. She mouthed the words "Your fault" and waved him away.

Eric stood in front of Tracy, the wind whipping her hair into a frenzied mess. Helpless to stop himself, he plunged a knife into her throat. Blood gurgled in her scream for help. She collapsed into a crumpled heap at Jason's feet. He knelt before her, bawling his eyes out, screaming "This is your fault" repeatedly. Each time, the sadness was supplanted with anger as the rage built inside him. Eric turned around to face Nick, driving the blade into his throat, opening a giant red smile. "This is all your fault."

Dana was running away from Eric. He chased after her, his outstretched arms grabbing fistfuls of hair. He was howling like a mad man. Somehow, she remained one step ahead, never looking back over her shoulders, remaining silent. They ran towards their old house in Corner Brook. A blood red sun died in the horizon, fading away to darkness. Eric found himself alone and cold, disoriented, no longer to tell up from down, floating in purgatory.

"Wake up," Dana shook his shoulders,

He startled awake. "What's wrong?"

"You were screaming bloody murder in your sleep. Is everything okay?" A stream of tears dripped from her eyes, falling onto his checks. Her fingers ran through his hair, sending a shiver down his spine. His head was foggy. S disconcerting feeling lingered, but he couldn't articulate the nightmares lurking inside. "They should be back soon, just hold on. Can you promise me that?"

Eric coughed blood over his chin. "I don't think I can do that." His face grimaced in pain and sorrow.

"Just get some rest." Dana held back tears, her voice trembling with fear. "You'll be okay. Here, it's a little early but I think it should be fine to take these now." She held out the black and red capsules.

"I don't think I can stomach those anymore." Eric shook his head.

"Please." She handed him a plastic cup filled with tap water, it chilled his hand.

"Come over here and take a look." Smith pointed towards a grate on the floor. "There's a trickle of light coming up from the floor."

A pale silvery light cast shadows over the wall, reaching towards the ceiling. Edwards rushed over, his hand finding a latch. He tugged on it, pulling the trapdoor open, revealing a ladder. "Is there anyone down there?" he called out.

"Help us," a muffled cry answered from below, echoing as it rose.

"We are coming to get you," Edwards replied. He glanced at Smith, who nodded his head, before heading downwards.

Smith watched as Edwards lowered himself down, his body disappearing below the floor. Edwards gave a quick wink before fading completely from sight. "You," Smith barked at the crowd, "bring the first aid kits we found here."

"Right away," one of the women from the Mount Peyton Hotel responded and dashed off to help.

"I'll help her," another girl added, departing with her.

Smith unslung his rifle. "If you hear gunshots down there, seal this grate and get everybody out of here." Then Smith handed his rifle off to the guy standing beside him. When the man took the weapon, he saluted his agreement. Making his way down into the pathway, Smith felt nauseous from the heat that ascended from the sublevel. Although it only took a minute to climb down, sweat soaked his undershirt. When he arrived at the bottom, his boots clanged off the grated floor, the vibrations ringing through the hollow space beneath. He turned around, finding himself staring at the back of Edwards head.

"What's going on down here?" Smith asked, pushing his way past Edwards. Innocent survivors, remnants of Pharmakon's discarded population, crowded the room. A collection of distressed, dirty faces glared back at him. "Is everyone okay?"

The room was silent, most of the inhabitants too afraid to glance up from the floor. "They haven't spoken a word since I've found them," Edwards said. A concerned expression furrowed his brow.

"If you let us, we can help you," Smith spoke up. "Bring you someplace safe. You don't have to be frightened anymore."

"You wouldn't understand what they've done," a familiar voice answered from the back.

Smith scanned the crowed, trying to locate a recognizable face hidden amongst the strangers. When it appeared that his mind was playing tricks on him, his eyes settled on the former premier of Newfoundland. "So, this is where you've been hiding yourself?"

CHAPTER 39
INTO BATTLE

Sirens blared, red lights flashed their warnings, and gears grinded loudly. The clamorous noises drowned out the hungry howling of undead ghouls. Running as fast as she could towards the mine's closing gates, Aliyah glanced over her shoulder at the zombies shuffling after her. It took some convincing to remember they weren't chasing her; they were following her, drawn towards the commotion. Once that door sealed, those undead freaks would be trapped inside until they starved to death and Aliyah would be free of the herd. If her plan worked, the majority of the shambling corpses on the island would get sealed underground, safely away from their sole food source. The faint stream of daylight narrowed as the doors slid together. Aliyah's feet slammed off the asphalt, her tired legs wanting to rest.

She squeezed past the heavy metal doors, having to turn sideways to press through. At the instant she escaped the compound, a resounding *whoop* boomed as the gates bolted shut. The siren's blare dulled and faded away. Sunlight was a welcome substitute to the ominous red glare.

There was a fetid stench of death lingering outside the cave, but the wind swept it away. With the putrid smell suppressed, breathing became easier now, the scent growing faint, replaced by the invigorating aroma of pine needles and crisp snow. She pulled the walkie-talkie out. A burst of empty static filled her ears as she fiddled with the knobs until she found channel two. "Come in, Smith."

"Go ahead," he responded after several minutes of nothing but static.

"I got them sealed in the underground lab. Now tell me what to do next."

"Go back to the hotel, we'll meet you there."

Aliyah felt her heart skip a beat. "Did you find them on Fox Island?"

"They must have just taken off, but we know where they're headed."

"Can you meet me in Miller Town? I don't want to walk all the way back."

"Roger that. I'll shoot off a flare when we get there. We should be back sometime this evening."

After she pocketed the walkie-talkie, Aliyah considered asking where the members of Pharmakon had moved, but she knew Smith wouldn't let her get a head start without him. She would have to be patient, but she promised herself she would be around when the final blow landed against Pharmakon. A decrepit zombie shuffled towards her, its lower jaw missing, a blackened hole where its neck should have been. It cocked its head at her as if it recognized her. She walked straight up to it, grabbed a handful of thin hair, and drove a hunting knife up through the creature's skull. Even after she yanked the blade out, the blood was so thick, it barely seeped out, turned a tarry black. She held onto the hair until it ripped from the scalp, the body crashing into the snow.

"I wonder how many more of you remain on the island?"

Aliyah searched the desolate landscape, finding a silhouetted pack of bodies shuffling towards her from the forest. If she would be sticking around, she never wanted to see another walker on the island. She picked up a heavy rock and headed towards the gathering swarm of dead. With several hours until Smith returned, Aliyah got down to the gritty business of her new purpose. The first skull caved in with a sickening *thunk*, the bone taking on the consistency of a moldy orange. Somehow, it didn't burst. Instead, it imploded, the liquids inside congealed into a thick sludge beneath the rotting scalp. Without noticing, the other zombies went about their business as if nothing happened.

By the time Smith and the rest of the Republic arrived, every muscle in her arms, shoulders, and back were strained and exhausted. The red glare of the flare blended into the bloodied massacre strewn about Aliyah's feet. When Smith walked over, a sly smile snuck on his face. "I see you kept yourself busy." A larger crowd than when he left now gathered behind him. The Republic was flourishing.

Dana sat by Eric's bedside, watching the rise and fall of his chest. It was shallow and laboured, his ribcage deflating more and rising less with every strained breath.

His body was slick with sweat, his skin a ghastly shade of grey. Early that morning, he started breathing through his nose, his lungs riddled with phlegm, producing a wet rumble. She reached out and placed her hand on his skin, feeling it burning up. It brought a warm tear tracking down her cheek. The baby kicked every time she reached out for him; she feared it was a warning. She took another look at the bandage. A blossoming black rose spread out from the center, the edges a reddish yellow. The foul odour reeked of death so strongly she could taste it in the back of her throat.

"Just hang in there a little longer," Dana whimpered, "they should be back soon." Then her eyes wandered over to the kitchen knife Stella insisted on keeping on the nightstand. Even though Dana had refused to keep it close, Eric begged her, insisting it was a necessary precaution. After Dana told Stella, they both agreed with Eric. Before being left alone, they all agreed the baby needed to be kept safe, and it would be a last resort.

She peered out the window, wishing she would see the headlights of the convoy or pick up the grumble of engines as they approached. Outside, the clouds parted, exposing a powder blue sky as the breeze faded into a faint whisper. Snow fell lazily from the sky, floating back and forth as it descended, hanging in the air periodically. She grabbed his hand, giving it a gentle squeeze. "Please don't let go."

Eric let out a gargled, choking wail. Phlegm rattled in his throat, suffocating him. With every breath, his chest deflated deeper. Turning a pale shade of blue, his lips parted slightly. Dana leapt out of the chair, straddling his chest after a single leap. She started giving him chest compressions, leaning all of her weight into the motions. His head wobbled back and forth as she pressed down. His sternum broke beneath her frenzied efforts. She pried his chin down, opening his jaw. A blackened slime oozing from his mouth.

"No, you can't die." Dana held his jaw down with one hand, trying to scoop out the blockage. The liquid flooded back in as fast as she her fingers would reach, scraping it out, leaving the side of his face covered in ropes of saliva. In a fit of rage, she pounded her fists against his chest. When an emphatic, dull *thud* answered her efforts, Eric's head lulled to one side. Strands of the black sludge seeped from his parted lips. Dana bawled, tucking her head into his chest, wishing desperately for his heart to beat once more. Agonized sobs seized control of her body. No longer able to control her emotions, she collapsed into him, her tears soaking his chest. A glimmer of light caught her attention outside. She glanced up at the window when she heard the rumble of engines.

"Why wouldn't you wait another ten minutes?" Dana let out a heartbreaking howl.

A stiff hand brushed her thigh. When she glanced down, she saw Eric's hand fumbling over her. His eyes opened. The hazel irises were concealed behind a foggy veil of white. A low, hungry growl crept up Eric's throat, his jaws cutting the air around his mouth.

"Don't make me do this," Dana begged, speaking through deep sobs.

His fist grasped the small of her back, trying to pull her forward into a lover's embrace, his neck straining to reach her. Dana stretched out for the knife she had left on the nightstand, reaching over his gaping jaw as she did. His teeth tore into her sweater, chewing on the cotton, not knowing the strange sensation in its mouth. Eric jerked his head back, tugging the sweater tight against her shoulder.

"You were always stubborn, Eric." She plunged the blade into his ear. Eric's eyes frozen open, his mouth fell wide open, and his arms flopped to his side. After she removed the kitchen knife, a trickle of blood spilled out of the wound.

"I love you," Dana cried.

Even outdoors, the rancid odor of burnt flesh hung in the air. A faint wisp of smoke carried on the breeze from the pyre above them on the hilltop. Too many bodies to bury, they voted and unanimously agreed to burn them. The entire town reeked of the putrid stench. Blood stained the streets from stray body parts frozen to the earth. It would be weeks before they could clean up Grand Falls, but this wouldn't wait.

Sweat rolled down Dana's forehead despite the bitter wintry wind tugging at her back. Staring down into the six-foot hole at the bundle of bed sheets, Eric's body concealed within, she flung the first handful of earth over him. After three gruelling hours of back breaking labour, her task completed, she leaned against the shovel. Stella stood beside her, a gentle hand caressing Dana's shoulder. The gravel landed with a low *thump*. Smith and Tina stood across from her, exhausted and freezing, adding their share.

"Our Father, who art in heaven, hallowed be thy name. Thy Kingdom come, thy will be done, on earth as it is in heaven. Give us this day our daily bread. And forgive us our trespasses, as we forgive those who trespass against us."

Dana watched the dirt and snow tumble over Eric's corpse as Tina and Smith filled the grave. Sobs crippled her, bringing her to her knees. The shovelfuls landed with lifeless *thumps* at a slow and rhythmic pace. She rubbed her belly, feeling the baby kick. The wind howled, but Dana refused to leave until they'd completely filed in the grave. They stood in the freezing cold together, helping each other deal with their pain. Before they left, they erected a small wooden cross at the head of the grave.

Here lies Eric Jones
May he rest in Peace
09 August 1984 - 07 October 2021

CHAPTER 40
BUT IT IS NOT MINE ALONE

In the days that followed Eric's death, Dana sought to fit the pieces of the world back together like a jigsaw puzzle. She needed to make Eric's vision a reality or else his death would have been in vain. The first step was bringing people together, keeping them safe. This would be his legacy. The torch was her own to carry. She led a search party back to the cabin where she'd left Janet and Clarence. After finding the cabin in a state of disarray, her hopes of recovering them evaporated. They discovered the bottom of the cabin torn apart, the door torn from the hinges and leaning into the porch.

"Janet?" Dana called out, not getting a response.

Climbing over the debris, she pushed her way into the living room. There were bodies strewn over the floor with heads caved in, and brain matter coated everything. Dismembered limbs and unidentifiable hunks of flesh were scattered about the room. In every direction, blood stained the walls, some crimson drops reaching the ceiling. From somewhere upstairs, a baby wailed, and the floorboards groaned and creaked. Then Dana noticed that they had barricaded the stairs with the loveseat, a bookcase, and the kitchen chairs piled into a tangled mess. With a sense of revived hope, Dana cupped her hands and called out.

"Clarence, are you okay?"

There was a moment of silence, followed by the muffled sound of Cooper's high-pitched wail, as if someone were trying to silence him. "Is that you, Dana?" his voice thundered. The entire cabin vibrated with his voice.

"It's me," Dana answered. A euphoric feeling washed over her at the sound of his voice.

"Just wait here." Dana held up her hand, motioning Tina to stay put. "I'll make sure everything is okay. You keep a watch over everything down here."

"No problem." Tina's eyes wandered around the room, examining every detail.

"I'm coming up, Clarence," Dana warned him, not wanting to catch him off guard. When she moved the debris out of the way, a pool of blackened blood flooded out. A dark stain had settled beneath everything, the chair legs stuck in it. As she pulled them away, long ropes of thick, congealed fluids came with it.

Clarence lumbered down the hallway. The upstairs shook as he made his way towards the staircase. Suddenly, he appeared at the top, Cooper swaddled in a grey blanket. "You came back?" A tired smile crossed his face.

"Is it safe?" Janet appeared beside Clarence. She was pale, in urgent need of vitamins and sleep, exhausted by everything motherhood threw at her.

"I can take you someplace safe." Dana nodded her head. "We have a doctor that can check on everyone. You will be all right." She turned to Tina, finding her wandering just outside the front door. "Tell the others we need transportation for three."

"Do you think we have enough room back in Grand Falls? Smith just brought back fifty people," Tina sighed.

"We'll find room," Dana said, thinking about Eric's vision for the future. "They are only the first of many we will save."

Smith stood in the entrance to Fort Louisburg. The neglected brick building was crumbling into the ocean, slowly eroded by the weather. "Another dead end," Smith complained to Aliyah.

"We don't know that yet." Aliyah stumbled her way over the rubble. "They may have left something behind."

"We've been tracking them for a year now." Smith shook his head in frustration. "There are herds of the undead roaming all over this province. It's safe back in Newfoundland. We should head back."

"What if they come back?" Aliyah snapped. "The years we spent vanquishing the biters from the island would have been for nothing. Yes, it's safe from those decrepit creatures, but as long as Pharmakon is out there...."

"Yeah, I know, I've heard your rallying speeches," Smith interrupted. "I should be back at the academy teaching people to fight."

"I'd go crazy if I started roaming around with those creatures again." Aliyah held out her hand. "I'd be lost without you."

"Then come back with me." Smith squeezed her hand. "I'm tired of fighting every day. I'm getting too old for this."

"You're not too old yet." Aliyah gave him a wink. "Besides, you'd go crazy teaching those kids. You don't have the patience for that anymore." She laughed as a breeze blew across the water, carrying the saltwater scent with her words.

"It's too dangerous over here for people like me." Smith approached a door. It hung open, held in place by a rusted hinge. "We can't all walk amongst the dead." Without stopping, he stepped inside, spotting some old broken furniture but no traces of Pharmakon. "This room's clear."

"Let's head over there." Aliyah pointed towards the center building.

As they strolled across the open, dirt field, the gravel crunched beneath their feet. Smith searched for signs of vehicle tracks. The ground was much too hard to leave behind footprints, but he didn't even see so much as a single cigarette butt. With relentless fury, the June sun beat down on them, drawing out sweat and dehydrating them. Smith took a long drink from his canteen, wiping his mouth with the back of his hand, leaving behind the bitter taste of salt on his lips. "I don't believe they've been here since the outbreak."

"Well maybe we can find some fresh intelligence or something," Aliyah sighed, tiring of Smith's persistent inclination to turn back. "It took us forever to get through Labrador and you nearly got us killed in Moncton. I'm not heading back empty handed."

"If I'm not mistaken, you were on watch when it happened," Smith reminded her.

"Yeah," Aliyah laughed, "but you were distracting me." She bumped into his shoulder playfully.

"A welcome diversion," Smith smiled, "if I recall correctly."

They paused at the main entrance to the primitive fort, the iron doors drawn closed. A broad, black iron bar was drawn across both doors, securing it against the dead. Decayed and deteriorating, the embankment was falling down around the door. Shattered pieces of stone littered the ground all around the edge of the perimeter. Out of nowhere, half concealed beneath the tall grass by the side of the door, something shimmering in the sunlight caught his eyes. He bent down and picked it up, holding it out in front to examine it.

"Is that an empty casing?" Aliyah questioned.

"It's a live round." Smith released his magazine, adding it to his depleted supply. "They must have been here recently."

"What makes you assume that they just left?"

"The weather and salt air haven't corroded the casing yet. If this were from a long time ago, it would be dull by now." Smith searched around, scouring for a used path. "Over there." He pointed towards a tower in the corner. "That must be the entrance."

"I'll run ahead and check for zombies." Aliyah dashed off before Smith could protest.

"What if they're still there?" he called out after her.

Aliyah threw the door open. It rattled on its hinges and banged off the cinder block wall with an emphatic thump. She disappeared behind a veil of darkness, swallowed up by the room, the door closing shut behind her. When Smith approached the doorway, he drew his weapon, made sure the safety was off, and burst into the room.

Huddled in the corner was a child, not much older than four, shivering and clutching a blanket. Aliyah knelt in front of the innocent looking girl, her skin an alabaster shade. For a moment Smith was tricked into believing it was Cooper; they shared the same haunting blue eyes. "Everything will be okay," Aliyah said in a hushed, calming tone. The timid girl turned her head away from Aliyah, her entire body trembling. She pulled the blanket tight around her shoulders. The folds of the blanket fell around her on the floor, fanning out all around her.

"What's your name?" Smith wanted to distract the child. "It's okay, we won't hurt you." Aliyah glared at him, thrusting her finger towards the rifle. He slung it over his shoulder, pinning it against his back, the muzzle pointed skyward. Ignoring them, the girl retreated into the corner, trying to become invisible behind her blanket. A sickening image crossed Smith's mind. "What did they do to you?"

Aliyah glanced over at Smith with an acknowledging nod, then she reached into her backpack. "Are you hungry?" She held out an apple, the child eyed it but refused to take it. "It's okay, we can help you."

"That's what they said." Her voice came out merely a whisper. Fragile, the blue of her eyes smoldered with swirling intensity. Her trembling hand reached out, her fingers balled into a fist. Aliyah nodded her head, inching the apple closer. At first the child's arm recoiled back into her cocoon, then it darted out and snatched the apple. She bit into it, chewing and swallowing large mouthfuls of the fruit in greedy gulps, juices flowing down her chin.

"Do you want more?" Aliyah rummaged through her bag. Smith realized there wasn't much left, but they always found more. "I still got a candy bar." The girl's eyes lit up. This time she didn't hesitate to take the food. She stuffed the chocolate bar into her mouth, smearing her lips and chin. The trembling faded and she allowed the blanket to slacken, revealing an arm full of track marks like. "What did they do to you?"

"They said they were running experiments on me," she whimpered.

"Did they say what they were doing?" Smith asked, the child shook her head. "When did they leave?"

"It was four or five days ago." Her frame was gaunt, just skin pulled over a skeleton, the illusion magnified by her ghastly appearance.

"Smith will take you somewhere safe." Aliyah nodded at Smith. "There's no more zombies there."

"Just me?" Smith objected. "You want me to leave you here?"

"I don't think there's any other choice," she argued.

"You have got to be kidding me? There's no way in hell I'm leaving without you."."

As Smith and Aliyah continued to bicker, the child sobbed louder the more their voices rose. She pulled back the blanket, revealing a trap door leading below ground. "Hey!" She raised her voice to a shrill bark to get their attention. "Is this what you're after?" She tugged on the rope and the trap door popped open. "Follow me." The girl disappeared down the tunnel.

"Age before beauty." Aliyah swept her hand towards

the entrance, a sly smile on her face.

Smith rolled his eyes. "That's getting old."

"You're getting old," she chuckled.

Smith let out a long, exaggerated sigh. "You're a chicken shit." He placed his hands on the iron rung, walking his feet down slowly. An electronic hum buzzed below and bright lights followed. When he got to the bottom, he looked up for Aliyah, making sure she wasn't having any problems climbing down the ladder. When he turned around, the familiar Pharmakon layout surrounded him. High tech computers and top-notch scientific equipment filled the underground lab. The walls were insane-asylum white; the doors matched.

The timid girl held a door open. "The boss's office was in here."

Smith looked at the name plate, *Purchase*, and could have laughed. "Arrogant son of a bitch, isn't he?"

"Do you think he would have left anything behind?" Aliyah asked.

"He never does," Smith said with dismay. "Even when we're nipping at his heels." The office was identical to the one they had torn apart on Fox Island. Even though they'd locked the drawers, he learned that he would find them empty from his encounters with Mr. Purchase. "Can you hand me the crowbar?"

Aliyah unslung her knapsack, taking out the black iron bar. "Here you go."

"Thanks," he mumbled as he pried the lock open. The drawer popped free, the bare white bottom taunting him. He refused to give up, prying them all open. "Fuck." He smashed the crowbar through the computer screen.

It shattered into pieces, glass tumbling off the desk and landing on the floor. He looked down at his feet and noticed a crumpled ball of paper in the trash can. "What do we have here?" He picked up the paper and straightened it out against the desk.

"What is it?" Aliyah asked.

"An email." Smith read through it. "It appears our friend Mr. Purchase is in big trouble with his bosses at Engen," he snickered, handing her the paper. "They're meeting him in Halifax to discuss moving back into Newfoundland."

"Holy shit." Stunned, Aliyah paused with her mouth hanging open for a moment. "We have to warn the Republic."

"We need to stop them." Smith knew they needed to cover both options. He wasn't about to put all of his marbles in one basket. "We have to act fast."

"I'll spy on them." Aliyah must have been reading his mind. "I know you don't want me out there alone, but I can handle myself."

Smith shook his head. "We don't have time to argue. I'll head back and wait for word from you."

"You realize it will be years before you hear from me again?" Aliyah was on the verge of crying.

"I understand that, but I need to run the Academy. We will need soldiers."

FROM THE AUTHOR

In my original plan for *Zombies on the Rock*, there was only one book, Outbreak. The first draft was, to put it kindly, terrible. Ask Jason Baker, he can confirm. But I kept working away, and by draft five, I knew I didn't want to end the series. A few simple changes to the ending allowed me to keep going. And I'm glad I did.

This fourth book, *Extinction*, is the end of the Eric Jones Chronicles, but not *Zombies on the Rock*. While this entry will certainly feel like and ending in a lot of ways, I will revisit the series after taking some time off. How long? I'm not sure. But like the title of the next book, *Zombies on the Rock Book 5: The Dead Will Rise Again*.

I hope this novel is your favorite (until the next one), and that you enjoyed the journey of our band of surviviors.

It's been a long journey, with a lot of people to thank. First, thanks to my wife for everything you do to make this happen. I couldn't do this without you. Thanks to my daughter Dana, who is always giving me great ideas and doesn't even know it yet. And of course, thanks Rick, for sitting in my lap over the 90,000 + pages and watching Peppa Pig with me the entire time. The ENTIRE TIME!

Thanks mom and dad for encouraging me to read when I was younger. Thanks to my big sis, Terri Lynn, and brother-in-law Steve, for always promoting my latest novel. Thanks to my entire family for always supporting me and showing off my novels to everyone you know.

A big shout out to all my friends. Some of you may recognize your name in the series and wonder if the character is based on you. Just remember, if I killed you off, it's nothing personal. I hope you enjoyed your time wandering The Rock and your eventual demise. I know I did.

Thanks to the team at Engen Books, for publishing my crazy books in the first place and allowing me to follow my dream and supporting my work. Big thanks to Matthew LeDrew for always believing in my work and never doubting me. A special thanks to Brad Dunne, for polishing my work and making it the best it can possibly be.

Thanks to Jason Baker for all the fantastic ideas and without our late night zombie chats, this series probably wouldn't exist. And last but certainly not least, thanks to you, the reader. Without you, this book would have no reason to exist.

Did you enjoy the work of Paul Carberry?
Read his other short fiction in the Bestselling From the Rock
series, including *Chillers from the Rock, Undead Rebirth*, and
Terror Nova, on sale now from Engen.

The From the Rock series features short stories written by a
diverse mix of the best authors in Canada, including award-
winning veterans of their craft, and brand new talent.

Featuring the work of Ali House (*The Segment Delta
Archives*), Matthew LeDrew (*Coral Beach Casefiles, The
Xander Drew series*), Jon Dobbin (*The Starving*), and more!

Edited by Erin Vance and Ellen Curtis, these collections
showcases the talent, imagination, and prestige that Canada
has to offer. From stories of censorship gone awry to sentient
buses, global warming to corporate-branded culture, these
collections have it all!

The early years of **Xander Drew** as he struggles with the evils of his small rural hometown of Coral Beach, Maine. Cursed with the heart of the Womb and the gift of seeing the world around him for what it really is, Xander must learn the hard lessons about the nature of humanity to traverse the minefield of criminals, gangs, and abusers that stand between him and ultimate happiness -- but most of all that **sometimes it takes a monster, to catch a monster.**

The Coral Beach Casefiles series by Matthew LeDrew:

Book One: Black Womb (February 2019)
Book Two: Transformations in Pain (March 2019)
Book Three: Smoke and Mirrors (April 2019)
Book Four: Roulette (May 2019)
Book Five: Ghosts of the Past (June 2019)
Book Six: Ignorance is Bliss (July 2019)
Book Seven: Becoming (August 2019)
Book Eight: Inner Child (September 2019)
Book Nine: Gang War (October 2019)
Book Ten: Chains (November 2019)

Epilogue: The Long Road (December 2019)

For more information, please visit

www.engenbooks.com

ABOUT THE AUTHOR

Paul Carberry is a huge proponent of the horror genre and its place in literature. He has two children, daughter Dana and son Rick, with his wife Leah.

Paul has published five novels with Engen Books: *Zombies on the Rock: Outbreak, Zombies on the Rock: The Viking Trail, Zombies on the Rock: The Republic of Newfoundland, Zombies on the Rock: Extinction,* and, *Carcharodon*. He has also had numerous short stories featured in publication, including The Light of Cabot Tower, Into the Forest, and Halloween Mummers.

His sixth novel will be released in 2022.